Readers like

Richard Puz's

stories –

Λ VENGE

. . . powerful account of frontier
violence and justice . . . excellent
dialogue . . . a fine novel capturing
vivid history . . . the setting is
terrific, as is characterization . . .
(MidWest Book Review)

His novels brilliantly capture the
essence of American pioneer experiences
in the 1800's –

If you are a history buff or
enjoy a good novel with
lots of excitement, then
you should love his books!

**Attention to detail brings
you face-to-face with two
families and their true-life
adventures**

Wholly absorbing . . . the ending
was so riveting that I was reading
way past midnight . . .

A wonderful story,
full of rich details -

**Read his books — I
guarantee you will
enjoy them.**

RICHARD PUZ
Books and Short Stories

NOVELS
(Print and E-Books)

Six Bulls — The Ohioans
The Carolinian
Avenge
Bride by Mail

SHORT STORIES
(E-BOOKS)

Abraham
Buzzard
Canyon of Death
Roaring River
Runaway Slave
Smoke
Sourdough Wind Minev

TWIN SHORT STORIES
(E-Books)

Arkansas Storm & Captain Jonathan
Beanblossom Creek & Stain
Danny Boy & Tennie
Three Bells & Newtonia

Λ VENGE

Richard Puz

EAST 74TH STREET PRESS*WASHINGTON

Copyright © 2014 by Richard Puz

Cover design by Julie Puz-Wilson

Library of Congress Control Number: 2014934235
East 74th Street Press*Washington, Lacey, WA

ISBN: 0985277998

ISBN: 9780985277994

Dedicated to the love of my life, as she fills my heart with purpose and happiness.

With K's encouragement, this novel was created. It brings me closer to his memory.

ELDEST SON

Lost Creek Valley,

Missouri 1853

Valor is a gift. Those having it never know for sure if they have it till the test comes. And those having it in one test never know for sure if they'll have it when the next test comes. **Carl Sandburg**

CHAPTER ONE

Baying mournfully, the hound dog sounded the alarm in the still of the night.

Curtis grudgingly rolled out of bed, drowsiness clinging to him like a wet blanket. Feeling about in the darkness, he found his pants, and stuffed one leg through, then stumbled, falling to the cabin's plank floor and striking his head against a stout bedpost. For a moment, he lay dazed.

He heard his agitated horses milling about in the corral, and his hound continued howling. Suddenly, men shouted, and he recognized the jangle of tack. The dog's howl changed, becoming deep-throated and ferocious.

"Who's out there?" he challenged. "Don't you touch my horses or dog!"

His hound yelped loudly, then the thunderous roar of a shotgun shattered the dark night.

"Damnation! What's that shooting all about?" he hollered. Grabbing his Hawken rifle, he flung the cabin door open. Instantly, a brilliant flash of gunfire blinded him and wood splinters stung his face as a bullet smashed against the cabin doorframe. Ducking low, he zigzagged, running for shelter behind the thickly built, wooden water trough.

"Who in thunder is out there?" he called again, clutching his gun. "What're you doing on my land?" Peeking above the container, he saw a horseman with a burning torch moving among dim shadows in the corral. Another gun blast struck the trough in front of him, drenching him with a torrent of water.

"Fence be down," a man loudly yelled from the corral. "Ya got the lead ropes on them horses? Then, let's get!"

Rising carefully, he saw figures moving, then the flaming torch curved high overhead, blazing a bright streak against the starless, black sky. Horrified, he saw it land on the peak of his barn, immediately igniting the thrush roof.

As the heavy beat of hooves faded, he hurried to the corral. His prized, coal-black "Tennessee Walker" and the black and white pinto were gone. Shocked by the brazen attack, he stood frozen for a moment.

The blazing fire behind him demanded his attention, and he turned and ran to the barn. He worked feverishly to save grain and equipment. The creaking roof gave a final loud signal before crashing to the ground in a blaze of sparks. The remaining stored hay and feed ensured that the inferno burned intensely. His frenzied activity gave way to inaction, as he grappled with his staggering loss.

"I'll be damned—I didn't even get a shot off," he grumbled. A deep, smoldering anger welled within him.

Searching among the items pulled from the barn, he found a lantern and lit it with a phosphorous-on-sulfur, Lucifer stick.

Hurrying back to the corral, he held the light high, carefully examining the tracks left behind. *There were six horses, including mine,* he figured. Looking about, he saw his hound, lying crumpled in the dust, felled by buckshot.

"Aw, you bastards," he cried, kneeling beside the dog and stroking its head, as a raging cloud of fury seethed through him.

Loudly, he shouted to the empty prairie sky, "You damn polecats—you ain't seen the last of me—not by a country mile. Those horses are mine, and that's the way it's going to stay, or my name ain't Curtis Sommer."

———————◆————————◆———————

Before daybreak, Curtis pounded on the door of his father's cabin. He had run much of the way and arrived winded.

"Who's out there?" Andres called out.

"It's me, Pa, Curtis." He heard shuffling steps inside.

Opening the door wide and holding his camphene lantern high, his father asked, "What in heaven's name are you doing up this early in the morning, son? And, why in heavens name are you puffing so hard?"

In a rush, Curtis answered, "Rustlers stole my horses, killed my hound, and burned down my barn. Pa, I'm going after them, and I need to borrow your sorrel horse."

There was a shocked expression on the older man's face, as his mother, Ilse, stood behind with a quilt wrapped around her shoulders to ward off the morning chill. Seconds later, he heard the sound of bare feet traipsing down the ladder from the loft above, as his brothers and sisters crowded around the doorway.

"Come in, boy," his father said. Turning, he moved to stoke the fireplace. "Jonah, you and Marion scurry up some kindling and split wood," he said to two of his boys. "Let's warm this cabin up."

His mother looked at the red bruises on Curtis' face and uttered a cry of concern. "How'd you get them cuts?"

He shrugged and wiped away a trail of dried blood. "There was shooting, and wood splinters must have nicked me."

"Well, you sit right down at the table and let me tend to your face."

Reluctantly, he sat as she ministered to him. At twenty-five years of age, he was of medium height, yet his wide-shouldered frame was brawny. Topped off with his mother's traits—dark hair, eyes, and complexion— his features were manly. Fidgeting with impatience, he was dressed for travel in a buckskin blouse that loosely gathered at the neck with a leather thong, tan canvas pants, and black boots match his hat.

He observed his mother as she bent close to him and cleaned his wounds. Her strong hands were coarse and reflected years of hard work, while birthing and raising ten children. She was also the family's gardener and healer, and had a seemingly endless list of added chores around the farm and homestead. She dabbed at her son's face with a wet cloth, then rubbed a fresh garlic clove over several areas with splinters. Magically, the wood seemed to pop out of his skin.

"It's nothing, Ma," Curtis said, wrinkling his nose at the pungent smell. "I'll be all right."

"Nonsense, young man, you sit still and let me finish," she gently ordered. "Why, if'n those splinters had been another fraction of an inch closer to your eye, they would've . . ." Ilse shook her head, as her voice trailed off.

"Ma, I'm all right. I have to get after them varmints that stole my horses and killed my hound." Seeing the fixed look on his mother's face, he knew it was faster to let her fuss over him, so he remained seated. "Pa, can I borrow your sorrel?" he asked, again.

"Ja," his father replied, his European accent apparent.

Curtis thought that his father's appearance—though disheveled in his nightshirt— was striking. *I wish I had Pa's light coloring and blue eyes. Well, at least God gave me his strength and willingness to work.*

Concern was evident in his father's voice, as he asked, "How many were there, and which way did they go?"

"Besides my horses, there were four other set of tracks, all heading west."

"Were they Injuns?" his father asked.

Curtis saw his mother's look of alarm and the wide-eyed stares of his brothers and sisters. "I'm not sure," he replied. "Some of the ponies could have been Injun, but two were shod. Besides, those gents fired a couple of shots, so I'm guessing they weren't Injuns. More likely, they're no-good rustlers."

"Ja, probably hiding out in Injun Territory," his father commented.

Several miles west of their farms lay the lands designated *Indian Territory* by the federal government. Curtis knew it was a vast slice of America, bounded by Texas to the south, Nebraska Territory on the north, and unexplored lands to the west. One of his early schoolmarms had told him that it covered an area large enough to hold half of the original thirteen American colonies.

It's possible that Injuns stole the horses, Curtis silently reasoned. *If so, it may have been a renegade bunch that just happened by. More likely, they were white men—known as bushwhackers in these parts,* the young man decided, as he sat at the family table, trying to be patient. *It would be just like them misfits. Such men travel in gangs, steal from lone riders and remote farms, and hide in caves along the Missouri border.*

For a moment, memories of his hound filled his head. *We followed many a trail, old boy,* he recalled, saddened by the loss of his constant companion. *And, those varmints stole my horses that I reared from colts, then torched my barn,* he recalled, as his seething anger returned. *Sure as hell, they'll have me on their trail in the next hour.*

"When you fixing to leave?" his father asked, with a worried expression.

"I'm starting out right after I pick up a few things at my cabin and say my farewells to Judy Beth." Mentally running through his list of supplies, he thought, *There'll be sparse outposts where I'm going. I'll pack enough food for a week. I'll also need my bedroll, rain slicker, rifle, and fire starter kit. I better check my "possible bag" to make sure that it contains enough lead balls, powder, patches, and percussion caps for this journey.* Thinking about the upcoming journey, he added a sack of coffee beans to his mental list.

"What about your crops and animals?"

The question bowled him over. "I plumb forgot about them, Pa," he replied, astonished that his everyday chores had completely slipped from his mind.

"Don't worry, son," his father replied, stroking his light-colored beard. "Your brothers and I'll tend to them."

"Pa, Curtis is going to need help running down those bushwhackers," Jonah said. "Let me go with him."

Curtis saw a look of excitement on his younger brother's face. *He thinks I'm going on an adventure, and he plays down the unknown dangers of going through Injun lands.* Jonah was nearing eighteen and had his father's looks, yet standing over six feet in his long johns, he was the tallest in the family. Curtis had heard that some women at church considered Jonah handsome, given his muscular build and square jaw.

"I want to go, too," Marion chimed in. "Can I, Pa, can I go?" pleaded his barefooted, gangly younger brother, who was half-boy and half-man.

"You're both needed on the farm, and we got to take care of Curtis' place while he's away," Andres replied. "Besides, chasing after bushwhackers is a dangerous matter."

"Oh, Pa," Marion muttered.

"Now, see here, boys, its bad enough that my eldest son is taking after four outlaws, without the two of you going about whining." He turned toward Curtis with a worried expression. "Son, I know you raised those horses and love them, but do you really figure on facing four outlaws alone? That's a mighty big load for one fella." As was his habit, his father stroked his beard, then continued, "Maybe, this once, you ought to let it go."

Lifting his eyes to his father, Curtis was calm but firm. "There's no way that them rustlers are going to get away with stealing my horses, even if it takes me clear across Injun country into Texas . . . maybe even farther south, all the way down to Mexico, if'n that's what it takes! Besides, I have in mind asking Braided Hair to ride with me."

"I'll pray that the good Lord also rides with you, son. Come back to us soon."

CHAPTER TWO

It was daybreak when Curtis left his cabin to find his Indian friend. As he rode westward, the sun rose behind him and the distant hills emerged from the deep shadows, revealing the marvels and wonders of God's creations.

Everything is fresh at this time of morning. If'n I wasn't hunting them outlaws, I'd think everybody was at peace, watching this marvelous sunrise.

I know Pa was seeking cheap farmland when the family came to southwest Missouri, but I wonder if he had any idea how good this soil would be for farming. He thought back to the journey twelve years earlier, when the Sommer family traveled two thousand miles on flatboats, down the great rivers of America from Ohio, to find their new home on the Missouri frontier. As the eldest, he worked beside his father, helping him carve out the family's new life.

All his life, he toiled with the demands of farming, first with his father and finally, on his own land. *When I was not much older than Marion is now, I often took the family wagon on the ninety-mile trip to Springfield for supplies.* He became an expert shot with the muzzle-loaded long gun and kept it nearby, as he spent lonesome nights on the trail, usually settling in the crook of a stream or river, where any unusual sound helped alert him to danger.

I began making them trips as a young whippersnapper and learned to handle my fear of darkness and being alone. Pa must have believed in me, even when I was a youngster. Then I started earning money by hauling farm goods to Springfield and returning with goods for our neighbors or for Pa's trading post. It's my guess that I've traveled with more grain, corn, chickens, and greens than anybody else in the whole county.

I saved enough money to buy me a Hawken rifle at Mr. Sparks' General Store down in Fort Smith, and it cost me more than three month's wages that I earned from my hauling work. My rifle's accuracy is exceptional. I've brought down many a deer at two hundred paces or more. Surprisingly, I've even grown to like the double triggers. You can fire the rifle using the forward one, but pulling the second sets up the front as a hair-trigger. Yep, it's handmade, and the curly-maple stock sure is a beauty.

When chores permitted, his best friend and cousin, Seneca, hunted with him. Growing up in Ohio and Missouri, he and the older half-breed Indian were inseparable, until his friend's tragic death several years earlier. Seneca, a natural-born hunter, taught Curtis how to track game, and he made him practice with the bow and arrow until he was proficient. As a result, Curtis was one of the best trackers in the region—and could drop a running deer with an arrow at fifty yards, making him an excellent marksman with both the bow and the long gun.

I also bought me eighty acres of virgin prairie farmland from the government—and I hadn't even crossed my eighteenth birthday at the time. At five bits an acre, it took me saving a hundred dollars. Not too shabby, I reckon, for a wet-behind-the-ears buck, he reasoned, reflecting the pride he took in being self-reliant. *And, it won't be long before I'll be asking Judy Beth to be my wife, because my farm is nearly complete. With help from my family, we cleared most of the land, and I finished my one-room cabin, the corral, and the barn last summer.*

His expression hardened, as he recalled his burned down barn. *Now I'm going to have to rebuild it, and that'll delay me asking Judy Beth. Those bushwhackers have changed everything. They singled me out, and until I return the favor, nothing will be right.* Again, he felt himself bristling with anger and the determination to find his prized horses.

———◆———————◆———

Curtis reined in the sorrel at the top of a low rise. Below, long rows of corn grew, their green leaves swaying in the light breeze. Squash plant vines thrived between the furrows as a deterrent to some corn-loving varmints. Beyond the field, smoke rose from the chimney of the cabin. The land, originally staked out by Seneca, was the home of Flower on the Water and her brother, Braided Hair.

His friend had been murdered a year after his marriage to Flower on the Water, on the very day when the nearby town had celebrated its founding. During the festivities, beer-laced rowdies shouted insults at her, and one began lashing Seneca with a bullwhip. As the fight progressed, his friend bested the man, but another drunken rowdy shot him. It was after that tragic incident that the small community had adopted the name *Seneca,* to honor the young Indian.

Curtis slowed his horse, as he saw the lovely Indian standing outside the cabin, washing clothes in a wooden tub. *Besides Judy Beth, she's the most beautiful woman I've ever known*, he thought. Her long, black hair fell straight down her back over a red, loosely draped blouse, bound around the middle with a braided belt of woven rawhide. Her soft, elk-skin skirt fell to the high-top moccasins.

"Hello, the cabin," he called. Years earlier, Curtis and Seneca had taught English to Flower on the Water and her brother, but Braided Hair only caught on to so much. She, however, was eager to speak her man's talk and learned well.

"*Hau,*" she responded with the traditional Indian greeting and a welcoming wave of her hand. Holding the horse's bridle as he dismounted, she smiled. "I heard you coming when you were well below the crest of the hill. Your noisy approach surprises me. I reckon every critter within the flight of an arrow is now quaking in fear and hiding from the great hunter," she said, laughingly, as she flicked her tresses over her shoulder.

Chuckling, Curtis dismounted and hugged the longhaired beauty. "You've been well?" Standing back, he continued, "You're looking mighty fit to me."

"Your words are kind, and I am fine. There's always work around the farm, as you know. You see," she said, pointing with pride. "My corn grows strong, like Seneca taught me, and just as your ma taught him. It'll be knee-high by July, and reaching for the sky in the fall."

"Yes, it looks like it'll be a fine crop." Looking around, he asked, "Any strangers pass by lately?"

"No," she replied. "Why do you ask? But, where is my proper greeting? Come help yourself to water from the clay jug. It sits there next to the cabin. You'll stay for supper and spend the night?"

Curtis paused. He was keenly aware that the outlaws had a half-day head start. Seeing her beautiful smile, he nodded. "I'd like that, as I wish to talk with Braided Hair. But in the morning, I'll be leaving before daybreak." Sipping from the dipper, he found the water refreshing.

"My brother is hunting, and I expect him any time. How are your folks?"

"Right well, thank you."

"Mention that I asked about them, the next time you are in Seneca."

"I'll do that."

She looked at him for a moment. "There have been no strangers hereabouts recently," she said.

After a supper of venison, winter potatoes, and boiled chard laced with bacon drippings, Curtis heard a horse approaching the cabin. Moments later, Braided Hair entered, hung his bow and arrow pouch on a wall peg, then turned, and saw Curtis.

Smiling, he raised his arm in the traditional greeting. "Cur-Tish. *Hau.*" Then, in sign language, he asked, "My friend well?"

When Curtis first learned Indian sign language, the shortened manner of communicating surprised him. To convey a thought, such as "I'm riding over the tall snow-covered mountain," he simply made a steeple with his fingers for "mountain" and passed one hand over the other for "snow." In sign, he then conveyed, "Me go." There was no need to add that he would ride his horse, and the journey would take days, because such facts were well known and assumed.

"I'm well." Curtis communicated. "Men steal my two horses last night. I track them," his hands moving to convey his thoughts.

Curtis saw the surprise on the woman's face, but Braided Hair only nodded and stared at him.

"You want me go, Cur-Tish?" he questioned.

Curtis nodded.

The man stood nearly six feet tall and wore his buckskins with an easy grace—a loose-fitting top with fringed sleeves, to help shed rainwater. Skin leggings and buffalo hide moccasins completed his outfit. His head was nearly bald, in the traditional Osage Indian manner, with a single roach of hair on top, running from front to back, and stiffened with bear grease to keep it ridged and upright. At the back, a longer mane fell to his broad shoulders.

"White men?" the Indian asked.

Curtis again nodded.

"When go?"

"Before sun rises," Curtis signed, raising his arm and arching it high.

"Moon rise first," his friend answered. "Then go."

Flower on the Water watched and listened, finally asking, "How many men were there?"

"Four."

The woman gazed at both her brother and Curtis. "Best you rest now. I will wake you when the moon is high."

CHAPTER THREE

For the next two days, Curtis followed the tracks of the horse thieves, with his Indian friend by his side. The bushwhackers had pushed hard before crossing into the Creek Nation, located deep within Indian Territory. By midmorning of the third day, they came upon the thieves' deserted camp. Curtis dismounted, looking for anything that would help identify the rustlers.

Testing the warmth of the extinguished fire with his finger, Braided Hair stood. "We close, Cur-Tish." Signing, he continued, "We catch before sun go down." Looking up at the sky, he added, "No rain. That good."

Checking the girth cinch of his saddle, Curtis looked at Braided Hair and smiled. "You, me," Curtis said, pointing, then used sign language to continue, "we talk first sitting under stars by campfire. You remember?"

Nodding, the Indian answered in sign, "Me remember. Night of falling stars," he added, referring to the meteors they had observed in the night sky years earlier.

"You teach me Osage talk."

"You teach me white man talk, Cur-Tish. Good time."

Smiling, Curtis signed, "You learn white man talk good."

Nodding, the Indian signed, with a tight smile, "You talk Osage like white man."

Curtis continued signing. "No warrior now for Flower on the Water. She troubled?"

"She happy. Believe Seneca spirit live on land. Maybe many more moons," he replied, with an arching gesture of his arm, "other brave come."

Looking at the tracks in camp, Curtis pointed and signed, "Some Injun?"

Braided Hair shook his head. "No moccasin tracks."

Curtis nodded and continued searching the campsite.

On one side of the camp, Braided Hair knelt to study hoof prints in the loosely packed dirt. "Cur-Tish," he called, pointing northeast.

There was a lone set of tracks, heading back toward the Missouri border. The men looked at one another, then Braided Hair swung onto his horse, following the trail.

Curtis continued walking around the campsite. He stopped at one end of a log that appeared to be covered with dried blood. Moving it with his boot, he was startled to see two human fingers lying on the ground. They had turned a pasty, gray-blue and still showed dirt embedded beneath the fingernails. *By Jove, this gang has had a falling out for some reason. I wonder what happened.*

His friend returned, hurriedly. "Cur-Tish," he said. Then, he signed, "Blood on trail. Man no return."

Curtis showed him the fingers. Both knew there was one less bushwhacker ahead of them.

"We follow man or horses, Cur-Tish?"

"Horses!"

As they rode hard, the tracks freshened. Just before dusk, they noticed a wisp of white smoke rising beyond a low hill. Dismounting, they crawled slowly to the brush-covered crest.

Pushing back his hat from his dark hair, Curtis slowly parted the greenery and looked down at the camp below, where two men sat on a log near the fire, drinking coffee. The horses stood quietly, picketed beyond the camp in a grove of trees. *Probably figuring anyone on their trail will have given up by now,* Curtis guessed, as the delicious smell of coffee, bacon, and wood smoke mingled and wafted in the air.

This was the first time that he had actually seen the features of the bushwhackers. One appeared to be middle-aged, wearing a dirty coat and badly stained leather leggings. His unkempt black beard and hair gave him a wild and mean look. The other was a lanky, redheaded man about Curtis' age. There was no sign of the third man.

Backing down the slope, both pursuers untied their bows from their packs. Bending the stiff, but yielding hickory wood, Curtis strung his bow, and his friend did the same.

Signing, Curtis conveyed his simple plan. Braided Hair would go around the knoll to the right while he went left. When Curtis was in place, he would give a mockingbird call, and Braided Hair would respond. In the fading light, the two hunters nodded, and each circled toward the outlaw camp.

With the Hawken strapped on back and an arrow fitted to his bow-string, Curtis stepped carefully in the dense brush. Abruptly he stopped at the sound of pounding hooves, as a horseman galloped toward the camp.

The rider slid his horse to a stop and hollered, "Tucker, Jens, stir your bones and grab your guns. Someone is following us. I came across the tracks of two horses a ways back. They could be Injuns." Suddenly spying Braided Hair, he raised his rifle and shouted, "There's one now."

Quickly, Curtis aimed for the rider. With a sinister, swooshing hiss, the arrow hit the man squarely in the chest, toppling him from his horse. Dropping the bow and swinging the Hawken off his back, he charged, yelling his blood-curdling Indian war cry, *"Yeooowaaawee!"* The need for birdcalls was past.

Similar sounds came from the other side of the camp, as Braided Hair made his move.

"Christ, we're surrounded by Injuns," one man yelled. "Let's get, and fast."

Braided Hair's arrow struck the younger man in the arm, tumbling him to the ground.

"Tucker, I'm hit," the man screamed, as he looked at the embedded arrow.

Running hard, the other outlaw fired wildly at Braided Hair before scurrying through the brush to the horses.

Curtis heard the anguished cry of his friend and saw him drop to the ground. Rounding on the man with the arrow, Curtis swung the butt-end of his rifle, knocking him unconscious. He looked toward Braided Hair, who motioned for him to go on. Curtis chased after the one called Tucker, the mean-looking outlaw with the black beard. Pushing aside branches, he caught a glimpse of him galloping away on his pinto with the Walker's lead in hand and the other horses strung out behind.

Turning, Curtis ran back to tend to his Indian friend.

Braided Hair rolled on the ground in pain, both hands tightly holding his bleeding leg.

With his belt, Curtis quickly tied off the leg above the wound to stem the flow of blood. There was a nasty gash in the leg, but fortunately, the bullet missed the bone.

Raising himself on his elbows, Braided Hair stared at him. With a slight nod of his head, he lay down, again.

He knows the wound needs searing to stop the bleeding. With quick moves, Curtis slit the soft leather leggings and fully exposed the wound. Stoking the outlaw's campfire, he thrust the blade of his knife into the embers. As he waited, he looked at the unconscious bushwhacker on the ground. The man was dressed in a faded, gray woolen shirt, dark pants, and a muddy, worn coat. *His scraggly red beard certainly could use a trim,* Curtis reflected.

Pulling the red-hot knife out of the fire, he returned to his friend. "It's going to hurt like blue-blazes," he said, handing him a stick to bite on.

"Cur-Tish, do now!"

The hiss and smell of burning flesh nearly gagged him, as tension and consciousness left his friend. Working quickly, Curtis dressed the leg and rested his friend's head against a saddlebag.

There was a groan and movement on the other side of camp, as the wounded outlaw gained consciousness. Grabbing the young man by the collar, Curtis dragged him several feet until he lay between two trees. Extending both arms, he tied each hand to a tree. *By golly, this redheaded fella smells rank. He needs a good scrubbing with a big dose of Ma's lye soap.*

"Gads, what hit me?" the man moaned, slowly trying to clear his head. Feeling the pain, he discovered the arrowhead sticking through his arm and coat sleeve. "Injuns got me good," he said. Turning toward Curtis, he said in surprise, "Thank God you ain't a redskin. Will ya do something about my arm, mister? Who are you, anyway, and what happened to the Injuns?"

"I'm the one asking questions," Curtis replied, harshly. "What's your name?"

Slowly, the bushwhacker focused on Curtis. "Jens Jensen," the man replied, groggily. He studied him, then continued, "I figure ya must be the owner of the Walker."

"That's right. Is Tucker the name of your pardn'r that rode off and left you to fend for yourself?"

For the first time, the man realized that he was alone with Curtis. Bewildered, he asked, "Eh, where did Tucker get off to, and where's Loren?"

"Loren must be that fella over there with my arrow in his gizzard. As for the man you call Tucker, he rode off with my horses, leaving you and your dead pardn'r behind," Curtis replied. "What's Tucker's full name?"

"I only know him as Tucker. What're ya planning to do with me?"

"What about the fourth member of your gang. Where's he?"

"Who're ya talking about?"

"There were four of you the night you stole my horses. Where's the fourth fella?"

"Ya must mean Veeko. He lit out this morning."

"And what's his full name?"

"Again, I only know him as Veeko. Mister, will ya please untie me so I can tend to my arm? It's really paining me."

Retrieving his long hunting knife from the fire, Curtis knelt down. "Not so fast. Where were you fellas taking my horses?"

The man's eyes widened as the point of the hot blade came close to his face. "I don't know where Tucker's off to," he gasped. "Look, mister, help me out here—I'm bleeding, and I'm hurting something fierce."

"Likely, you are, but first you're going to tell me where Tucker is headed."

"He's meaner than a gut-shot grizzly, that one. He'll kill me real slow, if'n he finds out I told ya."

"Well, it's your call. You can bleed to death here in Injun country or take a chance on living by telling me what I want to know. What'll it be?" Curtis stood and walked over to look at Braided Hair, who was still unconscious.

"Hey, you ain't leaving me tied up like this, are ya?" the man said in alarm. "Cut me some room. I'll tell ya what ya want to know, but ya got to tend to my wounded arm."

Curtis returned and stood over him with his knife still in hand. With a quick flick of his wrist, the hard-thrown blade tumbled in the air and buried itself in the ground next to the man's ear.

"Don't be doing that," the outlaw yelled, his voice cracking with fright. "All right, I'll tell ya. We were on our way to a big ranch down Texas way. There be a cattle rancher who fancies fine-bred horses, and ya got two of the best we've come across."

"Where's this spread located?"

"You go straight through Injun Territory and south of the Choctaw Nation, then across the Texas border. There be a one-horse village nearby called Wee-chi-tah, and his ranch is less than a half-day's ride south. The *adobe* compound is located on a bluff overlooking the Red River. Now, will you please have a look at my arm?"

"How do I get there?" Curtis asked.

"Mister, can't ya see that I'm in a bad way with this arrow?" the man pleaded. "Untie me so I can look after it." After a long pause, the outlaw resigned himself and continued. "Look, ya go southwest right through Injun Territory, cross the Cimarron and Washita rivers until ya come to the big Red River. Ya can't miss it. Still, it's mighty dangerous country, with bands of Cheyenne and Kiowa roaming the area and wild Comanches, to boot."

"What's the rancher's name?"

"Gilbert . . . his name is Captain Mabel Gilbert. Ain't that something—a woman's name for a fella? And the ranch, it's called Injun Red."

"You and this man, Tucker, must be thinking that you'll make good money selling my horses to travel through such country. How much were you expecting to split?"

"Damn, mister, are we going to chew the fat all day, or can ya do something about this arrow in my arm?"

Curtis calmly stared at the man, his face set with determination.

"All right, ya got high quality animals in them horses. We figured to divvy up maybe a thousand or more for the two, with the big black being the real prize."

Curtis was shocked. He had saved to purchase the colt from his friend John Leach, who had taken up breeding the Walker line years earlier, beginning with a pair of horses he had purchased in Fort Smith. Curtis had paid the outrageous sum of seventy-five dollars—more than it cost to purchase sixty acres of virgin land. *But, my God, a thousand dollars for two horses,* he pondered in disbelief. *By golly, I could buy and stock an entire ranch for that.*

"Tell me more about the fella that rode off this morning," Curtis said.

"Veeko? I reckon he's a yellow-bellied, sniveling coward. When he figured out that we were going to cross through the entire Injun Territory, he wanted out of the deal. It was strange because he wanted his share, and there we were, nowhere near our Texas buyer. His whining increased, as we went along, and that made Tucker mad. When our leader gets in that mood, things tend to turn nasty. Tucker booted him out of camp and flipped him two bits, saying that was all the little *hombre* was worth."

"Go on."

"Well, Veeko came storming back into camp, feisty and waving a rifle. That's when Tucker got real quiet, so I knew that he was in one of his rages. He knocked the runt to the ground and clobbered him with the stock of his own gun. Then he made us hold the runt down. With his big Bowie knife, he hacked off two fingers from Veeko's left hand, just as slick as chopping carrots, while the man squealed like a stuck pig. Tucker said that it'd show the coward not to cross him again. He threw him out of camp once more, and this time, Veeko didn't return."

"How old is Veeko?"

"Hell, I don't know. How about tending to my arm, mister? Won't ya do something to stop the bleeding?"

Staring at the man, Curtis remained silent.

Jens finally continued, "I reckon he be a couple of years older than me, with brown hair and a pinched face. And he's short, kind of plain-looking, and has broken front teeth."

"Thank you kindly for the information." Kneeling, Curtis broke off the feathered end of the wooden shaft near the man's arm. Firmly and quickly, he grabbed the arrowhead and pulled the rest through in one stroke.

"Christ, man, do ya have to be so rough?"

"Only way to get it out. Which one of you shot my hound?" Curtis asked, as he took the man's arm out of the coat sleeve and began wrapping the wound.

Swearing profusely with pain, the outlaw managed to say, "That would be Veeko."

Curtis tended to Braided Hair, who rested near the campfire, while he roasted a rabbit on a spit for their evening meal. They were more than one hundred miles from home—a long way for an injured man to ride alone. *If the wound stays closed and there's no sign of foul seepage, I reckon my friend can return by himself, as he's strong and fit. If not, I'll have to give up the chase.*

The next morning, in broken English his friend said, "Me go back. You follow, Cur-Tish. Trail fresh."

Curtis examined the leg, and found that the wound had closed cleanly. Yet, he was reluctant. In sign language, he replied, "I ride by your side. Take you home."

"No. Go now. Follow trail. Flower on the Water make medicine. Make Braided Hair better."

Nodding, Curtis helped him mount his horse. "I'm much obliged, blood-brother."

"Watch trail. Many warriors. Danger, Cur-Tish," his friend said, and finally, *"Hau."*

"Hau."

Turning his horse, Braided Hair disappeared among the trees.

With the burial of his partner accomplished, the youngest outlaw went on his way the previous evening, after having his arm tended. Additionally, the bushwhacker left behind one of his ears. It was the traditional way of dealing with thieves on Boone's Lick Trail bordering the Missouri River. Any outlaw caught stealing had a couple of choices— hanging or, depending on the crime, having one or both ears cut off as a warning to others about his thieving ways.

In this instance, Curtis figured that losing one was sufficient justice. He carefully wrapped it in a rag and stuffed it into his saddlebag. When he returned to Lost Creek, he would nail it to a tree near his corral.

There's no sense backtracking to try catching the fourth rustler, Veeko. I'll follow my horses and this gent Tucker. Maybe someday, I'll come across the last bushwhacker, and if so, that will be the time to deal with him.

CHAPTER FOUR

Days later, Curtis rested on his horse at the edge of a wooded area. Tucker's trail was becoming difficult to follow over the rocky ground; fortunately, the man led a string of horses, which laid down a wide set of hoof prints. *No question, this rustler is heading southwest to the Red River, just like his pardn'r said.*

Urging his horse on, Curtis made his way through the trees, then suddenly reined in, as a movement ahead caught his eye. He felt a strange tightening in his gut and a ruffling chill ran along his back. Drawing his long gun out of the sheath, he nervously waited, gripping the gunstock nervously in his gloved hands. He was unsure of what had attracted his attention. A snapping twig caused him to duck low over the sorrel's neck. Flashes of color between branches alerted him that someone else was in the woods. Suddenly, he glimpsed several Indians on horseback, slowly moving among the trees. They seemed to be carefully studying the ground.

Carefully, Curtis dismounted and led his horse down a narrow coulee. Tying the reins to a tree, he turned toward the redskins. Kneeling on the ground, he waited, as beads of sweat broke out on his forehead. *I think there're four or five Injuns up ahead. Most likely, they're a hunting party. Even so, they're making way too much noise to slip up on any game. Wonder what they're looking at.*

The stirrings stopped, but he waited a long time for them to clear out before slowly walking ahead. *No sense losing my scalp by bumping into these fellas,* he figured. As he approached, he realized what had caught the Indians' attention. *They're looking at the same tracks that I'm following. Well, how's that for stumbling on a bushel of souring apples?*

Hurrying back to his horse, he followed the Indians, wondering about his next move. *If'n I catch them, then what? What if they find Tucker and the horses before me? I guess that'll likely lead to a sorry mess. The only thing certain is that I have to be nearer for any chance to recover my horses.*

Following the tracks, he gradually became aware of a distant rumbling sound. At first, it was low, but the deep, throbbing noise rose rapidly. Curtis was mystified, and he reined in and dismounted with his Hawken rifle in hand. *What in the name of holy tarnation is that ruckus?* Slowly, he walked forward with his horse, until he could see a huge rolling cloud of dust in the valley below, moving fast like a wind-driven, brown fog. Dropping down, he placed his ear to the ground. The earth was quaking, and Curtis heard muted thumping.

Standing again, he felt vibrations traveling up his legs. "Good Lord Almighty," he exclaimed. Bits of dry twigs fell from overhead branches, and he heard sharp clicks, as small rocks toppled into a nearby gully. The earth was literally shaking beneath his feet, and, for the first time in years, he felt a dread of the unknown.

Surely, the small hunting party has no part in this, he reasoned. The low rumble swiftly became a swelling crescendo, as the reverberating sounds neared. *It has to be animals,* he reasoned. Moving to the edge of the hill for a clearer view, he looked across a valley and saw the answer—stampeding buffalo.

It was the largest herd that he had ever seen, heading up the broad basin and funneling between distant hills. He figured there must have been hundreds of animals; no, quickly changing his mind, thousands were streaming below him.

As his eyes traveled up the valley, he saw an uninterrupted river of brown beasts with black horns, churning up huge clouds of dust. He felt a surge of excitement as he watched the powerful herd streaming past; yet, he was nervously wary, knowing that the herd could instantly change direction and rush up the hill, likely trampling him and his horse.

Nothing can stop these animals until they've run themselves out, he decided. Looking to his left, he saw the Indians trailing the outside fringe of the stampede. They had quickly given up on the horse tracks for a chance to hunt buffalo, their primary food.

Curtis watched in awe from his vantage point for nearly an hour—and only then did the flow of animals dwindle. It was the most astonishing sight that he had ever seen. The prairie ground was churned up in a broad swath, a quarter-mile wide, up and down the valley. It was as though a thousand farmers had come together with their plows to turn over the dirt. Dust hung heavily in the air, obscuring the opposite side.

Well, so much for the Injuns, and that also goes for tracking my horses, Curtis judged. *I best get to the other side of this valley before those redskins come back to tend to their kills.* In the distance, he could see several animals on the ground or walking in a death stagger, with arrows in their sides.

He decided that his only course now was simply to follow the directions that earless-Jens had provided. After crossing the valley, he continued deeper into Indian Territory until early evening and then made a dry camp with no telltale smoke. For the next eight days, he continued to head southwest, while the high, dry heat of the sun beat down on him. He found himself squinting through half-closed eyes against the shimmering glare, looking for signs and tracks. Dust coated him, his horse, and everything in his kit. Each evening, he cleaned and oiled his Hawken.

During the long days on horseback, his mind wandered. Living alone on his own farm, he found that he missed the daily interaction with his two sisters and seven brothers, particularly Jonah and Marion. The three of them often hunted together in the woods, and he had taught them to track game, use the bow, and to shoot well with their long guns.

Additionally, he found that he missed the frequent interaction with his father. *He possesses the most penetrating blue eyes I've ever seen, along with a head of reddish-blond hair and a beard to match. He's medium in height, like me, but wiry from years of hard work, and as everyone in the family knows, he prides himself on discipline. We really got a lot done in those first few years after we arrived in Missouri—clearing the land, building the cabin and barn, and digging the leather tanning pits. Pa was also smart to come up with the idea of building the shed to trade with the Injuns. Later, we built the springhouse over the stream out of river rock. There, he stores his milk and cheese. Just thinking about the cool interior makes me thirsty. Yeah, the others in our family helped, but it was Pa and me that made sure it got done.*

At night, Curtis kept his cooking fire low, camping in protected glens. He crushed roasted coffee beans and dumped the grounds into a pot of boiling water to brew the savory drink. Afterward, a sprinkle of salt settled the grounds to the bottom. Turning in under the brightly spangled heavens, he had the gift of easily going loose, wrapping himself in his blanket to ward off the cold. His saddle was at his head, and his Hawken and possible bag were always nearby. Many mornings, he arose stiff and chilled to the bone, as he started another day.

It had been more than two weeks since Curtis began his chase. As he rode, he removed a small tin from his saddlebags. He always kept a supply of earwax, which he used to coat his lips in the dry heat. In the distance, he spotted a thin dust cloud rising against the horizon. *That could be my man,* he reckoned. *Or, perhaps it's nothing more than a dust devil heading off for some unknown destination.*

The land had become a rolling plain with rounded hills framing broad, shallow valleys. Prairie grasses, as high as his horse's belly, covered the ground. And, dense stands of shin-high, shinnery oaks, along with larger mesquite, cottonwood, and tall pecan trees, lined dry stream banks.

He forded several shallow rivers but had no real idea how much farther it was to the Red. *I'm guessing that it'll be big and wide and wet. Otherwise, I'll never know that I'm there.* At midday, the sun was hot, and his eyes smarted from sweat running into his eyes. Pulling loose his bandana, he mopped his brow.

Crossing still another shallow river, he stopped in midstream to drop into the refreshing water and wash away some of the trail grit. Splashing his horse, he rubbed the sorrel down with his hands, knowing the sun would soon dry both of them. Mounting again and raking his fingers through his wet hair, he replaced his hat and touched the horse's flanks with the heels of his boots, constantly heading southwest, in the direction of the dust swirl.

As he moved over a rise, a wide plain stretched below, with the bright glimmer of a river snaking along on the far side. Much to his surprise, there was a large herd of rangy-looking, longhorn cattle grazing in the tall grass. The lush setting looked like a heavenly pasture to him, after the dry, desert-like conditions of the previous week. Colorful blossoms, including greasewood, dogwood, and skunk-bush added to the splendor of the scene. Continuing the journey, horse and rider parted the herd.

Rounding a large, dense thicket of shrubbery, Curtis reined in abruptly, as three flinty-eyed, white men on horseback confronted him, their rifles pointing at his chest. Their clothes and leather chaps were well worn, and each wore a wide-brim hat with a tall crown, ringed at the bottom with sweat from many long days of herding cattle in the hot sun.

An older, white-haired man, with a tanned, weather-lined face, rode forward a few feet, his gun trained at Curtis. "Well, stranger, what's yar business in this part of the country?"

He shifted uneasily in his saddle, noting the man's drawn-together bearing. "My name is Curtis Sommer, sir, and I'm riding south to find the Red River." He realized that he must look like a down-and-out drifter to these men, with his trail-worn clothes and dusty horse and outfit.

The white-haired man was obviously suspicious. "Well, my lad, you found it. It's over yonder, behind me. Now I'm asking ya once more, what's yar business hereabouts?"

Unsure, Curtis took a deep breath before answering. "I'm from Missouri and following a rustler who stole my two horses."

"Well, horse thieves are considered lower than the bottom-side of a snake's belly hereabouts, and hanging is the justice we serve up."

Lowering his gun slightly, the older man asked, "But how do I know what ya're saying is true, Mr. Sommer?"

"I guess you don't know exactly, sir," Curtis replied, looking guardedly at the other men and their rifles. "I can tell you this, the thief had three pardn'rs. One man died in a fight we had seven or eight days ago and another got away. I captured the third, who told me that my horses were going to be sold to a Texas rancher that fancied fine horseflesh. Said his name is Mabel Gilbert. You ever come across a man with a name like that?"

At once, the man stiffened, and his face reddened. His gun rose again, leveled at Curtis. Slowly, the man let out his breath and spoke in a low voice, "I reckon I've heard of this Gilbert fella. Ya're saying that he's a horse thief, young man?"

"No, sir, I'm only repeating what I heard. The man I captured said that the rancher ran a big spread out here, and that his main operation was located on a bluff overlooking the Red River."

"What kind of horses are ya talking about, stranger?" the older man asked.

"One is a coal-black Walker filly, sir, eighteen hands high. The other is a black and white pinto. I raised them both from wee colts."

"And ya come all this way, and, I might add, through dangerous Injun country, risking yar life just for a couple of horses? That yarn sounds a bit fanciful. Maybe ya can spin me another that I can find more believable."

In a steady voice, Curtis replied, "They're my horses, sir. I aim to get them back, even if it takes me clear down to Mexico, if'n that's needed. I worked hard for what's mine, and I intend to keep my property, including those horses."

For the first time, the older man seemed to rest easier in his saddle, and a slight smile played on his lips. "Ya seem genuine enough, young fella, and I like yar spirit. We don't take any chances out here on the open range. There're too many savages and cutthroats in this part of the Red River Valley, and we've our cattle and ourselves to protect. And besides, we're the law as far as anyone is concerned, as the closest ranger station is more than two hundred miles from this stretch of Texas."

Curtis was relieved to see the other men lower their guns. "Then, I'm in Texas?"

"That ya are, and I guess ya found the rancher ya're looking for. I'm Captain Mabel Gilbert, and I own the Injun Red Ranch. Now, before ya get around to asking, I ain't seen hide nor hair of yar horses." The older man smiled, as he continued, "Pleased to make yar acquaintance, Mr. Sommer. Ya must be tired after that long journey. Maybe a hot cup of coffee and some victuals back at our camp will help perk ya up."

"Thank you kindly. I accept your offer."

"Speaking about miles, ya must have come three hundred or more, looking for that outlaw and yar horses," the man commented with a measure of respect. "Missouri is a far piece from here."

"I reckon."

Riding together, the rancher asked, "Now tell me again, Missouri . . ."

Curtis looked at him, with a startled expression. Then, he pushed back his hat and smiled.

Gilbert continued, ". . . what in tarnation is the breed of yar black horse?"

"Walker, sir—she's a Tennessee Walker. Some of them are medium-sized animals, but mine is tall with a long neck and a short back. Walkers have a smooth, four-beat running gait on the trail that makes sitting a saddle comforting. They are usually calm and gentle animals."

"Black, ya say and a filly?"

"Yep, a coal-black filly. And the pinto is also tall, with black and white markings."

"How old is the Walker?

"Let me see . . . she's four and a half."

"Has she foaled yet?"

"Nope," Curtis replied, surprised at the question. "I'm looking to breed her to a stallion of the same line."

They rode silently, until the rancher finally spoke. "No accounting for thieving scallywags these days. Stay the night in camp with us and rest a bit. Ya can catch us up on what's happening in yar part of the country, Missouri," Gilbert said, again calling him by a new moniker.

"Don't mind if I do. Coffee and a hot meal sound mighty good."

"We didn't bring the chuck wagon with us this time, but our grub is decent enough. We can fix ya up with a supply of beans and a thick bull's heart steak."

———————◆———————

Abruptly, Curtis awoke from a deep sleep. In the faint, first light of morning, he was sure that something odd had stirred him. Disoriented by the strange surroundings, he recognized the captain and the wranglers sleeping nearby, spread out around the embers of the campfire.

Slowly, he slid his rifle and possible bag closer, and he rose quietly to his knees, quickly glancing around, as his feelings of uneasiness mounted. *What woke me? Cattle shuffling about . . . maybe the nightrider . . . or is it something else?* On those many long wagon trips to Springfield, he had learned to trust his gut instinct.

His muscles tensed, and his grip on the rifle tightened. He slipped the strap of his ammunition bag over his shoulder and made his way toward the picketed horses. Off to his left, came the screech of a redtailed hawk. Almost immediately, a singing chirp replied on his right, making the hair on the back of his neck bristle. No small animal would ever call out with a predator screeching in the sky above. He maneuvered around the horses and then, keeping low, he hurried toward a small rise overlooking the camp. On one side, scrub oak and tall brush covered the ground, while a stand of trees on the left showed the way to the river.

Looking toward camp, a movement suddenly caught his eye. He slipped his Hawken around, peering at the area over the rifle sight. Immediately, loud war cries came from the cottonwoods behind him, and an Indian stood up in scrub oak near the camp.

Curtis quickly cocked his gun to set the hair-trigger, just as the sudden rustle of bushes behind him warned him of another threat. With his long gun raised, he wheeled around to face an attack—but the flat side of a tomahawk knocked him to the ground, as the musket roared in his hands.

Groaning, he cautiously opened his eyes. The pain in his head was fierce. He had no way of knowing how long he had been stunned, but now he heard more yelling, coming from the direction of the camp. Rising slowly, he saw his attacker lying on the ground, dead. The warrior was dressed in a shirt and leggings made from deerskin, with his hair shaved in a straight line along the side of his head to his ear and beyond, making him look fierce. Looking toward camp, two savages were holding the ranch owner, while others chased after his men.

Reloading quickly, Curtis looked up as a long, agonizing scream came from a cowhand off to the left who was losing his scalp to an Indian's knife. Moments later, the blade slashed across the man's throat, silencing him forever. Another drover was desperately fighting a losing battle, which ended with a spear thrust into his chest. The final wrangler hightailed it through the tumbleweeds, only a few steps in front of three Indians brandishing war axes. Near the center of the camp, the rancher was pale and looked unnerved beside his two captors.

Curtis crouched low and moved toward the trees, wondering how he could save the captain. Making his way through a thicket, he stumbled over the dead nightrider lying on the ground. Beyond the trees, he saw the Indians' ponies. There was one brave standing there, holding the horses' reins. He was watching the attack and standing with his back to Curtis.

Using the brush to mask his movements, Curtis moved closer. Setting his Hawken down carefully, he swiftly covered the remaining distance, while swinging his ammunition-laden possible bag like a heavy, weighted lasso. He surprised the guard, and the heavy bag caught the Indian squarely across the back of the head, knocking him to the ground. Curtis jumped on his back, wrapping the strap of the possible bag around the man's neck. With all his wiry strength, Curtis pulled back sharply, keeping his knee in the guard's back, until he heard the spine snap, and the body became limp.

Retrieving his gun, Curtis slowly approached the skittish ponies. He stroked the nearest horse to calm it. *There're nine ponies here plus a pack-horse, so seven more Injuns are attacking the camp,* he figured.

Quickly checking the area, he saw that the braves had left behind buffalo robes, extra spears, and other gear on their packhorse. The gear gave Curtis an idea. Unloading several hides, he bound them together with a long lariat. He tied the other end of the rawhide line around a pinto's neck. Holding its reins in one hand, he jumped bareback onto another. With his gun, he smacked a third pony on the rump and succeeded in getting all the horses moving at a gallop.

The pony dragging the skins immediately created an enormous dust cloud, as the hides trailed and skipped over the ground. Urging the horses faster and heading toward the longhorn cattle, Curtis yelled at the top of his lungs, *"Yeooowaaawee!"*

The herd was already uneasy from the commotion in camp and, seeing the horses galloping toward them, they stampeded. Almost immediately, Curtis turned all the animals toward the camp and shouted his war cry again. The swirling dust, pounding hooves, and the swelling tide of animals approaching the camp looked like a thundering wave of death.

Through the dense haze, Curtis saw the attackers scattering. Sliding to a stop, he dropped the reins of the second horse and shouted to the captain, "Climb onto the back of this pony."

Driven by necessity, the older man managed to clamber onto the back of the off-saddled horse. From behind him, an Indian suddenly grabbed the rancher's leg. Curtis leveled his rifle and fired, striking him in the back, as Gilbert shook off the attacker's grasp.

"Let's ride," Curtis shouted, galloping toward the river.

Riding bareback, the older man was right beside him, struggling to stay astride the pony. Pointing ahead, the rancher shouted, "Missouri, cross the river over there!"

Curtis looked behind and saw no pursuers. He slowed his pony, giving Captain Gilbert an easier ride, as the man desperately clung to the horse's mane and neck.

With tremendous splashes, both horses plunged into the wide river, found their footing, and continued across the belly-high water.

"That way!" Gilbert directed. "The ranch house is on top of a bluff a few miles west of here."

Finally breasting the hilltop, both men galloped into the ranch compound, with Captain Gilbert shouting, "Injuns attacked us and killed the others. Grab yar guns, boys, and keep an eye out for danger."

CHAPTER FIVE

The bushwhacker's trail had gone completely cold, so Curtis gladly accepted the captain's offer to have supper with him and to stay overnight at the *hacienda*. After many days on the trail, the prospect of sleeping in a bed was a treat he could not pass up.

Covered with grit, he decided to wash at the well located behind the large, rambling *adobe* ranch house. Using a gourd dipper to fill a washbasin, he cleaned up and gave himself a blind man's shave. Returning to the *hacienda*, he changed to clean clothes, provided by his host. Feeling refreshed, he looked through the window beyond the compound's whitewashed walls and saw a lush landscape with thick stands of trees and chaparral dotting the range. *This really is beautiful land. Wonder if it looks this green in the dead of summer?*

That evening, a servant showed him to the *hacienda's* large, colorfully decorated dining room, gaily lit by dozens of candles, many resting on tall candelabras, which gave the room a warm, soft glow. The amazingly arched, stucco ceiling was brightly painted, depicting mountains and steams.

"Welcome, Missouri," the rancher said in greeting, as he shook his hand. He was neatly dressed in a dark blue shirt, silver-tipped string tie, tan vest, brown trousers, a silver-buckled belt, and polished calfskin boots. "They've got a saying around here, '*mi casa, su casa.*' I owe ya my life, and I want ya to feel right at home on the Injun Red."

"Thank you kindly, sir. A real bed sounds like a wonderful change to me."

"How's your head? You feel any better this evening?"

"I'll be fine." Curtis replied. "I'm just feeling low at the moment, having lost my Pa's sorrel horse to them Injuns."

"I'm truly sorry about that," the captain replied, sympathetically. Moving to the table, he said, "Have a seat right here. Ya like beefsteak? The ones we're having tonight have hung in the storehouse out back and should be juicy and tender."

The platter of steaks looked and smelled heavenly to Curtis.

"And here, have some of these beans and take a few of these corn shells. Had the cook stuff them with a very tasty filling inside as a special treat for tonight."

The fried corn shells were new to Curtis. "What're they called?"

"*Tortillas.* We Texans eat it like bread. The Mexicans taught us how to make them, and they probably learned from the folks that originally lived throughout this area and south of the Rio Grande."

"And what's inside?"

"They're usually filled with either beans or shaved beef, sometimes chicken. However tonight, ya being my special guest and all, I asked the cook to fill them with my favorite. It's called *huitlacoche*." Seeing the puzzled look on Curtis' face, he laughed, explaining, "In English, the closest translation—are you ready for this—it's 'raven shit.'"

"Come again, sir?" Curtis asked, as he dropped the corn shell and fought down his sudden gagging.

Laughing heartily, the older man continued, "The stuff's good for ya. It comes from the smut that forms on corn. Ya must have seen it on yar crop back home. It's that brown sticky fungus that forms on husks."

Nodding, Curtis curiously opened the *tortilla* and sniffed.

"Mexican folks love it as a delicacy, and most Texans have a taste for it. I'm told Injun women even use it to ease their birthing." Looking down, he continued, "Before we begin, let's say a prayer for the fallen wranglers this morning, and give thanks for both of us being alive this evening."

> Lord, men lost their lives today but put
> up a good fight. Please welcome them to
> yar bosom. Thank ya for protecting my
> new friend and me this morning from
> them Injuns. And please, Lord, watch over
> Missouri. I reckon he's going to need an
> extra measure of Thy protection. Amen.

Curtis ate hungrily and thoroughly enjoyed the meal and his long conversation with the captain. The older man had led a colorful life.

"Yep, I came to Texas from Tennessee with the Stephen Austin party in the summer of '36. I settled outside the village of Houston, fought in our War of Independence, and became an officer in the Texas army. I came up here to the Red about twelve years ago and settled with my wife. She's gone now, but I love this country and this ranch."

"How many acres does the ranch cover?"

"As near as I can figure, about four thousand."

"Four thousand?" Curtis repeated, nearly choking on his food. "My Lord, sir, that's not a ranch, that's a county."

"Well, most of it was back pay for my service in the army and more came to me for serving in the Texas Rangers. For years, I did many stints chasing after Comanches and *banditos*—and I have a couple of holes in my hide to show for it. In those early days, the newly formed Texas Republic had lots of territory, but little money. So, they paid folks with land rights."

"I'm still amazed at the size of this spread. How many cows do you run?"

"Each acre supports about three animals, but we're down because of the drought last year. I figure after branding in another month, we'll have near seven thousand."

Again surprised, Curtis was sure his mouth hung open.

After dinner, the captain rose to the sideboard and offered Curtis a *cigarillo*. Lighting his own, he blew a cloud of blue smoke toward the brightly painted ceiling. Sitting down, he said, "That was right quick thinking on yar part this morning, young man. Not many men would have done what ya did. I reckon them Injuns must have had big plans for me after killing my men. I mean it when I say that I'm much obliged and in yar debt."

"I take no pleasure in killing anyone, and some of my best friends are Injuns, but I'm glad the ruse worked. Truth be known, I didn't know whether I'd get back in time." Smiling, he continued, "And once you climbed aboard that pinto, I wasn't sure you'd be able to stay on its back."

"Let me tell ya something, I wasn't sure, either," the captain said with a chuckle. "But, Missouri, it was that or losing my scalp, so I had a heap of reasons not to fall off. I don't recall the last time I clung to a horse's neck with no saddle, galloping at full speed, but I hope today was my last. My butt is still smarting."

"What manner of Injuns were they?"

He answered by holding two fingers horizontal at the outside edge of his left eye and moving them back past his ear. "Kiowa. Maybe you noticed their hair was shaved straight back over their ears. I heard tell that keeps it from tangling in their bowstrings. Still, it's a sure giveaway."

"Do you think those Injuns will attack in the morning?"

"Oh, I've no doubt we'll see more of the heathens, but I wouldn't expect to see that particular bunch soon. Ya jumping them and stampeding the cattle, which Injuns around here call white man's buffalo, has likely put the fear of evil spirits in their minds, and besides, ya took down at least three. They'll have to chew on that back at their camp. Ya were lucky to escape yarself."

"Yes, I reckon you're right."

"Say, Missouri, ya spoke of a fourth thief that stole yar horses, and ya said he got away. I assume we should be on the lookout for him. Do ya know his name?"

"His name is Veeko. And no, I don't think he's likely to be in these parts." Curtis told him about the quarrel that led to Veeko loosing his two fingers and heading back toward Missouri.

Silence followed as the housekeeper poured a clear amber liquid into goblets. The captain raised his glass in a toast. "Here's to yar health, young man from Missouri. This brandy will help what ails ya, but beware, too much of it will kill ya, and that's for damn sure," he concluded, with a broad grin.

Curtis took a sip and nearly choked. *What in blue-blazes is this firewater?* He wondered, as he smelled the pungent liquor. Then, he took another swallow. *I swear, I can feel it flowing down to my gullet. Likely, my toes will be tingling next.*

"Ya know, I could use a man like ya on the Injun Red. Ya're fast on yar feet, quick thinking, and there's no question about yar bravery. How about it? How would ya like to work for me? The pay is thirty dollars a month, plus room and grub. And, ya can have the pick of my horses to replace yars."

The offer surprised him. The wages were triple what he earned hauling freight; still there were other things on his mind, like his farm and Judy Beth waiting for him back home. "Thank you, sir, for those kind words and for your generous offer, but I'm fixed on what I aim to do, and finding my horses tops the list. Then I'll be off for home back in Missouri. It's like my pa says, 'a man works hard for what he has, and when needed, he fights even harder to protect it.'"

Nodding and smiling, his host commented, "Yar pa is a wise man. I felt the same way during our war with Mexico." Looking at him with a smile and a twinkle in his eyes, he asked, "Ya got yarself a pretty gal waiting back home?"

Curtis smiled.

"I figured as much. Well, where're ya going to look next for them horses of yars? You know, it won't be easy getting back on their trail, unless Lady Luck smiles down on ya."

"The bushwhacker that I captured said something about a small village being close by the ranch. I'd like to mosey there tomorrow, if'n I can borrow a saddle from you. It's been a while since I rode bareback, too."

"Sure, we fork our own broncos hereabouts, but ya can take yar pick out at the corral in the morning. Also, pick out a saddle for yarself and replace the kit you lost from the stores in the barn. Wichita Falls ain't much, and it's a few miles north of here. Ya go ahead and take a look, but the horses ya described would be hard to miss in such a small village. I'm doubtful that ya'll find them there."

"Thank you, sir. I'm much obliged for your generosity and your hospitality."

The next morning, Curtis was on the road by daybreak. He tried saddling one of the Indian ponies, but decided that breaking the horse to a saddle would take more time than he wanted to spend. So, he took the ranch owner's offer and picked another from the corral.

The captain was right; it wasn't much of a village. As he tied his horse's reins to a hitching rail, he saw about three dozen *adobe* houses, along with a dirt street lined with a general store, saddlery outfit, and blacksmith shop. He made inquiries about his distinctive horses, but no one knew anything about them. He heard *concertina* music coming from a saloon across the dusty road and made further inquiries, but he had the same result.

In the afternoon, he returned to the Indian Red. As he rode into the walled compound, he saw the captain leaning back in his chair on the ranch house *veranda*, with one leg propped on the railing, smoking a *cigarillo*.

"Anybody see yar horses?" the rancher asked.

"Nope."

"Well, c'mon around the other side of the house. I've got something to show ya."

Walking toward the well on the backside of the sprawling *adobe* dwelling, Curtis was surprised to see a dead white man lying facedown on the ground. His hair was missing from the top of his head; instead, there was a broad slash covered with dried, reddish-brown blood. His naked body was badly mutilated.

"One of my cowhands found this fella staked out on an anthill on the other side of the Red. Injuns use the ants to make a fella talk. It also assures that his life drains away slowly. This one was delirious, but alive, when my hand found him. He ranted about a big black horse, Comanches, and other things that made no sense. He died before reaching the ranch. Have ya ever seen him before?"

"I'm not sure." Rolling the man onto his back, Curtis continued, "I only got a quick glimpse of the rustler who got away during our fight, but yes, I think he's the one his pardn'r called Tucker. He had a shaggy black beard, like this gent."

"I figured as much. We don't get many strange white men around here." Seeing the look on Curtis' face, he asked, "What's yar next move? It seems obvious that the Injuns now have yar horses."

"Nothing has changed. I'm still going after them."

"What? Can't ya see how dangerous this country is?"

"I can't rest easy until I get my horses back. At the very least, I'm going to try my darndest."

"So, let me get your meaning straight, Missouri. Ya're going to search for the Injuns and ride into their camp. Maybe ya'll kindly say 'howdy,' as ya pass through, and possibly 'thank ya,' as ya depart. Then, ya're thinking that they'll all smile and wave goodbye, as ya make off with horses that they stole and figure belong to them. Is that about how ya see it?"

"Well, sir," Curtis answered, chuckling. "I hadn't figured it quite the way you picture it, but something like that."

The older man stared at him with an expression of disbelief on his face. "Holy Jehoshaphat, boy, yesterday I told ya that yar actions showed lots of smarts, but this sounds as loco as anything I've ever heard. Look at this man. That could be ya tomorrow or the next day. Ya're not itching to die here in Texas, are ya, son?"

"Not hardly, sir," Curtis replied, taking off his hat in the scorching sun and mopping his forehead. "But my horses are out there, and I've come this far to get them back. Nothing is going to stop me from trying, sir." Steadfastly, he returned the rancher's gaze.

"Young man, ya sure are set in yar ways, and I'm telling ya, it sounds to me like a fool's errand. But then, *quien sabe*, who knows?"

Curtis remained silent, his face set.

"I'm sorry, son, but I can't send any of my wranglers along to help ya. Before losing those men yesterday, I was already short-handed."

"I'm not asking for any help from your cowhands. They're my horses, and it's up to me to get them back."

"Boy, ya got grit. When ya figuring on leaving?"

"First light, I reckon. I'd be much obliged if'n your wrangler showed me where he found this man."

"Of course, that's the least I can do for ya." Breaking out in a big smile, he added, "Besides, that gives me an excuse to feed ya another fine meal tonight. Think ya can put down more of them *tortillas?*"

"Yes, sir, I believe I can," he answered, smiling.

That evening, the cook dished up another tasty meal, including the same smut-filled corn shells, which Curtis enjoyed more the second time.

After dinner, his host said, "Ya know, I still owe ya for saving my sorry, old ass."

Curtis whiffed the liquor in his glass and then stared at it. *I swear, the soles of my boots are curling, simply from vapors of this firewater.*

Lifting his sniffing goblet, the captain saluted his guest, "I've a brandy toast for ya tonight. Confusion to yar enemies," he said, raising his glass and drinking deeply. Pausing, he lit a *cigarillo* and drew heavily. "And I'm figuring ya're going to need a lot of confusion, if'n yar going to have any chance of success." Standing, he went to the side cupboard and returned carrying a beautifully lacquered wooden box. "Curtis, I'm truly obliged for yar actions out on the range. I'd like ya to keep the horse, rifle, and saddle ya picked out, and I'd like to add this as part of my thanks."

"There's no need for any more —"

The rancher's quick hand gesture cut him off. "Now don't be offending me by refusing my Texican hospitality."

"Sir, I can't —"

Raising his hand once more, the rancher stopped him. "Just hear me out. I admire yar grit and what ya've done. This is my small way of thanking ya. In this box is a newfangled thing that I picked up last month at the Texas Ranger Station down in Dallas. I think ya're going to need it where ya're going."

Curtis ran his hand over the finely finished case and read the inscription on the inset plaque.

To M. Gilbert
For gallant services ~
Texas Rangers

"Sir, this was a gift to you. I can't accept it."

"Nonsense, open the box."

Inside, a pistol gleamed, set in a green, velvet-covered mold. The highly polished walnut grip contrasted with the handle's bright brass frame. A polished bead at the end of the octagonal, gunmetal-colored barrel served as the front gun sight while the notched hammer, when cocked, framed the nipple for the shooter's eye. The burnished cylinder highlighted the engravings etched into the metal. Cradled below the gun were two boxes containing lead balls and percussion caps, along with a copper powder flask.

"The Colt Firearms Company sent a supply of these from Connecticut. Texas Rangers have been using Colt revolvers for twenty years, but this is the company's newest model, called the Navy Colt. It carries the name of our successful sea battle with Mexico when Texas became a part of the Union. See here, ya can make out the fighting ships on the engraving on the pistol's burnished barrel, commemorating that fight."

"It's a pistol, I know," Curtis began, unsure of exactly what was in the box, "but what's the cylinder for? The only pistols I've ever seen were single-shot, muzzle-loaders."

"The cylinder holds the powder and lead for this six-shot, .36-caliber, percussion-fired, single-action gun. It's light enough to stick in your belt or in a holster strapped around yar waist. The reading material says that it takes only a second to throw lead about a thousand feet. That's covering a lot of ground in a hurry."

Curtis was fascinated. "How does it work?"

Captain Gilbert bent over the wooden box and loosened the gun from its mold. "One thing to remember is ya can't fire it by just pulling the trigger. The weapon must be fully cocked first and then ya can pull the trigger. Or if'n ya want to shoot in a more rapid fashion, ya can fan the hammer with yar other hand," the former ranger explained, holding the pistol and simulating his hand slapping back the hammer repeatedly, while pulling the trigger. "Fanning surely sprays a lot of lead, but it's hard for me to hit anything that away. Ya can practice what works best for ya. It's much different from shooting a rifle. Some of my ranger friends find they can best hit a target shooting from the hip."

"You don't say," Curtis responded, expressing his surprise. Holding it, he figured it was nearly a foot long, as the barrel, alone, measured about seven inches. From its heft, he thought the gun weighed about two pounds. "How do you load it?"

"Half-cocking the hammer, like this," the rancher said, as he demonstrated. "The cylinder spins freely. See what I mean? Ya fill the front of each chamber with black powder and then the ball. The lead is a bit oversized, so you use this lever to firmly seat the ball and powder in each chamber." The man demonstrated, straightening the mechanical device tucked beneath the gun barrel to tamp the ball and powder in place. "Lastly, ya add a percussion cap on each on these nipples, right here at the rear of the cylinder. Then, ya're all set.

"A ranger pardn'r of mine had an earlier model called a Colt Dragoon. It misfired once, igniting all the chambers at the same time, and the explosion nearly took off his hand. They say this model is improved and won't do that. Still, I'd add a slick of grease on the caps, to be safe."

"How long does it take to load this gun?"

"Oh, it takes a few minutes. Some fellas carry a loaded, extra cylinder and switch them out. Ya have to remove this screw with a knife blade, but it's much faster than reloading all the chambers."

"Sir, I can't take such a magnificent gift. Such a gun must cost a heap of money. It's just too much. Please, I don't want to offend you, but it just wouldn't be right for me to take it and, besides, I was also saving my—"

Interrupting, the captain's face bore a serious, almost stern, expression. "Ya ever figured out what the value is of a man's life, young man from Missouri? What's more, how do you know what mine is worth to me? Only I can judge that, Curtis." Pausing for a moment, the rancher cracked a big smile that rearranged the sun-baked lines of his face. "I won't take no for an answer, and that's final—fair is fair. Ya did me a good turn by saving my hide, and this is my way of repaying ya. I'll be real offended, and I mean real offended, if'n ya refuse me."

"All right. Thank you, sir. I accept. It's like my pa always says, when manna falls into your lap, you best feast before heaven changes its mind," Curtis laughed as he spoke.

"Ya're welcome. Tomorrow or the next day, ya'll need all the firepower ya can get. In a close fight, this gun is like having a couple of extra shooters with ya." The rancher paused and looked squarely at Curtis before adding, "I want to see this gun at least one more time, when ya return. What I mean is, keep it and yarself safe. *Vaya con dios.*"

CHAPTER SIX

Captain Gilbert's wrangler returned to the ranch after leading Curtis to the place where Tucker was found. Curtis knelt over the soft ground, studying the tracks and gauged them to be three days old, with perhaps as many as eight horses involved.

Walking the area, he stopped and again knelt to remove a twig covering a hoof print. *It's my horse's shoe,* he thought, recognizing the notched imprint of his big black's left front hoof. He felt a rush of excitement, being on the trail of his horses once more.

Looking in the direction of the tracks, he saw that the ground sloped down to a distant alkali basin, with mountains to the right and on the far side. *I'll wager that those Injuns with my horses hole up in the high ridges beyond this dry lake. Likely, they'll have a watch posted that can easily see anyone riding across this sink. Well, there's more than one way to get there,* he thought, gazing toward the ravines and foothills bordering the side of the valley. It took him the rest of the day to make the trip, moving slowly to avoid raising a telltale dust cloud.

Early the next morning, Curtis set out on foot after leaving his horse hidden behind a thicket of brush. After a grueling climb up a soaring ridge, he had an unobstructed view on all sides. There was no sign of any living thing, as he gazed across the vast expanse of land and mountains, clear to the edge of sight. The clear line between sky and earth in the crisp morning air was sharp. He knew that the haze of heat later in the day would blur the distinction.

Returning to his horse, he checked the mouths of several ravines, which were on the backside of the high peaks that he had observed the previous day. No tracks were apparent in the loose sand and gravel. That evening, he made a dry camp in a grove of mesquite trees, and at first light, the search continued on horseback. Near a stand of scrub ever- greens, he suddenly reined in. Below, he saw an Indian hunting party on horseback. He quickly turned down a draw, dismounted, and hurried back on foot.

He watched, as three riders, leading a packhorse carrying a four- point deer, crossed the valley and rode into the high hills. Using an *arroyo* as their trail, the hunters disappeared beyond a bend. *That has to be the entrance to their hidden camp. Looks like I'll have to pay these folks a visit tonight.*

Creating a blind with brush and limbs, Curtis hid his camp for the night. Pulling several strips of beef jerky from his saddlebag, he sat and chewed, thinking about the Indians and waiting for dusk.

I'd best take only the revolver with me. A rifle could get in my way as I climb, or if I get into a tight situation. Yet, I've never fired the darned Colt and don't know if'n I can hit anything. Sure hope this incredible gift doesn't find a new home tonight in some brave's teepee. Well, it's no use complaining, as the cards in my hand ain't going to change.

He had no illusions about the difficulty of the night's work, and no amount of planning would help. He took off his spurs and tore an extra shirt into strips, so that he could tie them around the soles of his boots to muffle his steps.

The rest of the day, he found himself fidgeting with a leather thong, repeatedly tying and untying it. He closed his eyes, but sleep escaped him. He was tense and too aggressive in his thoughts. His nighttime stroll was the most dangerous undertaking of his life, and the odds of his horses being in the Indian camp were unknown—as were his chances of returning alive.

———————◆———————

After midnight, the three-quarter moon began to slide behind adjacent hills, as a coyote sang his sorrowful howl, seeking a mate. Curtis had followed the bottom of the ravine and was already at the top of a pass, using the moonlight to find his way in the crystal-clear night. He stopped often to listen, but everything remained quiet, other than the distant, mournful wail.

As he cautiously made his way still higher, the sagebrush thinned and gave way to heavy stands of Manzanita and scrub evergreen pines. The setting moon and faint starlight were his only means of penetrating the darkness, until he saw a dim glow in the sky ahead. *By golly, that has to be coming from campfires, which means I've found the Injun's village. Wonder where they keep their horses?* Figuring that the Indians would post lookouts, he paused frequently to listen. Slowly, he continued toward the light, until the low campfires became visible beyond a line of trees.

Curtis edged forward, until the sound of a faint cough stopped him in his tracks. He instantly crouched and waited. Finally, he distinguished the guard's dark form, sitting on a log. *Now what? Maybe I should scout the area and come back tomorrow night. I'm not even sure that this bunch has my horses. Still, risking another stroll up that black canyon seems chancier than I care to ponder. Best I get on with it.* Reaching down, he found a pebble and flung it high over the sentry's head to the far side of a clearing, where it lightly clattered on the ground.

The lookout froze and slowly stood, peering away from him and into the darkness.

Curtis moved with quickness and stealth, bringing the handle of the heavy revolver down on the Indian's head. Catching the man before he fell, Curtis eased him to the ground. He searched and found a bow and sheathed knife. Cutting the bow's gut string, he bound the Indian's hands and feet, shoving the man's waist pack into his mouth. Pausing, he strained to listen, but the village remained quiet. Relaxing his tense muscles, Curtis pushed the man's knife into his own belt and continued to the outskirts of the encampment.

Tall teepees surrounded a cleared area in the small valley, where dying bonfires provided weak light. Carefully, he scanned the camp, but nothing stirred. Moreover, no horses were evident. *I need to move ghost-like. These Injuns probably have dogs in camp.* He smiled tightly, wondering if they might have eaten theirs.

Circling around, he made his way to the other side of the village, where a fenced pen corralled the Indians' ponies. From the distant campfire light, it appeared that steep hillsides bordered most of the enclosure. A wide gate sealed the entrance, made from an assortment of misshapen limbs and strung together with braided rawhide. "Whoa," he said, in a hushed voice to calm the animals, figuring there might be another guard nearby.

Suddenly, he heard a dog bark. It came from the direction of the teepees but stopped. Then, he heard the crashing noise of an animal sprinting toward him through the low brush. Pulling the Indian's knife from his belt, Curtis anxiously waited, watching for any movement. At the last instant, he spotted a dog silhouetted against the dying campfires, as the animal leaped, snarling at him with bared fangs.

Curtis dropped to his knees and, instinctively, thrust the knife straight up with both hands, catching the animal in the throat, as the momentum of the attack bowled them over in the dirt. Pulling out the knife, he slashed the dog's throat.

Trembling, his heart pounded in his ears. Slowly, he stood, fearful that the clash had attracted the attention in the camp. Time passed, but everything remained quiet, as he calmed down. Dropping the knife, he felt sticky, warm blood on his hands, and unconsciously, he wiped them on his pants.

Backing away, he became aware that the horses were stirring about uneasily. Going through the odd gate, he could not tell one animal from another until he saw the finely chiseled head of a large horse silhouetted against the dim glow of the campfires. Carefully, he made his way among the ponies until he was standing beside the tall horse. Gently, he put his arm on her neck, rubbing her ear.

The horse softly nuzzled him.

It's my black, he concluded. Reaching into his shirt pocket, he retrieved kernels of dried corn that he had found in the captain's barn. The horse gently gave his hand a push with its nose and finished off the corn. It was a habit of his to have a treat for the black, and she began her usual prancing dance of appreciation, while pawing at the dirt and nickering softly.

"Easy, girl," he whispered, patting her neck, "settle down. We don't want to attract any attention just yet."

Another horse snorted, alerting Curtis, who quickly dropped to his knees. *Was another guard nearby?* He looked under his horse's belly. In the faint first light of dawn, he saw moccasin covered feet . . . and the hem of a deerskin skirt.

The sight stunned him. *I didn't figure on coming across no Injun female. Now what do I do? What if she stumbles over the dog and shouts an alarm?*

He saw the feet stop, as though the woman was listening and searching the darkness. Despite the night chill, Curtis' hands were clammy. He held his breath and tensed for his next move. *That's just it,* he thought in confusion. *What the heck am I going to do, if'n she shouts an alarm? What if she has a weapon?* he wondered. *Well, the die is cast, and I'll just have to deal with whatever comes up.* Waiting seemed like an eternity, as he quietly slipped the Colt out of his waistband.

The moccasin-clad feet shuffled around, as though she was searching the corral. Finally, the feet slowly moved away.

Shakily, Curtis let out his breath and stood. He stared through the darkness for any signs, but all remained quiet. Turning to his horse, he pulled out a short, thin rawhide rope from his pocket and slipped it around the big black's head. Patting the horse gently, he jumped and climbed onto her back, then lay prone along her withers and neck. Still, there was no sign of trouble.

Grasping the black's mane firmly in one hand, he pulled the rope, and the horse responded, walking to the rear of the corral. Now fully in the dark, with the camp on the other side of the enclosure, Curtis straightened. *This worked the other day,* he thought. *I pray it works tonight.*

He dug his boots into the horse's side, and the animal trotted in the direction of the camp. Letting loose of the mane and holding tightly with his knees, he drew the revolver, cocked it, and fired a shot into the air. The stillness of the dark night shattered, the sound cannonaded off the nearest hills, then leapt to the other side of the cleared area. The echo faded as it moved toward the other end of the crater-like valley. The big black bolted, nearly unseating him, as the gunshot continued to reverberate around the mountaintop hollow. Curtis grabbed the big horse's mane tightly, as though his very life depended upon it—which it did.

"*Yeooowaaawee!*" Curtis shouted, as he moved toward the gate. Once more, he fired the pistol. "*Yeooowaaawee!*" he let loose, again.

The gunfire and his hollering spooked the horses. Following an ancient instinct, they stampeded as one, easily knocking down the shaky corral fence and galloping headlong toward the camp.

Shouts of bewilderment came from the village, as Indians hurried out of the teepees and gathered around the dim campfires. Then, startled and unbelieving, they dove out of the way to avoid the deadly hooves of charging ponies.

Most of the animals knew the way in and out of the hidden mountain retreat, having traveled it many times. The man from Missouri moved with the flow, trying to keep low. Teepees, Indians, and campfires passed him in a blur, as he managed to stay atop the big black.

Near the outskirts of camp, a brave suddenly blocked his path. The man's eyes opened wide in astonishment at the oncoming horse and rider. The big black collided with the man, roughly tumbling him into the thicket.

Curtis drove the herd down the mountain, following the twisting bottom of the *arroyo* in the faint light of false dawn. Galloping out of the ravine, he cut to the right in order to retrieve his borrowed horse from the thicket hideout. Crashing through the brush, he dismounted and quickly saddled the black, tied on his kit, and slit the hobble between the other animal's legs. Mounting his big filly, he felt a sense of relief for the first time, yet there was much to do.

He returned for the Indian ponies, which were grazing on scrub grass in the mouth of the wash. With loud shouts, whistles, and using his twirling *reata*, Curtis managed to round them up, and he got the whole herd galloping in the early light of dawn. Setting a course directly across the broad alkali valley, there was no letup, until Curtis and the herd splashed into the Red River.

High on the bluff ahead, he saw the welcoming lantern hanging at the Indian Red Ranch. Slowing the pace, and flushed with success, he shouted to his horse, "Not a bad night's work, eh, big black?" Then, grinning widely, he yelled his Indian war cry one last time.

Most of the hands were already milling about, preparing for the coming day. Captain Gilbert was standing on the *veranda* with a cup of hot coffee in his hand. As the ponies galloped into the center of the compound, everyone scattered.

"What in heaven's name is going on here?" the rancher exclaimed, dumbfounded, as he dropped his cup. As Curtis slid his horse to a stop before him, a big smile creased the older man's face. "Ya went to find yar horses, and looki here, ya brought back a whole herd. There must be a dozen ponies . . . no by golly maybe two dozen, besides yar own. I see some blood on yar leggings, but I don't see any arrows or tomahawks sticking out of your hide. Are you hurt anywhere that I can't make out?"

"Other than a scratch, I was mighty lucky," Curtis shouted, in a rush of exhilaration.

The ranch compound was filled with sounds, as the wranglers shooed the ponies toward a corral gate, shouting, whooping it up, and waving their hats.

Now, the rancher was laughing so hard that tears ran down his face. "No . . . no question about it, Missouri, ya've done pissed off them Injuns something fierce." Beginning to catch his breath, he stared at Curtis, and continued, "Son, ya got to be one of the cleverest men that I've ever met. By Jove, when I spin yar yarn to my ranger friends down in Dallas, they're going to wonder how much locoweed juice I've been swilling. If'n I hadn't seen it with my own eyes—" He paused, at a loss for words.

"Thank you, sir," Curtis replied, grinning broadly.

Still beaming, the captain added, "Well done, Curtis Sommer from Missouri. Somewhere in yar past, ya must surely have some Texican blood in ya. And I'm right glad to see that Colt six-shooter again, too."

***

Curtis finished saddling his black horse and tied on his kit. The pinto and his pa's sorrel, part of the liberated Indian herd, were to one side, strung together on a line. The *hacienda's* cook had supplied him with a cloth sack—filled with fried *tortillas*, cooked cactus apples, and beef jerky, which he tied to the horn atop the pommel. Ready to leave, he turned to say goodbye to the captain.

Wearing a coat to help ward off the early morning chill, the ranch owner commented, "I aim to have a horse like yars. My ride yesterday on yar big black convinced me that the Tennessee Walker breed is just the thing for me, what with my lumbago acting up. That horse's cadence is remarkably easy."

"I think that's a fine idea," Curtis replied, smiling, "as long as it ain't my black."

"Of course," the rancher laughed. "I imagine ya get to Fort Smith from time to time, don't ya, Curtis?"

"Why, yes. Either my pa or I go there at least once a year. These days we get most of our supplies from Springfield. Still Fort Smith continues to have the advantage of being on the Arkansas River with steamboats pulling in regularly."

"Good. I'd like ya to do a favor for me and stop by the fort on yar return to Missouri. I know it's a bit out of yar way, but I'd be real obliged."

Mystified, Curtis said, "I'm not following you, sir."

Pushing back his wide-brimmed hat, the captain explained, "I want ya to buy me a Walker stallion and take him north to yar farm, so it can be bred with yar filly. Next year, send or bring the stallion back to the fort, and I'll have one of my men pick him up. Ya can leave him with Foster Wheeler. He's a friend of mine in town, and he publishes the *Fort Smith Herald* newspaper. How about it, will ya do that for me?"

The request was a surprise, yet the idea of adding a new stud's vitality to his and John Leach's breeding program was appealing. "And what happens to the colt?" Curtis asked.

"Ya keep it. It's my last gift to ya for this added trouble."

Curtis was stunned. "That's a mighty handsome offer, sir. Sure you want to do this?"

"Yep. I've drawn up a bank draft for a thousand dollars drawn on the Fort Smith Territorial Bank. Use what ya need to buy me a high quality stallion and leave any extra funds in my account at the bank."

"My word, Captain Gilbert, that's a lot of money. I'm not sure I'd do the same, if'n I was you."

"I know men, and I figure ya're a fella of yar word. I've taken many risks in my day, but I don't reckon this is one of them."

"All right, I'll do it."

Drawing a leather wallet from an inside coat pocket, he handed it to Curtis. "The bank draft is in there, made out to ya. What's more, ya'll also find three hundred dollars, which is yar share of the money I'll get for selling those Injun ponies to the folks down in Dallas."

Well, this is a day for surprises, Curtis thought. "Hey, Captain Gilbert, they're my gift to you. I can't take this money."

"Nonsense, ya not only liberated those horses, ya also left that band of Injun cutthroats without ponies, so I won't be having any trouble from them for quite a spell. I did my sums, and I'll easily sell that bunch for twenty or thirty dollars a head, so we're both getting something." Sticking out his hand, he asked, "How about it, Missouri, do we have a deal?"

"It's a deal, sir," Curtis replied, laughing and shaking the rancher's hand. "I'm much obliged for your generous hospitality, sir. I'll pick out the best Walker that I can find."

"Ya do that, son."

Swinging up onto the big black, Curtis touched his hat. "*Adios.*"

"*Vaya con dios, mi amigo.*"

CHAPTER SEVEN

As Curtis rode east, he had a great deal of time to think. *I kind of like the nickname that the captain laid on me,* he thought. *Somehow, Missouri sounds manly. I'll try it on and see how it fits.*

He remained dumbfounded by the rancher's proposal. *And him, a stranger, walking off with a draft for a thousand dollars, on my promise to buy a horse that won't be delivered for at least a year. I know I'm good for my word, but how does the captain know it?*

Suddenly, his thoughts cleared. *Captain Gilbert's wanted a Walker all along, even before seeing my black. He must have told drifters passing by the ranch, or maybe he spoke about it to his friends down in Dallas. Those bushwhackers that hit my place—they knew and were prepared to steal my horse and then risk their lives by traveling through Injun country to reach his Red River ranch. Furthermore, that fella, ear-less Jens, told me they expected to get as much as a thousand dollars for my horses.*

Laughing aloud, he said to his big black, "Well, I'll be damned. That old Texas Ranger is a true-to-life, wily old cougar. He's going to get himself a Walker, one way or t'other, ain't he?"

Still chuckling, he remembered his share of the money for the Indian ponies. *Three hundred dollars is more money than I've ever had at one time. No reason for me to put off marrying Judy Beth any longer. I'll ask her just as soon as I get back. Maybe we'll set a date right after harvest time. I think I'll also buy more land from the government and add it to my farm. After all, some day Judy Beth and I'll have a parcel of younguns, and that'll mean more mouths to feed.*

Riding on, he continued to think about his good fortune. *Maybe I'll pick up a memento for my brothers and sisters . . . and for the folks, too. Pa could use a new plowshare file and maybe I'll find a quilt for Ma. Judy Beth will be more difficult, but I can probably find a pretty shawl at the Sparks' General Store.*

Besides thinking about his family and the Walker, Curtis practiced every morning with his new six-shooter. At first, he tried alternative ways to hold and sight the weapon. Lining up the brass-tipped barrel within the V-sight of the cocked hammer meant holding the pistol straight out in his right hand and sighting down the barrel. Unlike his Hawken rifle, it seemed awkward that way, with his arm fully extended.

Accuracy was another real issue. If he took too much time to aim, the weight of the pistol took its toll on his extended arm, spoiling his shot. He tried holding it with both arms extended in front of him, and accuracy dramatically improved. Either stance required that he be upright, and this frustrated him. *I reckon it'll likely give me away to most critters that I hunt using this peashooter.*

After many attempts, he found that he could shoot with fair accuracy by firing from the side of his right hip, while fanning the hammer with his other hand. *I'll also get me some type of leather holster to hold this small cannon and look for a second cylinder in Fort Smith,* he concluded. *The Colt will come in right handy, if'n I ever catch up to that last horse-thieving bushwhacker, Veeko.* Memories of his hound overtook him, and he wiped away a tear, as he continued toward Arkansas.

The long days of hot, dusty travel continued, until one afternoon when he stopped atop a hill, looking down at a village. It was centered in a river valley, and it appeared to be an Indian compound, yet there was a white building with a cross sitting on the peak of the roof, situated among a smattering of *adobe* houses. To the south, widespread teepees dotted the encampment. Fish drying racks dotted the camp with several hides staked out on the ground to cure.

Riding slowly into the village, he saw many Indian boys and girls scurrying about, who looked at him curiously. As he came to the building with the cross, a young white woman came through the door, shooing little ones outside. She wore a blue gingham dress, beneath a cornflower-blue apron.

"How do, ma'am. My name is Curtis Sommer, and I'm on my way to Fort Smith. What place is this?"

Surprised to see a stranger, she replied, "G'day to you, Mr. Sommer. This is the Asbury Mission, which is a Methodist school for Creek Injuns. The village is Eufaula. My name is Sarah Jane Ish, and I'm the schoolmarm here."

"Pleased to meet you, ma'am," the Missourian said, tipping his hat. "I'm riding in from Wichita Falls over in Texas. Anywhere around here where my horses and I can rest for the night?"

Eyeing the Missourian briefly, the young woman seemed to make up her mind. "Sure, why don't you join my father and me for supper? You can tie the animals out back of our *adobe* home and throw your sleeping roll under one of the trees." She laughed softly as a stray breeze blew a lock of brown hair in her face.

He liked the friendliness in her eyes. "That's mighty kind of you, ma'am, but I don't want to put you out, and I'm a bit rank from riding the trail."

"Don't be silly. My pa and I enjoy talking to folks passing through. It's about the only way we get any news. See that white *adobe* house at the end of this lane?" she asked, pointing. "That's our place. Go ahead and settle behind the house. The river is just beyond, and you can wash off some of that heavy trail dirt before the meal. I'll be there shortly."

"Thankee kindly," he said, tipping his hat again and made his way toward the river.

An hour later, he was sitting down, eating with the attractive woman and her father.

"What brings you to the wilds of Eufaula, young man?" John Ish asked.

Cutis noted that the man was tall in stature, vigorous, and likely in his sixties.

As they ate, Mr. Ish quizzed him about his travels.

Briefly, Curtis relayed his experiences following the horse thieves, meeting Captain Gilbert, and battling the Kiowa Indians.

"My word, you must certainly love those horses," Sarah Jane remarked, a look of wonder on her face. "And you got them back, and you weren't injured?"

"Yes, ma'am, I was mighty lucky."

"Shows a lot of spunk on your part," John Ish opined. "I hear tell you're traveling to Fort Smith. Be that so?"

"Yes, sir, that's my next destination," Curtis replied. "From there, I'll be traveling north to my farm in Missouri."

"My daughter is also leaving for Fort Smith tomorrow. We got word yesterday that Lieutenant Frank Parke and his troop of Third Calvary from Fort Gibson is arriving this evening and will be escorting her. Why don't you go along with them? That way, you'll have company on the trail."

"I'd like that, sir," Curtis responded. "I'm not much of a talker, but I've had far too many nights on the open range, with just the stars and my horses to keep me company."

Mr. Ish laughed, and said, "Then it's settled."

The next day, Curtis' escorts were a troop of mounted bluecoats, Miss Ish, and Lieutenant Parke, on the six-day journey to Fort Smith. He found the army officer to be a striking figure of a man, who easily sat his horse. He wore traditional blue-gray trousers, high-top black boots, and a dark blue tunic, topped off with an off-white hat, and a yellow kerchief. Standing tall, he appeared to be five or six years older than Curtis. His tanned face, auburn-colored hair, and wide sideburns set off his light blue eyes.

Curtis and the man hit it off right from the start. This was also true for Parke and Sarah Jane. After the first evening meal, the three sat around a campfire and talked.

After a spell, Curtis asked, "Miss Ish, where do you hail from originally?"

"My pa was one of the first settlers in Arkansas, up in the northeast corner of the territory, right on the Mississippi River. The family migrated there after Cherokee Indians killed my grandpa back in North Carolina. My father came to the mission four years ago, and I joined him last year."

"Despite all the tragedy in your family," Curtis observed, "here you are, teaching white man's talk to Injuns in the middle of nowhere." He was impressed with this teacher. She had a quick smile, and she was bright.

Sarah Jane laughingly responded, "To us, it's not the middle of 'nowhere,' as you call it. It's our home and our work. Still, you're right about one thing—I don't fear the Indians at the mission. I figure we all have to learn to get along. So, I try to help where I can."

"Aye, there be nothing more touching than a sad account from such a pretty young miss," Lieutenant Parke remarked with a twinkle in his eye. Lighting his pipe, he smiled at the woman.

"And with that brogue, where do you hail from?" Sarah Jane asked.

"'Tis the country green of Ireland, me dear, which lies across the wide blue sea."

"Is it a pretty land?" she asked.

"My dear, 'tis the land of shamrocks and the home of me patron, St. Patrick."

"That's some lineage, Lieutenant," Sarah Jane replied, with a laugh. "Not everyone has an ancestral saint."

A twinkle of merriment lit the lieutenant's eyes. "Like we oft say, particularly to a pretty lassie back in the old country," Lieutenant Parke continued, "may the apple of yer eye always bring ye blessed happiness and may yer lips be touched with the sweetness of a good man's love."

"My, my," Sarah Jane replied, with a dimpled smile and a touch of blush on her cheeks, "you're a poet as well as an officer and a gentleman."

Turning serious, Lieutenant Parke smiled and turned to Curtis. "Tell me more, me boy, about the brush ye had with the Injuns."

Curtis told them about meeting Captain Gilbert and sneaking into the Kiowa camp to reclaim his horses.

"By all that's holy," the lieutenant stated in amazement, "ye slipped into their camp and stole back yer horses . . . and all of their ponies, too? We need ye in the cavalry, me fine new friend from Missouri. When can ye join?"

"Well, it sounds more dangerous than it really was," Curtis replied, sheepishly. "Besides, my pa says I sometimes spin a better yarn than the facts merit."

"Nonsense, what ye did was brilliant and, not to embarrass ye before the lovely lass here, it was the work of a hero. Having seen yer big black, I can understand the feelings ye have for that horse. But mind ye, they'll be clamoring to print yer news in Mr. Wheeler's *Fort Smith Herald* when he gets wind of it in town."

"Please, sir, let's keep this to ourselves, and not embroider it any more. If'n I didn't have some business to do for Captain Gilbert at the fort, I'd already be traveling north."

"All right," the lieutenant agreed, and winked conspiratorially at the young woman. "Let's keep his secret, shall we, Miss Sarah Jane?"

Laughing, the woman responded, "As you say, Lieutenant Parke. But, aren't you going to report Curtis' Injun experiences to your colonel?"

At that, they all laughed again.

With such company, the change was good for Curtis, and time seemed to fly. He was glad that he had stopped at the mission school.

During the Sommer family's journey from Ohio, Curtis first saw Fort Smith and the adjoining village as a boy, when he stood at the rail of a river steamboat, which was towing their flatboats up the Arkansas River. As the steamer rounded a wide bend, there it sat on the high ground of a peninsula created by the arc of the large waterway and the intersecting smaller Poteau River. The huge army parade ground stood out, outlined by ridged military lines, and it was bare as a baby's bum.

In the ensuing years, the fort had changed, as the army abandoned the post and moved its command farther west, to Fort Gibson. Later, the army re-activated Fort Smith, as a processing center for members of displaced eastern Indian tribes, in accordance with the Federal Government's Indian Removal Act of 1830.

Over the years, the small village had prospered and evolved into a major trading center, as steamboats made their way up the Arkansas River carrying Indians and cargo, returning downriver with cotton, corn, wheat, and livestock. According to the lieutenant, more than five hundred settlers now lived in town, in addition to the army garrison of several hundred.

Curtis saw a sizable Indian settlement camped on the banks of the Poteau River, just as he had seen many times before. They awaited word from the government agent at the fort on where their new homelands were located in the vast territory.

"Sergeant, see to the men," Lieutenant Parke commanded. "I'll be escorting Miss Ish to her lodging." He turned and waved to Curtis. "Glad to have met ye. Hope we'll see ye again. Keep yerself safe, my adventurous new friend, but mind what I've told ye. If ye want some Irish luck, wear yer bit of shamrock green."

___With a touch of his hat and a nod toward Sarah Jane, Curtis turned his horses toward the stable, where a blacksmith operated his furnace and anvil under a shed roof next to a corral. Curtis asked him to stable his animals and to look after their shoeing requirements. Then he inquired about horse traders in town, especially those selling Tennessee Walkers.

"There is a trader on the east side of town who sells fine horses. You can look him up. He goes by the name of Seabold—Frankie Seabold."

"Thank you kindly. I'll look him up in the morning." Walking down the busy, main street, he turned into a saddlery shop and looked at leather holsters for his Colt. He set aside one with a cover flap. The design seemed too cumbersome. Strapping another type around his waist, he slid the pistol in and out several times. A thong at the bottom kept the closed-end, gun sleeve fastened to his leg, and a buckled strap at the top secured it. It had a good feel, so he bought it.

The gunsmith shop across the road sold the new Navy Colt. There, he purchased more supplies and an extra cylinder for his revolver. He also traded in the replacement rifle the captain had given him, for a new Hawken with a beautiful maple stock. Continuing down the main dirt road, Curtis bought gifts for his folks and Judy Beth. A big bag of rock candy would be his gift to his brothers and sisters.

Tomorrow, I'll look up that horse dealer. Tonight, I'm looking forward to a good night's sleep in a soft, warm bed.

CHAPTER EIGHT

Curtis spent a restless night, as a loud, noisy crowd had a roaring good time in the saloon below his hotel room. The next morning dawned crisp and clear. Before setting out for the horse trader, he treated himself to a big breakfast of biscuits and gravy, three eggs, a slab of ham, and three cups of coffee in the saloon on the ground floor, which also operated as a restaurant.

Strapping on his new gun belt before leaving, Curtis made his way to the trader's place of business. He saw about a dozen horses in the corral, with a combination barn and cabin at one end. He made inquiries of a stable hand, who directed him to the owner.

"Are you Frankie Seabold?" he asked, seeing a man coming out the barn door.

With a wide, toothy smile, the fellow replied, "Indeed I am. I'm the purveyor of the finest horseflesh west of the Mississippi. Why, men ride from all over the territory just to buy from Frankie Seabold. Everyone knows they'll get an honest deal and a sound horse from me. What can I do for you this fine morning, young fella?"

Seabold was stylishly dressed in a linen shirt beneath a light charcoal-colored coat, with a white handkerchief tucked into his breast pocket. A gold chain and watch adorned his vest, and a string tie matched the man's hatband. His well-trimmed beard and moustache were the same color as his flowing hair—mostly white.

"I'd like to look at your horses, particularly your Tennessee Walkers."

"Why, sure enough," Mr. Seabold replied. The older man ran his eye up and down Curtis and his trail-worn clothes, and his smile slipped into a smirk.

He's wondering if'n I'm a no-account drifter, or maybe a rustler looking to steal his horses, Curtis guessed. Hurrying to dispel that notion, he continued, "My name is Curtis Sommer. I've just come to town from the Injun Red Ranch outside Wichita Falls, over in Texas. I'm looking to buy a horse for Captain Mabel Gilbert. Perhaps you've heard of him."

Immediately, the toothy, crocodile smile returned to the man's face. Taking his hat off, the older man ran his fingers through his thick, wavy hair. "Why, sure enough, I've heard of the Captain Gilbert. I expect he's one of the most famous rangers in all of Texas. I even met him once over at the saloon. Nicest man you'd ever want to meet. Why," he went on, "he told about the time he was chasing after some Comanche braves and how he—"

"I'd be obliged if we could get back to horses, Mr. Seabold. I'm looking for a Tennessee Walker."

"Ah, yes. Walker, you say. Well, as it turns out, I have three. They're fine riding animals, don't you know. Come this way, young man."

In a separate corral, three horses stood at a water trough, as the men drew near. The gelding and filly held no interest for Curtis. The third, a chestnut-colored stallion, stood tall, with a refined neck and a white stripe accenting his face. The horse seemed to arch his head, watching them approach.

Sliding between the rails, Curtis approached the animal and gently ran his hands over the horse's shoulders and glossy haunches. In turn, he picked up each hoof. Mentally drawing a line straight down the middle, he saw that they were equal-sided. *That's good. Even so, the walls of the hooves are thick and need trimming, and this stallion needs shoeing.* Curtis walked a short distance and turned to study the chestnut from the side. *Its top line is continuous, also a good sign.*

His friend, John Leach, had spent considerable time acquainting him with the finer points of horses. "From the top," he would say, "the body should be well balanced." From that starting point, they had meticulously covered other parts of a horse's configuration. "I can't overemphasize the importance of a horse's underpinnings," John had often repeated. "No sense breeding poor traits." The man had taught him to avoid mounts with front legs that were knock-kneed, toed-out, or splayed; and hind legs that were overly cow-hocked or sickle-kneed. This stallion had great composition, and Curtis liked the glint in his eyes, as the animal tossed his head.

Curtis became aware that the horse dealer had apparently been talking all the time he was assessing the chestnut. Curtis interrupted the man in mid-sentence. "Where was this horse bred?"

"Brought him all the way from Tennessee, don't you know? That's where this extraordinary line of horses was bred originally. Yes, siree, I picked him out myself, and he came by steamboat, and that cost a heap of—"

"You got any papers on him, showing his lineage?"

"Yes, indeed," the slick talker replied.

Attaching a lead, Curtis walked the stallion across the corral. He stopped and looked back at a straight line of prints. *Yep, this is a fine animal,* he thought.

"I can clearly see that you know a few things about horses," the talkative Seabold persisted, pacing and watching the young man, often curling the ends of his silvery moustache. "Where do you hail from, young man?" the man asked with more than usual curiosity.

Curtis ignored the man, as he ran his hand over the horse's broad chest. *His muscling is long and smooth. Good.* "Whoa, boy," he said, patting the horse on the neck and opening its mouth. *This male has all his permanent teeth, complete with tushes.* "What's his age?"

"As I recall, his papers say he be near five years old."

"That's about right," the Missourian replied. *At four or five years old, a horse sheds its milk teeth, and the canines are in place. There's a little wear,* he noted, *and the front teeth are showing some rounding on the backside. These signs are consistent with his age.*

"Captain Gilbert must be quite fussy about his horses."

"That he is, and so am I. Can I borrow a saddle? I need to walk and run him a bit."

"Sure, sure, I wouldn't expect anything else. You go right ahead, young man. Pick a saddle in the barn that suits you."

Curtis rode the chestnut around the sizable corral for the next ten minutes, taking the animal through various gaits. Following the ride, he was convinced that he had found the right horse for Captain Gilbert. With a sense of anticipation, he also figured it would be a fine stud for his black, but he made sure that his face didn't convey his enthusiasm to horse-dealer Seabold.

Returning to the corral, the older man began his nonstop gabbing again. "Course, all the finer points of this excellent animal run up the price. You understand how those things work, don't you, Mr. Sommer?"

"What'll you take for him?"

"Well, I usually have only one such fine animal, but today I have three, as you can see, so I've a mind to make you a good offer for a quick sale. Show me eleven hundred dollars, and he's yours, err . . . I mean, Captain Gilbert's."

With a skeptical expression on his face, Curtis stared at the horse dealer. Shaking his head and looking solemn, he walked to the corral fencing and stepped between the rails. "If'n that's your best price, you'll need to sell him to someone else. Captain Gilbert is no fool." Looking the horse dealer in the eye, he continued, "And, neither am I. Much obliged for your time. Have yourself a fine day, Mr. Seabold."

The shocked expression on the fellow's face said it all. The crocodile smile slipped and disappeared. Out came the breast pocket handkerchief, and the older man used it to mop his brow.

Curtis touched his hat as a farewell gesture and turned to walk away.

"Hold up there, young fella," the older man called out, his big smile firmly re-established.

Curtis turned, and he had a calm expression on his face. "Yes, Mr. Seabold, do you have something else in mind?"

"You never made me an offer, so I wasn't sure how interested you were in this chestnut. What say we step into the barn, where we can sit a spell and talk things over? Maybe we'll have a pull on the white-lightning jug to wet our whistles?" The silver-haired man was smiling and nodding, while attempting to guide Curtis toward the barn by grasping his arm.

Shaking the man off, the Missourian pushed back his hat. "My offer is nine hundred dollars. Will you accept?"

Curtis nearly missed hiding his smile at the expression of anguish on the older man's face, as his mouth opened and closed, resembling a gulping catfish. "Well, what's your answer?" he demanded brusquely.

"My good man, surely you jest," Seabold lamented, his big smile replaced by a look of anguish. "I've expenses to cover, like the costly steamboat charges and the grain and hay this horse has eaten and—"

Breaking in once more, Curtis added, "And I want his hooves trimmed and shoed, as part of the deal."

A further look of bewilderment, indeed astonishment, rippled across the horse trader's face. "You obviously don't understand how the trading business works, and the costs involved in maintaining such a fine animal for sale. Why, a man could go bust dealing with the likes of you."

Turning on his heel, Curtis began again walking toward his hotel.

"Now, don't be turning away like that, young fella," the older man said. "Hold yourself together and give me a minute, while I check my trading book, and think on your offer for a spell."

"All right."

Pulling a small black notebook from his coat pocket, the trader thumbed through the pages until he found what he was looking for. Running a hand through his wavy, gray hair, he stared at Curtis. "Is that your best offer?"

The Missourian nodded.

"You drive a hard bargain, but I'm feeling bighearted this morning, and after all, I still have those other two Walkers to sell. You've bought a great horse, my fine young friend." The crocodile-smile returned, as quickly as it had disappeared, and he held out his hand to seal the deal.

Shaking the man's hand, Curtis smiled. "I'll pick him up in the morning?" Seeing the nod from Mr. Seabold, Curtis added, "It's a deal."

As he walked away, Curtis smiled to himself and figuratively shook his head. *I wonder if all horse traders are as gabby and full of bull as this one.* Feeling good about the purchase, he made his way to the center of town and headed toward the Fort Smith Territorial Bank.

Curtis waited his turn at the bank, then presented the clerk with the bank draft. The man, wearing a visor and garters for his shirtsleeves, looked at the draft for a moment, then referred him to the manager, who sat at a corner desk.

Through small spectacles perched on the end of his nose, the primly dressed, balding man examined the piece of paper carefully. He looked Curtis up and down, taking in his grubby, trail-worn clothes and his shaggy, overgrown head of hair. In a nasal, high-pitched voice, he declared, "The signature certainly appears genuine enough, but I've never laid eyes on you before. What proof do you have that you're the fellow named on this here draft?"

The question stunned Curtis. Too readily, he responded, "Because I'm telling you, that's why!"

"Now, now, we'll need more than that. After all, Captain Gilbert is a much respected customer of this bank, and I'm obliged to look out for his interests."

"Well, how do you suggest that I prove who I am?" Curtis answered, showing his annoyance. "I give you my word. Isn't that good enough for you?"

"Don't you raise your voice to me, young man! Do you work for Captain Gilbert?

"Nope."

"How do I know you didn't steal . . . ah, acquire this draft under false pretenses, or, maybe, even using duress of force?"

"Are you calling me a thief? I don't take such talk lightly, sir."

For the first time, the bank manager seemed to take full notice of the holstered revolver strapped around Curtis' waist, and he began backing away.

"Sam," he called over his shoulder to the bank clerk, "close your window and go get the sheriff. Tell him we may have a situation here at the bank."

"Sir, this is a straightforward transaction," Curtis said. Seeing no give on the man's part, he continued, "Think on the matter and I'll take back the draft." Snatching it out of the bank manager's hand, Curtis turned on his heel, angry and frustrated. As he walked out the door, he saw Sam run across the street and enter the sheriff's office.

Ducking down a side alley, Curtis made his way to the blacksmith's shop, wondering what to do next. *There ain't no reason for me to hide, but how do I prove that I'm me,* he wondered. Suddenly, he remembered Lieutenant Parke. Cheering up, he quickly crossed the broad parade ground in search of the army officer. After asking several troopers, he finally found his new friend in the huge horse barn.

"G'day to you, sir," Curtis called.

The man was currying his horse. He was dressed in an undershirt tucked into his army trousers, supported by a wide set of braces. His blouse hung on a peg next to the stall. "Well, this is a surprise, Curtis. Top o' the morn' to ye. There must be something on yer mind to be searching me out so early on this fine day."

"Yes, sir, I've got a small problem and thought you might be able to help me." As Curtis explained, he observed the lieutenant's knotted forehead.

"Curtis, I'd be only too glad to help, as ye seem like a decent and brave chap, but we only recently met on the trail. Don't get me wrong,

I think yer genuinely the man ye claim to be. It's just that I can't vouch for ye any more than Miss Sarah Jane can, after knowing ye for only a few days."

Sensing Curtis' disappointment, he went on, "Didn't ye say that ye and yer folks have done business in town over the years? Surely, some shopkeeper in town must know yer family and can speak up for ye. Maybe there's someone at the mercantile store or the livery?"

"Of course," Curtis responded. "We've done business for years at the general store with the owner, James Sparks."

"Aye, I've yet to meet him, but I understand he's another fine squire from the emerald green island of me birth. Why don't ye look him up at the store? I'll be along directly, as soon as I wash up and slip me tunic on."

"I'm mighty obliged, Lieutenant," turning to leave.

"Kindly linger a moment longer, courageous fella that ye be from Missouri. Come with me," he directed. Parke walked out of the huge, double barn doors with a mystified Curtis following.

Outside, the army man paused, obviously searching for something. "Aha, there 'tis," he said. Bending over, he snapped off the end of a grass stalk.

Reaching up, the army man stuffed it beneath the band of Curtis' hat and stood back to admire his work. "Ye be a manly fella, me new-found friend, but 'tis luck that'll save yer neck someday. Now, ye're wearing a bit of green and are properly attired, so ye can go back to meet the foolishness at the bank, knowing that the good luck of the Irish be with thee."

Curtis was dubious, and his expression reflected his feeling.

Hastily, the lieutenant added, "Now, don't be going thickheaded on me about this. Get thee moving, me boy, I'll be there straightaway and meet ye at the mercantile."

Chuckling, Curtis started for the town, wondering about the lieutenant's tales.

Approaching the store, someone roughly collared him from behind and spun him around.

Curtis was startled and knocked the offending hand away, only to have two other men seize him roughly by the arms. "Who are you and what do you want?" he asked, voicing his anger. He never liked being manhandled.

"We're the civil law in this town, and I'm Sheriff Story," the man replied, moving aside a coat lapel to reveal his badge. "I heard tell that you were trying to pass a draft signed by one of the bank's best customers. How did you get it? Did you steal it?"

The matter was getting out of hand, and Curtis couldn't believe his ears.

"Captain Gilbert, the Texas cattleman, asked me to buy him a horse with the money from the draft."

"Surely the captain wrote out his instructions for you, considering the large sum of money involved," the sheriff said. "You could have shown it to the bank manager to back your claim. So, let's have it now."

"I've nothing in writing except the bank draft. It's really not a thorny issue, as Captain Gilbert gave me instructions to buy him a horse here in town."

"Well, we'll have to see about this back at the—"

"Here, now, what's this all about?" Lieutenant Parke spoke up behind them.

Responding to the authoritative voice, the sheriff spun around. Seeing the officer's blue uniform, he composed himself. "I'm Sheriff Story, and this man's been badgering the bank folks. They think that he may have stolen a valuable draft from one of their wealthy customers."

"Nonsense, I was just speaking to Curtis, and he's on his way to see Mr. Sparks who can vouch for him."

"You mean the mayor?" the sheriff asked in astonishment.

"Aye, now let's all calm ourselves, and we can go inside and straighten out this mess."

As two men continued to hold Curtis' arms, the party entered through the mercantile doorway.

Mayor Sparks indeed remembered the Missourian. "Curtis, me lad, it's good seeing ye again. How's yer pa? And John Leach? Be they both in good health?"

"The last I saw them, everyone was fine, sir. There's a problem, and I hope you can help. I've been over Texas way. Captain Mabel Gilbert gave me a thousand dollar bank draft made out in my name, and he wants me to buy him a horse here in Fort Smith. I've already selected the animal at Frankie Seabold's corral. I need to cash the draft to complete the purchase.

"The bank manager says that I need to prove who I am. You've known me and my family for years. Would you please tell the sheriff and these men that I'm Curtis Sommer, the same as the fella named on the draft?" He looked at the men holding his arms, then brusquely pulled away and straightened his coat.

Taken aback, the mayor recovered. "I see, me boy," he replied. "Sheriff, I've known this lad and his people ever since the day the steamboat dropped them off at the old fort landing, many years ago. They are fine, upstanding citizens of Seneca, Missouri, and I've been selling them equipment and supplies for years. Tarnation, sheriff, he and his kin, have always been good for their word."

With a look that suggested disappointment, the lawman shrugged his shoulders at the mayor's statement.

"Thank you, sir," Curtis said, "I'm much obliged. Let me introduce you to Lieutenant Parke from Fort Gibson. We traveled to Fort Smith together from the Injun mission at Eufaula."

"Pleased to make yer acquaintance," the mayor replied, shaking the army man's hand. "Now what say we all take a little walk over to the bank and get this matter resolved?"

<hr>

That afternoon, Curtis bought a new shirt and canvas breeches to replace his worn clothes, and he paid two bits for a bath to wash off the trail dirt. Then, in the early evening, he sat down for dinner with Lieutenant Parke and Miss Ish at Mayor Sparks' house.

"This be me wife, Lisa Annie," the mayor said, introducing the handsome woman at his side.

"Welcome to thee all," she said with a smile. She seemed considerably younger than her husband, and her sparkling blue eyes matched her dress. Her brogue had a lilt to it, like that of the mayor.

As they sat at the dining table, Mayor Sparks commented, "I've been admiring that gun ye wear on yer hip, Curtis."

"It's a revolver, sir, which holds six bullets. The Colt Firearms Company of Connecticut is the maker, and they call this model their *Navy Colt.* Captain Gilbert says it's the company's newest pistol and similar to the type the Texas Rangers have been using for many years."

"I've been meaning to ask ye about it, too," the officer chimed in. "Can ye hit anything with such a weapon. My muzzle-loaded, single-shot is accurate only to about thirty yards."

Curtis told them about his experience. He pointed out the hammer action, spun the cylinder, and unlatched the seating lever.

"May I hold it?" the lieutenant asked.

"Certainly."

Turning it over in his hands, the army man continued, "It's not like using a rifle, eh? Ye're obliged to be near the skirmish when ye use this weapon."

"Indeed," the mayor added, "no wonder the bank manager was a bit put-off his feed, when he saw ye wearing it. Ye may not know it, but he was robbed last year, and he's still as skittish as a mule with a blowfly on its backside."

The soldier expertly examined the long pistol, spinning the cylinder. "How long does it take to reload this weapon?" he asked.

"Several minutes," the Missourian replied. "That's why you carry a second loaded cylinder. In short order, you can fire off twelve rounds, if needed."

"Well, I'll be."

"You men and your guns," Sarah Jane piped up. "Surely, there's more going on than the latest firearms from Mr. Colt's forge."

"Yes, I agree with thee, Sarah Jane," Mrs. Sparks added. "Land's sake alive, ye men and yer guns. Why, a body would think that it be the only thing worth chatting about. In fact, there be interesting things happening all about us. James, surely we can change the topic to something else. Why not tell these folks about your preparations for the trip to California next year?"

"Of course, me dear," the mayor replied, soothingly. "There's nothing I'd rather talk about. We're well along in our planning to lead a group of folks to the gold country a year from now. We already have two dozen lads committed and just itching to go prospecting in California, and I expect that we'll be bringing along a thousand head of cattle on the journey. Long trip 'tis, straight through the Kiowa and Comanche nations. At the foot of Pike's Peak, we'll turn north to pick up the Oregon Trail."

Lieutenant Parke appeared quizzical. "That's a far piece. Isn't there a way around the big mountains by heading southwest?"

"Well, I suppose we could cut south into Arizona Territory, or perhaps Mexico, to get around the high mountains. We have to keep in mind that such a large herd needs sufficient water along the trail. The route I described is one that is proven, and that's why I prefer it."

"Where abouts is Pike's Peak?" Curtis asked.

"Let me show ye," the mayor responded, standing and leading the way to a large map spread across his desk. "We'll head northwest from Fort Smith to Fort Gibson, then travel almost due west, following the Cherokee Trail." He moved his finger over the map to trace the route. "It follows the Arkansas River to its headwaters. Pike's Peak is part of the Rocky Mountains and is right here, Curtis. When we have it in sight, we turn north to the Oregon Trail. Finally, we'll take the Mormon Trail south to the Great Salt Lake. Then, it's onward and westward to the gold country of California. Yes, siree, I can almost taste the milk and honey of that magical land," he concluded. He laughed, and an expression of excitement covered his face.

The mayor's enthusiasm rubbed off on Curtis. With a heightened sense of adventure, he marveled, "That sounds like a grand trip, full of wonderful new lands and amazing sights. How many miles do you reckon it is?"

"About two thousand, give or take a few."

"I've heard that some of the tallest mountains in the world are between here and California," Curtis said. "And you plan to drive such a large herd right over them?"

"Yep," the mayor replied. "We'll take South Pass to cross the biggest ones—really, more like going around the tallest. Here they are." He drew his finger over the diagram, "And, right here, is the location of the pass."

"That's some trip," Curtis responded, his imagination stirred by the thought of the trip.

"When do you expect that you'll be leaving?" Sarah Jane asked.

"It'll be in the spring of next year. By then, I expect that we'll have over fifty lads, itching to go. We should be outside of the Salt Lake area by October, and we'll likely lay over there for the winter. We'll continue to California in the spring of 1855."

"Are you going, as well?" Sarah Jane asked Lisa Annie.

"Well . . . yes."

"You must be excited?"

"Of course, me dear," the woman replied, with measured reluctance. "Yet, I hope it won't be . . . too exciting." She wrinkled her brow, as her bright smile faded. "I expect it'll be a long and difficult trip, and sometimes, when I think on it, the thought sends shivers down me back. I guess that's from the excitement of anticipation, and partly from the fear of the unknown—ye know, things that James and I will encounter before we reach civilization again."

Sarah Jane reached over and tenderly touched her hand.

Mrs. Sparks' concerns passed right over Curtis' head, as his mind whirled at the magnificent adventures of such a long trip and the idea of driving a large herd to the promised gold country beyond the mountains. *I'd love to be going with them, but dadgum it, I'm too set in my life to take off for the West. Maybe there'll come a day when someone else in the family makes such a journey. I hope so. It sure sounds grand.*

A week later, Curtis covered the final leg of his trip in the last light of the day. He was bone-weary, and every muscle in his body ached from long days in the saddle and sleeping on the hard ground. For some reason, the final stretch of his journey, turning north from Fort Smith, proved the hardest part for him. Finally arriving at his farm, he turned the horses toward his burnt down barn and the horse corral.

Ahead, the door to his cabin suddenly swung open, and he saw someone standing there, silhouetted by the light spilling out, a long gun in hand.

"Hold up there and make yourself known," the shadow demanded.

Recognizing Marion's voice, he replied, "It's me, little brother, Curtis."

"Oh, my gosh, it's you," his brother gushed. "Where in tarnation have you been, big brother? Some were about to give up on you ever returning home—but not me. I knew that you'd make it back." Holding his lantern up, he continued, "And I see you got all your horses back." After pausing, he raised the lantern even higher. "Where in tarnation did you pick up that beautiful chestnut stallion? He's really something. I'll wager that you have a grand yarn to tell me about how you came by such a fine animal."

Stopping at the rail, Curtis slowly dismounted, threw off his hat, and dunked his head into the water trough. Coming up dripping, he shook his head like a hound dog and ran his hand through his drenched hair. *This is where I got wet when the bushwhackers shot at me. Tarnation, it seems like a long time ago.* Before he could properly prepare himself, Marion had him in a crushing bear hug.

Bubbling with happiness, one question after another flowed from his little brother. "You weren't hurt, were you? Did you catch all the bushwhackers? Have you seen Ma and Pa yet? How far did the chase take you?"

"Whoa, boy, you've more questions than the nuts in a squirrel's hideaway. I'm too dog-tired to answer them all tonight."

"I just knew you'd make it back. The folks will be mighty happy to see you. Your setting off after them bushwhackers is all anyone talks about on the farm. And, the same is true in town, too."

"Little brother, I've just come seven or eight hundred miles, and I'm plumb tuckered out. All I can think about is taking off my boots, throwing off these dusty clothes, and sleeping for a good, long spell."

"Flower on the Water came along a couple of weeks after you left and told us about you and Braided Hair jumping the bushwhackers' camp. By the way, he's recovering well." With nary a pause for breath, he rambled on. "Did you get all four? Were there any more gunfights?"

"No more questions tonight, little brother. Sleep is the only thing that I want. I'd be obliged if'n you'd turn the horses loose in the corral and off-saddle my black. These animals have traveled a far piece, and they could use a good feed of oats tonight and a rub down. Will you do that for me?"

Enthusiastically, Marion replied, "Of course." Yet he was fairly itching with more questions, spitting them out in a torrent. "What's that you're wearing around your waist? It looks like the butt of a pistol stuck in that leather holder. How'd you get it? Can you hit anything with it? Did you have many run-ins with Injuns? Did you get clear to Mexico?"

"No, I stopped short at the Red River, in Texas."

"Gosh, I can hardly wait until I hear about your adventures. What happened to the fourth bushwhacker? We heard that he lit out from the rest. Did you ever come across his trail again?"

"No more questions tonight, Marion. There'll be time enough for storytelling, come another day."

BROTHERS

Two Years Later

Seneca, Missouri

CHAPTER NINE

Curtis sat on a log bench inside the big barn and looked out through the open doors. He loved the spring season, when everything was blooming. The magnificent sunset captivated his attention, as he watched the sky turn shades of blues, reds, and purples. Even with all the folks talking and laughing inside, he could hear the loud buzzing call of the cicadas. *This beautiful evening is warm for springtime,* he thought. *I guess that's why those insects are out so early this season.*

Surveying all the folks, he thought, *Them Vogel brothers had the right idea when they organized this get-together. Most neighbors from nearby farms and the town are here to help set aside the tragedies of the past year, "the winter of death," as Pa calls it.*

After Christmas, the ague had taken his mother and many friends and neighbors in Lost Creek Valley. The fast-moving sickness seemed to travel up the river and then back down. Her passing had been swift. Neither the new doctor in town nor any of the home remedies had helped.

The murder of John Leach, in late winter, shocked the community and added to the miserable times following the mysterious illness. John had been on his way to Joplin for supplies when the attack occurred. Curtis keenly felt the loss of his friend.

The outraged community took swift action, resulting in the formation of a large posse. Initially, hound dogs tracked the killers, but the animals lost the scent. Using his experience and hunting skills, Curtis took on the task and followed the gang for more than thirty miles to their hideout in Roaring River Canyon. There, the Lost Creek posse cornered the desperadoes in a canyon and finished them in an epic gun battle beside the raging river.

Just east of his father's farm sat the Vogel brothers' farm and their big barn. The oldest, George, expressed the opinion that the community needed an uplifting event after the misfortunes of the previous winter. He believed nothing was better suited to raise everyone's spirits than a hoedown and an old-fashioned feed. Most folks agreed.

A barrel of hard cider stood in one corner along with tables laden with food contributed by every family. A dozen or more lanterns hung from the barn's posts and beams, giving the interior a soft, warm glow.

At one end, fiddlers and a banjo player lit up the festivities, with a fourth man twanging a mouth harp, for good measure, as the group played one song after another. Folks swung in and out of the latest quadrille, as still another man called the moves, stomping his foot forcefully in time with the lively music. As the men swung their partners, and everyone clapped, it was just as farmer Vogel had predicted, a merry festival celebrating life on the Missouri frontier.

Beside Curtis sat his wife, Judy Beth. With so many people talking and laughing, he leaned toward her to be heard. "How are you feeling tonight? Any rumbles from the little one?" She was nearing her birthing time, and her flowing yellow and white frock did little to hide her advanced condition.

"The bench is a bit hard, but the baby's not doing his usual flips and turns tonight," Judy Beth replied, with a laugh. "It'll be a relief when it's over in a few weeks."

Watching the swinging couples, Curtis noticed that Marion was dancing with a girl from the farm situated north of his father's place. He leaned toward his wife again and asked, "What's the name of that gal dancing with Marion?"

"Ella Mae," she answered, "and Zacharias is her last name. Marion sure has a big smile on his face tonight, doesn't he? I'm glad to see him having so much fun."

Curtis nodded, "He does look happy." He did not know much about the Zacharias family. They had come to Newton County from somewhere upstate, and Mr. Zacharias had purchased his farmland in Lost Creek Valley from his father.

Looking at the dancers again, Curtis smiled at the grand time Marion and Ella Mae were having, whirling about, and laughing. *She's a mighty pretty gal, with her brown hair and dimples in her cheeks. And, she's tall, as she comes right up to Marion's shoulders. I always have a hard time figuring out the age of females, yet I'm guessing she's a bit younger than him, although her figure is full.*

He smiled to himself remembering how Marion had complained about being as willowy as a string bean. *I can't call him that any more, as he has added muscle, filled out, and grown as tall as me in the last few years. Looks like he dressed special for this gathering, as his clothes are neat, and he even combed his hair. Actually, he's become a handsome young man, and he's blessed with Ma's good looks. I've worried about him ever since she died, but Judy Beth is right, he's sure having a good time tonight.*

Curtis knew that his mother's death had changed many things at the family homestead. *There doesn't seem to be as much laughter as I recall when she was alive. Everyone misses her gentle ways but none more than Marion . . . and Pa.*

Beyond the musicians, Curtis noticed his father talking with Preacher Jason Hood. *The preacher is wearing his black Sunday frock and string tie tonight. But then, I can't recall when he hasn't worn his church-meeting clothes to any event.* He watched his father walk to the other side of the barn. Still in a reflective mood, he thought, *it'd be good for Pa to marry again, when he's ready. He needs a wife, just like the rest of us. Besides, there're too many little ones still under foot at home and lots to do on the farm.*

As the musicians began playing another high-stepping song, he recalled his trip months before to deliver the Walker stallion to Captain Gilbert's friend in Arkansas. Curtis had not seen any of the Injun Red ranch hands and had simply left the horse in the care of Foster Wheeler, the newspaper publisher. Two months later, much to his joy, his black filly had delivered a beautiful, chestnut foal.

While in Arkansas, he had visited with Frank Parke, a newly commissioned captain, and his new wife, the former Sarah Jane Ish. They were expecting their first child in the fall and were doing well. Watching the dancers, he recalled his parting words with the captain, as they had leaned on the rail outside the Parke cabin. The remembrance brought a smile to his face.

The Irishman had commented, "Me fine young friend, don't ye be forgetting me excellent advice—wear yer bit of green to bring ye luck."

Curtis recalled that it had taken a great effort to keep a serious expression on his face. Slowly and quite deliberately, he had looked the captain up and down before replying. "My blarney, Irish friend, you're wearing black boots, gray-blue trousers, and a dark blue tunic." Continuing to eye him, he had continued, "But on thee, I see nary a stitch of green."

"Wouldn't it be truly grand if life was only what ye see on the surface?" the Irishman had responded, laughing. "Seeing as ye're neither me wife nor me patron saint, ye'll simply have to imagine where it be that I keep my bit of green."

Curtis remembered the hearty laugh that they had shared.

He had also learned that Mayor Sparks and Lisa Annie had left in the spring of the previous year, for their trip to California. Again, he imagined the excitement and adventure of such a journey. *His party should arrive in California sometime this summer. Ah, well, maybe someday Judy Beth and I'll make such a trip. It'd certainly be a grand time.*

He knew there were stories making the rounds in the county about his tracking abilities, even though he had provided few details about his Texas adventures.

I guess it's enough that I returned safely with my horses, he reasoned. *Finding John's killers just embroidered it.*

He found that his six-shooter also held a certain fascination for many admirers, including Marion and Jonah. They enjoyed using it to shoot at targets when the three had their regular outings to hunt in the forest.

Curtis continued practicing with the Colt, until he could hit a darting squirrel at thirty paces. He found himself very attached to the revolver, yet he had mixed feelings. *It's a great weapon for a lawman or someone like Captain Gilbert, out in the wide-open savagery of the Texas plains. As a close-in shooter, it's truly unmatched, but it has limited value for hunting game. Other than varmints, I don't see myself using it often on the farm.*

Of course, coming across Veeko's cold trail could change that. Still, I'd have little stomach for a long chase these days. There's Judy Beth to consider and the coming little one. Besides, with the additional prime farmland that I bought, thanks to Captain Gilbert, my days are full with clearing and plowing.

Lost in thought, Andres stood facing the dancers, fingering his beard. Minutes earlier, his brief discussion with Preacher Hood was unsettling, as his friend urged him to consider remarrying. He admitted that the thought made sense . . . for some.

His friend had said, "Now that Ilse's in God's care, you got to think of the younguns, as well as yourself."

Andres had listened with increasing discomfort in the crowded barn. Friends and neighbors were standing close or walking by, as he waved to one and acknowledged another.

This ain't the place for this kind of talk, he had thought, feeling embarrassed discussing a personal matter with other folks nearby. *Besides, my Ilse is only freshly buried. Why then is my friend bending my ear so hard?*

The preacher had droned on, apparently oblivious to anybody who might overhear their conversation. "You're a successful man in your prime, with a big farm and an active trading post on your hands. After last year's illness, there're single women and men with families looking for someone to take the place of their recently departed. Think on it, Andres. C'mon by the church, and let's talk again."

Nodding to another friend, Andres walked toward the cider barrel, muddled in his thoughts. *I don't know about being in my prime, but I'm as fit as I ever was. I wonder how my brood would take to a new ma. They'd likely be right happy to have a woman tending to their needs again. Well, it ain't happening tomorrow, so there's no need thinking hard on it tonight. It's time for me to get more of George's cider. It's almost as good as my strawberry wine.* Moving between the dancers, he decided, *I'll talk to the preacher again—maybe next month.*

Marion sat near his mother's tombstone, and, as he often did, the teenager ran his hand over the words chiseled in the stone.

Ilse
Wife of Andres Sommer
1806 -1854
Be With God

Often, he stole away from his chores and the rest of the family to sit there, or to bring flowers, as he had just done. It was the one place where he could sort things out in his mind and where he felt she was nearby.

She was small in stature, he recalled, *but had boundless energy and always had a ready smile. After bearing ten of us, she looked older than her forty-eight years, and there were silver streaks in her dark hair.*

His mind wandered to his brother Curtis. The loss of their mother seemed to bring the two closer. *He's always been there for me,* he reflected. *We even share Ma's coloring, not like Pa and Jonah. In stature, I've obviously taken after Pa, as I'm now growing so fast that it won't be long before I'm taller than him.*

By golly, it must have been a grand adventure, when Curtis chased them bushwhackers all the way to Texas. Wish Pa had let me go along. As for the rustlers, Curtis only says, 'I got my man and brought back my horses.' He was following four and found three. I guess the last one skedaddled to parts unknown. Lucky for him, otherwise my big brother would have been after him, sure as shooting, just like he tracked down John Leach's killers.

I'd like to see more of this big country, but I'm thinking that I want to be a farmer, just like Pa and Curtis. It'd be wonderful to work on my own land. Around Lost Creek Valley, we have fine soil for growing crops and livestock. What's more, it has to be good for raising young ones, as Pa sure has a passel. When the time comes, I know my family will help me clear my land and build a cabin, just like we did for Curtis. Then, I can find me a wife. Wife hunting, he smiled, amused at the thought, *I guess that'll have to wait until I find the right one, unless it's that pretty gal, Ella Mae.* Thoughts of the barn dance filled his head, and he almost blushed, as he remembered that they had arranged a time to meet again.

Once more, Marion ran his hand gently over the words on the grave marker. *After Ma died, things changed on the farm. All of us do more to pitch in, and I have her garden to care for. That's in addition to milking, hoeing, mucking out the barn, and tending to the animals that thresh wheat by walking in circles on the planked barn floor.*

Ma always made time for private moments with each of us youngsters. While he had been close to her, it was a different matter with his father. *I wish there were stronger ties between me and Pa, like he has with Curtis. Jonah thinks Pa works the farm just like that steamboat captain we came across on our river journey from Ohio. Do this, do that, lift that bale, plow that furrow. There's no getting around it, Pa runs the place, and us younguns, with a firm hand. Chores begin before first light and finish after dark, particularly at this time of the year. Since Ma died, he also seems more withdrawn.*

"Marion," Jonah called from the hillside overlooking the family cemetery. "Where're you keeping yourself?"

Hearing his brother, Marion wiped his eyes and walked up the hill.

CHAPTER TEN

On a sunny and warm Sunday afternoon, Andres sat at the head of the table with his family. The lush setting for the evening meal in the woods used the wooden platform that he and his sons had built years earlier. Located several hundred yards from the cabin, it extended over the banks of Lost Creek River, and the rushing water provided a soothing backdrop of tumbling water. During previous summers, the deck was often the site for parties, picnics, and family meals like the one on that day.

After saying a prayer, Andres sat watching his family, as platters and bowls of food passed around the table. Curtis, Judy Beth, and his new, towheaded grandson, little John Wesley, were there, along with the rest of his nine children.

Conversations around the table dealt with the weather, crops, and some still buzzed about the Vogel barn dance, held months earlier, as they got down to the serious business of satisfying hearty appetites. Everyone was enjoying the spring warmth, and most still wore their go-to-church clothes. Andres, in shirtsleeves and vest, had left his string tie and black coat at the cabin.

Despite the jovial and spirited talk, he found himself lost in thought, absently fiddling with his beard. Taking small portions of spit-roasted possum, potatoes, and collard greens, he passed the platters on.

His thoughts turned to Ilse, his departed wife, and the end of their dream of having at least a dozen children. A private man, he had become increasingly distant since her death. His older children helped with the little ones, and that was a blessing. Turning away from the table, he pretended to look across the river, as he quickly brushed tears away from his eyes.

I miss my Ilse, and my youngsters have lost her comforting touch. Her smile was always there for the younguns, and she had a tender way of doing many small things to please them—making shawls for the girls, or perhaps, new dolls fashioned from scraps of fabric, tied off with straw strands to form the head and hands. Our rambunctious boys have always had boundless energy, and she insisted that I hang a swing rope down by the river and provide iron bands from old barrels for them to chase. On birthdays, she insisted on preparing their favorite meal, saying, "Everyone needs a celebration on their special day."

Smiling to himself, he remembered that she had been firm in her demand that everyone wash before attending Sunday church services. *She always said that cleanliness and God were the same. That's why we all had to take a bath once a month . . . unless the water was frozen in the well. By Jove, how the younguns complained, particularly during the winter months. Even though we reused the water many times, those last in line squawked the loudest and had the most goose bumps to show for their long wait.*

Ilse had unbending faith in her chicken soup, and its ability to cure nearly any ailment. When illness struck family or neighbors, I knew that the first thing into her cooking pot would be a chicken sprinkled with special healing herbs from her garden. When that sickness spread in the valley last year, many became ill, including Mary Rallemore, on the next farm. My wonderful Ilse sat at her bedside, helped with the family meals, and mopped the fever from her brow. When Mary died, Ilse provided the quilt to wrap her for burial.

She was my partner in making our Ohio farm a success, and, more so, here on the prairie. Even though the cabin is still full of noisy and busy younguns, I get lonesome at times. Again, he wiped his eye.

"Pa, you're not eating very much this evening," Curtis said, looking at him with concern. "You look like you're lost in thought. Are you feeling all right?"

"My appetite is poor tonight, that's all," he replied, as the heavy pot of mashed potatoes and turnips went around the table again. "You go ahead and enjoy," he added, sipping his strawberry wine.

After his last visit with Preacher Hood, he decided that the children needed a woman's hand, and he resolved to find a new wife. *Now, how exactly do I go about that?* he asked himself. *Other than the rare barn dance, seeing and meeting folks is limited to attending Sunday church services and going to town for provisions. Even then, there ain't much time to socialize, and most of my brood is usually close by.*

Ja, deciding to take a second wife is one thing, but finding a suitable woman is difficult out here on the prairie. Toying with his food, his mind continued to wander. *Women who've lost husbands will usually remarry. Life on the frontier is a constant struggle, tending to chores for both life and livelihood. Preacher Hood is right, better to meet the challenges as a man and wife,* he concluded.

It had been a different time in his life when he had courted Ilse. Finding someone now took time and effort, when his days were already full, working at both the farm and his trading post while tending to the family.

On top of that, I'm beyond all that moonlight and touchy stuff. When I was twenty, I did some things that seem downright silly to me now. His reflection turned to the many awkward situations that might confront him in the near future. As the thoughts flashed through his mind, he shuddered. *My God, can't you see me prancing after some female right in front of all my younguns, and with all my friends in town looking on? There I'd be, saying something like, "Out of the way neighbors—excuse me Preacher Jason—I don't mean to step on your toes, ma'am—I'm just trying to make my way to that pretty widow standing next to the punch bowl.* A shudder ran through him. *Ugh! That's more gut churning than I care to think about.*

When I remarry, I'd like the lady to be approachable and to have some womanly qualities that appeal to me. She doesn't have to be the finest looking or most shapely, but she has to be good people, love the Lord, and be mild in her ways. Most likely, any woman of age will already have younguns of her own. Ja, I would welcome them, but she has to want more younguns. I'm still in my prime, as the preacher keeps pointing out, and I want more little ones scampering about the farm.

The illness the previous winter had affected both young and old. Preacher Hood told him that other widowers in Lost Creek Valley were also searching for new partners. This was not news to Andres, yet it disturbed him. *The preacher makes it sound like I'm in a race—like one of them contests where each fella tries to rope the most heifers in a given period of time— except the prize now is a two-legged wife and not a fancy blue ribbon. Heavens, all this makes finding a woman even more complicated.*

I can see that this may become a thorny task for me, given my standing in the community. Maybe I should talk it over with Curtis. He and I've been close over the years. Looking at his eldest son sitting at the other end of the table, Andres considered the thought for a moment. *No, that'd be difficult for me, and probably for him, too. It's not an easy matter for me to talk about, except maybe with the preacher. I'd better go see him again next week.*

***

Andres walked along the dirt lane to visit Preacher Hood in the village. After exchanging views on the weather, his friend listened attentively, as he acknowledged that it was probably best for the family if he remarried.

Then, Jason continued advising him, pointing out that it was the right thing to do for his youngsters. "And for you, too, my good friend," he added.

They sat on the hard bench pews at the rear of the church. Andres looked up at the sunlight streaming through the stained glass window, one of only a handful located west of St. Louis. Patterns of fractured light cast colorful rays throughout the nave, and Andres always felt nearer to the Lord in this house of worship.

"You're hearing me, aren't you, Andres?"

"I always listen to you, Jason," Andres replied.

His friend asked, "What age are you, Andres? You're in your forties, aren't you?"

"I passed my fiftieth year some months back."

"Really? You're a vigorous man and you look younger." Thinking for a moment, his friend continued, "Did you know Shane McReynolds, down in the south county? He came down with the illness about the same time as your Ilse. His wife, Letha Sue, has four small younguns. Do you remember her?"

"I recall seeing her a few times," Andres replied, noncommittally.

"She's a fine Christian lady, but keeps mostly to herself. She's a mighty attractive woman. And, my goodness, her figure is something to behold. She reminds me of an image I once saw of a Greek goddess."

Andres blushed at the preacher's plainspoken comments. As he reflected on the preacher's matchmaking efforts, he wasn't offended, but his friend's straightforward approach surprised him.

"You keep her in mind, Andres, but don't take too long. I know some fellas in our congregation who've already started calling on her in the last month or so."

Back to the contest of roping heifers, Andres thought, recalling the widow from church socials. *Let me see,* he thought, softly scratching at his beard. *She's the one with that high-pitched voice. That quality about her plainly sticks in my mind.* Having stirred his memory, he also remembered that she always seemed to be talking at church socials, at least whenever he had been nearby. *Yes, I remember her, perhaps too well.*

The preacher looked at him, probably noticing the dubious look on Andres' face. "Look, my friend, at your stage of life, you got to be practical. Additionally, you already know that available women are scarce in the county. It's about time you let more sunshine into your life. You ain't getting any younger, and you have to set a course toward new horizons. It ain't likely that the Lord will declare an eighth day anytime soon."

Andres remained silent, fidgeting with his beard.

"That dark-haired lady, Mary Lou Boss, over on the other side of town is available. And let me think, the Methodist minister in Neosho told me recently that he had several widows in his congregation, looking for . . ."

At that point, Andres stopped listening to the churchman. He took his leave soon after and started the mile-long walk back to his farm.

I'm fifty years old and have a few white hairs in my beard—yet I can do more work in a day than any two of my offsprings, except for Curtis. I never figured Ilse would leave me so soon. She was my rock—the person I counted on as we made our life. I know, God, that she's in your good hands, but why did she have to leave so soon?

Still, I think the preacher is right. I need to find another wife, but going around wooing some female like a moonstruck calf ain't for me, not no more. He shuddered again, at what lay ahead. *I wish there was a way to avoid all the touchy-feely bits of finding someone. That would be a blessing.*

CHAPTER ELEVEN

M arion quietly moved through the forest, looking for telltale spoor. He loved hunting with Curtis and Jonah, and he recalled the many times the three had been together on similar outings.

Curtis got his attention by softly clucking his tongue. He gave hand signals, directing Marion left and Jonah right, while motioning that he would continue straight ahead.

Stepping carefully, Marion made his way over the heavily carpeted floor of the forest. The early morning air smelled fresh, while a light mist clung to treetops, awaiting the sun's warmth before it magically disappeared. He carried his new Hawken rifle, as he carefully stepped through the woods. *Best advice Curtis ever gave me was to save my money and buy this rifle,* he thought. *And, the tiger-maple stock makes it a real beauty.*

Making his way down a hillside, Marion paused at the bottom, listening. There were no sounds—not the twitter of birds, the scurrying of small residents on the forest floor, nor any breeze playing in the treetops. Into the quiet solitude, the memory of Ella Mae and the barn dance came to him. Never had he been so captivated, and certainly not by a girl, as they had danced and laughed. *It was one of the best nights of my life,* he reflected. Since then, they had met several times, beside the river and in the woods, looking for honey. It hadn't occurred to him that a girl could bring such feelings of warmth and affection. Nor could he have imagined holding someone's hand or kissing a girl, much less enjoying it.

Since that night, everything had changed for him and the pretty girl on the next farm. He was unsure at first, pulled back, and, all the while, she was patient. Expectantly, he looked forward to meeting her again, on Friday. In fact, most times, he couldn't stop thinking about her gentle ways. Their growing explorations were breathtaking, and such memories sent a delightful quiver through him.

In the utterly hushed forest, his measured footsteps seemed loud to his ears. Cautiously, he took another step—then abruptly stopped, as a gunshot shattered the deep silence of the forest.

He hurried toward the sound, knowing there was no need to be quiet, as all the animals within a mile now knew of their presence and were instantly taking cover and disappearing. Rounding a stand of tightly packed alders, he saw Curtis kneeling on the ground. As he approached, his brother held one finger to his lips, motioning for him to stop and kneel down.

Puzzled, he obeyed. Jonah approached, and he, too, knelt, as his brother directed.

Marion had no idea what his big brother had in mind. Surely, they weren't stalking game any longer. *Who fired the shot?* he wondered.

Curtis motioned for them to gather close. "None of us fired our guns," he whispered. "Somebody else is in this neck of the woods. Keep low, so we don't become targets. It's possible that the shooters are outlaws."

All remained silent until a distant shout rang out. "Hey, Benny, I shot me a deer. C'mon over here and help me drag it to the clearing."

"So, there're at least two of them," Curtis said softly.

"You think they're bushwhackers?" Jonah asked.

Curtis shrugged. "There's no sense seeking trouble. Let's just ease ourselves back to our horses."

Quietly, they covered the distance.

Entering the clearing, a raspy voice startled them. "Well, looki what we have here."

Whirling around, they saw three men holding rifles leveled at them.

One, sitting on a log, gave them a welcoming salute and flashed a yellow-toothed grin. "How do, boys," he called. In the next instant, his smile vanished. With a cruel sneer, he commanded, "Drop yar weapons on the ground and do it now! And, don't make no fuss about it! We have no patience for any guff from you boys. Now be quick about it and throw them rifles on the ground!"

The three Sommer brothers complied.

"Thankee. Now just calm yarselves and don't try to be heroes." The outlaw was dressed in a grubby dark coat, faded black pants, and a hat that looked ancient. The others wore similar-looking, tattered clothes. All had long, unkempt hair, shaggy beards, and dirt seemed to be ingrained in the creases of their faces and hands.

"Who are you and what do you want?" Curtis asked, his voice laced with anger. "Why are you pointing those guns at us?"

Marion could tell by the tone in his brother's voice that he was concerned for their safety.

"Let's just say that we happened to be riding through and saw yar horses. Mighty fine-looking animals ya have there, particularly that big black filly. So, we figured that you all were hunters and cooked up all that shooting and hollering in the woods, so ya'd come back for yar horses."

"Now what?" Curtis asked.

"As long as we're relieving ya of yar animals, we figured it was only fitting to steal anything else ya got of value. Benny, ya and Jimmy Joe get their guns and search them, while I keep my rifle on them. Here, ya three, spread out and don't be trying no tricks."

One outlaw roughly patted Marion's pockets and took his few coins and his Hawken rifle.

Nervously, Marion looked at the gang leader, and a trickle of sweat ran beneath the collar of his coat.

"Hardly worth keeping ya alive," the leader noted, as he counted the money. "Ya ain't got but a few coins between ya, but these beautiful rifles will fetch enough for many nights of good times in the saloons up in Joplin," he continued, turning Marion's long gun over in his hands, and admiringly running his hand over the tiger-maple stock. "As for ya fellas, guess we'll just leave yar carcasses right where they fall, so the turkey buzzards can have a Sunday feast."

Marion saw Jonah give Curtis an ever-so-slight nod toward the horses. *Don't try something stupid, brother,* he thought.

Then, taking a tentative step forward, Jonah said, "If you gents kill us, you'll never know about our real treasure—our sack of gold eagles. I'll show you where it is, but you have to promise to let us go."

"Eh, what the heck are ya babbling about, young fella?" the leader asked in a dubious voice. Still, his interest was scratched. "I don't like being joshed."

"We've buried our loot in the forest, not far from here, and I'll show you where it is. But first, we need your word that we can leave here unharmed."

"Well, howdy-you-do," the leader replied, smirking. "Ya'd like that, I reckon. Now looki here, ya got something on yar mind, then speak yar piece, or I'll put a bullet in that young lad standing next to ya."

Marion saw the man pointing the gun at him, but his mind was busy. *What's my foolish brother up to?* he wondered. Uncontrollably, his began shaking. *I don't see any way out for us. They're aiming their guns right at us, and we're disarmed.* In a gesture of resignation, he dropped his eyes to the ground.

"I give you my solemn oath," Jonah continued, "that we'll make it worth your while. Just let us be on our way."

"Now yar severely trying my patience, son. Where would the three of ya come up with a bag of gold eagles? Tell me quick or ya're all dead meat."

"Our pa owned a log mill near Springfield. After he died, we sold the land and have the gold to show for it."

"Are ya messing with me, boy?"

Without looking up, Marion felt his stomach tighten as his throat suddenly went dry. *My God, they'll never believe such a cock and bull tale.*

With increasing agitation, the gang leader demanded, "Ya tell me everything right now, before I drop that young fella."

"Our gold is buried down by the river. We drew a map to make sure we could find it again. The map is in the kit on my horse. So tell me, are we agreed?"

There was a crafty look on the wedge-shaped face of the outlaw. "Sure, boy, sure."

"That's not good enough. I want you to swear by God."

"Young fella, my patience ain't never been very good, and yar stretching it a far piece."

"Swear it!" Jonah demanded.

The man on the log stared hard at Jonah. Then with a wicked chuckle, he responded, "All right, boy. I swear by God that ya fellas can walk away from this glen, if'n ya show us where ya hid yar valuables. Now, get on with it, and let's stop messing about."

"I need to walk over to my black horse. Is that all right?"

Suddenly, the bandits' three guns swung around, trained on Jonah.

Marion's heart skipped a beat. *Brother, I think I know what you're up to, but we're holding very poor cards in this game.* Looking again at the leader, sitting on the log, he saw a definite spark of interest on the man's face. *Can it be that he's swallowing my brother's lame story? I hope so, Jonah, because you've just bet our lives on getting hold of Curtis' pistol. Then, what happens if he does grab it out of Curtis' saddlebag? They'll surely see what you're doing and shoot us down. This is a very risky play.*

Standing, the leader approached Jonah and jabbed him hard in the ribs with the barrel of his rifle. "No hanky-panky, ya hear me, boy," the man said, prodding him again and then stepping back to resume his seat on the log.

His brother nodded and slowly approached the big black.

Out of the corner of his eye, Marion saw Curtis cautiously sliding several steps, lining himself up with their brother.

Reaching up, Jonah untied the saddlebag and pulled it off. For a moment, he faced the big black with his back turned to everyone in the glen. Awkwardly, he seemed to stumble against the horse nearly dropping the leather satchel.

What's he going to do now? Marion questioned. *Good Lord, I think Jonah may have the pistol. He can't get it to Curtis, can he?*

The outlaw leader watched, as did his men. "C'mon, c'mon, show me the map!" the man demanded, impatiently.

Turning, Jonah tossed the bag underhanded with one hand, in a lazy, high-arching throw, right over the leader's head.

The eyes of the three outlaws followed the bag.

Pivoting quickly, Jonah's other hand flew inside his coat and brought out the hidden Colt. In a blur of motion, he tossed it to Curtis.

Recognizing something was afoot, the leader swung his rifle back to where Curtis had been standing.

It was an instant too late, as Curtis caught the big revolver, thumbed back the hammer, and fired three times.

"Good God in heaven," Marion exclaimed, stunned and gagging at the horrific sight of gushing blood and the overpowering sulfurous, rotten-egg smell of burnt black powder.

"You got those two, but the leader is still alive," Jonah noted. Kneeling down, he turned the man over. The dying outlaw moaned and motioned for him to bend down. Moments later, Jonah stood and said, "He's gone."

"That was fast thinking and mighty brave on your part, Jonah," Curtis said.

Thoroughly shaken, Jonah replied, "I'm glad the hoax worked, but an instant ago these men were alive and bent on killing us."

The quickness of death stunned Marion, as he stared at the men on the ground. Suddenly, he felt lightheaded and bent over and heaved. His brothers rushed to him, but he waved them off. "I'll be all right. Just give me a moment." Wiping his mouth on the back of his sleeve, he hesitantly asked, "What . . . what do we do now? And what will Pa say?"

After a long pause, Curtis responded, "Pa would say a prayer over them and figure that they came looking for trouble and found it. Anyone else's memory of them will grow fainter until the great void of time renders them into nothingness—which, I suspect, will be quick for these varmints. As that one outlaw already said, the buzzards *are* going to feast today, only there's been a change in the bill of fare. We'll take their guns and horses and post a notice at the general store. I can't see doing all the work of digging them into the ground. They sure wouldn't have done us that favor."

"I expect you're right," Jonah agreed.

Marion's leg was quaking, and he still felt queasy. He'd seen death before, but he had never witnessed such savage men up close, both alive and now departed.

"Are you all right, Marion?" Curtis asked, concern evident in his voice. Stepping closer, he placed his arm around his brother's shoulders.

"I think so," he answered. "It's only that I've never been close to such violence before."

"I know, little brother." With a final squeeze of Marion, Curtis turned and stared down at the bandits. "It ain't a pretty sight. Still, a man does what's needed. Little brother, gather up the reins of their horses."

Nodding, Marion obeyed and mounted his horse.

"And get yourself thinking about something else," Curtis advised, "like something that makes you happy."

Immediately, the smiling face of Ella Mae came to his mind.

As the Sommer brothers turned toward home, Curtis slowed his horse until he was riding beside Jonah, letting Marion ride ahead, handling the bandits' horses.

Reacting to the violence and their near miss with death, Curtis' hands began to shake. Unconsciously, his right one hovered over the revolver's grip, holstered at his side. *The gun came in mighty handy to defend us. It's a fearsome weapon and definitely made for killing.*

"Good Lord in heaven above, big brother," Jonah observed, "you look like you've seen a ghost. Are you feeling all right?"

"Yeah, I think so. Even when men are evil like them fellas, there's a great emptiness in taking a life. I hope none of us ever has to go through anything like this again. I'm also very worried about Marion. He's been so easily upset since Ma left us, and today has been a nightmare for all of us."

Jonah remained silent.

How can it be right to take a life—three lives? Curtis corrected himself, as he pondered the killings. *Yet, I was defending myself and my kin. I'd be feeling real agony if'n my brothers were lying dead in the woods right now.* He rode silently, questions of right and wrong tugging at his mind. *Does the Almighty think less of me for what I did? What would he think if'n I'd done nothing, and the three of us were lying back there full of bullet holes?*

The dilemma occupied his thoughts until a different question occurred to him. Turning to Jonah, he asked, "Did that last fella say anything to you before he died?"

"I couldn't make out everything, but he whispered something about there being another member of the gang. I guess he was the fella making all the noise about shooting the deer in the woods. The leader said his last pardn'r would hunt us down, and that his name is Geeko or Beeco or some such. I couldn't quite make it out."

Sharply, Curtis reined his horse in, and his startled brother stopped, too. In a strained voice, he asked, "Could the name have been Veeko?"

Jonah nodded in surprise. "Yeah, that's the name. Why, have you heard of this fella?"

"Not really," Curtis replied, controlling his outward reactions with difficulty. Inwardly, he was shocked and his mind reeled, realizing that the last bushwhacker, from years earlier, was somewhere in their very forest. *What I can't figure out is how we've passed each other more than once, and yet, if he stood right here in front of me, I wouldn't recognize him. This fella keeps drifting into my life, almost like a spirit from the dead of the night. And, don't you know, he's always trying to steal my big black and do me dirt. I suppose that if we ever do meet, one of us will have to die to settle things.*

There's no need upsetting my brothers any more than they are already. I'll just keep these run-ins with Veeko to myself. I'll come back later to pick up his trail in the forest. Maybe I can rid the frontier of this ghostly bushwhacker.

Recalling Marion's earlier reaction to the violence, he looked up and saw that his young brother was lost to sight beyond a stand of trees. "Jonah, best we keep this Veeko business to ourselves," he said in a hushed tone. "Our little brother has had enough unsettling action today, and I think it's unlikely that we'll see that last bandit again. Finding his partners shot will surely put the fear of death in him."

"I expect you're right," Jonah replied. "I'll say nothing to Marion about it."

CHAPTER TWELVE

Veeko heard the distant gunfire and cautiously returned to the forest glen. Carefully entering the clearing, he found his three bloodied partners sprawled in the dirt. There was no movement, as he nudged the gang leader with his boot. Checking the other two, the result was the same.

Pushing back his hat, he pondered the situation. *I never did see the owners of them horses. Sure glad I missed this get-together, given how things turned out. Them fellas must really be handy with their guns.*

He searched his former partners for anything of value and was annoyed when he found nothing. *It was stupid to take chances not knowing who the strangers were,* he thought. *Stealing their horses, particularly that big black, would have been enough. There they were, tethered, with no one around, and we could've just ridden away with them, simple and easy. So why take more chances when their animals would have fetched us a pretty penny? I tried to convince my partners, but they paid me no heed. Well, to hell with them, I sure ain't going to bust my gut digging in this hard ground to bury them. Let the forest critters do the work.*

The outlaw sat on a log, thinking about his next move. *That damned ornery mare of mine! It took off during all the commotion back yonder in the forest along with my kit and every bit of money I have. Well, it's gone now and good riddance to that old nag. Still, I ain't walked more than a mile, and my feet are getting mighty sore.* Kicking at a small limb, he lamented his problems. *I have to get onto other things, like getting me some money and some food and stealing another horse.*

He had the predatory instincts of a solitary, yet cautious, coyote, with no scruples. Veeko's sole interest was himself. Now, the mess left him with little choice; he had to find temporary work on one of the farms in the area.

Finally making his way to Seneca, a man told him that a farmer east of town by the name of Zacharias was looking for help, and Veeko slowly rambled in that direction. *I've covered my tracks well all my life. Still, around these parts, I think that I'll use my other name, Shorty Younger. It's smart to play it safe, and little tricks like this have kept me alive more than once.*

Having passed his thirty-third birthday, he drifted as a crook and a ne'er-do-well. When dry spells occurred in his preferred line of thieving, he looked for temporary jobs, to keep his belly full. When coins jingled in his pocket, he had flings with saloon women, but such flings usually left him strangely uneasy. His unkempt, mousy appearance and broken front teeth left most women unmoved. Even his missing fingers drew little sympathy.

In an unusual twist of pity for her plain-looking brother, his older sister had initiated him into lustful ways years earlier. That had lasted until their father had found out and promptly booted him off the farm and into the life of a drifter. From that day forward, he had stayed alive by stealing and moving from one straw tick to another. He was cunning when relieving folks of their valuables—waiting for "safe opportunities," as he called it.

Trudging the woods, he looked for a low-hanging beehive. The thought of chewing on a thick cone of honey made his mouth water, and it would surely satisfy the hunger rumblings in his stomach. Paw paw trees, loaded with fruit were abundant in that part of the forest. The fruit was sweet and succulent, but they would not be ripe until late summer.

Nearing Lost Creek River, the short man heard loud, cheerful laughter. *Sounds like some folks are having a grand time in the water,* he reasoned. Warily, he took extra care to avoid detection, as he made his way along the heavily wooded riverbank.

Kneeling and moving aside one last branch, he was unprepared for an eye-opening encounter, as a young woman emerged from the river, streaming water. She walked straight toward his hiding place and stopped a few feet away. Mesmerized and afraid to breathe, he gawked at the shapely figure, as her wet shift molded soft, rounded curves. Bending at the waist, she stretched toward the ground, and her water-soaked camisole fell away, unveiling her stark-nakedness. *Hot damn, she's one fine-looking filly,* he thought, completely enthralled. *Her skin looks like peaches and cream, topped with twin strawberries for nipples. Tarnation, I could almost reach out and grab . . .* Suddenly, the girl's long hair swept down over her head, blocking the enticing sight. As he stared, she ran her fingers through her hair, separating the strands.

Quickly, she straightened, then flipped her hair behind her and turned around to face the river.

Veeko nearly gasped, as he ogled her rounded backside, tightly confined and outlined by the wet shift.

A boy in the water shouted, "Turn your back, Ella Mae. I want to get out and put on my breeches."

Posing with her hip tossed to one side and her hands on her waist, the young woman answered in a sassy tone. "Marion, c'mon out. Are you afraid that I'll see something new that I haven't already seen on the farm?"

"You promised you'd turn around and not peek."

"Well, la-de-dah," she said, with an amused expression on her face.

"Wait until I catch you," the boy said, laughing. "I'll smack your backside if you don't behave yourself, young lady."

"You're such a willy-nilly," she scolded, mockingly. She stood provocatively, placing her hands on her waist and cocking one hip to the side, before continuing. "I'll think about it and let you know tomorrow." Teasingly, she added, "C'mon out, and don't be such a big baby."

"Baby, is it? When I catch you, you're going to pay for all this misbehaving."

Flushed and fully aroused, Veeko reluctantly let the branch slowly bend back. Stealing away, he heard the girl say, "When you see a blue towel hanging alone on my ma's clothesline, I'll be in the barn about midday, and if'n you've a mind, you can come and visit me. That'll be our signal."

Veeko distanced himself, while remaining hidden by the brush. Even so, the thief tried to overhear more of the teenagers' conversation, with no success. He caught glimpses of them and saw that both had become fully dressed. A safe distance away, he peeked around from behind a tree.

With no saddle, the boy easily jumped onto the back of his horse but labored to pull the girl up behind him. Struggling, Ella Mae's skirt hiked higher, tantalizingly exposing her long, shapely legs.

She's just pleasuring me with one delightful sight after another.

Astride the horse, the young people slowly rode away from the river and through the woods.

Impulsively, Veeko decided to follow. *I hope I can see much more of her today.*

The two were having a lively conversation, but the distance was too great for Veeko to hear them clearly. The horse stopped before a farm gate, which opened to a wagon way, leading across plowed fields.

Hidden, he watched, as both slid off the horse. The boy—she called him Marion,—swept her into his arms and kissed her deeply, all the while pressing against her. *This lumbering farm boy is getting ready to make his next move, and I reckon that he'll bed her down on that soft grass right under them trees.*

Instead, the boy remounted his horse, reining it south.

Eh, don't tell me he's going to leave that pretty young woman at the gate? Holy tarnation, he's actually riding away. Now what kind of nincompoop does that to a pretty female like this one? She'd not tease me like that and get away with it.

The girl opened the gate and slowly walked across the field, often look-ing over her shoulder after the boy. For the first time, Veeko noticed the cabin on the other side of the field, a thin line of smoke rising from its chimney. Some distance beyond, he saw other farm buildings, including a barn.

The girl disappeared into the cabin, as Veeko waited in the bushes. The short man's passion dissipated, but emblazoned on his mind were the images of the girl bending toward him and then walking toward the river with the shift plastered against her backside.

Cautiously, he made his way along the fence to the gate. A wooden sign read "Zacharias Farm" in rough, burned-in lettering. *Hooray and hot damn*, the short man thought excitedly. *This is the farmer looking for hired help. I'll not turn down anything this fella offers nor haggle about wages. You can bet that I, too, will be looking for that blue towel on the clothesline. Maybe I can catch that hot-blooded, young gal romancing again, even if she's with that backward yearling of a boy. She needs real loving by a man, while that dumb fella's mind likely dwells on feeding the chickens back at his farm. Who knows, maybe I'll even get a turn with this pretty vixen.*

My pardn'rs are gone, but the prospects for Shorty Younger have taken a most favorable turn.

———————————————

Sweating heavily in the humid afternoon heat, Veeko buried the heavy pick in the ground to begin digging still another posthole for the new fence. Leaning on the handle for a moment, the hired hand rested and mopped his brow with a dirty rag.

"I pays an honest day's wages for an honest day's work, Shorty," farmer Zacharias said, unloading split rails from the nearby wagon.

Veeko looked around to see who the farmer was talking to, then recalled that "Shorty" was the name he was using. Grunting, he picked up the shovel and cleared dirt from a new posthole. *Working is pure hell,* he thought. *Why for two bits, I'd tell this jackass where he could stick his damn fence posts. Yet, there's . . .*

Ever since that first day at the river, he found himself fantasizing about Ella Mae. His mind constantly filled with images of the young woman, dwelling on how the wet covering had fallen away, revealing eye-catching curves. Now, chores on the Zacharias farm were nearing an end, and he would be drifting down the road again. He worried that he would never have another chance to secretly spy on Ella Mae and her fumbling farm boy.

As the days wore on, he sought guarded moments to watch her from a distance, and his agitation mounted. His ate his meals outdoors, but he sneaked glances through the open doorway, trying to catch a glimpse of her. At night, he bedded down in a shed, where he punched out a knothole so that he could keep a close eye on the outdoor washbasin, located atop a barrel beside the cabin. He hungered for the times when she stood there, rubbing the wet, soapy cloth over her neck, arms, and face. Yet his favorite view was watching her lean into the crank atop the well, winding the rope to bring up a heavy bucket of water from below, her arms pumping up and down, and her body straining against the thin fabric covering her shapely curves.

Twice before, he had seen the blue towel fluttering alone on the clothesline, but farmer Zacharias had kept him digging postholes. In his mind's eye, Veeko imagined what the young couple was doing behind the closed barn doors. Repeatedly, he remembered the pretty girl bending toward him on the riverbank, revealing her milky-white breasts. Envy and lust consumed him until he could think of little else.

In the early morning, he saw the blue signal hanging on the line, and his spirits soared. More amazingly, old farmer Zacharias hitched up the wagon and said he was taking his wife to town.

"You keep building the last part of that fence, Shorty," the farmer instructed him. "I expect this section to be done by the time we get back late this afternoon. I'll pay your wages tomorrow and then you can move on down the road."

Nodding and smiling crookedly, Veeko could not believe the lucky timing, as he watched the farmer's wagon disappear. Then, he sneaked into the barn early. *To hell with them fences,* he reasoned. *Nothing is going to stop me from seeing her next romp in the hay. And, maybe afterward, I hope, I hope, I hope, this'll be my day.*

Waiting in the hot barn loft, time passed slowly. Shifting uncomfortably in the humid, cramped space, he used his old rag to wipe the sweat from his face and neck. From time to time, the handyman stood, looking down for any signs of the young people. He fantasized about Ella Mae, dwelling on the swell of her womanly curves in his mind's eye and again seeing the unveiling of her breasts, as her thin shift fell away.

He also remembered the young boy's hesitancy following their romp at the river. *Too bad that boy wasn't culled a long time ago, as he's too green to handle this gal who is yearning to be a woman. There she was, waiting for the fool to make his move, while he acted like a newborn calf taking its first, stumbling steps. What a ninny!*

Suddenly, sounds below announced an arrival, as the creaking barn door opened and then closed. Veeko dared to glance down just in time to see the girl climbing the tall yellow haystack with a quilt beneath her arm, followed, in short order, by the young man crawling between loose planks in the side of the barn. Immediately, he ducked back to his hiding place. He heard a few initial words whispered between the two and then there was silence, with only the faint rustle of hay to break the stillness.

Passing seconds seemed like hours. Finally, he dared to look down on them. He carefully rose until they came into view. The amorous couple was sprawled on the coverlet atop the haystack. Sweating heavily, the handy man's eyes were transfixed.

The top of the girl's dress was unbuttoned and lay open. Veeko could scarcely contain his excitement, and his breathing became ragged, while his eyes devoured her naked breasts. A sound from outside the barn made him reluctantly duck back to his hiding place.

Sweating heavily, and fully aroused with burning desire, he remained motionless for a long time, until he shifted his cramped position in the loft. Telltale sounds of creaking floorboards made him freeze in mid-step.

Did they hear me? the hired hand wondered. The thought heightened his excitement, and his breathing came faster. *So, what if they did. I'll just go down there, thump that fumble-assed boy in the head, and have it over with. And then, I'll have the gal all to myself,* he reasoned. Looking around at the stored items in the darkened loft, he grabbed a short, wooden axe handle.

Once more, he rose and peeked at the entangled pair. *They're too busy fiddling with one another to notice floorboards squeaking,* he concluded, as he watched the boy passionately kiss the pretty girl. Veeko's heart nearly stopped as the boy's hand slowly crept down the girl's shapely figure, pausing frequently to hold and caress her. Finally, the meandering hand reached the bottom of her skirt. Deliberately and ever so slowly, the hem began rising.

C'mon, you lamebrain throwback, Veeko raged, emitting a ragged breath and feeling his pulse beating wildly. *Pull the skirt up. Let's see everything.*

Unexpectedly, the boy paused to brush aside strands of hay from his face.

Why are you stopping, you possum-brained, weak-kneed, muddle-headed simpleton, the short man nearly shouted. Frustrated and sweating heavily, he was nearly beside himself with fury.

Panting from the heat in the high loft and his wild state of excitement, Veeko suddenly caught his breath, and his anticipation soared once more. The boy's hand leisurely wandered down the length of the girl and again gripped the hem between his fingers. Once more, the skirt edged higher in a tantalizingly slow manner, revealing first her ankles, then her shapely legs.

CHAPTER THIRTEEN

"Lordy be, Marion, we have to stop," Ella Mae panted, grabbing his hand and pushing him away. "We mustn't," she persisted, lowering the hem of her skirt. Pulling together the top of the blue gingham dress, she began refastening the buttons. Despite her aroused state, she knew there was a line that they dare not cross.

Flushed and excited, Marion pleaded, "Come on Ella Mae, you know you like what we're doing. Why don't you admit it? Tell me you don't like me kissing you and—"

"Now you listen to me, Marion Francis Sommer," she interrupted, breathing deeply, "I love it when we're together and particularly here, snuggled in the hay on this old quilt. You make me happy, and I feel so womanly. Even so, that don't mean you can do whatever you like with me. There're limits, and I expect you know them as well as me," she said, straightening her dress.

"Ah, Ella Mae, you know I wait for these moments, when we steal away by ourselves." Kneeling on the quilt, bits of straw clung to his hair and clothes. His forehead and upper lip were damp from the heat of the day and their passionate kissing.

"You're just a randy fool," she whispered, reaching up and kissing him. "Of course, you know I like you touching and kissing me. You're a real bezel bum, you are. We both know that my papa and mama may come looking for me at any moment, and if they find you here, kissing me and doing all these things, why they'd be after you with our scatter gun, sure as bees make honey."

Lying back once more, she looked up at him, as the afternoon sun filtered between the planks of the barn, casting a bright ray of light across his handsome face. Bits of hay still dangled from his disheveled dark hair. She wanted him as much as he wanted her. Closing her eyes, wonderful thoughts floated through her mind, just as they did when she was alone at night. She often dreamed about them getting married some day and starting a family.

He bent down and a long, exploring kiss stopped her daydreaming, as he loosened the dress-top once more, slipping it aside. Her breasts rose, as he kissed one, then the other.

Once more, Ella Mae felt his hand moving down her leg. Shaking her head and breaking away from him, she scolded, "Marion Francis, you stop this tomfoolery right now.

"Dadblast it, I suppose you're right."

Oh, why do I always have to be the strong one, she bemoaned, silently, *even when I don't want him to stop? He's so handsome and his body is hard and strong. I love his tousled hair, and those dark brown eyes set me tingling. All he has to do is give me that certain look, and my heart starts racing.*

He smiled at her. "You know, I've fancied you ever since that barn dance. Then, that first time we were alone down by Lost Creek, I was so happy that I felt like I was walking on clouds for a whole week. Do you remember our first kiss?"

Blushing, Ella Mae nodded and gave him a demure smile. "I remember. It was kind of a short peck, wasn't it . . . like two chicks going for the same speck of corn," she added teasingly.

"Ah, Ella Mae, that's not the way I remember it."

"But it didn't take long before your kisses were warmer and much longer. Where did you learn to kiss like that, anyway? Say, how many gals have you been squiring about in this county?"

Now it was his turn to blush, as he let out a self-conscious laugh. Turning serious, he said, "You're the first and the only one that I want to be with. You're my gal, ain't you? I mean, you don't fancy any of my older brothers or them Vogel fellas, do you?"

Coyly, she asked, "Would it bother you if I looked at another boy, ah, I mean, fella?" *Boys,* she giggled to herself, *are such contradictory beings. One minute they have their chests stuck out, cocky and strutting their stuff; the next, they're bashful, clumsy, and helpless as lambs. Even so, this boy is special. He makes me feel so alive, especially when he loosens my top and touches me.*

Indignantly, he responded. "What's that supposed to mean? So tell me! You are my gal, right?" Marion was half-angry. "I'm sixteen and you're fifteen. Why, I know some folks that were married at our ages. So, tell me straight out, are you my gal or not?"

"Of course, silly, but you've got to grow up more."

"What? Grow up more?" he asked, angrily.

"You know what I mean. We've both got to be older before we make any plans for our future and—"

"Now you're the one that's being silly. Why, heck, I've been plowing, milking, and farming for my pa ever since I was knee-high to a sapling. Furthermore, I'll have you know that I can turn over a straighter furrow than most of my brothers when I get behind the plow. Besides, I can out-hunt and out-shoot all my brothers, even if they are older than me, except maybe Curtis."

"Oh, you dimwit, I just meant that in a couple of years, you'll be more manly, and I'll be older, too." She wanted Marion with all her heart, but her upbringing told her to wait.

Miffed, he replied hoarsely, "More manly, you say . . . *more manly,*" he repeated angrily, and he stood. "Maybe you're just too young to have deep feelings yet," he said, tucking his shirt into his pants. "Maybe you're the one that needs to grow up more," he continued, delivering his hurtful words with a hard edge. He reached down a hand to help her up, but she brushed it aside and turned over on her stomach.

"Pshaw, how you talk, Marion Sommer. Even with the sisters in your family, you're just plain ignorant," Ella Mae replied, indignantly. "I'll have you know that I've been a woman for near two years now, as if you even have the slightest idea what I'm talking about."

"Even so, you sure know how to make a man feel small," he countered, brushing straw from his clothes and hair.

"Marion Francis Sommer, sometimes you just say the wrong thing at the darndest time." Snappishly, she continued, "You best be going before my pa comes looking for me and sticks a hayfork in your backside."

"All right, have it your own way for now. Anyway, I have to check the cows pastured in the upper meadow." He turned and slid down the front of the haystack.

"I'll see you tomorrow, won't I, Marion?" she asked, anxiously, looking over the top of the stack. "We can meet right here." She stopped and blushed.

He looked up at her and demanded, "So, tell me, are you my gal?"
She nodded.

"In that case, not even stampeding horses will keep me away," he added, smiling broadly. Giving her a wave of his hand, he left.

"You're such a bezel bum," she whispered tenderly, watching him stoop to go through the loose planks.

He paused, sticking his head out first.

He's peeking to see if Papa is nearby, Ella Mae figured. She watched his firm backside, until he disappeared; then she reclined on the hay again, smiling to herself and buttoning her top. Recalling their recent kissing and touching, she blushed, turned over on her stomach, and buried her face and body into the yielding haystack. *He's such a silly, sweet boy. I love him so.*

Sneaking a glance from his hiding place in the loft, Veeko watched the farm boy depart. His pulse raced, as he saw Ella Mae snuggling deeper into the quilt. Unsure of his next move, he crouched down to think.

Slowly, he let out his breath and waited. There were no sounds from below, so he cautiously rose once more.

Stretched out fully, the pretty girl lay with her head cradled on her arms. A small smile of contentment creased her lips, as filtered sunlight cast warm rays of light across her face, highlighting her brown hair.

She's positively glowing, laying there in that streak of light, just like an angel. I think she's the prettiest gal I've ever seen. Still, she's teasing the daylights out of that young buck. She'd not be baiting me that away. No, sir, it's a man she needs, and today's my day. It's got to be! I'm going down there right now, he thought, breathing rapidly.

His face was beet red, and excitement knotted his stomach, while the wooden handle felt clammy in his trembling hand. He continued to hesitate, wondering about his next steps. *This gal's like a ripe peach that's ready to drop from a tree. Even so, how am I going to get down there before she hears me and maybe calls out for help or scampers away?*

Carefully, he stood and once more stared down at the girl. Slowly, he became aware that the beauty on the quilt was asleep. *Looki there,* he thought. *Well, I'll be a ring-tailed possum that's been hung out to dry. That sunlight and her romancing have lulled her to sleep.*

With her eyes closed, Ella Mae's breathing was slow and regular.

Hell, this really is my lucky day. I'm going down there right now. This wooden handle will come in handy, if she tries taunting me like she does that boy. I got to hurry so I don't miss out, he concluded. His heart pounded and his work shirt was soaked through with sweat, as he mopped his face once more with the rag.

Cautiously, he crept to the ladder, fearful that creaking floorboards would give him away. Tight with anticipation, his legs trembled as he descended.

Each rung of the ladder was a cautious step downward. At last, he made it to the barn floor. Quietly, he dropped to his hands and knees, slowly moving toward the haystack. At the base of the hay, he began crawling on his belly, clutching the wooden handle, steadily slithering upward.

As his eyes came level with the girl's bare feet, he got a fleeting glimpse under the hem of her blue dress, as Ella Mae's skirt was askew. Fearful that his uneven movements on the pile of hay would awaken her, he inched forward slowly.

The young girl continued to breathe gently, as the warm light played over her.

Dreaming about romancing, don't you know, Veeko figured. He shifted ever closer until he was within arm's reach. Carefully getting to his knees, he paused to admire her shapely figure, from her long brown hair lying softly along her cheek, back to the swell of her backside and down to her bare ankles.

He considered his options. *She'll likely welcome me with open arms and pull me down to her, once she knows she has a man to please her,* he fantasized, as a lopsided smile creased his sweaty face. *No matter, I best not take any chances.*

Slowly, he pulled the sweat rag out of his back pocket and mopped his brow. *Yep, I'll just use this old rag to gag this filly, so if'n she yells, it'll be no mind to me—and I can take a good long time giving her what she's yearning for.*

Swiftly, he slipped the cloth beneath the sleeping girl's face and around her mouth, pinning her down by placing a knee in the middle of her back. Roughly, he knotted the dirty rag behind her head.

Ella Mae's eyes flew open in surprise. Her first reaction was that Marion had returned and her body glowed for an instant. Twisting her head, she saw Shorty's homely face and wicked leer. Enraged, she screamed, only to find her voice muffled. Twisting, she tried turning over.

The hired hand leaned heavily on her back, pressing her down into the yielding hay. "Now you hold still, little darling," he whispered hoarsely, licking her ear.

She felt his sweat dripping onto her face, as she nearly gagged.

"I'm the man who's going to pleasure you, not like that calf-brained farm boy who's still searching for his manhood," the short man rasped, whispering wickedly, while one of his hands traveled down her body.

She cringed as she felt his hand groping her buttocks beneath the thin material of her dress, and she nearly gagged at the overpowering stench of his man-sweat. Struggling with all her strength, she turned so that she could see him.

A sneering smile split his face, drawn over yellowing broken front teeth.

She quickly heaved up and managed to throw him off. Rolling on her back, she freed her arms, slapped him hard, then raked his face with her fingernails. The dirty rag stifled her yells of outrage.

Stunned, Veeko drew back.

Taking advantage, her knee came up fast and hard, smashing into his thigh.

The short man's face was even more flushed with anger, as blood trickled down his cheek. He came down on her with all his weight, an arm stretched across her throat. "You're a sashaying little taunter, aren't you? I saw what you and that whippersnapper were doing today and at the river. You think you can tease me and get away with it, like you do with that mooncalf farm boy who pretends he's a man. Not with me, you can't." Quickly, he threw a leg over the girl, sitting on her while pinning both arms between his knees.

Ella Mae was confused and frightened by his words but determined to fight.

The hired hand grabbed the collar of her dress and ripped it open as buttons flew.

The next thing Ella Mae knew, the sour-smelling man was pawing her breasts with his rough calloused hands. "Get off me," she tried to scream. A chill of terror ran down her back, as she twisted and squirmed to throw him off again, inadvertently hiking the hem of her skirt higher.

The short man cruelly grabbed a breast and squeezed hard, causing her stomach to turn over.

Where did this foul creature come from? she wondered wildly, as her heart pounded. *I have to get out of this barn, but first I have to get this evil-smelling brute off me.* "Help," she attempted to scream. "Stop, you monster! Marion, where are you? Get off me, you sour smelling swine!" The results were only muffled sounds.

"You got to be taught some proper manners, you tormenting vixen," he shouted, slapping her face once, then again and again, until her cheeks were crimson. "It ain't fitting to pester a man, not even that young greenhorn. I ain't going to stand for none of it. You hear me, missy?"

Dazed, Ella Mae's face smarted from the stinging blows. She continued to struggle, beginning to feel the strains of exhaustion and the cold claws of dread.

Veeko looked around the haystack and found the wooden handle, while continuing to imprison the girl between his legs. Lifting the club high above his head, he brought it down hard.

Searing pain shot down the side of Ella Mae's head. Stunned, tears clouded her eyes. "No," she moaned into the gag, shaking her head from side to side. "Please don't hurt me," she pleaded. Suddenly summoning her remaining strength, she rolled violently to her right.

The hired hand lost his balance in the soft hay and fell to the side.

Ella Mae tried to knee him in the groin, but he blocked her.

Out of his head with raging passion, Veeko scrambled on the yielding haystack and dove on top of her. Sitting up, he quickly rose on his knees and came down heavily on her chest and stomach.

The wind went out of Ella Mae. Gasping for air, terror gripped her, and she intuitively crossed her legs tightly. Then, she looked up and cowered in even greater fear.

The twisted expression on Veeko's homely face was a wild mask of desire and emotion. Panting heavily, he again raised the wooden handle above his head.

As the blow came down, she instinctively raised her arm for defense, then screamed into the rag, as she closed her eyes and saw exploding stars in her head. "No!" she sobbed in pain, tears streaming down her face. "Pa, Marion, someone—please help me," she shrieked into the gag. "God, help me!"

"You'll not tease the likes of me again, you sassy, wretched woman.

For the third time, the axe handle was poised high over the short man's head. Ella Mae opened her eyes and immediately went ridged, panic-stricken and horribly afraid.

Down it crashed, sending her into a void of unconscious darkness.

CHAPTER FOURTEEN

Marion made his way up to the saddle-like ridge overlooking the Zacharias farm, as he did almost everyday, hoping to catch sight of Ella Mae. He peered at the farmyard below, and saw the barn. Chickens were scattered about the yard, but there was no sign of the blue towel. His pulse quickened, as he remembered the last time he and Ella Mae had been together.

Since that day, nearly three weeks had passed, and the only time he had seen a blue towel was when a gaggle of wash hung from the clothesline and flapped in the breeze.

There had been no sign of her. She missed Sunday church services with her parents, and when he asked, her little brother said that she was feeling poorly and stayed at home. When he asked the following Sunday, other excuses were given—something about chores piling up at the farm. It was as if she had simply vanished.

As the days slowly passed with no news, he became glum, wearing his worries like a prickly, cactus coat. He picked at his food. Even visits to his mother's grave became fewer. *Did I offend her, asking if she was my gal,* he wondered? *It was silly of me to badger her. Is that why I haven't seen her?*

One evening after supper, he slowly walked down to Lost Creek, kicking a small stone, his hands stuffed in his pocket. His spirits were low, as he continued along the riverbank, lost in thought.

"Hey, wait for me," Jonah called.

The two of them had always been close, but they had become inseparable since their mother's death. Walking together in silence, they sat on a fallen tree, watching the swirling water rush downriver.

"Young brother," Jonah asked, "what's eating at you? For days, you've been acting like something that our hound dog dragged home, and you do chores as though your mind is in the next county."

"Nothing." Marion replied. "I've just been thinking about a few things,"

"About what?"

"Oh, just things."

"Well, dopey, what's actually going through your mind? C'mon, you know you can tell me."

Marion remained silent.

"All right, sunshine," Jonah replied, with a laugh, "I'll wager that you're pining, because you haven't seen that pretty gal on the next farm. Isn't that right?"

Self-conscious, Marion blushed.

"You do know that she's staying over in Jasper County, don't you?"

Startled, Marion demanded, "How do you know that? You hear something you ain't told me about?"

Giving his brother a sympathetic look, Jonah continued, "I overheard Mr. Zacharias talking to Pa about his mortgage. I was working in our barn behind a stall, so they didn't know that I was there. Pa asked him when he would repay his loan for the land that he bought from us, and Mr. Zacharias answered that he wasn't sure. I think he may have trouble meeting the due date."

"I hope you're wrong. I'd sure hate to see my gal leave."

"And then Mr. Zacharias told Pa that Ella Mae was hurt real bad and went to her granny's to recover."

"What? How did she get hurt? How bad is she? When did she leave?"

"I don't have the answers to those questions, but I did hear our neighbor say that he's been looking for his former hired hand, a fella named Shorty. Have you ever seen him?"

"Yeah, I've seen him a couple of times, but I didn't pay him much mind. You're saying that he harmed Ella Mae?" Marion asked, his brow wrinkled with worry.

"Yep, old man Zacharias said that when he found him, he was going to string him up and gut him . . . and that would only be after he cut off his private parts."

Marion stared at his brother, trying to comprehend. Recovering, he asked in quick succession, "How did it happen? Will she be all right? Do you know what ails her?"

"I told you, I don't know any more than I'm saying, and I don't know what's ailing her."

"No wonder I haven't seen her. I've got to go to her. Whereabouts in Jasper County is she staying?"

"Old man Zacharias never did say."

Marion's head was swimming with worry. *There must have been an accident. What's the hired hand got to do with it? Why didn't she send me a message with her brother before she left? My God, I hope she's going to be all right.*

Jonah looked at him. "She's the reason you've been going around with that hangdog look on your face, isn't it? You like her real bad, don't you?"

Marion continued to gaze at the river, nodding.

Trying to distract his brother, Jonah asked, "How soon do you expect it will be before Pa takes himself another wife?"

The question took Marion by surprise. Turning and staring at his brother, he demanded, "Why are you asking me such a damn fool thing? You must have heard something else that you ain't told me. Go on, what is it?"

"Stop and think about it," his brother replied. "Why, our pa is fit and vigorous for a man of his age. He's a widower with ten younguns ranging from young Andrew to Curtis. You also know that Pa is working a section and a half of fine, prairie farmland, as well as his trading store. Our family has small ones to bring up, clothes that need stitching, gardens planted and tended, and, every single day, they're hungry mouths to feed. No question, he'll remarry, and I'll wager that it'll be soon."

Marion stared at him. All the things his brother recited were true. It just had not occurred to him that his pa would remarry, and certainly not so soon after his mother's passing.

Marion recalled his mother's kind smile and gentle face. Then the memory of her funeral came back to him, seeing her wrapped in the old quilt and slowly lowered to her final resting place in the Sommer Cemetery. He could never tell anyone, including Jonah, how often he stole away to lay a wildflower on her grave. Sudden feelings of sadness choked him, as he quickly brushed away a tear.

Then Jonah's words ran through his head again, bringing him back to reality. His brother had said "soon." Angrily, he snapped, "That's the damndest thing you ever did tell me. Our ma was laid to rest only recently, and you're saying that you want someone else to take her place. How could you think that?"

"Look, brother, facts are facts. And the truth is that we're short a woman and mother on our farm."

Bristling, Marion responded, "How can you be so coldhearted when you talk about such matters? It's like you're talking about the next cow our bull will service. My God, don't you miss Ma?"

"You know I do. You're just not thinking straight at this moment, because you're worrying about Ella Mae. So let me tell you, Mr. Smarty, I heard Pa tell Mr. Zacharias that very thing—that he's looking to find himself another wife."

Marion was stunned into silence. His mother and father had been married for over thirty years. Purposely sounding spiteful, he asked, "Well, what else did you hear? Do you have any more salacious details to tell me?"

"Only that Mr. Zacharias and Pa talked for a long time. I couldn't hear much more except when our neighbor raised his voice once, saying, 'you're as old as me,' whatever that means. And here is the best news that'll put a big smile back on your face—Ella Mae is coming home next week."

Marion's face lit up at the news. "Hallelujah, brother," he shouted.

The following day, Marion was in the barn with his father, repairing harnesses. Both he and Jonah knew that his father and Mr. Zacharias had talked again. *Maybe I can find out what's happening with my gal by asking him,* he reasoned.

"Pa, have you heard when Ella Mae is coming home?"

"Why are you asking?" his father responded, sharply.

"Well, it's just that I ain't seen her around for a long time, and I heard that she was visiting her granny in Jasper County, and her brother told me that she'll be returning soon." Marion rambled on, suddenly unsure of his ground. "And so I was just wondering. Maybe you've heard how she's doing."

His father gave him a long look before saying, "There's plenty of work for us to do here on our farm and at the trading post. Best you not be meddling into other folk's business. I expect you to mind your chores and leave the doings of others alone."

Persisting, Marion continued, "But I heard that she's been hurt, and that's why she went to stay with her granny. Is she feeling better?"

Crossly, Andres answered, "Boy, you got yourself a mighty big tongue and a nose for things that don't concern you. You can either shut your mind to this busybody meddling, or we can walk over to the woodshed, and I'll give you a taste of the switch to settle you down. You're not too old for that, you know. Which is it to be?"

Marion was surprised at his father's stinging words. *What did I say to anger him?* Lowering his eyes to the leather harness in his hands, he replied, "Sorry, Pa."

CHAPTER FIFTEEN

A few days later, Marion was working with his father in the trading shed, when he saw a rider approach and dismount. The man informed them that he was with a wagon train headed for Independence, Missouri, the jumping off place for settlers on their way to California and Oregon Territory. He said his people were from Alabama and Mississippi, and that they would be camping along Lost Creek for a few days. Further, they would be restocking provisions at the Sommer Trading Post.

Lost Creek Valley and the small town of Seneca were not located along one of the main westward trails, but there was enough wagon traffic coming from the southeast to establish it as a stopping point.

The arriving settlers became a favorite topic for Marion and Jonah. They had often talked and fantasized about running off with a wagon train, seeking adventures in Oregon Territory or, maybe, even in the goldfields of California.

That night, Marion declared to Jonah, "Pa's taught us how to work hard on our farm, and we can use what we learned to hire on with a wagon train headed west."

"You got that right, little brother," his brother agreed. "And we have the calluses on our hands to prove it. Between driving wagons, making repairs, milking, plowing, harvesting, and building things on the farm, we're experienced enough to be good outriders for any wagon train captain."

"We could easily tend to the livestock and remuda."

Jonah added, "We can also hunt and shoot with the best of them to supply food for settlers in a train."

Marion dreamed about going to Oregon . . . when he was not thinking about Ella Mae.

Eighteen wagons arrived two days later, with more than one hundred folks, settling temporarily on the banks of Lost Creek River.

Marion and his brother kept busy at the trading post, filling and delivering orders to settlers. Even so, his mind often turned to Ella Mae.

On the second afternoon, a man and his family entered the trading post.

"G'day to you," his father greeted them. "I'm Andres Sommer, and these are some of my boys, Jonah and Marion."

"And a fine day it is, my good man," the short, portly fellow answered. "My name is J. Heinrich Possard, but you can call me Henry." He was dressed in a light-colored felt hat, cutaway coat over a trim white shirt, and black wool trousers. Only his worn boots gave any indication that he might be part of a wagon train. "This here is my wife, Sylvie, and my three daughters—Tennessee, Bess, and Pansy. We're on our way to Oregon Territory and them gentle valleys beyond the rugged snow-capped-mountains. Even so, today we need some supplies. You selling any dried beans today? How about a crock of butter? We could use some fresh eggs and some greens."

Marion looked at the family and noticed that Possard's wife was diminutive in height, and she wore a patterned dress of blues along with a white bonnet. He glanced at Jonah and saw him staring at Tennessee, the oldest of the man's three daughters. *Well, go figure,* he thought. *My brother looks downright smitten with that gal. She's pretty enough, with her long hair.* As the girl turned toward him, he saw her face. *Gosh, she has the greenest eyes I've ever seen.*

Tennessee did not seem to notice him, or his brother. She was not acting highfaluting or uppity—she simply seemed to have no interest in either of them. Instead, the young woman was busy fingering gingham cloth from bolts stacked on a shelf.

"Ja, we got all them," his father replied. "Take a look in the corner at them bushels of turnips and potatoes. Over here, we have deer-tongue lettuce, picked fresh this morning. And, we put up our own strawberry and red currant preserves. Do you need any flour or maybe feed grain for your stock? We have wheat, barley, and corn. How about some honey? And if you've got a hankering, we still have a few jugs of strawberry wine left from last fall."

As Henry and his wife continued ordering and talking with his father, Marion kept glancing at his brother. Unusually flushed, Jonah worked his way toward Tennessee, while pretending to do his chores.

"Here, you boys," Andres commanded. "You start stacking Mr. Possard's purchases outside. Later, you can take this load to them, when you make your deliveries." Turning back to the shorter man, his father asked, "Anything else we can be doing for you today, Henry?"

Marion guessed that Tennessee was about Jonah's age. Her long, honey-colored strands of hair fell down her back, and her luminous eyes seemed to twinkle. Her occasional smile revealed pretty dimples in both cheeks.

His brother appeared to be under a spell, until Marion nudged him hard in the ribs to get his attention.

"Yes, sir, Sylvie and me, we be originally from New York State, up near Buffalo," Possard said. Seeing Andres's blank look, he went on, "You know, up near the Great Lakes."

"Ja, I've heard of them," his father replied.

Marion quickly turned to the side, hiding his smile.

"I worked first in Maryland, where I was the overseer on a tobacco plantation. Then we moved to Tennessee. That's where our oldest daughter was born," he noted, gesturing toward the girl with green eyes. "My last job was in Mississippi, managing a cotton plantation. We stayed there until we had enough money for this journey."

"I can tell that you're a well traveled man," Andres replied.

"I hear tell Oregon Territory be filled with giant trees," the portly man continued, "that grow as plentiful as weeds. I aim to go into the logging business when we get there. With all the newcomers arriving, there's sure to be a great demand for logs and milled wood, don't you know. I'm going to hire some hands, build a sawmill, and make ourselves rich. A place called Grants Pass is our destination, and we got friends there. Sylvie and me are going to file claims for some of the land that the government is giving away free. Think on that, Mr. Sommer, free land for the asking, and filled with them huge trees."

"The government is giving away land in Oregon?" Andres asked in surprise.

"That's right, Mr. Sommer, but the giveaways end this year. The program's name is 'Donation Land.' No question about it, the U. S. Government is trying to get more American settlers to that part of the country. Sylvie and I can claim six hundred-forty acres. After we live on it four years, it'll belong to us. Think about that, sir, a full square mile of land—*free*—and covered with them magnificent trees." J. Heinrich Possard repeated the last phrase for emphasis.

"That sounds mighty tempting, Henry. You ever done any logging?" Andres asked, as he fingered his beard. He was a little overwhelmed by the information.

"Sure enough, logging was part of the cotton plantation that I mentioned to you."

Marion noticed Jonah, as he continued to sneak long glances at the pretty girl.

Tennessee had stopped fingering the cloth. She looked bored, as her father continued talking about Oregon and a river called "Rogue."

J. Heinrich Possard rambled on. "Yes, sir, men have told me that there are an unbelievable number of massive trees in Oregon—and I mean colossal-sized trees, where two, maybe even three, men with outstretched arms can't reach around and touch hands. They say these giants grow to be a hundred or two hundred feet tall . . . maybe more." Dramatically, he raised his arm and appeared to be looking through the shed roof toward the heavens.

"Ja, it must be a wonder," Andres noted.

Marion knew that his father could not determine what to make of Mr. J. Heinrich Possard and his nonstop talk.

The portly man continued, again staring at Marion's father, "And, they grow packed together tightly, making it difficult to even count them. Imagine, Mr. Sommer, gazing from the top of a mountain at such a forest spread out before you," he explained, his eyes slightly glazed. Mr. Possard extended his arm a second time toward the trading post door to a distant horizon. "It must look like an endless blanket of green, stretching, I expect, clear to the edge of sight . . . or at least to the ocean. Think on that, my good man. Why, a man can make a fortune from all of them trees."

"Is there anything else you require today, Mr. Possard?"

"Where do you folks come from, Mr. Sommer?"

"We farmed in Ohio before coming here to Six Bulls country, which is what we call this area of Missouri. The prairie around here be tough ground to turn over when it's virgin, but after that, crops do right well in Lost Creek Valley."

"Well, nice to make your acquaintance, Mr. Sommer. We have to get back to the train, so we can be ready to move out tomorrow at first light. Listen, if'n you're ever out our way, you be sure to look us up, right there in Grants Pass. Just ask for Possard." Turning to Jonah and Marion, he asked, "You boys will be delivering these provisions this afternoon?" Seeing the boys nod, he added, "Good. Come Sylvie, girls. Have a nice day, sir."

"Thank you. They'll deliver your supplies before suppertime. Is Independence your next destination?"

"That's right."

"Well, stay safe and may the good Lord watch over you."

After loading the wagon in the late afternoon, Marion was startled when his brother suggested that he stay behind.

"C'mon, Marion," Jonah pleaded, "I can do this delivery by myself, and I have to talk to that pretty girl with the green eyes from Tennessee. If'n you come along, you'll just get in the way."

"In the way?" he responded, as indignantly as he could, but he was already laughing.

"What's so funny?" Jonah asked. Yet, he was chuckling, too. "You got yourself a gal. Why not me? Maybe she'll let me sneak back and see her after supper."

"I wouldn't wager on it," Marion said with a grin. "Why, she never looked at you in the store, and she probably doesn't even know you exist. And if'n she does, her train leaves tomorrow, and you'll never see her again."

"Could be, but something tells me different."

"And something tells me that you're just like a young, randy bull striding through the cow barn," Marion replied, laughing even harder.

"Now you're beginning to sound just like Preacher Jason Hood giving one of his Sunday sermons," Jonah replied. "All you need is his proper black Sunday go-to-church clothes."

CHAPTER SIXTEEN

The Independence-bound wagons left the following morning. Marion had no idea where Jonah was, as he had bolted down his breakfast and left, saying something about getting an early start on chores.

The family was working in the upper fields, as Curtis helped Marion pitch hay to the grazing cattle from the back of a wagon in the pasture. Their little brother, Festus, handled the two-horse team.

Marion looked toward the next field, where his father tilled the soil, preparatory to seeding a new crop of barley. They relied on dry farming to grow grain, and it was important to take advantage of spring rainfall to help seedlings get a good start. His trance-like rhythm continued, as he methodically swung his wooden hayfork back and forth. *This is rich land for growing grain and livestock,* Marion thought, lost in his daydreams. *This is where I want to do my farming someday, on my own place with Ella Mae.*

As he worked, thoughts of her filled his head. *When am I going to see my gal again? It's been too long.* He remembered her warm smile and bright eyes that greeted him every time he came through the broken plank in her father's barn. It always made him feel special when she called him by the pet name that she had given him, "bezel bum." *I like the way she tosses her long brown hair to one side when she pretends to be vexed,* he thought.

The night of the barn dance was the best of my life. I turned around to get some apple cider, and there stood Ella Mae, dressed in a blue and white frock, with a ribbon and bow in her hair. We said hello and talked for the longest time. As the banjo and fiddlers played, I summoned my courage and asked her to dance. She smiled and said yes. Afterward, we danced to every tune, while I maneuvered to avoid other fellas trying to cut in. Later, she and I went out of the barn to cool off in the moonlight, and we walked down to Lost Creek.

On an impulse, he had reached out to touch her hand, then held it in his. In his daydreaming, he recalled feeling the inner glow that night from the warmth of her hand in his.

At the river, Marion had asked, "With you living on the next farm, how come I ain't noticed you before?"

With the moonlight reflecting on her face, she had turned and looked at him with a quizzical frown. "Well, you looked, but you just didn't see, because I saw you!"

He remembered being surprised and embarrassed by the remark. Overcoming his embarrassment and self-consciousness, he had asked, "Do you think I can see you again, I mean, after tonight?"

"What for?"

Marion remembered how he had fumbled for words and finally managed to say, "Ah, I don't know. Just so we can talk again, I suppose."

"What about?"

"Well, I want to know more about you, that's all." Then, in a rush, he had rambled on, "You know, find out where you and your folks are from and what you like to eat and what you like to do after chores. You know, things like that."

"Well, that doesn't sound like very much fun," she had teased.

Unsure how to respond, he had been speechless.

"I suppose you'll want to hold my hand again, won't you?" she had asked, staring at him in a fashion known only to females.

"Yes, ma'am," was all he had thought to say.

And so, the banter had gone. They met again behind her barn the following Saturday, and many times after that. When they went to the swimming hole, she held tight, sitting behind him, as they rode the horse bareback.

Marion glanced at Curtis, who was working on the other side of the wagon. *I'm glad to be close to my big brother. He's always ready to help Pa or to teach me something new about hunting. Folks around this valley know he's a man that can be trusted. And, to boot, he can bring down an elk on the run with an arrow, slick as a whistle. His newfangled Colt is really something. He must have done that Texas rancher a really big favor for the rancher to give him such a wonderful gift. I can only guess at what it might have been, because Curtis keeps things like that to himself.*

"Curtis," he asked, as still another fork load pitched over the side of the wagon, "was Seneca as good at hunting and tracking as you?"

"Better," his brother replied. "He was older than me, and he knew the hunting ways of the Injuns. As my closest friend, he taught me good."

"Do you still think about the day he died?"

"Uh-huh."

"Tell us the story again, you know, about that day."

Curtis straightened and leaned on his hayfork. "I've told it so many times to you boys," he replied, with a grin.

"Yes, but I never get tired of hearing it—about how Captain Renke Vogel took on all them rowdies single-handedly." The captain was a family friend and had traveled to Missouri with them from Ohio.

Young Festus reined in the team and turned around, eager to hear the story again. "Please, Curtis, tell it one more time."

Looking around the field, Curtis seemed to be lost in his memories. "Well, it was sunny and warm, just like today. Folks came from all around the county to help celebrate our new town. John Leach even arranged to roast several lambs over a fire pit, and he had contracted for the delivery of a wagonload of beer from Neosho to please the hoot and belch folks. There were games for the younguns and contests. Our Ma won for her fried berry pie. Near the end, they held the last event, which was a horse race. I was a contestant and tried my best, but Seneca won the ribbon that day."

"Isn't that when the rowdies started acting up?" Marion asked.

"Yep, a dozen or more had been drinking free beer all day and got liquored up as the afternoon wore on. When the big crowd started to break up, one fella began shouting insults at Seneca's new wife, Flower on the Water. My friend confronted the man and, in a drunken haze, the fella uncoiled his bullwhip and began flogging him. Can you imagine?

"Well, Seneca caught the end of the whip and proceeded to give the roughneck a good pounding. All at once, another beer-laced drifter cocked his gun and shot Seneca dead. My friend's violent death shocked everyone in the crowd. The silence was thick, like a heavy blanket of snow in the dead of winter. No one moved—there wasn't even the sound of a cough from the crowd. That's when big Captain Vogel charged into the gathering on his gray stallion."

There was a moment of silence, as both Marion and Festus hung onto the image of a large man scattering folks with the flying hooves of his horse. At the time of the town's celebration, Marion was a wee youngster, yet he knew the stories were legend in Lost Creek Valley and throughout the county.

"My God, the captain looked fearsome that day," Curtis continued. "All by himself, Captain Vogel took on the rowdies, who were puffed up from too much beer. In the fracas, the captain killed two. First, his knife found its mark in the throat of the gunman who shot my friend. Then, he fought the bullwhipping-rowdy, lifted him over his head, and brought him down on his upraised knee, breaking his back."

Marion noticed Festus flinching, as Curtis' description hit home. The young boy's eyes were as big as saucers.

"And then what happened, Curtis?" Marion prompted, as his favorite part of the story came next.

Dead serious, Curtis resumed, "Well, the captain stood in front of the rest of those drunken ruffians, slowly swaying on his feet, with the look of death on his face. None of the rowdies moved, and the crowd continued standing in stunned silence. That's when the captain challenged the rest of the drunks. 'What's it to be?' he roared. 'You leaving town or are you dying this day?'"

"And all the bad men ran to their horses and galloped out of town," Festus added, quickly ending the story.

"That's about the way it was," Curtis agreed, with a chuckle. "And from that day forward, no one has seen the captain again in the land of the Six Bulls."

"Hey, you fellas," came a shout. "You working today or are you just going to lollygag and beat your gums?"

The three turned to see their father shouting from across the field.

"Sorry, Pa," Curtis responded, waving his hat. Turning to his brothers, he said, "Come on, boys, let's pitch some more hay. And, Marion, don't you go poking young Festus with that hayfork."

Laughing, they returned to their chores.

Working the hayfork back and forth, Marion's mind drifted to Flower on the Water. *She's gone on to live on the land Seneca homesteaded and, with the help of Braided Hair, works the farm. Despite her beauty, she hasn't remarried. That's amazing. How can you be married to someone for a short time, yet love them so much that no one else can take their place?*

Does Ella Mae love me? She's never said the words. Do I love her? The young man pondered the question. He knew that he liked her and thought about her constantly, as their relationship had deepened.

I've never been in love before, so how should I feel? he asked himself. *I guess it must be love between her and me,* Marion concluded, pitching out still another load, *just like it was between Flower on the Water and Seneca.*

———◆———

That evening, after dinner, Marion was daydreaming when Jonah poked him in the side. "Do you know where I was this morning?"

"Nope."

His brother had a surprising answer. "I was seeing my gal off on that wagon train to Independence."

"You saw her again?"

"Yep, a couple of times."

"I forget, what's her name?"

"Tennessee, but she likes to be called 'Tennie.'"

"How did that come about?"

"Well, it took some doing." With a faraway look on his face, Jonah continued, "She's the most wonderful gal that I've ever known. After my deliveries, I went back and talked to her last evening, and we walked to the river by ourselves. She pines for some fella back home in Mississippi named Jerome, and says she misses him."

"Oh," Marion answered, unsure of how to respond.

"Don't you say any more, brother. I think I got her attention. I gave her those soft deerskin moccasins this morning that I made last winter. She got kind of bleary-eyed and gave me a quick kiss on the cheek before we parted."

With an impish smile on his face, Marion needled his brother. "So, you've taken a fancy to a gal that you'll never see again, and you gave her a present which took you months to make. Brother, I'm lost, and your reasoning is a mystery to me."

"I can fancy a gal, if'n I want."

"Sure, sure," he replied, beginning to chuckle.

"Well, at least I don't fret and I'm not a grouch-hog like you. And besides, smarty, you did see Ella Mae, didn't you, since she's been back?"

"She's back? When did you see her? Where was she? How does she look? Is she well?"

Jonah was grinning. "Of course, I've seen her. I was up in the meadow repairing a fence and saw her riding in a wagon beside her pa. All I can tell you is that she had on a pretty, blue bonnet. They must have been coming home from Jasper County."

"Well, you darn fool, why in holy thunder didn't you tell me?" Marion asked indignantly, wondering how his older brother could be such a dunce.

"I'm telling you now, ain't I?" Jonah replied, bursting out with laughter. "I kind of figured that news would get your attention."

"Did you talk to her? Is she all right? How does she look?"

"She seemed fine to me, and no, I didn't talk to her. The wagon was a ways off, and I just kept working on the fence. Strange, though, it must have been less than a half-hour later, and I saw Mr. Zacharias riding over to our farm. Did you see him?"

"Yeah, I did. He came to the cabin. Pa took him inside and shooed out the younguns, but I didn't pay it much mind."

CHAPTER SEVENTEEN

Marion scrambled along the hillside overlooking Ella Mae's farmyard, as he had done every day since her return. There still was no sign of her and no blue towel hung on the clothesline. Increasingly desperate, he was beside himself to catch a glimpse of her.

As he hurried back to his cabin, his father said, "Marion, you and Jonah hitch up the wagon. We're going to town for provisions." Soon, he and his brother were bouncing around in the empty wagon bed, as his father drove the team to Seneca.

Pulling up in front of the general store, Marion jumped down to the boardwalk, just as the door opened, and Ella Mae stepped out of the store. It surprised him and he saw the shocked expression on her face. They stood staring at each other for a long moment. She looked different, somehow older. She seemed as pretty as ever in her bonnet and home-spun brown dress. Then, he noticed an angry scar running down her right cheek.

"Hello, Ella Mae. It's been a long time. I'm sure glad to see you again and glad that you're home. How are you feeling?" He saw tears cloud her eyes, and her face was ashen.

Gathering her wits about her, she responded curtly, "Well enough, thank you. I've no time for idle chitchat this morning. Papa is waiting for me around back of the store." She walked away without a backward glance and disappeared around the corner.

For a moment, Marion stood with his mouth open. He felt as though he had been gut-punched. *What did I do? Did I say the wrong thing? She's as cold as a cut block of ice from the river during a winter freeze.*

On the following Sunday, Marion's father insisted that everyone scrub good and wear clean clothes, adding that the Zacharias family was coming to supper after church.

Hooray, I get to see my gal, Marion thought excitedly. He was puzzled by the visit but wildly happy at the prospect of seeing Ella Mae again.

Jonah whispered to him, "Is there some reason our neighbors are coming to visit today?"

Noncommittal, Marion shrugged. His mind was on his gal. He might not have a chance to talk to her alone, but at least he would be near to her.

That afternoon, his father hurried to meet the arriving wagon. First, he helped Mrs. Zacharias step down and then Ella Mae. She wore the same blue bonnet that he had seen in town and a pretty, blue dress. She turned away quickly, avoiding his welcoming smile, as everyone took a seat around the outdoor table, with Ella Mae sitting on his father's right.

Marion felt an unexpected chill. *That was always Ma's place at mealtime.*

His father stood and got everyone's attention. He was dressed in his Sunday's finest, including a pocket watch, with its chain strung through his vest. Bowing his head, he folded his hands in front of him, and with his eyes closed, led them in prayer.

Our Father, thank thee
for this bountiful meal,
as we welcome the Zacharias
family as kin. Amen.

"Amen," everyone responded.

Marion's head snapped up. *What did Pa say? He's welcoming them as kin? What's that all about?* He watched, confused.

His father continued to stand, and he extended his hand toward Ella Mae, inviting her to rise. "The Zacharias family already knows the good news," his father began, with a wide smile on his face. "I'm happy to announce to mine that Ella Mae and I will be married next Sunday, right after church services."

Marion was stunned and disbelieving, as the words hung heavy in the air. He had heard them, but his mind refused to accept the meaning. *My Pa is getting married next Sunday. And, he's going to marry my Ella Mae?*

He suddenly felt light-headed, as shock and bewilderment buffeted him. Staring, he saw Ella Mae's tight, unnatural smile as she glanced around the table. Their eyes locked for an instant before she dropped hers. Puzzled, he saw his father still holding her hand.

Everybody was strangely quiet, until Festus cried out, "When is our real ma coming back? I already got me a Mama."

Little Andrew joined in and asked, "Ma is coming back, isn't she, Pa? I don't want no one else—just my real Mama. When is she coming back?" he managed to ask, before he broke down and sobbed. Large tears rolled down his cheeks, and his face turned red.

Marion was dazed. Glancing around the table, he saw Jonah's surprised look, while Curtis stared down at his hands. His other brothers, and even his eldest sister, appeared stunned. The youngest were crying, or openmouthed, unsure of their emotions. They looked about for a sign from the older family members. Still, his younger brothers had already voiced their views.

Tears filled Marion's eyes, but he roughly brushed them away. Abruptly jumping up from the table, he quickly ran toward the river. Beyond the barn, he clutched at a tree branch and bent over, heaving. Wiping his mouth, and blinded by his tears, he ran on, as the meaning of his father's words echoed in his head. *Pa's going to marry my Ella Mae.* Unseen branches ripped at his face, and his father's words repeated in his head. *She's going to marry my Pa. What about her and me? Don't I count? Someone please tell me this ain't true.*

Aloud he screamed, "Good God in Heaven, how can this be?"

Upset, Andres leaned forward on the table, resting his forehead in his hands. Not only had Marion been rude, in his unexpected departure, but now his youngest ones were crying and carrying on. He turned toward farmer Zacharias, who shrugged and looked away. Ella Mae was crying softly, with her head bent low. Her face was ashen.

Andres had envisioned this day as being festive, believing that his children would rejoice for him and themselves, happy to have a woman on the homestead again.

With an age gap of thirty-five years between Ella Mae and Andres, seven of his young ones were older than she.

Yes, Ella Mae is somewhat youthful, but that's yet another reason to rejoice, as she'll have the stamina for the many chores around the farm. Her years ain't that important, he justified to himself. *I need me a wife, and the younguns need a woman's touch. Next Sunday, we'll get us both.*

Andres had told Curtis the news the previous day, and he remembered his son's surprised reaction.

Seeming to recover, Curtis had responded, "Pa, you're a successful farmer here in Lost Creek Valley, and a hearty man who has a parcel of growing younguns. I think it's good for them to have a woman around. I guess I'm just a little surprised."

"Surprised at what?"

"I've seen this Ella Mae, and I reckon she be about half my age."

"So?"

"No disrespect to you, Pa, but she's very young."

"Ja, I know. Yet, being a bit young gives her the strength to keep up with our big family and all the work on the farm."

"Still, it might be difficult for her, she, being so . . . uh, untried in the ways of our family."

"Look, son, I just don't have time to go out courting females, like I did with your Ma, and the way you did with Judy Beth. It was fine and proper for me when I was Jonah's age. Now, all that takes time, and I'm full-up, working the farm and trading post."

Curtis had nodded.

"Son, if truth be known, I'd feel kind of silly courting another woman in front of you as well as your brothers and sisters. I've done a heap of talking with the preacher. He says there're more women over in Neosho that lost their husbands this past winter, but he never seems to stop talking about the Widow McReynolds down in the south county."

Curtis smiled and commented, "Uh-huh, I remember hearing her at church socials."

"That's about right," Andres replied, smiling and stroking his beard.

Pausing for a moment, his son had said, "With Ma being gone less than a year, it might be better if'n you asked the younguns to call Ella Mae 'auntie.' It'd likely ease the way for my brothers and sisters and might make it more comfortable for her."

Andres looked at his son and sensed his sincerity, yet he had responded with a measure of reluctance. "Well, all right, if'n you think it will help. It doesn't make much difference, one way, or t'other to me."

Is it just having another woman in the family? Andres wondered. *Is that what all this fuss is about? Age ain't that much of a concern for a fella. Ja, it's different for a woman. After all, she'll have all the usual chores, and someday soon, raising her own younguns.*

Preoccupied, he remained seated at the table, his appetite gone. What should have been a joyful afternoon had turned sour.

Ella Mae, seated beside him, was still quietly sobbing, her head down, and the meal untouched.

That evening, Andres slowly walked in the orchard, lost in his own absent-minded woolgathering. He had seen the Zacharias family off a short time before. It troubled him that Ella Mae looked so sad. He could not shake the images of his little ones wailing. Then, there was Marion's rude departure. *What in heaven's name got into him? I know that he was close to his ma, but why did he have to leave the table that way? He was downright disrespectful to the Zacharias family. I've always had trouble understanding him.*

Nearing a corner of the barn, he stopped short and backed up as he heard some of his youngsters talking, while they fed the chickens.

"I don't want anyone taking my real Mama's place," Festus sobbed.

Andrew replied, "I wonder if she'll read to us like our Ma did?"

There was silence and then his youngest daughter, Martha, voiced her question. "She's younger than Pa, ain't she? I heard Jonah say that she's about the same age as Marion. Ain't that kind of young for Pa?"

Andres quietly turned around. He felt as though a dark cloud had descended over him and over his family.

CHAPTER EIGHTEEN

Marion abandoned his chores on Monday afternoon and took his lookout place on the ridge above the Zacharias farm. A blue towel hung on the clothesline, beckoning him to the barn. Running down the hill, he literally dove between the broken planks.

And there, sitting on a barrel, was Ella Mae. She had on the same blue dress as the day before, but her face was more drawn, and her eyes were puffy, as though she had been crying.

Startled by his sudden appearance, she half-rose and then sat again.

"Hello, Ella Mae, I've really missed seeing you."

She remained silent and stared at him, as her fingers entwined themselves in her handkerchief. Hesitantly, she began, "I wasn't sure that you'd look for our signal after yesterday, but I took a chance, because I want to talk with you."

He saw tears forming in her eyes, and he reached out his hand to touch her shoulder.

Quickly, she shook it off and wiped her eyes. Looking away again, she asked softly, "Do you remember the last time we were in this barn?"

"I sure do," he replied.

Staring at the dirt floor, she continued in a whispered voice, "Something happened to me after you left."

He could see how difficult this was for her, and he longed to comfort her and hold her in his arms; yet he patiently stood apart, watching.

She remained silent for a long time and then began to sob, holding the handkerchief to her pale face and dropping her head.

"Tell me," he said, softly.

In a husky voice, her whispered words came haltingly. "I fell asleep on the hay . . . the next thing I knew, our hired hand . . . he tied a rag over my mouth . . . I fought him and then he tore my dress . . . and he hurt me bad."

Marion was stunned as anger swelled within, imagining the handyman harming Ella Mae. *The drifter hit her and tore her clothes. What kind of lowlife fella does that?*

She stood and began pacing back and forth, as the color slowly returned to her cheeks. Stopping, she met his eyes. "I fought him, Marion, I really did—you got to believe me, but he was strong, and he had me pinned down. The next thing I knew, it was evening, and I ached all over, and—"

"And what?" he asked, anxiously. "What else are you trying to tell me?"

The pretty girl sat on the barrel again, staring at the dirt. Her face was deathly pale once more.

Ugly pictures formed in his mind. Impatiently, he asked again, "Tell me . . . he didn't . . . the hired hand didn't—"

"Marion, I'm going to have a baby."

"Good Lord in the heavens above?" he said, shocked to his very core.

"Yes," she sobbed, "the evil man told me that he'd been spying on you and me down by the river and here in the barn." She paused, seeming to gather more strength before continuing. "He tore off my clothes and . . . put his filthy body against mine. I guess that wasn't good enough for him, because he kept slapping me and then . . . then he used a wooden handle to beat me until I was senseless. My arm was broken and I think a rib, and I've got several scars, including this one." Gingerly, she ran her fingers over the red mark on her cheek. "I've been healing at my granny's place. That's where I learned that I'm going to have his baby."

Speechless, Marion's mind raced, and unimaginable thoughts went through his head. His first reaction was anger at the man who had hurt his girl. Grimly, he asked, "What's happed to the bastard, and what's his name?"

"I don't know where he's gone. My folks told me that he didn't show up for supper that evening. Shorty being a drifter, they figured that he'd just moved on."

"What's the rest of his name?"

"'Younger,' I think." Looking miserable, she continued, "Then my folks came looking for me." Again she stopped, sobbing into her hanky. "No one knows about you and me, Marion, and now . . . it's too late."

Her words suddenly pulled him back to reality. "What about yesterday and my Pa talking about marriage?"

"When I came home, my Papa told me that townsfolk would likely brand me as a loose woman, being unwed and in a family way, forever figuring that I was the one who had tempted that evil form of slime."

"Why would your papa say such a thing? Surely, he knows it isn't true."

"My folks talked on and on about me shaming the family," she continued, lost in her thoughts. "They said your pa was looking for a wife, and told me that he's a successful farmer—an upstanding, devout man who organized the building of the new church, and a leader in the community. The first evening I was back, my folks just put it to me—about marrying him. Your pa knows about Shorty and the baby, and he's willing to marry me anyway. Considering everything that's happened, my folks say that I'm very fortunate to have such a successful man caring for my baby and me. And I guess they're right."

"But you don't love him," Marion protested, astounded by her story. "It's me that you love. Besides, my Pa is too ancient for you. Heavens, most of the brood in my family are older than you are."

Tears ran down her face, and she sobbed uncontrollably, her hanky twisted beyond recognition.

He stood, uneasily, and read the unhappiness expressed in her face. For the second day in a row, swirling emotions tore at him. At that instant, all he could do was stare at her, his face flushed, and his emotions barely under control.

Slowly, she regained a degree of composure, still looking downward. With a shrug, she continued, "They say a fella's age doesn't make that much difference, like it does for a woman."

Marion's frustration was evident. "You can't do this, Ella Mae," he added feverishly. "I won't let you. You and I have our whole lives before us. Pa can find someone else to wed who's more fitting."

The girl continued, as though she had not heard him. "Well, one thing quickly led to another, and very soon I was standing alone with your pa. He told me that he'd take care of me and the baby, and . . ." She paused, before continuing in a soft voice, "he asked me to be his wife."

"And, what did you say?"

An eternity seemed to pass until she whispered, "I said yes."

"But you and me, we love each other." He protested, urgently. "We can manage somehow."

Shaking her head, she pleaded for understanding. "It's been hard keeping my wits about me, with everyone telling me how to act and what to do. Besides, your pa and mine have settled the mortgage on my family's farm."

"What do you mean?" he asked, almost hesitantly. "What's the mortgage got to do with that lowlife Shorty and everything else that you've been telling me?"

Once more, the pretty girl shrugged. "I don't really know—something about my papa's loan on the farm being satisfied."

Wild thoughts and ugly questions battered him, as his face became beet red. Clenching his fists and erupting in an emotional rage, he shouted, "You mean my Pa bought you?" Then like a rush of venting steam, he went on, his voice loud and harsh, "He paid for you by canceling the note and mortgage on your land . . . and your folks, they traded you like . . . like a sow in heat. And for what . . . lousy farm dirt! AND YOU AGREED!"

Embittered, Ella Mae's back straightened and her cheeks flushed red with hurt and anger at the crude remarks. "Those are the facts. Why can't you try and understand what I've been through, and the burdens that I'm carrying?" she asked, heatedly, yet pleadingly. "I've been badly wronged! Can't you understand that? Still, everyone's pushing me to do this or do that. FOR THE LOVE OF GOD, WHY IS EVERYBODY BADGERING ME?" she screamed, utterly exasperated with her emotions boiling over.

Harshly, he asked, "Surely, you told them about Shorty sneaking around and watching you."

"Of course," she replied, curtly.

"Then why didn't you tell them about us, too?" he asked, the lump in his throat making speech difficult. His heart was pounding, his head throbbed, and his mind raced. Before she could answer, he said bitterly, "You know you could have come to me! I would have helped! How could you allow all of this to happen, Ella Mae?"

Standing, her back was ramrod stiff, as she bluntly answered his self-righteous accusation. "What for? You don't have two coppers to rub together—much less, any way you can support a family. You have no land, no cattle, no crops—no nothing! My situation is plenty hard without you flogging me with your wounded pride, Marion Francis!"

"I can hire out. We can find a way. You and me, we can build our lives together."

"Now you're babbling like a ninny."

He stood in stunned silence, glaring at her.

Her next words were bitter and icy, "My mind is on the future and a life for my baby. And I've got to figure things out right now, not next year or when it's more convenient or it suits your vanity."

Sagging under the weight of her words, Marion demanded, "Ella Mae, how can you say such words? I do love you, and I know you love me," he pleaded. "Why, if I was in your place, I think I'd rather —"

"DIE?" Furiously, she finished his thought in a voice that was sharp and cutting. Blistering mad, she demanded, "You'd rather that I killed myself than live? Destroy my baby?" She took a step toward him, her mouth strangely curled and her eyes piercing. "Face the facts as they are, boy. It's time you grew up."

Hurt to the quick, Marion snapped, "It has to be the mortgage, isn't it? You're selling yourself for the money. That's why you're letting all of this happen."

Silently, Ella Mae glared at him, her eyes rimmed in red from crying.

"You've gone bad, just like your papa . . . and my pa," Marion blurted out. "Why, you've become nothing more than a money-grubbing woman."

Humiliated by the slur, she slapped his face hard. "BOY, YOU KEEP A RESPECTFUL TONGUE IN YOUR HEAD! I'M TO BE YOUR NEW MA."

Bitterly, he replied, "That's never going to happen, Ella Mae—not today, not tomorrow, not in a million years! It won't even happen if'n hell freezes over! NEVER! DO YOU HEAR ME? NEVER . . . YOU . . . YOU USED WOMAN!"

CHAPTER NINETEEN

Marion stumbled home. In a daze, he managed to make it through the barn doors on his farm. Emotional crosswinds buffeted his thoughts, as Ella Mae's bitter words rang in his head. *She called me a boy and said I need to grow up. She talked to me like I'm a wee youngun—or maybe a knee-high halfwit. As for her being my new ma—that money-grubbing woman will never be kin to me,* he repeated to himself. *And my Pa—he's an immoral bastard, preying on other people's misfortunes! I'll never forgive him for ruining my life!*

He sat on a crate and blankly stared at the floor, oblivious to everything else. The actions of the Zacharias family made him shake with anger, and thinking about the hired hand brought feelings of hatred deep into his soul, darker than any he had ever experienced before.

Still, his most disturbing thoughts lay with Ella Mae. *In her time of need, I'm not good enough! I don't have no cows or land or money . . . and my love is not enough to satisfy her. Instead, she betrayed herself and me—and she gave up on our love.* Suddenly, his agonizing self-righteousness came to a jarring stop.

"Marion, I've been watching for you," Jonah said, hurrying through the big barn doors. "Are you all right? My God, you're as white as a sheet. What's happened?" Pulling up another keg, he sat across from him, his brow furrowed with worry.

Surprisingly, Marion's head cleared in an instant, as he decided on his next move. Setting aside his swirling anger and self-pity, he slowly stood. His voice was quite calm, as he said, "I'm leaving the farm tonight and going to Oregon or, maybe, even to California, just like you and I have talked about." He saw the astonished expression on his brother's face.

"What's happened? Why this sudden decision?" Closely peering up at him, his brother continued, "It's about Pa marrying Ella Mae, isn't it? You're upset with them and that's the reason you're running off. I'm right, ain't I?"

Marion steadily stared at his brother. "Our Pa is going to give you a new ma, Jonah, just like you predicted. Do you want to know how he arranged the marriage? Ella Mae's folks sold her, and Pa bought her, just as if he was buying a heifer for the herd. He paid Mr. Zacharias for his daughter with farm dirt—by canceling their mortgage. And, my God, she agreed to the arrangement." Pausing, his voice cracking with emotion, he continued, "I can't live in Lost Creek Valley any longer, and I won't be part of Pa's family ever again."

"How in the world did all this get arranged?" Jonah asked, in disbelief. "We know Mr. Zacharias and Pa met, and Ella Mae went to Jasper County, but how—?"

Marion's face was grim and hard-set, as he answered, "The Zacharias' hired hand attacked her in their barn and beat her bad with a wooden handle, but he didn't stop there. He raped her, and now . . . God help her . . . she's going to have his baby."

"*What?*" Jonah replied, totally stunned.

Marion continued, "She went to her granny's to recover, because her folks are dying of shame. They're fearful that townsfolk will get wind of her being with child and think the whole family is morally wicked. Our scheming father is taking advantage, getting himself a young filly to bounce around with in bed. And remember, she's not even as old as you or me. Think on that Jonah, she's fifteen and he's fifty. Our Pa's nothing but a devious, conniving, lecherous, son of a —"

"Marion, stop this talk," his brother interrupted. "All this is happening so fast that my head is spinning."

"So, I'm leaving right now. Are you going with me?"

Jonah stood staring at him. Mixed emotions played on his brother's face, until replaced with a flush of excitement.

"Hell, I wouldn't let you go off alone, little brother. If'n you're leaving, we're doing it together. But hear me good, I'm going for the adventure. What's happened between you and Pa and with Ella Mae—that has nothing to do with me joining you on this trip. Do I make myself clear?"

"Yes, I get your meaning."

"Besides," Jonah continued, grinning for the first time, "I've got this strong hankering to see *my* gal again."

They quickly determined what to take—rifles, clothes, bedrolls, coats, and a cloth sack filled with beef jerky and other food stores from the root cellar. With the horses saddled, they started out in the last light of the day, as Jonah held a lantern to light their way.

"Hold up a minute," Jonah said, pausing atop a hill as the sun set. "I want to take in this view one last time." The farm and Lost Creek Valley spread below in a broad panorama, and beyond, he could make out the river and the trees that lined its banks. *I wonder if'n this is the final time I'll ever see Pa's farm and the valley. Well, I've made my decision.*

Turning their horses north, it would take them four or five days to reach Independence.

As they rode, one thought kept nagging at Jonah, and he kept looking at his brother. Making up his mind, he suddenly reined in. "Hold up there, little brother. I'm worried about something and need to tell you what I did."

Surprised, Marion came to a halt. "You forget something?"

"Nope, but I couldn't just leave with no word, so I left a note for Pa, telling him that we're leaving."

"You did what?" Marion shouted, in stunned belief.

"I had to do it," Jonah answered. "So I simply wrote goodbye, and that we were going off to seek our fortunes out west."

"Well, if'n that don't beat all. You realize what this means?"

"Uh-huh, I've been thinking about it, as we've been riding. Pa will come looking for us, or more likely, he'll send Curtis."

"It'll be Curtis," Marion echoed. "No question, our brother will do as Pa asks." Sarcastically, he continued, "You do recall his reputation as a hunter and tracker, and you know that he'll follow us as long as it takes."

"Yep, those thoughts have been crossing my mind and are bothering me."

"Well, what do we do now?" Marion asked. "We've lost any advantage that leaving tonight would have given us."

"Un-huh, I reckon you're right."

Thinking for a moment, his brother finally said, "Curtis will likely guess we're headed north to Independence. Maybe we can put him off our trail by traveling east until first light. At daybreak, we'll cut to the northwest and try to avoid towns and farms. We have our guns. We can hunt along the way for our food."

Jonah nodded. "That sounds like a good plan."

Marion looked at Jonah and knew what he was thinking. "You're wondering what I'll do if our brother catches us, aren't you? Well, know this, whatever happens, I'm never coming back here."

There had been no sign of Curtis as they neared Independence, and Marion was growing more confident that their meandering ways had thrown him off their trail.

Riding down the dusty main street toward the center of a small town, Marion noticed two saloons, one at each end of the settlement. In the center was a cluster of dwellings, a general store, stable, and several other places of business. An oncoming rider told them that they were in Raytown.

"Does it have a blacksmith?" Jonah inquired of the stranger. He needed a new cinch for his saddle, as his had broken, forcing them to rig a temporary replacement.

"Indeed it does. His name is Billy Joe Ray, and he's the best smithy this side of the Mississippi. He does a lively business, as all the big salt wagons bound for Santa Fe come this way from Boone's Salt Lick. You'll find his forge and shed behind the stable."

"How much farther is it to Independence?"

"About a half-day's ride, I reckon."

"Thank you kindly, sir."

Marion tied his horse to the hitching rail in front of the stable. "I'm going to wander about the town, while you get that cinch fixed," he told his brother.

"You stay out of them saloons, young brother," Jonah replied, laughing and riding around the corral to the blacksmith shed.

Large in-tandem wagons pulled by teams of ten to twelve mules moved slowly along the road. *Likely forming up into a train outside of town that's headed to New Mexico Territory,* Marion figured.

Walking to one end of the village, Marion found himself in front of a saloon, just as three men and a woman came through the swinging doors, laughing and talking. His eyes centered on the woman, who had the most amazing shade of red hair that he had ever seen. She was dressed in a gaudy gown that seemed to glitter in the weak light spilling out of the saloon doors, and her wide mouth was smiling and red. *I reckon even a stone-cold woman, gone to meet her Maker, wouldn't have the gumption to wear such a getup in Lost Creek Valley,* he thought, smiling to himself. *Preacher Hood would have a fit, if she walked into his church service, revealing bare shoulders, ankles, and deep-cut dress, not to mention that blazing hair color. He'd likely chase after her and throw his bible at her.*

The three men with the woman were rough looking. They wore dusty trail clothes and sweat-stained hats. One was tall and large, while the second was slim and younger. As Marion finally glanced at the last man, he stopped dead in his tracks. There walked Shorty Younger.

Dumbfounded, Marion immediately tensed and retraced his steps quickly, until he was back around the side of the saloon. He watched as the four walked in the opposite direction. Staggering arm-in-arm on a boardwalk designed for three, at most, the group rounded the far corner.

He hurriedly followed, briefly noticing the smoky haze and noisy crowd through the batwing doors. He arrived at the other end of the building in time to see the four talking in the alleyway. Shorty was dressed in a brown coat, canvas pants, and a felt hat, pushed back at a jaunty angle.

At first, Marion could not hear their words. The men seemed to be arguing with the woman, and the big man was doing most of the talking. Suddenly, he saw Shorty reach out to fondle the woman's breast, a crooked smile on his face.

Instantly, she slapped his face. "Touch me again and I'll scratch your eyes out," she said, angrily. "Do you hear me?"

Shorty answered in a whining tone, "C'mon, Shelley, what's wrong with a little friendly groping? Nobody is going to notice us here in the alley." Mockingly, he continued, "Surely, you ain't afraid of your reputation being tarnished in this backwater town."

"Looki here, you short, miserable excuse for a man, I may be a dance hall gal, but you'll show me respect—or else."

The crooked smile on Shorty's face made it clear that her words had no effect on him.

Then, the big man pushed between them, all the while talking to the redheaded woman. "Shelley, we only want a good time, and that's all ya want. Let's go on up to yar room. I'll see to it that my pardn'rs behave. Now, let's get back to the money. How about we give you ten dollars for the three of us?"

The woman continued to throw Shorty angry looks. With further persuasion from the big man, she finally seemed to agree, as the four continued down the alley and climbed the steps to the landing above. As they were about to disappear through the door, Marion saw Shorty give the woman a slap on the rump, and, surprisingly, the woman giggled this time.

Marion slowly returned to the blacksmith shop, confused and angry at himself for not confronting the man. *Why didn't I just walk up and poke Shorty in the face or do something instead of backing away?* Raw ends of hatred buffeted him, and he reeled under a barrage of self-incrimination. *This matter has to be set right,* he reasoned, *and it's up to me to do it. I get that. However, what, exactly, do I do,* he wondered, as he continued on the boardwalk. Then, like a revelation delivered from on high, the answer crystallized in his mind—*Shorty Younger has to die, and I'm going to kill him.*

The young men settled in the woods outside the village and laid their bedrolls near their campfire. Marion sat thinking about his near run-in with Shorty. *Never have I hated anyone as much as I do that runt-sized fella. Losing Ella Ma, Pa's scheming ways, and that evil hired hand have changed my life forever. Now, I want revenge, and Shorty has to die.*

Jonah looked at him quizzically. "You look like a hound that's lost a possum trail. What's biting at you tonight, little brother?"

"I saw old man Zacharias's hired hand, Shorty Younger, while you were at the blacksmith," Marion replied. "He and two other fellas walked out of a saloon in town with a fancy, painted woman with strange red hair."

"Are you sure?"

"Yeah, it was Shorty."

"What happens now?"

"He's going to die for what he did to Ella Mae—and I'm going to be the one that kills him dead."

Stunned, Jonah paused. "Ah, you've got me plumb tongue-tied, little brother." Not knowing how to break the awkward silence, he continued, "Let's put the coffee pot near the fire and talk about this."

After a while, the pot began steaming, however, neither of the boys spoke, preferring to sit and stare at the flames, each lost in separate thoughts. Their hobbled, off-saddled horses were in the trees behind them, feeding on spring grass. As the pot began to boil, Jonah dumped in the crushed beans, and soon the pleasing aroma of coffee and campfire smoke wafted in the evening air.

Marion rested on the ground with his head against a saddle. He figured that his brother was waiting for him to speak and lay out a plan. *That's the problem. I have no plan! If'n Shorty and the other two head to Independence, it'll be a devil of a time to find them in a town that's bound to be crowded with westbound settlers. Jonah hopes to catch up with Tennie's wagon train before it starts down the trail, but my task is more important.*

"Howdy, boys," came a deep, familiar voice from behind them.

Startled, the young men jumped.

There stood Curtis, with a blade of grass dangling from his mouth, as he leaned against a tree. His holstered six-shooter hung from his waist, and he held his bedroll, saddlebags, and Hawken rifle. Pushing back his hat and smiling, he asked, "Aren't you going to invite me to your camp and offer me some coffee?"

"How . . . how did you find us?" Jonah stammered. "And where in tarnation did you come from?"

"Been on your trail for days," Curtis replied.

"But how could you?" Marion stammered. "We lit out east."

"Uh-huh, I know, but I've been hunting all my life and have to say that you boys weren't much of a challenge, particularly when I figured that you were headed to Independence. I just came north using the main trail, while you two were wandering over the prairie, trying to leave a confusing set of tracks."

Marion was dumbfounded.

"Come morning, we can saddle up and start back to the farm. Pa's worried."

"I'm not going back, not today, not tomorrow, not ever," Marion harshly stormed.

With quiet confidence, Curtis replied, "We'll see." He moved from the tree to spread his bedroll and then sat near the fire.

Marion was outraged. "You can't order me about like I'm a youngun that's under foot. Even if you hogtie me to my horse, I'll just run off again. I'm not going back to Lost Creek Valley, and I'll never live on Pa's farm again. Are you listening to me, big brother?"

Curtis remained silent, looking at him.

"He can't go back," Jonah added, "and I don't want to. I'm going to travel the Oregon Trail, and Marion is coming with me."

"Uh-huh," Curtis grunted. "And why can't our brother go back?"

"None of your damn business," Marion replied, angrily. "I got my reasons, and they're private."

Curtis reclined, resting his head against a saddlebag. Adjusting his holster and coat to a more comfortable position, he tilted his black hat to cover his face. "Tomorrow, first light, we'll start back," he answered from beneath the hat.

Marion looked at Jonah, who shrugged. Frustrated and seething with anger, he plunged ahead, "You're still not hearing me, big brother. I reckon you can follow me all the way to hell and back, if'n you want. I'm telling you flat out—I'm never going back to Pa's farm or living in Lost Creek Valley again."

Speaking through his hat, Curtis asked, "And why is that?"

"I told you already, I got my reasons."

Jonah blurted out, "Because he and Ella Mae were sweet on each other, and he won't live under the same roof with her and Pa."

"Figured as much," Curtis replied from beneath the hat. "Anything else you have to tell me?"

Furious, Marion replied, "You're always so cocksure about yourself. How are you going to make me go back to the farm, big brother?" he asked, his words taunting and dripping with sarcasm. "I'm no longer a gangly string bean. Are you going to use force? You going to knock me down and thump me, then maybe tie me to my horse? Maybe you'll draw your Colt. Huh? Is that what you're going to do? Are you going to threaten me with your Texas six-shooter? C'mon, big brother, speak up."

Curtis sat up like a shot, his hat falling away. Staring at Marion, his mouth was tight with anger. In a low voice, he said, "I realize you're hurting, little brother, but you've got no call to talk to me that away."

"Hear me good and hear me clear, I'm never going back."

"We could have a more harmonious chat, if'n you'd tell me your thinking."

Stomping out of camp, Marion replied, angrily, "I've already said my piece."

———————

Jonah watched his brother disappear into the darkness beyond the campfire's circle of light. He and Curtis sat silently for a long time before he spoke. "Marion's got something else he has to do that he hasn't told you. He reckons he needs to kill a man."

Already upset, Curtis' head snapped around. "What in damnation are you talking about, Jonah?"

"You're the one who always knows everything that's happening on Pa's farm, but I'll wager you don't know that our new ma is already with child?"

"What?" Curtis asked, in astonishment. "You'd better tell me the whole story. Go on, get it out."

Jonah told his astonished brother about Shorty, the assault on Ella Mae, and Marion's heartache. He ended by describing the mortgage deal, as well as the Zacharias family's shame, and their fear of becoming the butt of town gossip.

Curtis made no comment, as he listened to his brother's account. Pouring himself a cup of coffee, he said, "Well, if'n that don't beat all. You say this hired hand's name is Shorty?"

"Uh-huh, Shorty Younger."

"Where is this gent?"

Jonah relayed that Marion had seen him outside the saloon in town.

"What does he look like?"

"He's a double-dealing, evil bastard," Marion replied, striding toward the campfire. "He abuses women to have his way, and he's going to die, or my name ain't Marion Francis Sommer."

"Curtis knows about Ella Mae's condition, the land deal, and that you saw Mr. Zacharias's hired hand," Jonah told his younger brother.

"I asked what he looks like," Curtis repeated.

Unsure, Marion responded, "He's short and plain-looking. He's older than you and has brown hair, broken front teeth, and he's missing a couple of fingers."

Startled, Curtis asked, "What did you just say about his fingers?"

"Yeah, he's missing two fingers," Marion repeated.

"Which hand?"

"Left, but why do you ask?"

"And you say he's short?"

"That's right."

"And his front teeth are broken?"

"Look, I've already told you all that. Why are you asking me all these questions?"

Curtis shook his head and had a befuddled expression on his face.

Jonah saw the look on his big brother's face and was mystified. *Now, what's bothering him? How can Shorty's description mean anything to him? Is this someone he knows or has heard of?*

Saying nothing, Curtis laid down, his hat once more covering his face.

Marion and Jonah banked the campfire coals for the morning fire and silently stared at the embers until sleep overtook them.

CHAPTER TWENTY

Haunted by her horrifying experience in the barn, Ella Mae vividly recalled the brutality and everything that came after she regained consciousness—pain, humiliation, and being shunned by her folks. The dark memories, and the knowledge that she would give birth to Shorty's baby, doggedly reminded her of that terrible day.

Following her wretched argument in the barn with Marion, she worried about their next confrontation. His reactions and hurtful words wounded her deeply. *I was the victim,* she thought, resentfully. *Yet, he seems wrapped up in his feelings, while blaming me for everything that's occurred. Where is his righteous anger at the brute that beat and raped me?*

In her miserable state, there was no one she could turn to for advice. Her mother and father made it very clear that they feared the town's gossipmongers, and the moral condemnation from the community that would follow, if this event became widely known. She considered talking to Preacher Hood, but his position in the church and community intimidated her, so she reluctantly dismissed the idea. She could not turn to Andres. He was too much of a stranger, and besides, his son was the thorn in her side. She finally concluded that living under the same roof with Marion was going to be a prickly affair, leading to many tense moments.

Ella Mae was sick every morning, and the apron over her dress felt full, yet she was sure that no one other than her family and Andres would suspect that she was with child. Her daily nausea assured that every morning started out miserably.

On the wedding day, her mother helped her pack and tied everything together in a shawl. Looking at her daughter, she said, "Now girl, I'm not much on giving advice, but above all else, don't you resist your husband on your wedding night."

Unsure, Ella Mae asked, "What was it like for you on your first night? I mean, is it hard learning to sleep with a man? " All her life, she had slept with her sisters and brother, snuggled together in the cabin loft.

"Them's not memories I regularly summon up, and I surely ain't discussing them with any of my younguns. All you need to know is that most every woman survives the first night. Now you wash up good before going to bed and be sure to put on this clean nightshirt," she said, handing it to her. "I did it up fresh for you." Seeing the expression on her daughter's face, she continued, "You'll be all right, Andres is a good man. Are you hearing me? A husband's got his rights. You just try to act natural."

That's your advice, Ma? she asked, silently, looking at her mother with a perplexed expression on her face. *You think just because some fella in a black outfit says that I'm married that it's all right if a stranger undoes my nightshirt and feels me up, maybe lifts the hem and . . .* A shudder went down her back. *And, to soothe my doubts and prepare me, all you can say is act natural and don't resist! If you only knew what's tearing at my guts. Think on this, Ma— while the boy I love sleeps in the loft above, I'll be below in an unfamiliar cabin, while his papa beds me down. Act natural? How is that possible?*

Again, a shiver came over her. *Why haven't you or Papa ask me how I feel, or what I want, or what I need? How can it be that everyone else knows better than me? From all sides, everyone keeps punching at me. Good Lord in heaven above, give me the strength to go on! Why, dear God, is all of this happening to me?*

Ella Mae steeled herself well before the wedding ceremony, imagining Marion furiously staring at her backside, as she stood before the preacher. At the church, the need for her resolve suddenly disappeared, as she learned the astonishing news that her bezel bum had run away with his brother. A huge wave of relief swept over her, as one immediate worry temporarily washed away.

Andres was caring, asking how she felt. He told her how nice she looked, and he admired her blue bonnet.

Her mother had pinned spring flowers to her best blue and white dress. She was thankful that the hem covered her scuffed shoes.

Events swirled about Ella Mae during the ceremony. At times, she felt distant and removed, as though she was watching someone else go through the motions. Her vow of marriage was a single, soft-spoken response to Preacher Hood's question. Afterward, well-wishers visited with her new husband, while she remained slightly behind him. Most folks simply nodded to her, mumbled a few words, and smiled.

After church, she accompanied Andres to her new home. The busy life of the big family took over, as chores needed tending. She managed to set the table for super and helped carry the food. The meal passed with her taking small portions and saying little, as everyone ate in near silence.

She knew that the abrupt disappearance of Marion and Jonah had dampened the family's mood and added confusion. She learned that Curtis was looking for the two, and she assumed that he would bring them back. The thought of Marion's eventual return was unsettling, but it was not happening immediately, so she simply blocked it from her mind.

Her uppermost concern now was her first night of marriage and being alone with a strange, older man. The few words from her mother earlier in the day provided no comfort or insight. Tonight, she would have to find her own way.

Young Festus asked, "Auntie Ella Mae, will you please pass the potatoes?"

She was glad for the interruption, as her mind moved to another question. *How in heaven's name am I ever going to step into the daily life of this big family? I'm untried in their ways, and most of the younguns are wary of me. The eldest are dismissive, and they're bound to look down on me, given my age. Then, this silly game of calling me 'auntie' must sound as peculiar to them, as it does to me.*

Glancing around the table, the mood was far from festive, and nothing like the Rallemore wedding that she had attended the previous year. After that ceremony, the celebration went into the late hours, and the groom became tipsy, in a happy sort of way. *Still, I'll not forget the bride. It was obvious that her smile was forced, and she wasn't able to still her nervous hands. She gave a brave show of appearing unruffled, but she was clearly embarrassed at the coarse, suggestive remarks made by some of the guests about fulfilling her wifely duties. Late in the evening, her burning cheeks clearly attested to her dread.*

In the Sommer cabin, the evening wore on, until it was bedtime. Farm-raised, Ella Mae knew the acts of procreation, yet, now fully a woman with child, the memory of her lost personal intimacy and innocence in the barn was largely blank. *Mama says that Andres has his just rights tonight. Do I have any?* Involuntarily, her leg twitched, and she began trembling.

All the children said their goodbyes, as they were sleeping at Curtis' cabin with Judy Beth, or at the neighbors, in order to give the newlyweds privacy on their first night. Preacher Hood had seen to the arrangements.

Swiftly, the cabin quieted, and the bustling noise and clamor of the big family subsided. Andres stoked the fire and began blowing out candles.

Ella Mae shyly made her way outdoors. The trembling in her leg increased as she washed at the outside basin and let her hair down, purposely delaying her return. *Wouldn't my new husband think I was a strange one, if I kept walking all night between the cabin and the outhouse?* Staring at the open cabin door, she thought, *Well, here goes.*

Self-conscious and nervous, she entered, but Andres was not there. She hurried into the bedroom, drawing the draped material behind her that served as a separation. Her shawl-bagged clothes were on the floor, and she decided to undress quickly in the candlelit room. Slipping on her clean nightshirt, she covered the distance to the bed in a few steps. Then, she slid under the quilt, pulling it up to her chin. Tense with anticipation, she heard Andres come into the cabin and part the drapes.

"That be my side of the bed, missy," he said, softly.

Immediately, she moved to the other side, straightening her long nightshirt beneath her. She turned toward the wall, where flickering shadows danced, cast by the candlelight.

She felt the quilt being drawn back on the other side, followed by Andres's weight on the bed, as he blew out the last candle. The sudden darkness seemed stifling. For an instant, she recalled her passionate embraces with Marion, but reality quickly thrust the memory aside.

Tightly shutting her eyes, one thought after another chased around in her head. *I know his runaway sons weigh heavily on him, yet he was considerate at the church today. Mama said that nearly all women survive the first night. Was that supposed to reassure me? Moreover, what did she mean when she said I should act natural?*

Only night noises, drifting in through the curtained window, broke the cabin's silence.

What's he thinking? Ma and Pa say that he's an upstanding man. Even so, being alone with him gives me the collywobbles. I wonder if he knows how frightened I am. It's not that I dislike him. He has my respect, just as I have for my steppapa. Even so, I simply don't know him. Abruptly, her self-reflections ended.

"Over time," Andres said softly, "we'll get to know one another better. You've gone through a terrible experience, and you're probably uneasy about tonight. I'm guessing that it'd be fine with you if we don't rush things. Once we get better acquainted, you'll see that it'll be less worrying. For now, it's best to take it slow."

What does he mean? Is there something I'm supposed to do or say? Maybe I should thank him!

Turning over on his side, he whispered, "Goodnight, Ella Mae. I'm glad you're here and part of my family."

For the second time on that day, her apprehension washed away. Still, her mind raced. *What's my life going to be like from now on? I may take my feelings for Marion to the grave, but those times are over. Now I have me a husband, and it's up to me to make things right by him and his family . . . our family. Someday, maybe I can find my own peace.*

"Good . . . goodnight . . . sir."

CHAPTER TWENTY-ONE

"All right, get yourselves up and we'll have breakfast before we break camp," Curtis called out, cheerily. He stoked the fire, added more wood, and put on the skillet and coffeepot. He had slept poorly, while wrestling with the turn of events, including Marion's description of Zacharias' hired hand. Yet, he was in a surprisingly jaunty mood and began whistling.

For that effort, his grumpy brothers gave him nasty looks.

"Top o' the morn', brothers."

"Ah, morning, big brother," Jonah managed to grumble.

Just as I expected, Curtis reflected. It made him smile, as he thought of what was coming next. *Ah, my brothers, I'm sorry for the way things have turned out. At this moment, both of you are smarting, especially you, Marion. Even so, I'm feeling good, because I've finally put together the series of events that have plagued our family for years. There's more going on here than the boys know. They're in for a surprise.*

The three ate breakfast in silence, with Marion picking at his bacon and fried bread, while Jonah appeared distracted. The boys reluctantly broke camp, smothered the campfire with the remains of the coffee, and uplifted saddles onto their horses.

"I want the two of you to listen to me for a moment," Curtis said, adjusting his black hat.

With sullen expressions, his brothers turned to face him.

"What I heard last night puts a whole new light on everything, at least as far as I'm concerned. I'm not one to defy our Pa, but I've come to the conclusion that some matters are best left alone."

Marion bristled. "What does that mean?"

Curtis stepped next to his young brother and put his arm around his shoulders. "It means that I've heard you, little brother, and Jonah, too. You boys go on with your journey west. Considering everything that's happened, it's the right thing for you to do. If'n I took you back, you'd up and leave again, just as you said. I think you both have grit and gumption. Why if'n I wasn't married to Judy Beth, I'd go along and seek my fortune with you boys."

Marion twisted around and faced him, grinning from ear to ear. He grabbed his brother's hand and shook it. "I'm grateful for your understanding, big brother. I'll go, just as soon as I settle an important matter."

Curtis stared at him for a moment and then replied in a low voice, tight with emotion. "By now, Ella Mae is Pa's wife, and she's part of our family, whether you like it or not, little brother. You boys get on with your travels. The fella that wronged her is now my concern."

"Now, see here, Curtis—" Marion responded, but he got no further.

Curtis interrupted, "No, you listen to me. As it turns out, I have prior issues to settle with this short fella. You don't know it, but years ago, he was the fourth bushwhacker in the gang that stole my horses, killed my hound, burned down my barn, and tried to shoot me."

Marion stared at him with a dubious expression. "Aw, Curtis, you're making that up, aren't you?"

"Just calm yourself and hear what I have to say."

"You can't put me off Shorty's trail with such a thin cock and bull yarn," Marion responded, defiantly. "There isn't any way you'd have let that fella stay in Lost Creek Valley without challenging him."

"That's just it. To this day, I've never laid eyes on him. How was I to know that he was working for Mr. Zacharias, or even that he was in the area?"

Marion was dubious. "That explanation still sounds weak."

"Look," Curtis continued, "for one thing, his name isn't Shorty—it's Veeko. When I was chasing those bushwhackers, he had already left before Braided Hair and I came on their camp. The one fella that we did catch described Veeko as a short, plain-looking man with broken front teeth, who wanted his share of the rustling right away, because he thought traveling through Injun country was too chancy. This really made the outlaw leader mad, especially when Veeko made threats and pulled a gun on him. Out of mule-headed meanness, the headman cut off two fingers from Veeko's left hand. Now tell me, doesn't that sound exactly like the fella you describe as Shorty?"

Marion stared, his mouth open. "I guess so," he tentatively agreed.

"There's still more, little brother. When those bandits jumped us in the forest, you remember that we didn't see the last outlaw. It was Veeko."

"Now, you're really making up stories, aren't you?" Marion responded.

"Nope."

"He's right, Marion," Jonah added. "The dying bandit whispered his name to me before he died. He told me that the last outlaw, Veeko, would get us for the shooting."

Curtis continued, "After I left you boys that day, I went back and found Veeko's horse tracks. He'd left in one heck of a hurry, heading south. It didn't suit me to follow him, with Judy Beth and the new baby being left alone at the cabin."

The three men were lost in their thoughts, until Jonah broke the silence. Baffled, he said, "I don't understand how this runt of a fella keeps moving in and out of our lives with none of us ever seeing him. You're the exception, Marion, but then you thought he was someone named Shorty Younger."

Getting Marion's eye, Curtis slowly went on. "Brother, you'll never know how sorry I am for not going after him on that day in the woods. If I had . . . well, many things might have been different. I hope someday, you can forgive me."

Shaking his head, Marion tried to clear his thoughts, as a tear slid down his cheek.

"Our family," Curtis continued, "yours and mine, has been dishonored. I'm the eldest, and it's my obligation to deal with Mr. Veeko or Shorty or whatever he calls himself. Besides," he added, with a twinkle in his eyes, "you two would most likely muck it up and get yourselves thrown in jail or hanged. You needn't fear about the family settling our grievances. To prove it, I'll bring his ears back with me and nail them to a tree in Lost Creek Valley. You can see them when you return for a visit."

"I appreciate your understanding, Curtis," Jonah said. "I think it best that the two of us leave for Independence. Let's be off, young brother."

Marion was still staring at Curtis. "This is really my fight."

"Use your ears and listen one last time. This man stole my horses, killed my hound, burned down my barn, tried to kill us, and stained our family. Taking care of him is *my* job. Now, you two get along."

Slowly, Marion walked toward his horse. Then, he stopped and quickly returned, giving Curtis a bear hug. "Much obliged for your understanding, big brother. I know this mess isn't of your making. I'm grateful for you standing by me."

Jonah also gave Curtis a hug. "What're you going to tell Pa when you return?" he asked.

"Oh, I'll think of something. You can tell him all about your adventures someday when you come back for a visit."

In a quiet voice, Marion replied, "I'm never going back."

Curtis looked at him and then shrugged. "The passage of time is a mighty strange thing. For some, it heals. For others, the festering never stops. I'll not be letting on to Pa that I know about Veeko or the land deal with Mr. Zacharias." Fishing in his shirt pocket, he continued, "Here is half of the money I have with me. It'll buy you a horse and some grub, when you need it."

"We're much obliged, brother," Jonah replied.

"Good luck, boys, I pray God always rides in the stirrups beside you."

CHAPTER TWENTY-TWO

Riding down the dirt road of Raytown, Curtis recalled Ella Mae dancing with Marion at the community gathering at the Vogel barn, and how happy they were. He found himself increasingly bewildered by the happenings on the Sommer and Zacharias farms. As Jonah had continued with the tale the previous evening, Curtis had felt his knife-edged anger rising, though outwardly appearing calm.

Finally, he thought grimly, *I'm on the trail of the fourth bushwhacker. I'll always regret not finding him before all the tragedies that followed.*

After seeing his brothers depart in the morning, he set about finding Veeko. He reckoned that the starting place was with the painted lady at the saloon. Knowing he was unlikely to find her until evening, he spent the day talking with men congregated at the blacksmith shop and, later, with the Santa Fe drovers at the end of town.

After sunset, he went to the saloon, where Marion had seen Veeko leaving. He whiled away much of the night, but he had no luck. There were three women mingling with the customers in the smoke-filled hall, but none of them had red hair. *I guess I'll have to come back tomorrow night,* he concluded.

The second night, there still was no sign of a woman with bright-red hair. *Maybe these gals change the color of their hair often. If so, I'm going to have a devil of a time finding her.* Late in the evening, a bright redheaded woman walked through the swinging front doors, quickly sizing up the men in the room. She made her way to the bar and began talking to the barkeep.

Now that's an eye-catching color, Curtis observed. *She has to be the one my brother saw.* Making his way toward the bar, he stood and watched her reflection in the looking glass hanging behind the bar.

Meeting his eye in the mirror, she smiled and turned sideways, displaying her ample bosom. "Howdy, handsome. You new in town?"

"Yes, ma'am. May I buy you a drink?"

"Well, of course, young man." Laughing, she continued, "This country would be awfully dry, if'n there wasn't any whiskey to drink. My name is Shelley. What's yours?"

"Curtis," he replied. "I'd appreciate a little company tonight, as I'm pulling out for Santa Fe in the morning. Maybe we can get a table and do some talking. Sound all right to you?"

"Sure, big fella. No one is as good as me, when it comes to talking and listening—and there're a few other things I do well, too." She laughed, brashly. "Why don't you buy us a bottle and then we can talk a spell."

Sitting at a table, with their glasses filled, Shelley held hers up to make a toast. "Here's to you and me tonight, Curtis. What say we have a fun time?" she added, emptying her glass.

Curtis sipped his and smiled. *I'm gonna have to pace my whiskey drinking with this gal. Otherwise, I'll be crawling out of this saloon on my hands and knees.*

"I suppose you've been in town a short spell," the woman remarked. "No one stays hereabouts, unless they have to."

"Yep, I got in yesterday," Curtis, replied.

"Then, I drink another toast to wish you a safe journey tomorrow," she said gaily, emptying another glass.

"Uh-huh, to us," Curtis responded, barely touching the raw liquor to his lips. "I'm a muleskinner with a train that's camped outside of town." He saw her nodding and giving him a knowing look. Up close, he noticed that the roots of her hair were darker and that her lips and cheeks were brightly rouged. Her dark, blue dress covered her shoulders and closed at the neck, finished off with a black ribbon tied around her throat. The garment was fancy-cut, but it had seen better days.

They talked for an hour or more, drinking the bottle down to the bottom. Grabbing his knee under the table, she leaned over and asked in a slurred voice, "What's ailing you tonight that you ain't drinking more, handsome?"

"I got a hold of some bad water a few days ago, and I'm taking it kind of easy."

"Well, that's the problem with water," she quipped, "...it's unwashed." She laughed gaily at her silly humor. "But even with you sipping, Curtis, we've done in this bottle. Why don't you buy us another, then we can talk about some other things that may interest the both of us?"

Cheerfully, he replied, "Sure. I'll be right back, Shelley." He rose and unsteadily walked to the bar. *By golly, this gal must have an iron-cast stomach to put away so much of this firewater. I sip mine and feel woozy, while she tosses back full glasses like it's milk laced with honey.* When he returned, he said, "Let me have your glass, young lady."

She laughed, "Ain't as young as I used to be, but I'm good for some things, especially up in my room."

Going along with her game, he smiled, and started to sit down.

"How about you and I take a wee walk upstairs?" she asked, smiling and fluttering her eyes. Her voice slurred as she spoke. As she rose to her feet, she stumbled.

"Steady there, young lady."

"Thankee, kindly. You're a real gentleman. We'd be more comfortable in my room, and we can take the bottle with us."

"That's a right good suggestion, and the best I've had this week," Curtis replied, returning her smile. He reached for his hat and rifle, and the woman carried the bottle. "To tell the truth," he continued, "I was counting on us going somewhere else."

They managed to support each other, while weaving through the swinging doors, locked arm-in-arm.

They took the same outside stairs that Marion had described. When the door to her room closed, the woman shook off her shawl and pressed against him, running a finger along the edge of his jaw. "C'mon handsome, let's make a night of it."

Curtis gently pushed her away and saw the questioning look on her face. Locking the door, he guided her to the bed and sat her down with a firm push.

Alarmed, she responded in a hoarse voice, "Looki here, muleskinner, do you want to do it or not? I'm a working girl, and I ain't got time to be just wasting the evening. It'll cost you two bucks for me to get your spirits roaring, and three, if'n you stay the night, but I draw the line at any rough stuff, and I mean it. What's it to be?"

"Take it easy, Miss Shelley. I just want to talk with you and ask you some questions," Curtis replied, in a soft voice. He noticed that his slurred words did little to ease her fears.

She stiffened, as she answered. "Big fella, are you buying or not?"

"Ma'am, I'm looking for some information, and I'll pay you for your time. You need not worry your head about that." He saw the dubious expression on her face but continued. "I'm looking for a man, and I'm told that you know him. He's short and goes by the name of Shorty Younger or Veeko. When did you last see him?"

Unconsciously, she started rubbing her shoulder. "Are you a lawman?" she asked, her eyes narrowing. "How can you be sure I know him, this Veeko fella?"

Not answering, he asked again, "Tell me about the last time you saw him."

Shelley started to rise, but he sat her back down.

Frowning, she looked at the locked door, then at him. "I don't want no trouble. I had more than enough the last time I saw that miserable bastard. Why are you asking me, anyhow? Is he wanted by the law for something? Are you a bounty hunter?"

Curtis saw her rubbing her arm again. "My young brother saw you come up here with him and two other men several nights ago. You remember the short man, don't you? He likes to rough women up." Seeing her anxiety, he asked, "Did Veeko do the same to you?"

"So what if he did," she asked, tossing her bright hair back with a flick of her head. "Lots of fellas have followed me up them outside steps."

"You can be sure that I'm not here to hurt you. Veeko brutally beat and raped my brother's young sweetheart. I'm looking for the fella to make things right, and you may know something that'll help me find him." Still seeing her hesitation, he continued, "I mean to catch him and avenge the wrong he's done my family."

Her face softened, as she replied, "I've already spoken plainly. I don't want any trouble, and I mean it."

"I need your help. Please tell me about that night."

"This short man you're looking for—" She paused, blinking back tears and staring at him. Then, she slowly undid the drawstring collar at the neck of her dress and slid it down over one shoulder, showing him the angry looking welts and discolored bruises marking her shoulder and breast. "I've met him, as you can see," she answered, shrugging back into the dress and tying the top, "and the other fellas. That short excuse for a man and his pardn'rs hurt me so bad that it kept me in bed yesterday, and I couldn't work last night."

"Tell me what happened."

"Veeko's as vicious as they come. Have you ever seen him?"

"No, but he's the one with the missing fingers, ain't that right?"

"Yeah, I remember because his pardn'r, Butch, kept joshing him about having put them in the wrong holes too many times. He's older than you, plain-looking as sin, brown-haired, and has crooked front teeth."

"That sure seems to describe what my brother told me. What does Butch look like, ma'am?"

"He's uglier than all get-out and has a big, crooked nose," the woman replied. "And there's a deep scar that runs clear across his forehead."

"Is he tall or short, ma'am?"

"Big fella, he is," the woman replied. "He's heavyset, about six feet tall, has black hair, and his full name is Butch Baker. And the other fella, Billy Joe, he's about your size with brown hair but much younger and acts kind of foolish."

"Go on," he said in a husky voice.

"Veeko beat me and then took his way with me. After they used me, that miserable runt beat me some more, saying it was good for my soul. Can you imagine the wickedness of such an animal? Fact is, he had trouble with his manhood until he roughed me up." She rubbed her shoulder again and continued, "That also goes for the big man who was with him. They were meaner than chained dogs."

"I'm sorry they hurt you, Miss Shelley."

In a whiskey-laced voice, she continued, "I hope you catch Veeko and throw him into the river with his legs tied to his head. He's a no-good, mean-ass mongrel."

Curtis listened silently. He tried to steady himself by leaning against the metal footboard of the bed. His head hurt, which made it difficult to focus on her words. *The firewater has me in its clutches*, he reasoned.

A look of fear came into her eyes, and she blurted out, "I don't want none of them coming back here and hurting me again. Veeko beat me real bad the last time."

Looking into her eyes, Curtis replied simply, "I give you my word—they'll never bother you again."

Tears flowed down her face, streaking her powder, as she dropped her head into her hands. In a low, husky voice, she sobbed, "After . . . after they finished with me, I huddled in the corner over there, scared for my life. The three of them drank more whiskey and talked. I couldn't make it all out, but I heard them say that they're going to work the Oregon Trail west of Independence and waylay wagons—the ones that can't keep up with their trains. They plan to kill the settlers and steal their outfits."

"Did you hear them mention any particular place or landmark other than Independence?" Curtis asked.

"I heard them say they'd be scouting the area beyond Shawnee Mission."

"Thank you, ma'am," Curtis concluded, as he fished three dollars out of his pocket. "I appreciate the information, and I'm sorry they roughed you up."

As he turned to leave, Shelley grabbed his hand. "Please, do me one favor, Mister Curtis," she pleaded, tears streaming down her face.

"If'n I can."

"Just keep your promise. Never let them hurt me again!"

FORKED ROAD

Independence, Missouri

1855

CHAPTER TWENTY-THREE

The size of Independence astonished Marion, as he and Jonah arrived in the teeming city. It sat on the banks of the Missouri River, on land previously home to Indians from the Missouri and Osage tribes. Over the years, settlers converged on the town, making it the major departure point for the Oregon and California trails.

Never had Marion seen such a collection of folks, mingling with a seemingly countless number of oxen, mules, horses, and cattle. Flanking the main square, a gaggle of stores sold their goods, each busily catering to the needs of westbound travelers. The bluffs on the south side of the Missouri River appeared to be a sea of billowing white, representing the many canvas-topped wagons waiting to form into trains.

He and his brother spent the first couple of days wandering among the wagon camps, seeking the Possard wagons. Today, he was determined that the two of them find jobs with a train headed west. "How do we go about finding trail-hand jobs?" he asked Jonah.

"I don't rightly know, but I'm still going to keep looking for Tennie's group. You keep a sharp eye out for them, too, little brother."

Stopping at the livery, Marion made inquiries of a stable hand.

"Folks are arriving in town," the man began, "from every state and territory across America. Some have even come over the ocean to be part of this annual westward movement. Each wagon train's captain does his own picking of fellas he needs as scouts, outriders, cooks, herders, and the like. Then, all the wagons form into different trains of anywhere from fifty to a hundred. I suggest you move from camp to camp, until you get hired on. You can start anywhere, but the closest encampment is on the hill over yonder."

Anxiously, Jonah asked, "How long ago did the trains start moving out?"

"Haven't," the liveryman replied.

Marion was surprised, and he saw the eager look on his brother's face. That news meant Tennie was most likely still in town. "Why is that?" he inquired.

"Spring grass on the plains has to be at least knee-high, before there'll be enough feed for all the stock that'll be moving down the trail. Three or four scouts left a few days ago to make an evaluation, and they'll likely be back any day now. When there's sufficient feed for the animals, the trains will begin leaving."

Cheered by the information, Jonah intensified the search for Tennie among the thousands camped on the banks of the river. Finally, a man told them to inquire at Abe's Mercantile, where folks listed their family name under each wagon train master, and some posted notes for friends or relatives who were following later.

"I got to find that mercantile store," Jonah said.

Laughing, Marion pointed across the street. "Well, there it is, right over there."

Stepping up to the big wooden board mounted on the side of the store building, Jonah looked down the long lists, patiently scanning the names. He finally found the Possard family listed under the train of Captain Barry Shaw.

Suddenly, there was a hullabaloo at the far end of the busy street. It seemed to be a combination of cheering, hooraying, and clapping. As they peered down the main dirt road, the joyous sounds swelled, heading their way. In front, a man galloped his horse.

"CLEAR THE WAY! the rider shouted, wildly waving his hat. "GRASS BE UP! START THE TRAINS! GRASS BE UP!"

Several men fired their guns into the air in celebration, as though it was Independence Day.

Jonah and Marion smiled at each other. They joined the cheering and clapping as the rider made his way to the town square, still shouting his news at the top of his lungs.

Jonah turned back, urgently reading the posted notes, scribbled on every type and scrap of paper.

Marion noticed one entitled "For Jerome from Alabama" in large letters. He plucked it off the wall and handed it to Jonah. "This may interest you, big brother."

Jonah's face turned red as he studied the note. Crumpling the paper, he threw it on the ground.

Marion picked it up and read it:

Jerome ~

I pray that you are reading this, for it means that you are on the trail, following me to Grants Pass in Oregon. Ride fast and stay safe.

Yours, Tennie

"If that don't beat all," Jonah commented bitterly. "She's still mooning about that easterner and wants *him* to find her."

Marion could not help chuckling. "Those hand-stitched moccasins you gave her must have really impressed her," he teased.

Angrily, Jonah replied, "Why are you joshing me? At least I'm not running away from the gal I love."

The barb stung, as images of Ella Mae raced through his mind. Shaking his head, Marion led the way, as they set out to find the Possard wagons and secure jobs.

<hr>

The first train left the following day. Marion agreed to help his brother watch the departing wagons, checking each for any sign of Tennie and her family. That proved to be impossible, as they were standing in the middle of the staging area for most of the morning, where inexperienced wagon drivers were trying to form up into a column. It was, without a doubt, mass chaos, as unholy curses and shouting accompanied the muddle. More than once, the boys maneuvered quickly in order to avoid certain injury or worse, as greenhorn drivers tackled the daunting task of driving a fully loaded wagon hauled by up to six draft animals.

In exasperation, Marion asked, "Brother, how are we going to find work with a train headed west, if'n all we do is watch every wagon that leaves town?"

Reluctantly, Jonah agreed. The next day, they arrived at an empty campsite. By asking folks in the surrounding area, they learned that the Shaw train had left the previous day.

"Ah, if that ain't the worst luck ever," Jonah moaned, with a forlorn expression on his face. Brightening, he said, "You know, if'n we rode out of town right now, we could catch them in a few days. What say you, little brother?"

"We've no way of knowing if we could hire on with that train. If there's no work, then how do we live? Maybe you're figuring that we can stand alongside the trail." Mockingly, he continued, "That way, we can ask for scraps of food from passing travelers. Come on, big brother, you're not making much sense."

Grudgingly, his brother nodded, and they doubled their efforts to find jobs with a train. The next day, a man referred them to a captain by the name of Ernie Fudge. Searching until they found him, the man was busy getting his settlers ready for the trip. He was lanky and leather-lean, wearing a fringed deerskin coat, denim pants, and a hat with a feather stuck in the band.

Finally getting the busy captain's attention, Jonah said, "I'm Jonah Sommer, and this is my brother, Marion. We're farm-bred and learned hard work from our pa. We'd like to hire on with your train."

The wagon train captain looked the boys up and down. "So, you want to work yourselves west, do ya? You both look fit. Let me see your hands."

The two obliged, and the trail boss ran his finger over their rough palms, hardened by years of calluses.

"How are you with horses and cattle? You got any experience handling draft animals?"

"Yes, sir," Marion replied. "We've been tending stock on our pa's farm ever since we could walk."

"Can you shoot and hunt? You know, a train has to rely on game to help feed the folks over the long months of the journey."

"We sure can," Jonah replied. "We've both hunted since we were knee-high to a hitching post. I'm good, but Marion here, he's a dead-eye with his Hawken rifle."

"Do tell," the captain said. He took off his hat to mop his brow.

Both young men stared at Fudge's hair in amazement. Reddish-brown hair covered about half of the man's head, and the other was white as snow. Never had either boy seen anything like it before.

Seeing their flabbergasted expressions, Captain Fudge snapped, "Stop your gawking and pay no mind to my hair. It goes back to the days when I ran into some Injuns years ago. They were looking to relieve me of my scalp. It was a right good fight, as I recall. Don't you know, within a week, one side of my head turned white. Darndest thing, it was. You two hear me good, I'll not have you gossiping about it. You get my meaning?" Seeing the nods, he continued, "Now, let's get back to business. Any lawman chasing after you boys, or maybe your pa?"

"No, sir," Jonah answered.

"Are you well mounted? You know, we'll be traveling over two thousand miles, and they got to last."

"Yes, sir, our horses are fine bred."

"All right, I need a few more outriders and herders for the remuda. The job pays ten dollars a month plus all the beans and salt beef you can eat. You'll likely sleep under the supply wagon. Maybe I'll even let you drive the team, but let's get one thing clear. I'm in command of this train, and what I say goes. You got that? You work for me."

"Yes, sir," the boys said in unison.

The captain fished in his vest pocket, until he came out with a small notebook and a stub pencil. "You, boy," he said, pointing to Marion, "tell me your name again."

"Marion, Marion Francis Sommer, sir."

The wagon leader stared at him, his eyes squinting in his tanned, weather-lined face. "That sure is a mouthful, son. I used to know a lady by the name of Mary Ann, and my ma's name was Frances. I ain't ever had a trail hand working for me with a female's name. How about we just call you Frank? Is that all right with you?"

"Fair enough," the newly christened Frank replied. "But I got to tell you something, Captain Fudge, I never expected to hire on to work for a fella with a candy for a name."

That statement stopped the older man for a moment, until he responded with a roar of laughter. Turning to Jonah, he asked, "And you, what's your name?"

"It's Jonah Hiram Sommer."

Captain Ernie noted it in his book, and stuffed it and the pencil away. Sticking his hand in another pocket, he pulled out two coins. "Here's a five dollar piece for each of you. Consider it an advance against your first month's wages. You get yourself outfitted at Abe's Mercantile. If'n you don't have them, buy several boxes of lead, gunpowder flasks, boots, and a change of clothes. While you're at it, make sure you have a rain slicker, water canteen, and a warm coat. There's one more thing, put your horses up at the livery until we leave, and feed them oats. It'll only cost you two bits a night. Got all that? All right, get along to that wagon over there and look up a fella named Shep. Tell him I hired you milk-fed farm boys. You can take orders from him, as he's my ramrod on this train."

"When do we leave?" Jonah asked anxiously.

"Our turn will come in two days. Now get along and find Shep."

Just like that, Frank and Jonah were part of a wagon train headed to Oregon.

CHAPTER TWENTY-FOUR

N ewly named Frank knew that his brother was eager to get started west, but he would just have to contain himself. Their chances of finding Tennie on the vast plains seemed far-fetched, at best.

The train's ramrod turned out to be a seasoned trail man in his late thirties, sporting shaggy brown hair. In the style of many, he wore a black hat, a faded green shirt, and an ancient leather vest. His eyes were quick, and his face was well tanned, broken by a ready smile. Walking with them among the many wagons, he was full of information.

"Yep, this is my third train in the last six years. Some wanted to put me up for election as captain of a train, but that don't fit my nature. I shy away from holding the hands of all these tenderfoot greenhorns, yammering over every little dadgum thing that comes up. I'd rather work for Captain Fudge, and let him fuss with them folks."

Shep pointed to a wagon. "If'n you don't know, these are called 'prairie schooners,' as a line of them looks like sailing ships. Mighty pretty picture, they be, strung out on the vast plains. They're smaller and lighter than the old Conestoga wagons. See there," he pointed, "a wagon's body is made of hard woods to keep them from shrinking in the dry heat of the plains, and the sides are slanted to keep the rain out. Inside, many are tarred, making them watertight, and they'll float, if need be. Them Studebaker brothers make most of them, clear back in South Bend, Indiana.

"Greenhorns all make the same mistake. They start out with over-loaded wagons. It doesn't seem to make any difference what we tell them. They'll get halfway to Oregon and find that their animals are plumb worn out from pulling the heavy loads. Then folks will have to chuck out stuff, just to keep going, figuring it's better to lose a few possessions rather than family members."

"Why are the rear wheels taller than the front?" Jonah asked.

"The smaller ones permit the wagons to turn sharper," the ramrod replied.

The young men learned that hickory wood bows held up the white, billowing canvas bonnets. Overall, the schooners stood some ten feet tall. On the sides of most wagons, spare wheels nested, as well as water barrels, toolboxes, and other gear. A number also had coops attached, housing chickens, rabbits, or ducks.

Frank reckoned that the wagon beds measured about four feet wide by twelve feet long, and all the wagons had a bucket hanging below.

"Them buckets hold a mixture of animal fat and tar that's used to grease the wheel hubs and moving parts," Shep explained.

"I notice that folks use all manner of draft animals—oxen, mules and horses—to haul their wagons," Jonah observed. "Why is that?"

"Depends—most folks use oxen, as they're cheaper, stronger, and forage better along the trail," Shep replied. "A man can buy a yoke for twenty-five dollars down at the corral, compared to a hundred dollars for a single mule or horse in this highfaluting, pricey town.

"Horses are faster, but they need grain in their feed, which adds weight to a wagon. Besides, the heavy hauling plumb wears out some horses before the journey ends. Mules are more reliable and eat less than horses.

"For my money, oxen are the best draft animals for our journey. Ya do know, don't ya, that men handle and drive the ox teams walking along side."

"Some make the long trip walking?" Jonah asked in astonishment.

"Yep, most settlers prefer it. See that single spring under the wagon seat?" Shep asked, pointing. "That's the only one ya'll find on any of these schooners. Riding in the wagon bed can be hellish, even over the smoothest trail. Besides, I've already told ya that an overloaded wagon is a killer for the draft animals and walking saves weight. By the way, there's a ring of anvils on the edge of town manned by smithies. See to it that all the draft oxen are shod before we depart."

Surprised, Frank asked, "Folks shoe their oxen for this journey? But, sir, they have cloven hooves."

"That's right, so there're two shoes nailed on for every hoof."

"What's the routine, once we get started?" Jonah asked.

"We wake before sunup, yoke the animals, and breakfast on johnny-cakes and bacon or leftovers from supper. Then, we hit the trail. At mid-day, we stop for an hour, and we end the day before dusk. Some trains have fewer wagons than us, and they mostly laager each night with their livestock in the middle. We'll likely have more than five hundred draft animals, in addition to milk cows, cattle, and horses. That'll be way too many to corral with our hundred or so wagons, so we'll set night watches, and ya boys will draw that duty."

"I see that some wagons have spare parts tied to the sides, and some don't," Jonah noted. "What's best?"

"We encourage them to bring along any spare parts they want. At the very least, Captain Ernie and I insist that these folks carry additional wheels as well as coils of rope to use for possible repairs and for slowing wagons down steep grades. Moreover, ya see to it that there's an extra tongue, coupling bolt, yoke, wheel jack, and axle for every two or three wagons. Folks can go in together to buy them. These wagons are sturdy and can be repaired, but a major breakdown on the trail without spare parts can be a disaster and cost lives."

"Yes, sir," Jonah replied.

Frank noticed a butter churn lashed to one wagon and pointed it out.

Shep stopped to explain. "Most folks tie a cow to the tailgate. After milking in the evening, they'll let it sit until the cream rises. Each morning, they'll skim the fat off the cream and pour it into the churn. As it bounces along the rough trail, they have butter for their supper."

"That's a great idea."

"Yeah, it works well," Shep, added. "Now, listen, you two. Ya get yarself each two lariats. Rawhides are the best for what ya'll be doing. It'll cost about two bits for twenty-five feet. And, both of ya buy a fold of buckskin. Ya can mend yar clothes and do most anything with soft leather and an awl. Be sure ya have plenty of ammunition. Now, get thee off to the mercantile in town."

As Frank walked with his brother toward the center of town, he recalled his last bitter words with Ella Mae. He had come to realize how frightened she must have been, beaten by the hired hand, then finding she was with child. *Damn, there she was, needing my help and understanding, and me calling her a loose woman. I reckon she's right—I got more learning to do.*

His thoughts turned to his father. *I'll never forgive him, the lecherous old bastard. Pa's ruined my life and Ella Mae's, too. I'm never returning to Missouri. Pa can rot in hell for all I care.*

His mood turned even uglier as he pictured Veeko's face. *You had better start looking over your shoulder, you lowlife. My big brother is on your trail.*

CHAPTER TWENTY-FIVE

E verywhere Curtis looked, people in Independence hurried about—
going into Abe's Mercantile, scrutinizing draft animals for sale at
the stable, or busily rushing to complete their many tasks before heading
west.

*The towns of Joplin, Seneca, and Springfield, combined, can't compare in
size,* he reckoned. At one end, he was surprised to see a tall, three-story
building with a cupola-styled structure topping it. *This town must have
come a far piece,* he thought, staring at the tall structure.

Walking the dusty streets, Curtis knew that there was little chance of
finding a short man with two missing fingers, along with his partners, in
such a busy town. He could have tried the saloons, but a passerby told
him that there were a dozen or more in town. That was too many to
search. He wondered where his brothers were, but figured that he had
already said his farewells to them several days earlier.

I need more information about the trail ahead, he decided. *I reckon the best
way is talking to folks. Abe's Mercantile looks like the busiest place in town. Think
I'll sit a spell in one of the chairs out front.*

As he approached, he saw a large, roughly drawn map of the Oregon Trail painted on the store's side. Studying it, Curtis noticed that Shawnee Mission was directly west of Independence. From there, the trail generally went northwest, following the Platte River through Kansas and Nebraska territories and on to Fort Laramie in Wyoming Territory. *Heavens, you travel all that distance and it's only one-third of the way to Oregon,* he mused.

Planting himself in a chair, with his foot propped on the hitching rail, he looked like the soul of patience to any passing stranger, as he whittled away on a stick with his knife. Over the next hour, several men occupied seats next to him.

Finally, an old, silver-haired man sat down, and they struck up a conversation. Curtis noticed the man's weathered face and white flowing beard, stained with tobacco juice. He wore a faded blue shirt, dark britches supported by wide suspenders, a dented hat with a high-crown, and dog-eared boots. The fellow reached into his pocket and produced a plug of tobacco. Chewing off a chunk, he pouched it on the inside of his cheek.

"What route do the trains take when they leave Missouri?" Curtis asked.

"For darn near half of the way, the valleys bordering the rivers are the main guideposts," the old man replied. "The trail goes due west from Independence for about a hundred miles before turning northwest. That allows the trains to cut off the big dogleg created where the Platte and Missouri rivers meet. That river junction is about five days ride, due north of here. Anyway, after each train reaches the Platte, folks follow it, right up to and beyond its headwaters, and on to Fort Laramie. From there, it's a matter of following the trail west to South Pass, which leads you over the tall mountains, until ya pick up the Snake and Columbia rivers."

"You sound like you know the trail well. You must have made the trip a few times?"

"Made four in my earlier days. Twice, I returned by sailing ship. But, riding horseback for months on end and sleeping on the ground ain't for me no more—or maybe I'm too old for it," he said with a chuckle, expertly sending out a stream of tobacco juice to the road.

"When did the trains begin moving out?"

"Ain't none left yet," he replied.

Startled, Curtis asked, "Why is that?"

"Can't. Spring grass has to be tall enough to feed all the livestock going down the trail."

"How soon will that be?"

"Oh, anytime now," the old-timer replied. "And, of course, the huge gaggle of wagons gathered hereabouts can't leave at the same time."

Curious, Curtis asked, "What's the reasoning behind that."

"Think on it, young fella. If everyone left at once, there wouldn't be enough prairie grass to feed all the stock, water holes would soon be overrun and, most likely, tainted, and the continual dust in the air would choke every man, woman, and youngun, as well as all the animals. No, siree, train captains pick lots out of a hat at the beginning and leave in the order of their draw. It's a matter of surviving on the trail, in spite of all the eager, greenhorn settlers, who are just itching to get started."

"How much time passes between departing trains?"

"With the new grass, a train leaves every few days, except on the Sabbath. Within a few weeks, the early rush gets sorted out and then trains leave about once a week, if it ain't raining hard."

"I notice that folks are mostly using oxen to haul their wagons," Curtis commented. "That would allow the trains to make, what, about fifteen to twenty miles a day?"

"That's about right. A wagon train boss will try to cover about a hundred miles a week—traveling six days, with the Sabbath off for prayers, rest, and repairs."

"So, if'n it's two thousand miles to Oregon, that's a trip of four to five months, ain't that right?"

"Yep, it's about three weeks shorter, if'n ya're headed to the gold diggings in Northern California. That last bit of the Oregon Trail from the Snake and Columbia rivers is the most treacherous part of the entire journey for folks."

"I'm trying to understand how wagon train bosses can learn a trail that stretches for thousands of miles. Even very experienced men can't memorize a route that long. How is it marked?"

The old man gave Curtis a long stare. "Pshaw, son," he answered, chuckling, "for most of the way, a blind man could follow it. That's because the ruts are so deep in the hard-packed ground, from years of heavy wagons traveling over the land. Secondly, like I've already told ya, the trail goes along the river valleys, for the most part."

"Huh."

"Don't get me wrong, the captains have a lot on their minds, particularly trouble with Injuns, sickness, weather, and scarce water, as the trains travel across hundreds of miles of desert after leaving Fort Laramie. Most of them fellas are seasoned hands and have been shepherding pioneers for years."

"Is there much trouble from Injuns on the trail?"

"They'll steal ya blind and maybe lift yar scalp, if'n ya don't pay heed. Most run-ins happen because Injuns are after horses."

"Do many folks get injured or killed?"

"A few, but more settlers die from being run over by teams or wagons. Those big schooners weigh in at near fifteen hundred pounds, empty. Packed to the brim, they're nigh onto double that. If'n ya get in the way, they'll squash ya faster than I can spit my chaw juice across the road," he said, cackling at his humor.

"You don't say," Curtis chuckled.

"Ya better believe it," the old man continued, still smiling. "On top of that, more folks get killed by carelessly shooting someone or themselves," he said, sending a new tobacco spray to the road. "But mark my word, all of them dangers on the trail pale compared to folks dying from the 'golden showers.'"

Curtis looked at the man questioningly. "What in God's creation is that?"

"I don't rightly know, as I've never come across it directly. But, from tales I've heard, it's the mysterious, silent killer of western trail."

"How do you make it out?"

"It's pretty simple. Everything runs out of folks . . . from both ends . . . and then folks suffer from terrible cramps. I always reckoned that they must have come across bad water. Ya know what I mean, likely corrupted by man or beast. Anyway, I've heard of folks coming down with it in the morning, and by midday, they're a shrunken shell and gone off to meet their maker. Why heck, there were a few times when I've seen a grave that looked like it was filled with every member of a single family, all felled by that evil illness."

"Well, if that ain't something," Curtis commented.

"Yes, sir, and I've seen other folks laid out along the route, dead and abandoned, cause their kin and friends feared they'd die, if'n they touched or buried the fallen. Damnation, that misery truly is the biggest killer of settlers on the trail west."

"You don't say," Curtis added, following along.

"You mind my suggestion, young man. I lived by a simple rule when I rode the trails for all them years. If'n the water ain't rushing, boil it!"

"That's sound advice."

"Don't ya know, young fella," the old trail hand continued, sending out another spray, then staring at him and arching his brow for emphasis. "Folks making redeye from corn and grain boil it off, so it fits my simple rule. Kind of—lucky, ain't it?" he added, slapping his leg and guffawing in delight at his sense of fun.

"I get your drift," Curtis said, with a chuckle. Getting back to his task of finding Veeko, he asked, "How many days ride is it to Shawnee Mission?"

"It's only a twenty-mile jaunt, but it takes two days for most outfits to get there, what with the many greenhorns driving those big rigs. Many trains stop there to straighten out the messes and screw-ups that happen at the beginning of a trip, what with the new drivers and all."

"How large is the village?"

"Sufficient size, given all the Injuns camped nearby. The folks at the Methodist mission are a welcoming group. They teach Injuns to speak white-man's talk, the basics of farming, and the ways of the good Lord. Farther west, trains encounter days of rolling hills, which eventually dwindle away to the flatlands of the plains. Ya're hard-pressed to find a tree of any size out there. What once grew there was cut down long ago for firewood. Well, I got to get and be moving on. Nice talking with ya, young fella, and good luck on the trail."

"Thank you, I'll need it."

Curtis wanted to stretch his legs, so he strolled into the store. Near the main counter, he stopped to read a sign hanging on the wall.

FOLKS HEADING WEST
- HEED THIS AVICE -

This is the minimum supplies for a five month journey to Oregon City for a family of four. Ignore this at your own peril!!

Flour - 500 lbs
Rice - 3 sacks
Beans - 70 lbs
Coffee - 40 lbs
Dried Fruit -60 lbs
Tea - 1 keg
Beef Jerky - 250 lbs

Cornmeal - 150 lbs
Cured bacon - 400 lbs
Salt -20 lbs
Sodium bicarboate -
     leavening - 3 lbs
Lard - 200 lbs
Sugar - 100 lbs

. . . and don't forget your other needs!
Ax, shovel, hoe, scythe, hay fork, lever bar,
crop seed, hay rake, skinning knife, rifle or shotgun (pistol optional), plow lariat, sheet of leather, cloth, Spinning wheel, thread, awl . . . and
spare wagon parts - wheels, tongue, axel, hub nuts, canvas, harnass chains, coupling bolt, block/tackle, wagon jack, axel grease, rope and ??

Good luck and may God be with you ~ Abe

That's a parcel of supplies, Curtis figured. *You can either trust storekeeper Abe's word or take your chances that you'll have enough food for the long trip. Either way, you'll know who was right at the end.*

He walked the aisles, looking at the sky-high prices. *Good Lord Almighty, they're asking two dollars a pound for flour. And looki there,* he thought. *Abe wants eight cents for a pound of beans, and bacon sells for five dollars a hundred-weight. A farmer could make himself a small fortune by bringing a wagonload of greens and cured meats to Independence and selling it through the store, or directly to westbound settlers. I'm going to keep that in mind.*

Studying the list again, he figured his sums. It must cost a family nearly a thousand dollars—for a wagon, two or three braces of oxen, as well as supplies for the journey. Then, they have to carry enough stores to see them through the trip and extra for the following year, until they can plant and harvest their first crops.

So, that's what Veeko and his men are up to. They're stealing wagons full of supplies from stragglers and selling it to other folks going west. What a ghastly reason for plunder and mayhem.

Storekeeper Abe approached, asking to be of service.

"I saw the posted list of supplies for a trip west and have one question."

"Well, I'll answer the best I can. What is it?" the older man asked, smoothing his long apron.

"The bacon you pack in kegs, is it well cured?"

"The best I can get."

"Still, it must get rancid out there in the hot sun."

"We pack it in bran and that works well to keep it from spoiling."

"Good idea. How much are you asking for that old army spyglass?"

"Looking to get seven bits for it," the merchant replied.

"I'll take it. I'll also need more supplies for my Navy Colt."

As Curtis left through the front door and stepped out into the sun again, he saw a rider coming fast down the crowded dirt street shouting, "PRAIRIE GRASS BE UP. START THE TRAINS."

CHAPTER TWENTY-SIX

C urtis mentally laid out his field of search, as he rode west. *Veeko's most likely a sly fella—probably one of them cautious types that stay in the shadows until it's safe to strike. He and the others will be looking for easy targets, like wagons traveling alone or in small groups. That'll minimize their risks, while providing teams, wagons, and full loads of supplies to resell in Independence. They'll also want to stay clear of Injuns farther west along the trail. That leaves an area bordered by the Shawnee Mission on the east to, say, twenty or so miles—a day's ride, northwest along the narrow stretch of the rutted trail that the old-timer says a blind man can follow.*

He passed the mission on the first day but did not stop. For the next five days, he crisscrossed the countryside. From ridges and hilltops, he used his new spyglass to view seas of white bonnets moving along the rutty trail.

He realized that various twists and turns of chance could make Veeko impossible to find, but he had the patience of a hunter seeking his prey. His promise to his younger brother was uppermost in his mind. Thinking about the hired hand, Curtis found the little man loathsome.

Any fella who roughs up women and weaker folks has no honor and damn little moral backbone.

As he rode a ridge, the Platte Valley lay ahead and to the north. It resembled a shimmering, meandering ribbon, stretching to the far reaches of the distant horizon. Haze obscured the far edges of the visible world, but in it, shapes moved. He focused his glass on a train, trailing huge clouds of dust. He only saw the outline of the wagons' bonnets through the dense, choking haze. *Sometimes, trains stay in line; other times, wagons travel two, three, or even four abreast in the broader sections of the valley—each trying to eat less dust.*

Replacing the glass in its leather case, Curtis followed along, dipping down to cross a small valley and then urging his black up the next set of hills. The sun was bright and the soft breeze was warm and humid, carrying the fresh smell of prairie grass.

At the hilltop, he stopped to drink from his water skin. Again, he scanned the vast territory ahead through his glass scope. *Veeko's trail is absolutely cold at this moment,* he acknowledged. *Am I on a fool's errand? By now, Judy Beth must be wondering what's become of me.* Though longing for home and family, he rode on.

Curtis decided to broaden his crisscross field of search, until it stretched to a two-day ride from Shawnee Mission. On the following day, he sighted black smoke rising behind a low hill, dead ahead. Spurring his horse, he moved in for a closer look, easing up as he approached an outcropping of rock. Suddenly, he heard gunfire.

Cautiously riding around the knoll, he saw three wagons set in a triangular pattern, with horses and settlers in the middle. A fourth wagon was burning some distance away. *What're they shooting at?* he wondered.

His answer came moments later, as seven or eight Indians quickly swooped out of a gulch, heading for the wagons and loudly whooping and hollering.

For an instant, Curtis paused to appreciate how well the Indians sat and maneuvered their horses. They rode low, leaning to one side, partially shielded behind the necks of their horses, which made them difficult targets. As they circled the wagons, he was surprised to see that two had rifles. Others carried bows or lances, and one carried a torch.

Curtis quickly dismounted, smoothly pulling his long gun out of the boot beneath his right stirrup and slinging off the soft, protective deerskin sheath. He knelt, while cocking the gun hammer. Lining up the front nipple on the gun barrel through the rear, buckhorn sight, he squeezed the set trigger of his Hawken rifle. Focusing with deadly intent, he swung the rifle to follow a rider circling the wagons. Just as he fired the hair-trigger, the horseman rode behind a wagon, and the bullet cleanly sliced through the wagon bonnet.

Did I get him? A cloud of smoke and the odor of rotten eggs filled the air from the burnt black powder. He saw a riderless horse round the backside of the wagons, and that answered his question.

He was experienced with the Hawken and could shoot, reload, and fire several times in the space of a minute. But, the settlers needed a hail of bullets at that moment. Dropping the rifle, Curtis drew his pistol and ran beyond the rocks, yelling at the top of his voice to attract the Indians. He stopped and fired at the nearest one, who fell from his horse. He ran another dozen paces and dropped to his knee, then aimed the Colt in a two-handed, straight-armed fashion. As he fired, his face wore or an expression of determination, and he recalled an old saying—*there's no better defense than a charging offense—particularly when you're throwing a hail of lead.*

The Indians were surprised by the attack, and astonished to see a white man running toward them, shouting, and firing a gun that didn't need reloading. The leader paused for a brief moment, then motioned to the others, as they galloped away.

Curtis continued cocking and firing the heavy revolver, until it clicked on an empty chamber. With the flick of his knife, he removed the single small screw holding the pistol's cylinder, exchanging it for the loaded spare. Before mounting, he reloaded his Hawken from the supplies in his possible bag. Joyful shouts from the settlers greeted him as he rode toward the wagons. There were several men, women, and children within the wagon-formed compound. "Anyone hurt?" he asked.

Several answered at the same time.

"Hold up," Curtis shouted. "You can't all talk at once. You," he said, pointing to the oldest man, "tell me what went on here."

"I'm J. Heinrich Possard, but you can call me Henry."

The fellow's hair and beard were beginning to turn gray, and he wore a blue woolen shirt beneath his cutaway coat, which Curtis regarded as an odd choice in trail garb. The portly man smiled widely, and continued, "Two of our four wagons broke down, and we had to stop for over a week at Shawnee Mission for repairs. We've been traveling by ourselves these last two days, trying to whip up to a train ahead of us."

"Then what happened?" Curtis asked.

"This morning, them redskins jumped us. They torched one wagon and drove off the team. I guess they were looking to steal the rest of our livestock and lift our scalps to boot. They wounded one fella, but he'll live. We were mighty glad to hear your guns helping us out." Pausing to look at Curtis, he continued, "That was about the bravest thing I've ever seen, you firing away with that pistol. How were you able to reload it so fast?"

"It's a Colt repeater, and it holds six shots," the Missourian answered. "My name is Curtis, and I was attracted by the smoke from your burning wagon. Let's look to the injured and take stock of the situation."

"Thank God you arrived when you did," a woman said. Others echoed the same sentiment.

"That be one fine looking horse you're riding, young man," Henry observed.

"Thank you." He was listening to the man, but he was looking at a beautiful young woman with the most luminescent green eyes he had ever seen. He noticed her blonde hair, which was tied back, and gunpowder smudges on her cheek. Holding the reins in her gloved hands, she wore a red and white gingham dress. Her smile was dazzlingly bright.

He returned the smile, tipping his hat.

"My name is Tennie," she called out. "I drive the second wagon for my father."

"How do. My name is Curtis." Turning once more to Henry, he asked, "Is someone tending the wounded man?"

"Yes."

"Then, let's get these wagons moving. There's no sense waiting for the Injuns to come back. Another train is some miles up the valley. I'll see that you get there."

"How do you know that, young man," Henry asked, with a puzzled expression.

"I spied their dust cloud from a hilltop," Curtis answered.

As the Missourian glanced at Tennie, he saw her watching him with a particular smile on her face. Then, she blushed.

"Are you hurt?" he asked.

"I was scared during the attack, but I'm fine now. And no, I'm not hurt," she replied. "I don't know how providence delivered you to us this morning, but it surely was the hand of the Almighty."

Curtis led his horse to the downed redskins. Tilting back his hat, he studied their outfit and weapons. Mounting and riding close to Henry's wagon, he observed, "We'll have to make better time, if we're going to catch that train ahead of us before nightfall. I'm going to ride ahead and find the most direct route. You keep the wagons moving at a good pace."

Henry looked at him and smiled, "We're in your good hands, my boy. I saw you poking around that downed Injun. Were you looking for anything special?"

"I was trying to figure out which tribe attacked your party. These were probably Pawnee."

"How can you tell?"

"Oh, I can pretty much guess by the designs etched on the knife scabbard and the look of their arrows."

"They be the dangerous ones, aren't they, attacking helpless settlers like us?"

Looking at the man for a moment, Curtis replied, "Some of my best friends are Injuns, and killing any man isn't my way. But understand, Injuns love horses, and this band was trying to steal yours."

"So, they tried to kill us for our horses?"

"Well, maybe not entirely."

"They're nothing but beastly savages."

"Some folks have that view, but there's more to it. Everything here-abouts was Injun land before white settlers arrived and started travel-ing through. More than once, I've seen many displaced Injuns living in makeshift camps on the banks of the Poteau River, down in Arkansas Territory. Our government forcefully removes them from their home-lands east of the Mississippi River. Why do you suppose that is, Mr. Possard? I'll tell you the answer—because we white settlers covet their land. Those Injuns on the Poteau River—they were waiting to learn where they'd be *allowed* to live. Can you just imagine the gall of us white men, after Injuns had the run of the whole damn country—probably forever."

Henry started to remark, but Curtis cut him off. "Just hear me out, sir. Our government enters into treaties with the tribes on the plains. The Injuns agreed to safe passage for settlers. In return, our government promises them money and supplies for the next fifty years, and promises that these lands will remain theirs for as long as the rivers flow and the eagles fly.'"

"Then, why in heaven's name did they attack us?"

"Things happen on the frontier. No piece of paper is going to stop prospectors, emigrants, and squatters who hunger for land, gold, and other riches. Besides, our government has a poor record of keeping the white man's end of the bargain. Soldiers make treaties out here and send them to Congress, where they get stuck in a political stew. Before you know it, we've reneged on the deal, and the Injuns damn well know it! Get my meaning?"

"I didn't know those things," Henry replied, unsure of his ground. "You reckon them Injuns will be back tonight?"

"Possibly. Still, it may have only been a small hunting party that came across you folks, figuring that you wouldn't put up much of a fight. You and I can be thankful that there weren't a couple of dozen of them."

Riding off, Curtis dismounted at the top of a hill several miles ahead of the Possard wagons. He knelt and took in the view before him. To his north, the Platte River gleamed in the late afternoon sun. Near the far end of the broad plain, he saw a telltale cloud of wagon dust.

Sweeping the area with his spyglass, he saw no other movement. *Looks like the Injuns aren't following us, but we'll not catch that train ahead of us until tomorrow.*

When he returned, he spoke to Mr. Possard. "No way to catch that train today. There's a glen about five miles farther. We'll stay there tonight and set out at first light in the morning."

"What about the Injuns?" Henry asked.

"We don't have much choice. We can't travel after dark, and we won't catch the train before sunset. Besides, I didn't come across any new signs of danger. We'll just have to take our chances. Keep up the pace, until it's twilight."

"All right, Curtis, whatever you say."

Henry Possard's response sent a chill down Curtis' back. *I never intended to become a nursemaid for settlers headed to Oregon. It just happened, yet I think that the Possard group is exactly what Veeko and his bunch are looking for—a small party on their own. I don't relish using these folks as bait. Still, they're on the trail and the gang is out here. Those are the facts, plain and clear.*

A couple of miles before arriving at the glen, Curtis rode point, when he heard a scream coming from the wagons. Looking back, Tennie's team had stopped and the back end of her wagon dragged to one side. He spotted the rear wheel lying on the ground. As he approached, he asked, "You hurt, Miss Tennie?"

"No, I'm fine. I was mighty startled when the back end of my wagon dropped down and the axle dragged on the ground."

"Restraining nut probably came loose, but the wheel still looks to be in good shape." Looking around, Curtis saw that they were in a narrow valley between low hills on the treeless plains. "Where is your wagon jack?" Curtis called to Mr. Possard.

"It was in the wagon that burned."

There are no tree trunks around here to use as a lever for lifting the backend of the wagon. Yet, there had to be some way to make repairs, otherwise it would be necessary to abandon it and much of the contents. Pausing to think, he asked, "Henry, do you carry a block and tackle?"

"We sure do," the portly man replied.

Smiling, the Missourian said, "Good, we can use the tongue of your wagon as a lifting post. We'll unhitch the horses and tie the block and tackle to the end of the tongue, then manhandle it upright. When the team pulls one rope dangling from the block, the other one, fastened to the back of your daughter's wagon, should lift it enough to allow us to reset the wheel. Sound like a workable plan to you?"

"Why, sure. That's quite inventive, young man."

Nearly an hour later, the job was completed.

"This'll have to be our stopping point for tonight," Curtis told the group. He motioned the third wagon into place, to form a defensive triangle. "Make a dry camp. No fires! Understand? We don't want any smoke giving away our position tonight."

CHAPTER TWENTY-SEVEN

Captain Fudge's train stopped for the night after a hot grueling day under the sun, and everyone busily set about establishing their nightly camp. Jonah walked down the long line of wagons, thinking about Tennie and wondering if their trails would ever cross again.

"Hold up there, Jonah," the captain called to him. "I need to talk with you about guard duty tonight."

"Yes, sir," Jonah responded, turning around.

"Our scout came across more Injun signs today, maybe six or seven ponies. With these and the other tracks yesterday, we need to stay alert. We'll double the nightriders with the livestock tonight. You and Frank take the last watch, until dawn."

"Yes, sir, Captain, I'll tell my brother," Jonah replied. *Maybe there'll be some excitement tonight,* he thought.

Early the next morning, darkness covered the land, as the moon had set hours earlier. Jonah, chilled and wrapped in his blanket, gazed at the black, night sky and the vast array of stars sprinkled across the heavens.

"I'm always amazed," Frank commented, "at the huge horizon that we see on the plains and the number of stars at night."

"The night sky surely is God's greatest creation," Jonah replied, as he looked at the canopy in silent wonder. He gathered his blanket tighter around himself, and he scooted closer to the warmth cast by the campfire.

Time passed slowly in the early morning darkness, broken only by a lone coyote serenading the night. The train was camped in a wide valley with the ever-present Platte River to the north. The wagons were nested together just beyond the remuda and livestock. On that moonless, dark morning, it was chancy to circle the herd on horseback, so they took turns walking. Otherwise, they stood watch and tried to keep warm near the campfire. Each had two, single-shot rifles.

It was Jonah's turn to check the animals, and he walked softly among them, careful not to make any sudden movement that might startle them. He loved this time of morning, when dew formed and everything smelled fresh. A few animals shuffled along as he walked about.

From a distance, he heard a noise like an owl hooting. Many times, he had heard similar calls on the farm, as the predators used their calls to flush out smaller game. Any movement then sent the birds swooping down to feast. This time, something was different about the sounds he heard, and a raw tingle of alarm touched his spine.

He made his way back toward the campfire, holding a rifle in each hand. The fire was low, and shadows appeared deeper. Rounding a tree, a movement caught his eye. He froze, trying to identify it. He set one gun down and cocked the other. Very slowly, he moved closer to the campfire, thinking that his brother might have dozed off.

Nearby, he heard a twig snap. Immediately, he crouched down, unsure. *Was it one of the animals? Or, was it—?* His grip on the rifle tightened.

On a low rise before him, a shape crossed—a momentary silhouette against the first faint light of dawn. "Who goes there?" he challenged. Suddenly, he saw more movement. "Frank, stir yourself! We have visitors."

"Easy, brother," Frank replied in the darkness, touching him on the arm. "I figure there're three or four of them," he whispered, obviously worried. "You circle left, and I'll go the other way."

"We have to take care, so we don't shoot each other in the dark," Jonah whispered. "As our signal, let's use the mockingbird call that Curtis taught us."

"Right!"

Silently, Jonah moved toward an outcrop of rocks that was barely visible in the morning's first, half-light. After several steps, he abruptly stood face to face with a stranger.

The man reacted quicker, raising his tomahawk and slashing it down.

At the last moment, Jonah ducked below the swinging implement of death and pulled the trigger. The Indian's momentum carried him into Jonah, who stumbled and fell with the warrior on top. Jonah rolled him over and stood, staring at the fallen warrior.

Suddenly, another man materialized out of the gray shadows, standing on top of a boulder.

Jonah heard a mockingbird call, followed by a rifle shot, and he saw the savage tumble backward. *Good work little brother!* Picking up the second gun, he looked in the other direction and saw more movements. Quickly, he aimed—then stopped. No target was visible.

"BROTHER, WATCH OUT—BEHIND YOU!" Frank shouted.

Turning quickly, Jonah raised his rifle, as a war ax came crashing down.

Frank hurried toward his brother and rolled him over. In the gray light, he saw a dark smear of blood on his brother's head. He removed his bandana and pressed it against the wound, as armed men from the wagon train arrived.

Captain Fudge was the first. Holding a burning torch high, he knelt and examined Jonah, as the others hurried to secure the animals.

"Lucky thing," the captain commented, "the ax just grazed him. Otherwise, it would have split his skull. As it is, he'll be minus a patch of hair for a while."

Shep arrived and squatted on his heels beside Jonah, removing the neckerchief to examine the wound. "Here, ya men," he directed, "we'll take this young fella to my wagon, where I can tend to him." They hoisted Jonah and carried him toward the camp.

Frank stood up, a bit light-headed. He looked at the nearest fallen Indian and then at the other.

Captain Ernie arrived and stood beside him.

"Are they dead?" Frank asked.

"Yep, you boys got two and wounded a third, who skedaddled. That was quite a run-in you fellas had this morning. Tell me how it happened."

Frank told him about the birdcalls, moving shadows, and hearing Jonah's gun.

"I'll say this much, you and your brother are proving to be real good trail hands."

Frank suddenly slumped, as the enormity of the dead men hit him.

The older man grabbed his arm to steady him.

The young man recalled an earlier time, when he had stared down at three lifeless bandits lying in the forest glen.

"You've never killed a man before, have you, son?" Captain Ernie asked, probably knowing the answer before the young man shook his head. "Those Injuns were after our herd, and they were prepared to do whatever it takes, even if it meant killing you and your brother. You were defending yourselves and the entire train. Keep that in mind."

"But, we killed those men, sir," Frank replied, almost choking on the words.

"That's right, son. If'n you hadn't, we'd most likely be hauling you and your brother back to camp about now, and you'd be dead and missing your hair."

Frank turned away and walked to the other savage, where several men were standing. He saw a fierce-looking warrior lying on the ground, with his long, dark hair held back by a leather band. The man wore buckskins and leather moccasins. A red stain blossomed on his deerskin shirt, and his war ax lay nearby.

Captain Fudge picked it up and turned it over in his hands. "This is a fine weapon." Handing it to the young man, he continued, "I reckon it's yours. You and your brother earned it this morning."

Frank hefted it, running his finger along its fine edge. "It has good balance, but it's no match for the speed of a lead ball from my long gun."

CHAPTER TWENTY-EIGHT

On the second day, the small Possard caravan failed once again to catch up to the train ahead, as a broken harness required repairs and delayed their departure.

Dadblast it, Curtis fumed. *I can't leave these folks out here on the plains by themselves, with Veeko and his pardn'rs on the prowl. These settlers have already encountered way too much trouble—probably more than most settlers do traveling the entire way to Oregon. I have no choice, I'll just have to see it through, but I really need to get back to Missouri.*

Captain Parke's voice came back to him once more, making him pause. Then, Curtis smiled, and his mood lightened. *'Patience, me boy, everything comes to the man who is patient. Ye've set yerself a task. Now, see it through.'*

The Missourian selected a campsite for the night under the overhang of a hill. "Henry, I'm going to hunt game for our cooking pots tonight."

"Won't gunfire attract the Injuns?" the older man asked.

"I'll use my bow."

"How about the smoke from our fires, won't it let the Injuns know where we are?"

"Not likely in this glen," Curtis answered.

"Will we be all right without you?"

"There have been no signs of trouble." *But, it might flush out a short fella with a couple of pardn'rs,* he thought.

Grudgingly, Henry replied, "Well, if you say so. We're very indebted to you, and we're in your good hands."

"Always have an armed man on guard," Curtis warned. "And, keep everyone near the wagons and don't be going off alone, no matter what the reason. Make your cook fires over there and keep them small. I should be back by nightfall."

As darkness neared, Curtis started back with rabbits tied across his horse's flanks. Nearing the camp, he suddenly reined in, alarmed. There were fresh horse tracks in the dirt headed toward the Possard camp. *Shod hooves made these marks, so the riders are unlikely to be Injuns. Maybe Veeko is finally going to be within the sights of my gun.*

Curtis rode toward camp in the lengthening shadows, on the hunt for two-legged *hombres.* Leaving his horse in a wash, he quietly crept toward the wagons and heard a strange man say, "Hot damn, ya got mighty pretty golden hair, missy."

Tennie's voice immediately declared, "Keep your filthy hands off me, you stinking, ugly brute."

Crawling under a wagon, Curtis heard the sound of a slap and felt the hairs bristle on the back of his neck.

"Shut yar mouth, Missy, and sit with the others."

Moving aside a bedroll, the Missourian viewed the camp and saw Tennie sitting next to her father, rubbing her cheek. *One of them brutes must have hit her for being sassy,* he figured, as he fought to control his anger. *Patience, me boy,* he said to himself, mentally mimicking the Irish tone of his friend, Parke. *There'll be time enough to deal with these scallywags and then you can stick their bloody heads in a bucket of water.*

The rest of the family sat on the ground, with their hands on their heads. A man stood to one side, with his rifle pointed in their direction. He was the younger of the two, dressed in a scruffy-looking coat and pushed-back hat.

The other man, standing behind the family, was tall, heavyset, and rawboned. His dirty and shabby outfit matched that of the younger man. As Curtis looked closer, he saw an ugly scar across the big man's forehead, just as Shelley had described Butch. *No doubt who that fella is, but the other one doesn't appear to be Veeko. He's probably the one she called Billy Joe. It looks like it's just the two of them.* He felt a keen sense of disappointment that Veeko had apparently eluded him again. *Well, these fellas likely know his whereabouts, and they're going to tell me everything tonight.*

Butch continued to stare at Tennie, as he clenched and opened his meaty hands several times. A lopsided smirk split his ugly face.

Nighttime was fast approaching, as Curtis backed away. Making no sound, he found his way to where the men had left their horses. Untying the reins, he drew the animals to the swale where his black was tethered. When he returned, he again slid under the wagon.

"Hell, these be nothing but poor dirt farmers," the young man shouted, standing on the sideboard of a wagon. "They ain't got but chicken feed in here for money, and no gold."

Food, clothes, and equipment haphazardly littered the ground. Curtis saw Butch holding his gun on the settlers, as the younger man jumped down.

"Not a very big haul of gold inside," Billy Joe whined. Brightening, he continued, "Of course, we'll collect a heap of money when we sell their outfits and supplies. That'll buy us many nights with Shelley and her friends. C'mon, Butch, let's get the animals hitched up and move out."

Curtis saw the ugly man staring at Tennie, a nasty sneer on his grimy face.

"Not so fast," Butch replied. "I've never seen a gal with such green eyes like this pretty one has. I'm figuring to take a turn with her, out where we left our horses."

Henry Possard's red face expressed his anger. His wife wailed and carried on, pleading with the outlaws to take their wagons and leave them alone. The two youngest girls were huddled together, sobbing, while the rest of the party stared at the ground, fearful of making eye contact with the ruffians—all except Tennie. Defiantly, she stared at Butch, her lips tight and her cheeks flushed with fury.

The Missourian tensed. He wanted to face the men on his terms, without further endangering the Possard family.

Plainly, Tennie's pale face expressed defiance and determination, despite the wailing around her.

That gal has a lot of gumption, he thought with admiration. *I know she's frightened, but she's determined not to show it.*

"Tie up the rest," Butch commanded, "but not this pretty filly."

"You stay away from us and leave our womenfolk alone," Henry blustered. "I suppose that drifter is a member of your gang," he shouted.

"What in the hell are ya talking about, ya old coot?" Billy Joe asked.

"Didn't you send a fella to lead us right to you? You know you did," Henry shouted, angrily. "You're nothing but lying, no-good scallywags that ain't got the gumption or backbone to live like decent folks." He quickly rose and confronted them.

"Ya've gone plumb daft, and ya talk too much," Butch answered, as he quickly spun around, hitting Henry across the head with the butt of his rifle and knocking the older man senseless.

Tennie immediately moved to help her mother tend to her father. Beside herself with concern and righteous fury, she screamed, "Both of you are more godless than any wild animal roaming the plains." To emphasize her disdain, she continued, "And you both smell worse than any skunk that I've ever come across."

Throwing her a dirty look, Billy Joe roughly commanded, "Sit ye down and stay there." After binding everyone's hands, the younger man broke out into a broad smile. "I surely do like yar idea of bedding down this filly,

Butch. She be mighty fine looking, but don't ya forget what ya said the last time. It's my turn to be first, just like ya promised at Shelley's place."

The scar-faced man seemed to growl, as he swung around toward the younger man. There was a frightening scowl on his face and a fanatical glint in his eye. "Ya heard me," he replied in a low, gravelly voice. "I ain't going to say it again. I'm first with this green-eyed gal," he continued, staring at Billy Joe with a menacing look,

"If'n ya say so," Billy Joe grumbled, casting his eyes lower and turning away. "But ya make it fast, ya hear?" Smiling crookedly again, as though a sudden idea had occurred to him, he continued, "Ya settle her down, so she'll be eager and waiting to pleasure me." Facing Tennie, he ordered, "Now get up, little lady, and behave yarself, proper-like. Ya're going to be treated to some really fine times tonight with me and Butch."

"Don't you dare touch me," Tennie screamed. "I'm not going anywhere with the likes of you or your stinking pardn'r."

Her mother sat beside her with her arm around the two younger daughters. Tears streamed down the faces of the terrified girls, as they wildly looked from their mother to the bandits.

Butch took out his fixings and rolled a thin cigarette, ignoring Tennie. After lighting it, he swiftly grabbed a fistful of her blonde hair, yanking the young woman to her feet, and blew a cloud of smoke into her face.

"You let me be, you witless ox," Tennie shouted.

Curtis saw her pale face and knew that she was bent on resisting. He forced himself to control his rankling anger, as his right hand tightly clinched the butt of the six-shooter.

"Get moving," Butch directed, pushing the girl in front of him.

Unexpectedly, Tennie turned and kicked the man in the shins.

Letting out a howl, Butch slapped the girl hard across the face, sending her to the ground. "Ya want to play, do ya? Well, come along. You and I can play the rest of the night, because I'm yar man," he said, dragging her by the arm.

Mrs. Possard screamed, "You leave my little girl alone, you animal. Dear God, someone, please help us. Take me instead. Please don't harm my little girl," she sobbed.

Tennie was wild-eyed with terror, and a trickle of blood ran from the corner of her mouth. "Let me go, you big, revolting jackass," she screamed, kicking him again.

Gruffly, Billy Joe seized her arm, yanking her around. "Get moving," he said huskily.

Looking at her father, she wailed, "You killed my pa."

Menacingly, Butch spoke in a raspy voice, "Missy, yar pa is out, but he's alive. Now shut yar trap and stop yar sniveling."

With all the conviction Tennie could muster, she angrily replied, "You'll get no cooperation from my kin and certainly not from me. You're nothing but filthy pigs, and thieving murderers, to boot, taking advantage—"

The big man swiftly drew his knife. Kneeling, he roughly grabbed her father's hair, raising his limp head and placing the sharp knife-edge against his throat. With a growl, Butch rasped, "Missy, say one more word, and yar pa is a dead man with his throat slit from ear to ear."

Startled, the girl was shocked into silence, as were the rest of the settlers.

Butch roughly grabbed her by the arm and made her stand in front of him. "Now, Missy, this is the way it's going to be," Butch said, waving his knife in front of the horrified girl's eyes. "I'll say it real slow, so it don't clutter yar pretty, little head. Yar going to oblige me, as only a woman can, and then my pardn'r, Billy Joe, and ya're going to do it without whining or fussing or kicking. Refuse me and this knife is going to gut yar pa, right here in front of ya. If'n that don't convince ya to be obliging, then I'll slice up yar ma next. And if yar still being crusty, I figure I'll do the same to yar sisters, one by one."

Flinching, the bloodcurdling words hit Tennie like a sledgehammer.

Everyone in the Possard group remained dead silent, as the brutal man's intentions were clear. Even her young sisters were hushed.

Butch glowered and then gave her an evil smile, giving him the appearance of the grim reaper. "So, make up yar mind, Missy. Be friendly and pleasure me, or watch me cut yar kin? Now, do we understand each other?"

Curtis saw Tennie's reaction. Her face said it all—horror, loathing, and fear—as she grasped the full meaning of his words.

With a soft moan, she tilted her head ever so slightly. Then, another hard slap knocked her to the ground once more, and an empty expression of surrender seemed to cloud her face.

Butch snatched the back of her coat and dragged her outside the ring of wagons, beyond the view of Curtis.

"Oh, please take me instead," Mrs. Possard, pleaded, as she struggled to her knees. "Don't harm my daughter, please," she wailed, crying in mortal fear for her daughter's safety.

"Shut up," Billy Joe commanded, moving his gun from one to the other. "Sit down, the lot of ya."

Curtis backed out from his hiding place and drew his Colt. He followed Butch and the struggling woman, as they made their way toward the grove of trees where the bandits had tied their horses.

In the still evening, there came the fearful, distant cry of a wolf, mournfully signaling the plains that he was on the hunt.

As the man from Lost Creek silently closed on them in the dimming light, he heard the ugly brute's labored breathing. *That fella has only sheer lust on his mind. I'll take this gully and wait for them behind the thick brush.*

"This is my night, my little beauty," Butch said excitedly, pulling the girl along by the arm. "Maybe Billy Joe and I'll just take ya with us when we leave. There's no sense paying for saloon gals, when we got a fine looking filly like ya—besides, yar free for the taking. Just ya wait and see—pleasure us a couple of times, and ya'll like it as much as we do. Just ya wait and see." The big man let out a gruff laugh at his stupid jest.

As Butch rounded the dense shrubbery, Curtis hit him in the face with the butt of the pistol, knocking the big man down. Still in his grip, Tennie found herself dragged to the ground.

Dazed and sucking wind, Butch tried to sit up and found the barrel of a pistol pointed at his nose. Releasing Tennie, he grabbed his broken nose, blood spewing between his fingers, and shouted, *"Who the hell are ya?"* Looking back toward the wagons, he was about to call Billy Joe, but stopped as the gun barrel whipped across the side of his head.

Tears rolled down Tennie's face, as she frantically looked from one man to the other, completely unnerved, and wide-eyed with fright.

Curtis turned to her and put a finger to his lips, hoping that she would keep quiet. He motioned for her to move away from Butch and to come and stand behind him. Whimpering, she scurried to obey.

The big man groggily got on his knees, blood flowing from both wounds.

"Stand up, Butch," Curtis commanded. Coming up behind him, he drew his long knife and prodded the large man with the blade. "Where's your pardn'r, Veeko?" he asked, as he heard Tennie sobbing behind him.

Surprised at the question, Butch asked, "What do ya want with that runt?"

"Butch, you're one bad *hombre*, but it's Veeko that I'm after. Now, you tell me quick, where is he?"

"Who are ya? Why should I tell ya anything? I think ya broke my nose, ya rotten son of a whore. And how do ya know my name?"

Another hard prod from Curtis' blade shut him up. "Your just brimming with questions, aren't you? But, it's mine that you're going to answer. I'm looking for that snake, Veeko. If you want to live, you'll tell me where he is."

"Ain't no skin off'n my nose," the big man replied, craftily. "He has himself a job driving a wagon to Oregon for an old couple. He must be halfway to Fort Laramie by now. That all ya want to know? Now can I go play with my gal?" he asked, his voice rising hopefully.

Once more, the big man found himself on the ground, as the Missourian's pistol whipped around for a third time, ripping down his ear. "Butch, you're a cantankerous, evil cuss, and that's a little present from a mutual friend that we both know," he said. "Let's go over this again. When did Veeko hire on for the driving job?"

Unsteady, the big man replied, "He left about a week ago from Independence, right after the grass was up."

Curtis stared hard at him. He could still hear the girl sobbing behind him. "Perhaps I should use the Injun way of making you talk. I hear it works every time. They stake a fella on the ground over an anthill. Slowly, the ants do the work of making a man talk and draining away his life. And that's exactly what your fate will be, if'n you don't start telling me the truth."

"But I'm answering ya—Veeko's traveling with a wagon train. He sure ain't around here. Somewhere along the way, he'll get rid of the old man and woman that hired him and steal their rig. He figures that he can bring the wagon and supplies back to Independence, so he can sell everything. That's what he has in mind."

To the Missourian, the story had a ring of truth to it. "Stand up, you big ox. I want you to call Billy Joe to come out here. You tell him that it's his turn with the girl. Be mighty careful what you say, Butch, or my knife is going to go fishing for your innards. Now do it, call him to come take his turn."

Emotionally distraught, Tennie was still sobbing.

Softly, Curtis said, "Pull yourself together, young lady." Seeing the puzzled, fearful look on her face, he knew that she was still very frightened. "You've been very brave tonight, and you're going to be fine. First, I have to deal with these mongrels. Just stay behind me and calm yourself."

"What're you going to do with only a knife and a puny gun, when there be two of us with rifles?" Butch asked, belligerently. "I've never seen a long pea-shooter like ya got. It don't look big enough to bring down a squirrel." he said, sarcastically, wiping blood off his face with the back of a dirty sleeve.

"I'll tell you what it'll do, you big ox. It'll kill you six times before I have to reload for your friend," Curtis replied, as his knife sliced through Butch's coat and shirt, drawing blood.

Butch's eyes bulged, as he looked over his shoulder at Curtis. "All right, but be careful with that knife."

"Now, call out to your friend. And remember, you're only an inch away from dying."

"How is it that ya know our names?" the big man blustered again. "I never laid eyes on ya before."

"Stop stalling," Curtis commanded, as the point of his knife again pricked him. "Call him now, or be gutted. What's it to be?"

Hesitantly, Butch shouted, "Billy Joe, c'mon out here. I've had my fill, and ya can take your turn with the gal."

"Tell him she's a fine filly, Butch," Curtis commanded.

Another hard prod in the ribs caused Butch to grunt, as he called a second time, "Billy Joe, ya be hearing me? Ya're going to have fun with this pretty gal. She's really something."

The younger man came in a rush, paying no mind to the noise he made. He stopped short as he came around the bushes and face to face with the Missourian.

"Drop your gun, Billy Joe," Curtis ordered, holding his Colt and knife.

Startled, the man started to raise his rifle, as Curtis' flying knife caught him in the thigh. Dropping to the ground, the bandit howled in pain.

Curtis quickly picked up the young man's gun and, with quick back and forth jerks, retrieved his knife.

Billy Joe shrieked in pain, as blood gushed between his fingers, "*Damn,*" he yelled in pain, "why in the hell are ya so rough?" He undid his bandana to wrap it around the wound. "Who are ya, anyway? What're ya doing here?" Then for the first time, he saw Butch's bloody face in the fading light. "What in the hell did ya do to my pardn'r?" he demanded.

Ignoring him, Curtis turned to the woman. "Tennie, you take these guns and return to the camp. Your folks need tending. I've some unfinished business with these gents. Tell your pa to be ready to move out at first light and to follow the Platte. That'll lead you in the direction of the wagon train ahead."

The actions of the previous few minutes had sobered the girl. She stood, trembling, and her face was ashen, as she surveyed the two bleeding men. Raising her eyes to his, she nervously said, "Pa claimed you were one of them, but I never believed it. Thank you for saving me from—"

"Tennie!" Curtis cut in sharply. "Pull yourself together. It's over now, and you need to get back to the wagons and see to your people."

"What are you aiming to do with these murdering coyotes?" she asked, still wild-eyed and shaken. "And who is Veeko?"

"It's nothing you need worry about. Now, get along and help your kin. You can find your way, with the campfire as your guide."

Rattled and unsure, Tennie moved away. She turned once, gave a slight nod, and was gone.

CHAPTER TWENTY-NINE

The three horsemen rode north along a dry streambed for a mile or more, the horses picking their footing in the final light of the day. Overhead, a rising quarter-moon reflected off the surface of the Platte. Stopping, Curtis dismounted and tied the horses' reins to a shrub oak. Holding his Hawken on the men, he commanded, "Get down."

"What're you aiming to do with us," Billy Joe asked, his voice cracking with fear. "Why are ya after us anyway? We ain't done ya any harm." Cocking his head expectantly, he soon lost patience and demanded, "Answer my questions, will ya?" With his hands tied together, the man dismounted awkwardly, then stumbled.

The Missourian reacted instinctively, reaching out to steady him.

With surprising quickness, Butch threw his leg over the saddle and slid to the ground. With the momentum and his size, the big man landed on Curtis and pushed him to the ground, simultaneously pulling the six-shooter from the holster.

Pointing the gun awkwardly with his hands tied, Butch shouted, "Say goodbye to yar days of living, ya no-account bastard. Now it's my turn to

fix ya once and for all." Butch aimed the single-action revolver, squeezing the trigger. Nothing happened. His finger jerked harder. "Why don't
the damn thing fire?" he shouted. Uncertain, he finally cocked the hammer and pulled the trigger again.

By then, Curtis was on him and shoved the pistol barrel to one side,
just as it fired. Quickly, he pulled the gun free and slammed the butt into
the big man's head, knocking him unconscious. He picked up his pistol
and heard the agitated sounds behind him. Without looking, he knew
that the bullet had hit one of the horses.

Billy Joe was cowering on the ground, terrified.

"Crawl over next to that scrub oak, Billy Joe, and make it fast," Curtis
panted. "I'm in no mood for any more tricks." After tying the young
man's hands and legs, he returned for Butch. Dragging the big man to a
large tree—one of the few on the plains, he bound him securely.

Moving to the horses, he saw his black hobbling, her eyes wild with
agony. Tightly grasping the reins, the Missourian ran his hand down her
leg. "It's busted, girl," he said, in a voice filled with anguish. Leaning
heavily against her, he tried to keep the animal from moving but her
powerful muscles spasmed uncontrollably.

A feeling of loss overcame him, and numbness spread through him.
Even so, he knew what he had to do. *There's no choice—I have to put her
down.* "It breaks my heart, old girl, but I've got to send you off to a better
place. I'll never forget you." He drew his revolver and fired.

Standing over the body, he was grief-stricken. He remembered the journey to Texas, rescuing the Walker from the Indians, and Captain Gilbert
eyeing good horseflesh at the Red River Ranch. He remembered the many
times the black had stood just inside the barn door, impatiently watching
for him to arrive with her daily oats. As soon as he was through the corral
rails, the big horse always ran lickety-split, straight for him and slid to a stop
at the last moment, prancing in happy anticipation of a meal. *Thank God you
delivered the colt,* he thought. *Still, it'll never be the same. All of my troubles started
with that bushwhacking son of a bitch, Veeko,* he silently raged.

Struggling mightily, he managed to pull off his saddle and gear.
Moving away and still in shock over his loss, the Missourian off-saddled

the two remaining horses at a deliberate pace, lost in thought. Then, he searched around and gathered buffalo chips for a fire, using his tinder kit to light it. Soon, firelight flickered in the night's blackness.

As he went about the chore, he found his deep sense of loss slowly turning to a burning rage. *Men like these can't be allowed to ride roughshod over people—stealing, murdering, raping, and destroying. Tonight, I'm going to have me a "come to Jesus" talk with these outlaws—and that goes double for the big, ugly one.*

In the distance, the eerie howl of the night wolf called out again to the darkened sky, as the quarter moon slid behind a cloud.

"What're ya going to do with us?" Billy Joe asked, wide-eyed with fear. "Why are we tied up like stuffed pigs?" Beside himself with worry, he shrieked, "Who are ya, mister? Are ya deaf? *Why don't ya answer me?*"

"Yeah, what happens now?" Butch growled, as he regained consciousness. His narrowed eyes burned with hatred.

The Missourian knelt near the crackling fire and looked at both men with a steady gaze. Finally, he broke his silence and said in a hoarse voice. "Folks in Missouri have a special way of dealing with nasty *hombres* like you boys. Each gets a choice. Either a fella prefers hanging or chooses to have his ears cut off. Most want to live. Missourians reckon that it's fitting justice because rogues like you ain't using your ears anyway to listen to the law. And being earless gives proper warning to others—for as long as you live."

The outlaws were deathly still.

"Which do you fellas prefer?"

Butch spoke up first. "Ya can't be doing that. You ain't a judge, and I'm figuring you ain't a lawman either. Be that right?"

"True enough," Curtis replied. "But I'm your worst nightmare, because I'm the only man out here on the plains who is bent on avenging your sins. To the long list of grievances, I've added the severe harm you meant those settlers back yonder. You men heap your ruthless deeds on innocent folks and then expect to simply walk away, and do it again the next time. You low-lifes need to face justice. And what's more," he continued, looking steadily at Butch, "you cost me the life of my prized horse, and that cuts me to the quick. I can't right all your wrongs, but I sure can deliver the punishment."

The look on Butch's bloody face turned from arrogance to uncertainty and then to deepening concern.

Turning toward the younger man, Curtis asked, "Now, Billy Joe, tell me about Veeko's whereabouts. Is he signed on to drive a wagon for an older couple going to Oregon?"

Fear etched Billy Joe's face as he looked from Butch to Curtis before answering. "Un-huh, that's right," he said, nervously gulping as he spoke.

"What're their names?"

"Hills—Rodney and Carla Hills. That's what Veeko told us before the train headed out."

"When did the train leave Independence?"

"It was about the time the trains first began leaving. Veeko was going to take care of the Hills along the trail and meet us at a campsite near Shawnee Mission."

"What's the name of the train captain?"

"How in the hell should I know," Billy Joe replied, in a shrill voice. Immediately, the young man quieted, suddenly panicked that his overly abrupt reply might further anger his captor. "Listen, I don't mean no disrespect, but I just plain don't know."

"Well, Butch, now it's your turn. What's the name of the man who's ramrodding that train?"

"Go to hell."

"You still need to learn proper manners, don't you?" Curtis noted, as the butt of the Hawken rifle came down hard on his left leg.

"All right, all right, I'll tell ya," Butch replied, hastily, shifting his leg to ease the pain. "His name was like a type of sweet. Let me think for a moment. Fudge, that's his name."

"Thank you, boys." Curtis swung his rifle hard, knocking the big man unconscious once more. "Now, Billy Joe, let's get back to our previous discussion. Have you made your choice?"

Billy Joe, his eyes wide and round, stared at Curtis with his mouth open and his jaw slack. "Ahh . . .," was all he managed to choke out, as he began shaking.

"Speak up—you can't walk on one leg. What's it to be—you living or dying tonight?"

———◆———◆———

Curtis sat by the campfire, watching Butch slowly regain consciousness.

The big man tried to move his hands, only to find them tied behind his back. Blood trickled down from his head where his ears had been.

I wonder how long it'll take him to figure out that he's hanging upside down from this lonely tree, Curtis mused.

In the distance, and just under the wind, the desolate sound of the wolf came once more, but it was closer than before. Ghostly and utterly frightening, it filled every living thing on the prairie with fear.

Twisting on the rope, Butch's eyes finally focused on Curtis, who was wrapping a package and placing it in his saddlebag. "Yes, Mr. Butch, your ears will look mighty fine nailed to a tree in Lost Creek Valley."

"Ya cut me while I was out, didn't ya, ya son of a—"

"Now, now, don't get jumpy and say something you'll regret. Remember, you and I still must decide whether you're living or dying tonight. So, let's take a tally and see how you'd stack up if you're standing before St. Peter's gate right about now."

"Ya ain't no preacher, so don't be giving me yar cock and bull from no Bible."

Ignoring his comment, Curtis continued. "I begin with you terrorizing those folks back at the camp, and your plan to strip them of all their worldly possessions. Would you have left them to fend for themselves on the wild prairie without horses and food? Or would you have just slit their throats and been done with it?"

Butch's eyes were half-closed and his face was puffy and red from hanging upside down.

"Well, I don't know the answers to those questions, but either way, their chance of living was poor. Then, there was your threat and lust-filled intention to force that young woman to your evil ways. Surely, these add sinful marks on your soul. Lastly, there is the personal matter between you and me. Because of you, I had to put down my big black horse." Shaking his head, he continued, "Mr. Butch, let's just say that you're a very lucky gent to still be alive. I can't even guess why God allows an animal like you to roam this land."

"What have ya done with Billy Joe? I only see one horse standing behind you."

"That's right. Billy Joe rode off a short time ago. Don't expect we'll see him again."

"Ya're going to let me go now, like ya did Billy Joe, ain't that right?"

"First, there're just dues to be paid. I've already told you that. And tonight, I'm your judge, jury, and I'm the one who carries out the verdict, so hold yourself together, if'n you can."

"What does that mean," Butch asked, his voice edged with increasing uncertainty and fear.

"Well, I don't know what the future holds for you, so I'll let you decide. One alternative is that I can leave you hanging here, when I ride off, and let nature do the rest."

"My head's still buzzing from that last wallop ya gave me, so I'm having difficulty understanding yar meaning. What does nature have to do with anything?"

"With you bleeding and my dead horse over there, I figure it won't be long before your company arrives. I've heard a wolf howling all evening. Some say that a wolf can smell fresh blood on the wind more than a mile away. Do you reckon that's true, Butch?"

"Please, have mercy and cut me down. Ya've hurt me bad and ya have yar revenge."

"Not yet—at least not proper Missouri vengeance."

Curtis laid his horse blanket on the back of the remaining animal and heaved up his saddle.

"Ya're not leaving me here like this, are ya?" Butch pleaded, as tears filled the ugly man's squinty eyes.

Curtis looked at him for a time. "Your other choice is for me to cut you down and let you find your way. It's only a few days walk to Shawnee Mission. That's not too far."

"Ya mean I should walk all the way back? Ya wouldn't leave me on the plains without a horse and a gun, would ya?" he asked, his voice rising hopefully "Ya don't really mean that, do ya? Yar just saying it to scare me, ain't ya?"

"Remember, there's only one horse because you shot mine."

"We can ride double. I'll not give ya any trouble. You have my word—take me with ya. I don't want to be out here alone on the plains in the dark."

"You're a miserable excuse for a man, Butch. It's time for you to change your ways, and walking will give you time to think about matters like human kindness and the Lord's ways. And if'n walking doesn't suit your sorry ass—you can run or crawl for all I care." Remembering Shelley's words, he added, "Besides, a long walk will be good for your soul."

"No, please, I'll die if'n ya leave me out here with no horse and no gun and no water. Please, I'll do anything ya say, but—"

Curtis harshly interrupted, "So what's it to be, Butch. You want me to leave you hanging from this lonely tree? On the other hand, maybe you prefer being cut down, so you can try to save yourself? It's your call, but make it now."

The big man was silent for a moment. Then in a husky whisper, he replied, "Cut me down."

With a flash of Curtis' knife, the ugly man hit the ground. "Your water bag is over there next to your saddle and there's a knife stuck in the ground, so you can free yourself. Goodbye Butch, and best I never lay eyes on you again." Then, he added, "Next time, there'll be no choices for you."

"No! Please, don't leave me. What about that wolf that's prowling hereabouts?"

"I suggest you figure it out quick."

"I'll die if'n ya leave me. *No, ya can't do this!*" he shrieked, as he saw Curtis pour the coffee remains on the fire and then kick at the embers. In the last weak light, Butch fearfully watched him mount.

Without another word, Curtis spurred the horse.

"NO, MISTER, C'MON BACK. YA CAN'T LEAVE ME IN THE DARK! I'M SCARED TO BE ALONE. MISTER, PLEASE COME BACK! MISTER, DO YOU HEAR ME?"

In the blackness, a spine-chilling howl on the quiet night air was the only reply.

CHAPTER THIRTY

"Going to be another hot one today, little brother," Jonah said, as they rode at the rear of the train, with the herd. He took off his neckerchief to mop his face.

Frank grinned as he waved his hat at a lagging bull. "You got that right."

"Hi-ho," Jonah called out, "get up there."

They were on the trail that Shep called the "Great Platte River Road." It would take them to the foot of the tall mountains, still hidden beyond the far-off horizon.

Day after day, the trail was hot and dusty, as the train's one hundred and three wagons moved along. The deep ruts, baked into the ground, looked like running scars on the land. In fact, drivers had to be careful on hard-packed dirt in some areas, as ruts were deep enough to jostle a wagon badly and shift its cargo.

From a promontory, Jonah saw the wagons traveling ahead in multiple columns. Fine grit permeated everything, adding to the humid afternoon's discomfort. He slowed his horse, falling back to the rear of the herd.

Frank also reined in, looking over his shoulder. "Hey, Jonah," he shouted and pointed. "There's dust in the sky off to the east."

Jonah turned and looked in that direction. "So there is."

"What do you make of it?"

"I'm not sure. It could be from another train, or it could be Injuns."

"Here comes Captain Ernie."

Stopping his horse quickly, the train boss commanded, "Jonah, you come with me. In this country, where there's dust, trouble could be lurking. Frank, you keep a sharp eye on the livestock. If'n you see trouble acoming, you shoot your gun to attract the attention of Shep and the train. C'mon, Jonah, let's ride."

They rode hard and only eased up as they approached a small rise with a cloud of grit billowing into the sky from the other side.

Reining in, the captain held a rifle in his hand. "Jonah, let's take it slow and easy and see what this is all about. No sense us charging blindly into trouble. You go right, and I'll go around the other side. Now hear me good, if'n they be Injuns, don't wait for any orders, you turn and hightail it back to the train. Have you got that?"

Nodding, Jonah continued toward the bend of the hill and down into a draw, holding his long rifle. Moving cautiously around thick shrubbery and up the other side, several wagons moved toward him at a quick pace.

Captain Ernie came around the other side and raised his hand, signaling the leader. "Hold up there," he called to the driver. "What's your hurry, and where in tarnation are you headed?"

The man's face was grim, as he leveled his rifle at the strangers. In a raspy voice, he demanded, "Who are you fellas? Speak up, because I have a mighty itchy trigger finger this morning, and I don't take to strangers calling me out. Could be, you're with the wagon train ahead?" he asked, pushing back his hat to reveal his bandaged head.

"That's right. I'm Captain Ernie Fudge, and this is my trail hand, Jonah Sommer. Who're you?"

Lowering his gun and breaking into a big grin, the man replied, "Thank God, we found your train. I'm J. Heinrich Possard—but you can call me Henry. These are my wagons and my kin."

"Mr. Possard," Jonah exclaimed. "I didn't recognize you with all the dust and that bandage on your head. Do you remember me? I met you at my pa's trading post in Lost Creek Valley, back in Missouri."

Peering closer, Henry's grin got even wider. "Sure, I remember you, young man. You delivered the supplies to our wagon when we camped at the river. What're you doing here?"

"Galldarn it," Captain Ernie interjected, "you fellas can catch up on your life stories tonight, back at camp. Right now, I want to know what happened, and if there's any immediate danger lurking hereabouts."

Jonah stood in his stirrups and looked for the other wagons, wondering where Tennie was. Then he looked heavenward and silently thought, *Thank you, Lord,* before focusing again on Mr. Possard.

"We've been having nothing but trouble. We left our train at Shawnee Mission and stayed there for nearly a week, so the blacksmith could make repairs. Then we started out by ourselves, trying to catch the train that had left the previous morning."

"You tried going it alone?" the wagon train leader asked, in amazement. "That was a dadgum foolish thing to do."

"You're right. A band of Injuns jumped us and burned one of our wagons. We got a man back there that be hurt."

"So, then what happened? You folks must have fought them off. Is that right?" Captain Fudge asked, again fidgeting and looking around for any sign of trouble.

"Ah . . . not really. A stranger came along, and he attacked them and scared the Injuns away. He's quite a fella, and he has one of those dadgum new pistols that fires six times without reloading."

Sounds like a Colt revolver, Jonah thought.

"So you saw the dust from my train, and you were trying to catch us," coaxed the captain impatiently, trying to hurry the account along.

"We were hurrying, but then other things happened. We camped last night and two outlaws jumped us. They wanted to steal our rigs and supplies. They also tried to force our women . . ." He broke off, unable to finish.

Now intrigued, the captain urged, "Well, go on man, get the whole story out."

"Again, the stranger came to our rescue. He got the drop on them bandits, and they all rode off. We saw him again this morning when he got us started toward your train."

"Does this fella have a name?"

"Only one we know is Curtis."

Jonah was shocked. *It must be my brother.* "Where is he, Mr. Possard?"

"Why, he's right back there, riding drag," Henry replied, jerking his thumb toward the rear of his caravan.

Spurring his horse, Jonah rode toward the other wagons and saw Tennie at the same time that she saw him. Seeing her flashing green eyes and long golden hair was the best treat of his life. *I just knew that I'd see her again,* he thought, excitedly.

"Where in thunder did you come from?" she asked, surprised. Smiling broadly, she continued. "I thought I might see you another time, but I didn't figure it'd be so soon."

"I'm glad to see you, too," the young man replied, grinning widely and taking off his hat. *She looks even prettier than I remembered. That green dress matches her eyes, and she's even more beautiful with her face baked by the sun and framed by that white bonnet.* "Remember, my name is Jonah Sommer. I knew it in my bones that we'd meet once more. You must have thought the same, given what you just said about seeing me again. Did you really think that I'd follow you all the way to Oregon?"

"Don't be silly," she replied, turning crimson. "I was just surprised, that's all."

"Heard you had some trouble and a fella came along to help you folks." A shadow seemed to cross her eyes that puzzled him.

Quickly, she looked away. "We had the Injuns attack us and then those evil men tried to . . ." She paused, looking distant for a moment before continuing, "They tried to rob us. Why, if'n it hadn't been for

Curtis, no telling what would have happened. He drove those dastardly fellows off all by himself."

"Howdy, brother."

Turning in his saddle, there sat Curtis sitting on a strange horse. "My God, big brother, I'm sure surprised to find you out here on the plains. Why are you riding that horse instead of the black Walker?"

"It was shot by one of those outlaws that hit the camp last night. I had to put it down."

"Heavens, I'm sorry to hear that," Jonah replied, as the wagon train leader rode up. "Sir, meet my oldest brother, Curtis. And, brother, this is Ernie Fudge, captain of the train ahead."

"How do," the captain said, "I hear you and this group have had a busy few days. You see any signs of trouble this morning?"

Jonah noticed the odd expression on his brother's face.

"Nothing at all today," Curtis replied. "I'm pleased to meet you, Captain Fudge, but you caught me by surprise. You see, I was just about to leave these folks and go search for you."

Jonah was confused, and he saw the strange look on Fudge's face.

"Well, whatever it is," the captain said, "I hope it'll wait until we get back to the train. I don't like us chawing out here in the open. Let's get these wagons moving again."

◆————————————◆

Curtis rode beside Jonah at the rear of the column, as the Possard wagons continued over the plains.

Jonah asked, "So, tell me what's happened. And why were you leaving to search for Captain Fudge?"

Curtis told him about Butch and Billy Joe.

"So you killed them?" Jonah inquired, wide-eyed.

"No, but they got their just dues. They'll think twice before they rob folks and pester women again," Curtis replied.

"And it was one of them outlaws who shot your horse?"

"That's right, her leg was busted."

"I know how much she meant to you. I really feel for your loss." Pausing, Jonah asked, "What happens now? Are you coming with us or are you riding off to look for Veeko?"

Unsure how to answer, Curtis replied, "I've not changed my mind about traveling with you boys. How many wagons are there in the train?"

"More than a hundred."

"Know a family named Hills?"

"No, why do you ask?"

"Hold that question until I've had a chance to talk with your captain. I'll be back soon, and we'll talk more." Curtis spurred his horse and rode to the head of the column.

The captain looked around, as Curtis rode up.

"Sir, I've been tracking a man that did my family harm," Curtis began, "and I think he's with your train. The men who attacked this group last night were his pardn'rs. The three of them plan to rob and kill settlers who are traveling alone and can't keep up with their trains. They aim to steal their supplies, wagons, and teams and then sell the plunder to other folks back in Independence. Do you know a man by the name of Veeko?"

Reining his horse to the side to let the wagons pass, Captain Fudge replied, "No, not that I recall." Looking at him, he pushed back his hat. "Some folks sure do follow an ungodly and dastardly road through life, don't they?"

"The two last night told me that Veeko's driving a wagon for an old couple by the name of Hills, Rodney and Carla Hills, and that they're part of your train."

"I know the Hills, but let me look in my book for the other name," the captain commented. Pulling out his small, pencil-marked notebook from an inside coat pocket, he flipped through the pages. Finally, he said, "Aha, now I remember the fella. This man, Veeko, he's kind of short with broken front teeth?"

"Sounds like him."

"He's their driver. Regrettably, they're no longer with my train. Old man Hills was confined to his bed in the wagon. His wife told me that he was suffering greatly and was too weak to talk, so I never did see him. She insisted that they needed to return to Independence as soon as possible, so a doctor could treat him. I tried talking them into staying, reminding them about the many dangers of traveling alone, but nothing I said changed her mind. I believe that they pulled out yesterday morning at first light."

"Was Veeko driving for them?"

"Most likely."

"Did Mrs. Hills talk or act strange to you?"

"Now that you mention it, she was as white as a sheet. She kept saying that she'd been down with a cold. Come to think about it, I also recall that she kept looking at her driver—that fella you mentioned."

"I'm much obliged for the information, sir. I'll say goodbye. I'm leaving to find them, if'n I can. I think those folks are in serious danger."

"You don't say. And you come to this conclusion knowing something about their driver and what his pardn'rs told you?"

"That's about the size of it."

"I gather that we should have no fear of more trouble from them polecats?

"That's the size of it."

"I notice you're carrying that new Colt six-shooter strapped around your waist."

"Yes," he replied, as they continued riding side-by-side.

"Can you hit anything with it?"

"I'm fair to middling."

"Did it take you long to get the hang of using it?"

"Months."

"And you wear the gun all the time, do you?" the captain inquired.

"No, I don't," the Missourian responded, surprised by the question.

"Then you're not a lawman or, maybe, a bounty hunter?"

"No, sir, I'm not." Looking at the older man, Curtis continued, "I'm a farmer and a concerned member of a family that's been badly wronged by Veeko."

"I see. Sometimes, a man's emotions can get him tangled up like a calf snared in a tangle of ropes."

"I try to avoid such circumstances," Curtis replied, softly.

"I'm thinking of getting me one of them Colts."

"If I was herding a flock of wagons like you, I would, too. It isn't much of a gun for hunting game, but it has its uses."

"Good luck, young man. I hope you catch that fella before he hurts the Hills."

"I'll need luck to sort out their tracks on the busy trail."

"And thanks for what you've done for these people," the captain added.

"God bless. Please keep an eye on my brothers." Wheeling his horse about, he rode to Henry's wagon. "Goodbye, Mr. Possard. You're in good hands now, and I've business elsewhere."

"Young fella, we'll never forget how much you helped us, and, truth be known, saved our womenfolk and our lives. I don't know what I'd have done if'n them roughs had taken my Tennie. I'll be forever indebted to you."

"Keep your family safe.

"Come look us up in Grants Pass, if'n you're ever in Oregon. We'd love to share our hospitality with you."

"*Adios.*" Tipping his hat, Curtis rode next to Tennie's wagon. "I'm leaving you folks now, and I just wanted to say goodbye. I admire the grit you showed last night. You are one feisty lady with lots of iron in your backbone. I hope your future travels will be less exciting than those of the past few days."

"You're leaving us?" she asked. "I'm sorry to hear that. You know, I had no idea until this morning that you were Jonah's brother. I'm sure glad you came across us."

"Well, ma'am, sometimes things just sort themselves out, don't they?" Curtis replied.

"Why don't you stay and at least have supper with us this evening?"

"Thank you, but I have another matter to attend to. Then I'll be Missouri-bound and returning to my family and farm."

Tennie let out a short laugh and tossed her long hair over her shoulder. "You're going off to find that fella that you asked those men about last night? Veeko's his name, isn't it?"

"Yes. Say, how did you and Jonah meet?"

"We met at your pa's trading post, when we stopped for supplies," she answered, blushing. "He delivered them, and he seems kind of sweet on me."

Chuckling, Curtis responded, "He comes from good, strong stock. Give him a chance, Miss Tennie. He's a fine young man."

Laughing easily, Tennie replied, "Someday, I may do just that, Mr. Sommer. May God always be with you. I owe you for all you've done for us . . . and for me."

"Godspeed, miss," Curtis replied.

Jonah was trailing the small group, as Curtis rode up.

"You boys didn't know that Veeko was driving a wagon in your outfit?"

"Ah, you're joshing me, aren't you?" Jonah replied, astonished.

"Nope, Captain Fudge says he pulled out of the train yesterday morning headed back to Independence, driving the Hills' wagon. I'm going after them."

"My God, Veeko was in our train, and Marion didn't know it. Wait until our brother hears about it. I'll say again what I've said before, this fella Veeko is just like an evil spirit, moseying in and out of our lives, and leaving behind a trail of trouble and misery."

"Anyway, I'm headed back to Independence."

"Thank God you came along and saved the Possard family—more than once in the last few days."

"And particularly, that pretty lady named Tennie?" Curtis inquired.

Blushing, Jonah smiled and nodded. "You got that right—particularly her."

"She's a brave one and has lots of sand. She's also mighty pretty, too. You keep your eye on that one."

"I'm going to do exactly that," Jonah replied, grinning.

"All the best, brother, and give my regards to Marion. Come back to Lost Creek someday for a visit."

"I might just do that. I'm much obliged for all you've done, Curtis. May the Good Lord watch over you."

———◆————◆———

Frank lamented, "I can't believe what you just told me. How could I be so blind and miss seeing Veeko?"

"Don't beat yourself too bad, brother. After all, we have more than a hundred wagons in the train and over four hundred folks. And remember, that fella's been like a demon spirit, drifting in and out of our lives."

"It means that the family is still shamed."

"Yes, but don't forget that Curtis took care of Veeko's pardn'rs." Seeing the crestfallen look on his brother's face, Jonah continued, "I reckon you're right. All we know is that Veeko is now headed back toward Missouri."

Brightening, Frank asked, "And ain't it amazing that you came across that green-eyed gal who caught your fancy back at the trading post? That surely has to be destiny. What did she say when she saw you?"

"She was very surprised, and I think a bit pleased," Jonah answered.

"Well, maybe I was mistaken. Could be that something will come of your moccasin gift after all," Frank said, needling his brother.

Jonah grinned. "You'll recall that I told you we'd meet up again. I knew it in my heart and felt it in my bones."

CHAPTER THIRTY-ONE

Monotony was upon the Sommer men, as they herded livestock several days later.

Jonah and Frank presented a strange sight. Red-rimmed eyes looked out from beneath weathered hats pulled low, while bandanas covered their noses and lower faces. Otherwise, a fine layer of trail dust coated every inch of them, their horses and saddlery.

Jonah called to his brother, "Hey, look at Shep riding our way. He's coming fast, like demons are chasing after him. Sure hope he doesn't break his neck."

Shep slid his horse to a stop in a blur of even more grit. "Hey, boys," he shouted, "ya got nothing better to do than dawdle along with danger headed straight toward us?"

"What's wrong?" Frank asked.

"Look over yonder," Shep pointed.

For the first time, Jonah noticed huge black cloud formations in the southwestern sky. As he watched, the clouds seemed to boil, signaling the advancing fury. "I guess you're right, Shep. Sure looks like a thunderstorm is headed our way."

The trail boss looked at him, perplexed. "I guess ya green-tailed farmers haven't ever seen a real blow on the plains before. I've seen storms that can come up fast and lash ya with buckets of rain that turn gullies into raging streams in minutes. Then hail as big as rocks comes down from the sky that can plumb knock ya off yar horse and collapse wagon bonnets. And if'n ya're in a really dangerous storm, lightning strikes are near-constant with several occurring every moment."

"You think that's the kind of downpour headed our way?" Jonah asked.

Brusquely, Shep replied, "Yar asking questions, when I haven't finished telling you about the *really* big ones they have in this territory. Rain and maybe flooding are bad enough. All of that pales before the greatest danger—wind. Why, I've heard of it blowing so hard and funneling itself into a terrible, whirling cloud that can easily pick up a loaded wagon and carry it clear across the river with the team still in harness. When hail starts falling, keep a watch out for the whirlwind."

"What do folks do for protection?" Frank asked.

"Sink as low as ya can and stay down," Shep replied.

"I don't understand what you mean?"

"Get down, preferably in a gully or streambed, wherever the lowest place is."

"What about the wagons?"

Shep shrugged. "I'm not sure. Captain Ernie wants everyone heading for the valley just south of us, and *pronto*. He hopes that we can ride it out, with the surrounding hills giving us some protection from the winds. Now, let's get these critters moving fast! We don't have much time."

Spurring his horse, Jonah flanked the herd, along with his brother and Shep, driving the animals toward the low-lying hills. He continued to watch the black clouds moving swiftly toward them in the late afternoon sky, punctured by frequent lightning strikes. Out of the gloom, a gray veil of showers marched toward them, and the wind freshened considerably. He reached behind his saddle and pulled out his rain slicker.

Sensing the oncoming storm, the animals became restless, and many were lowing and wild-eyed. The herders kept busy, moving the stock south. Jonah saw that the train was already at the base of the hills. Many settlers had driven their wagons into shallow, dry creek beds. Everyone was rushing about, unhitching teams, and strapping down loose supplies before seeking shelter beneath the wagons. Thunder was all around them, as the curtain of heavy rain swept over them.

Shep yelled, "Ya take cover anywhere ya can find it."

"What about the animals?" Jonah asked.

"We've done about all we can," the ramrod shouted. "They're just going to have to fend for themselves. Tie yar horses' reins tight to a wagon. And find shelter right now, because it won't be long before the full fury of this storm is on us."

Jonah shouted to his brother, "Let's see if we can find the Possard wagons. I'd rather ride out the storm with them."

"So you can be near your gal?" Frank teased, as water dripped from his nose.

Blowing rain made all the wagons appear to be the same shade of dingy gray. Oxen bellowed, men shouted, and horses wrenched in their harness. The brothers saw folks battling rain and wind and roping draft animals to their wagons. Finally, they found the Possard wagons in the bottom of a deep dry creek bed. Henry was attempting to get an extra rope over one wagon's bonnet.

"Let me help," Jonah offered. "I'll heave it from the other side with the wind, and you tie it off on your side. In this storm, I'm not sure it'll do any good."

The ground was turning to rubbery mud, as the Possard family gathered beneath their wagons. Jonah grabbed Frank by the arm and made sure they were under the same wagon as Tennie.

The young woman tried laying a tarp on the ground before hunkering down, but the wind kept blowing it up around her. Giving up, Tennie closed her eyes tightly, burying her face in her arms.

"Come slide between us," Jonah shouted to her.

Without hesitation, the pretty young woman squeezed in.

Jonah felt her shivering. He undid his slicker, and tentatively, he placed his arm across her shoulders and pulled her gently beneath his rain gear. She did not resist, and he could hear her sobbing with fright. "There, there," he said, soothingly, "nothing will happen to you while I'm here."

He looked at the darkening sky, just as a brilliant flash of lightning slashed to the ground, blinding him momentarily. An instant later, the heavy crash of rolling thunder enveloped him, and even the ground quaked from the titanic boom's power. From somewhere in the train, the wind carried the sounds of youngsters screaming in terror from the shrieking wind and the electric tension of everyone. Thick, relentless sheets of rain pounded them.

"Oh, God, please spare us," Tennie cried, her voice cracking with fear, as the rumble of thunder rolled toward them. Another lightning strike momentarily illuminated the drab looking wagons, hunkered down in the gully.

"We're safe in this streambed," Jonah whispered in her ear, trying to comfort her. "We'll be all right. Just you wait and see," he continued, drawing her even closer. At any other time, the soft touch and smell of her hair against his lips would have thrilled him, but not in the middle of such a dangerous storm.

Suddenly, they heard a loud, terrible ripping sound. A flash of lightning lit up the scene. The bonnet above them snapped one leather tie-down after another, in rapid succession, until it was wildly flapping in the wind and rocking the wagon above them.

Tennie screamed in terror and held him tightly. An instant later, the bonnet was gone.

Lightning lit the sky in jagged bursts, outlining the heavy clouds as the wind howled and rain came down in slanted sheets.

Then, Jonah saw white balls striking the ground hard. *Hail. My God, this is just like Shep described. Is the whirlwind next? Dear Lord, shelter us from the terrible wrath of this storm and help protect this beautiful woman next to me . . . that I love.* That sentiment was an unexpected self-revelation, and the thought startled him. Smiling to himself, he continued, *Well, I finally said it, at least to myself. I hope there'll be a time when I can hold her in my arms and say it to her.*

Over the drumming of the wind-lashed rain and hail came a new sound—deep, penetrating, and rising in an ever-louder crescendo. *Oh my Lord, the noise is louder than a thousand stampeding horses. What is it?* The hairs on the back of his neck stood stiff, as a shiver of fear swept over him. Looking up, Jonah saw little through the thick, blowing rain.

Suddenly, lightning strikes flashed in a twin salvo of brilliant streaks. Then, he saw it.

Ominously poised over a hill was a monstrous cloud, layered under others of varying shades of black, gray, and even green. While the sky was lit for no longer than a blink of an eye, he saw two thin columns dangling below the thick cloud, resembling short pigtails hanging from the head of a young girl, and centered between, a massive whirlwind funnel extended to the ground. In that instant of light, he also saw a billowing aggregation of rubble spinning inside the broad, pedestal-shaped base.

Holy tarnation, here it comes, as if it's plowing the prairie. Instinctively, he ducked his head. The frightful whirlwind howled wildly, and the deep, penetrating sound was more menacing than anything he had ever heard. *Good Lord in the heavens above, is this the end?*

Trembling with fright, the pretty girl pressed against him.

Jonah tightened his hold. He found it difficult to think, with the overwhelming sound of the wind. Even breathing was a struggle. *We're in your hands, God,* he prayed. *Give us the strength to see this through.* Resigned, he closed his eyes and waited, as the shivering, young woman huddled next to him. The feel of her body against his gave him a measure of solace, knowing that they were together, whatever might happen.

Sheltered beneath the wagons, time passed, but it seemed endless to Jonah. *Please, God, make this stop,* he prayed.

Ever so gradually, the screaming wind lessened, as the fast-moving, twister-led storm traveled onward. The falling rain slowly dwindled down to a fine mist and then stopped.

Peeking out from beneath the wagon, Jonah watched the swirling clouds rapidly moving eastward. Continuous lightning strikes lit the backside of the storm, which outlined the dangerous, dark clouds. From his vantage point, Jonah thought it looked unreal, though, somehow magical. He had never seen anything like it.

"Look, Tennie, the storm is moving away from us," he said, pointing to the immense dark clouds. "Look at those lightning flashes. Isn't that a wondrous sight?"

Carefully, the girl stirred and raised her head. "Is that what ran over us?" she asked, incredulously.

"Yep, it's unbelievable and strangely beautiful to watch from here, isn't it?"

For the first time, she seemed to be aware that she was close-fitted between the Sommer boys, with Jonah's arm over her, holding her tightly. "I'm fine now," she said, regaining her composure and pulling away. "Would you boys give me some space, so I can breathe? I'm beginning to feel like a caged possum."

Jonah blushed, releasing her and retrieving his rain slicker.

"That's the wildest dadgum storm I've ever seen," Frank said in amazement.

Jonah saw bawling animals milling about everywhere. "It's going to take us the rest of the night to round up the stock. Best we get on with it."

"You got that right," his brother replied, as he eased himself from under the wagon.

As Jonah joined him, he saw that Tennie remained below the embankment and under the wagon, perhaps afraid that the storm would return.

In the dim light, Jonah heard something—not the wind—but a new, sinister noise. Rapidly, the intensity increased, like a giant rushing and tumbling sound, and clearly coming toward the wagon train. It was not a second whirlwind, yet it was almost as terrifying. Startled, he looked for new signs of danger and saw other folks anxiously doing the same. The frightening, swishing roar defied comprehension and the source remained a mystery.

"*Jonah, help!*" Tennie screamed, in a loud shrill voice.

He looked back at the wagon and saw her swallowed up by a wall of water that barreled down the gully, fed by furious runoff from the surrounding hills. Quickly, the former dry streambed became a rain-glutted, raging river, rising higher than the wagon wheel hubs.

Jonah turned and ran toward Tennie, shouting, but the din of the rushing torrent swept away the sound of his words.

Swept off her feet, she hung onto a wagon wheel spoke to avoid washing downstream.

Running at full speed, Jonah slipped and fell in the mud. Quickly arising, he rushed toward the water-swollen gully.

In horror, he saw the wagon begin to move with the flow, grudgingly at first, as the ground beneath eroded. The prairie schooner suddenly wheeled about, broadside to the current. Battered by the floodwater, it balanced briefly on two wheels, then, ever so slowly, it tilted farther to one side. In the next instant, the interior load shifted and over it went, floating downstream with Tennie clutching a wheel.

The wagon's tongue abruptly jammed into the opposite side of the gully, wedging the rig broadside in the streambed and creating a temporary dam.

"HELP!" the terror-stricken young woman screamed, as the rising water kept her off-balanced. Floundering and thrashing, she managed to raise her head above the rushing torrent, while the water's force pinned her against the underbelly of the wagon.

Jonah stopped at the edge and stripped off his rain slicker. Holding it by the sleeve, he flung the rest toward the terrified girl—and missed. It was too short.

Frank slid to a stop beside his brother. "Here, tie the sleeve of my slicker to yours."

Jonah quickly knotted the two together and threw the longer lifeline out again, farther upstream—and let the swift current carry it to the struggling woman. Tennie lunged for it and hung on with both hands, as he hauled her toward the bank of the newly formed river. The tied sleeve suddenly ballooned, filling with water, and pulled both into the current.

Frank shouted, "BROTHER, WATCH OUT! There's another wagon floating downstream, and it's heading your way."

Looking up, Jonah saw another Possard wagon looming above him. It looked like a gigantic, wayward ship, as it rapidly bore down on them. *Oh, my God, it'll crush us.* He struggled against the raging, cold water, striving to regain his footing.

Protecting Tennie with both arms around her, Jonah watched in horror, as the looming wagon appeared gigantic against the darkened sky. Closing his eyes tight, he waited for the inevitable. Strangely, nothing happened and the force of the water lessened. He opened his eyes and was astounded.

At the last moment, the oncoming wagon's larger rear wheels grounded on the bottom of the gully, skewing the cumbersome floating vehicle about into the full force of the current. Then, it, too, toppled over, creating another dam, which briefly blocked the on-coming water. Quickly, Jonah scooped Tennie up and carried her to higher ground, where he gently set her down.

She was shaking with fear, as her arms tightly encircled Jonah's neck.

"It's all right now, Tennie," he whispered softly into her ear. "I've got you. You're safe with me."

The calmness of his voice reassured her, yet she continued to cling to him.

Frank came running to them with a dry blanket and wrapped it around her shoulders. "That should help warm you up."

Slowly, she broke away from Jonah and rose on trembling legs. Looking around frantically, she shouted, "Pa, Ma! Do you boys know where my family is? Have you seen my sisters?"

"Look over there," Jonah said, as he pointed. Hurrying toward them was the entire Possard clan. Everyone was laughing, happy that all had survived both of nature's greatest calamities.

As he watched the family hugging and joyously laughing, Jonah felt fulfilled, with the knowledge that his love was safe.

His sense of relief was brief. A woeful, haunting shriek came from behind him, demanding his attention. Turning, he saw a woman tightly clutching her small child, praying that life would return, while sorrow-fully crying to the heavens above.

———◆———————◆———

It took three days for the settlers to make repairs. Several dozen wagons had been damaged in the nightmarish flood. When righted, tandem teams of oxen hauled them out of the mud and muck of the gullies. Supplies were spread about to dry, and repairs were completed on damaged wagons. A number also needed new bonnets.

Frank and Jonah rode the plains during those days, rounding up the animals that had scattered widely before the storm.

Early on the fourth morning, Captain Ernie said a prayer over the graves of the three children and two men whose lives were lost in the violent whirlwind and flood.

> God, the memory of family members
> and our neighbors lost in that terrible
> storm will live with us forever. Gracious
> is Thy love, and we're commending the
> souls of our brethren to Your bosom.
> Amen.

"Amen," the pioneers echoed.

As men replaced their hats and women wiped away tears, the train leader addressed the group. "Folks, it breaks our hearts to lose our friends and loved ones. I know all of us are hurting, but life is all about moving on and, for us, that means getting back on the trail. Be ready to head out in half an hour."

Soon, the captain shouted his familiar command, "Wagons, ho!"

CHAPTER THIRTY-TWO

Jonah often gazed down the long line of wagons after a hot day on the trail, hoping to catch a glimpse of Tennie. The terrible storm and flood were behind them and weeks had passed. He usually appreciated Sundays, which provided a chance to catch up with needed chores. However, he had other matters on his mind on that Sabbath, as he walked toward the Possard encampment.

He hummed a melody under his breath to bolster his spirits, with the words repeating in his head—

My lady love, she stands a-waitin'
Away, you rovin' river
On the banks, I hear her callin'

Away, I found the way
Across the wide Missouri

I'm pushin' on, when dawn's a-breakin'
Away, you lovely river
Where my love, she stands a-waitin'

Away, I found the way
Across the wide Missouri.

Coming around the corner of a wagon, he spied the green-eyed beauty standing next to a good-sized pot, which hung from a stanchion over a fire. His false bravado and humming ended abruptly. He was hesitant. Even so, he summoned his courage and called out, "Top o' the morn' to you, Tennie. Is everything all right here at the Possard camp?"

"Of course," she answered, using a thick wooden paddle to stir the steaming pot.

"What're you cooking?"

Looking at him and turning away quickly, she replied, "I'm not cooking anything, just boiling clothes to get them clean. There's mud and grit in everything. Why aren't you out hunting with the others?"

"I've been helping a man fix his wagon wheel."

"What can I do for you today?" she asked, a bit more formal and brisk than necessary. She brushed aside a tress of hair from her face as she spoke.

"I brought your quilt back. Thank you for lending it to me."

"You're welcome. Just lay it on top of that barrel right there."

Jonah had hoped for a warmer reception, but today he was determined to overcome his shyness. "Would you like to walk with me down by the creek this evening?"

"As you can see, I've got my chores to do around here, trying to clean the dirt out of these clothes," the blonde-haired woman responded. "And later, I'll be helping get supper ready. Afterwards, I'll be plumb done in."

Disappointed but not put off, he rambled on, "Captain Ernie says that we should reach Fort Laramie by the end of the coming week. Then we have another six weeks of travel before we get to Fort Hall. That's where the California Trail hives off, and many folks are talking about taking it to the gold country. Frank and I've been thinking that we might head that way, too."

"Oh?" she asked, derisively. "You've decided to go mindlessly trekking over deserts and mountains searching for illusive riches in grains of glitter, like all the other aimlessly wandering fools?"

"Ah, Tennie, I'm just sharing with you what we've been thinking. I'd never leave this train if'n you'd give me a kind word."

"We'd all like something that we don't have. Look, Jonah, I've been straight with you ever since we first met. I'm greatly in your debt for saving my life during that evil storm, but don't go thinking that you have a rope over me. My heart is with my Jerome, and he promised to follow me clear to the Pacific Ocean. I think of him every day, hoping that he's already on the trail."

At that moment, lovesick Jonah felt as though something died inside him. Swallowing became difficult. Staring at her, his mind had become blank. Finally regaining his thoughts, he voiced his sorrow, "Every now and then, some apples don't ripen, and I guess this is one of those times. I'm sad that you love another fella, who isn't here and may never come. Yet, I understand. I don't believe anyone could love you more than me. I knew it the first time that I saw you at the trading post."

She was touched and her eyes glistened. "Those are very sweet and touching words, Jonah," she replied, quietly. "I've told you what's in my heart. I'm sorry, but I don't see that changing anytime soon."

"I know that I'm not about to share your heart." He saw her nod, and to his surprise, tears were rolling down her cheeks. "I'd do almost anything, but I won't stand in line. You'll have no more bother from me," he continued. "I thank you for your kindness to me and your gentle ways. My wish for you is that your life will always be filled with love and happiness." Turning on his heel, he walked away, feeling a suffocating burden of sorrow and despair.

———————

"So," Frank asked, as he and his brother rode the trail together the following morning, "there'll be no more talk from you about Tennie? You're through with her! And, she certainly sounds like she's through with you. Do I have that right?"

"I reckon," a dejected Jonah responded. "I'd hoped that our being near one another and part of the same train would bring us closer together. She made it very clear that her love is with that easterner, and nothing I do or say is ever going to change that."

Frank felt for his brother, as once again he recalled Ella Mae standing in the barn, shaken to the quick by his angry outburst.

"Her love for another has really hit my soul a couple of hard licks.

They rode in silence for a time, each lost in his own thoughts.

Finally, Jonah looked at his glum brother and said, "I've heard that a broken heart mends itself in time. Think that's true?"

Shrugging, Frank replied, "I guess neither of us is destined to be lucky with the ladies."

Slowly, a broad smile came to Jonah's face. "Little brother, don't be so eager to write off our whole lives with fair young maidens, before either of us has even sprouted his very first gray hair. We know how to work, and we ain't the worst looking fellas. Why, we're still young and full of vinegar. Let's just say that our first attempts with fair maidens haven't been satisfactory, but, my young brother, there are many others for us to meet."

"So, how do you suggest that we brighten your sour mood?"

"Some say to start anew, you have to shuck off the old. So, brother, let's start shucking."

Frank grinned at his brother, wondering if he really believed his own words or was just trying to make them feel better. *Well, given time, we'll both know.*

REAPER

Nebraska Territory

CHAPTER THIRTY-THREE

Backtracking on the Oregon Trail, Curtis searched in vain for signs that would lead him to Veeko. Slowly—painstakingly—he attempted to separate a pattern of tracks heading southeast from the many headed in the opposite direction. *Dadblast it, how am I going to do this?* he questioned. *The ground is a muddle of prints, laid down over many years. Weather and wind sweep many away, yet we're at the start of a new season, and already, there're far too many to sort. I hope I sort out the riddle soon, as I'm itching to see my family again. Still, Veeko is out here somewhere.*

Pondering the problem, he came to several conclusions. *I know that the man's destination is either the Shawnee Mission or Independence. That means he's traveling southeast. My guess is that he'll avoid all trains—there'd be way too much explaining for him to do about Mr. and Mrs. Hills.*

Looking immediately to the northeast, he reckoned, *What with the hills and added distance, it seems unlikely that the fella would go that way in a loaded wagon. So, I should find Veeko's tracks on the southern flank of the trail.*

Having set his plan, Curtis rode on the fringe of the broad Great Platte River Valley Trail, looking for a lone set of tracks. Finally, he found prints heading east. Then he lost them among the multitude. The "find and lose" contest continued, until the jumbled ground became unreadable, and pickings went from slim to nonexistent. By nightfall, he had nothing to show for the day's effort.

That evening, he considered his next move. *Well, so much for my vaunted tracking skills,* he thought, frowning in consternation. *My brothers would likely be laughing themselves into stitches, watching me out here on the prairie—well, maybe not Marion, given what he's going through.*

If Veeko chooses a different route, what would it be? He isn't heading west or east, and I've found no signs of him going south. There's only one direction left—due north to the Platte River. Once there, he'd follow it to the Missouri River. According to the old-timer at Abe's Mercantile, all the wagon trains avoid going that way. Still, he's less likely to run into other folks, and that has to be the answer.

Early the next day, he began riding the main trail west once more, this time along the northern edge. Self-doubts continued to plague him. *Maybe I've totally misjudged what this devious man is up to. Was it foolish for me to head this way again?* he questioned. Beneath the huge sky, he continued, searching, hour after hour, his eyes fixed on the ground. His frustration only increased, as he looked up at an unending sea of tracks ahead and wondered whether his hunt was doomed to failure.

His concentration drifted to his last visit to Fort Smith and Captain Parke. Smiling and mimicking his army friend's brogue, the Missourian muttered to the horse, "Patience, me boy, and find yerself a bit of shamrock green." Chuckling, he thought, *Well, why not.*

He stopped and dismounted. The air was fresh and clear, and the sharp-scented smell of prairie dirt was on the wind. Plucking the head of a hip-high bloom from a blade of grass, he took off his hat and stuffed it into the band. Once more, using his Ohio-Missouri-Irish-laced voice, he muttered, "Now ye're properly dressed, with the luck of shamrock green on yer side, and ye can better meet the craziness of yer search. Curtis, me-boy, mount yer steed, and get thee back to the hunt."

Possibly, there was a kernel of truth to the captain's Irish tales, or perhaps that very day, a particular saint watched him on the vast plains of Nebraska Territory, because he spied a lone set of wagon tracks heading north. Feelings of vindication and euphoria shot through him, as he roared, "Hurrah and hallelujah, I finally found his trail. This has to be Veeko with the Hills' wagon." Looking upward, he smiled and continued, "Thank ye, good patron of Captain Parke."

Almost immediately, his excitement diminished and abruptly ended. Another set of tracks—a lone horseman—accompanied the wagon. *Where in tarnation did this rider come from? I thought that I was down to hunting one hombre, not two.*

As he had expected, the tracks led to the Platte, where they turned eastward. For nearly two days, he hurried along after the slow, ox-drawn wagon and horseman.

During the second afternoon, he often looked over his shoulder, watching the gathering of heavy black clouds that stretched across the southwestern sky. *Going to be a big blow coming my way,* he thought, suddenly concerned that the rain would wash away Veeko's trail. *This one looks like it's going to be a gully-washer.*

An hour later, heavy sheets of rain poured down on him. He looked for shelter, but none was apparent. There was little choice, so he buttoned the top of his slicker and pushed on.

Lightning lit the area, as he adjusted his rain-soaked hat and looked at the trail ahead. Startled, he was surprised to see glaring eyes staring at him from the trail. His horse became skittish and reared, and he reined his mount tightly to regain control. Peering through the downpour was a big, shaggy coyote ten yards in front of him.

Intently, the critter watched him, ears laid flat along its rain-slicked head, and a ridge of raised hair bristling from head to tail. Its nose lifted slightly, sniffing the scent of man and horse. Then, standing fixed and lowering his head, the predator fiercely looked up at him from hooded eyes, which glowed eerily in the dim light. With lips drawn back in a vicious snarl, blood dripped from its jaw.

That's one mean looking coyote, Curtis thought. *His stare is downright chilling and almost ghostly in this dim light. It must be guarding something. It's probably food, because he's not backing down at the sight of me and my horse.* "I'm just passing through, big fella," he called to the shaggy animal.

The coyote did not move, and his rumbling snarl increased, as the beast bared its teeth.

The Missourian was about to give him a wide berth, when another lightning bolt lit the area. Beneath the predator, there appeared to be a shirt. "Are you standing over a dead man, Mr. Coyote?" He was unsure until the next lightning strike confirmed his suspicion. "I'm sorry, but I can't leave, if'n that's a settler's final resting place." Despite his worries about the sound of gunfire carrying on the wind, Curtis shot a round from his pistol, trying to scare the coyote away.

The animal tensed and crouched lower, but stood fast, its eyes fixed on the horseman.

Firing a second round, the loud boom and the whoosh of a bullet hitting close by finally persuaded the predator. The animal grudgingly slunk away and was soon lost to sight in the dim light of the rainstorm.

The man from Missouri dismounted, as still another lightning flash showed the grizzly scene of a partially buried, gray-haired, old man. *This has to be Veeko's work*, Curtis reckoned. Kneeling, he saw that the man's throat had been cut from ear to ear, and that the remains had been ripped and mauled. *Good God in heaven, can this be Mr. Hills? By his appearance, the body hasn't been here very long. I wonder if the short man knows that I'm following him. If so, he may figure that I'll stop to bury this fella, which slows me down. Yet, I don't see how Veeko could have learned about me. Maybe he's just being very crafty. Whatever the reason, this evil killer has gone bad . . . real bad, killing this old settler.*

Curtis stood staring at the body, shaken to his core, as tears streamed down his face. *That bushwhacker must still have the woman with him. When I catch you, Mr. Veeko, there's going to be one less monster out here on the plains.*

———◆——————◆———

Rain, darkness, and weariness finally stopped Curtis for the night. It also occurred to him that sitting tall in the saddle was a ripe invitation to attract one of the many lightning bolts ripping across the sky.

In a makeshift refuge made of brush with his slicker spread over the top as a covering, he tried to light a fire—but everything was too wet. He would simply have to shiver the night away. Seated on his saddle in the soggy weather, he attempted to console himself by chewing on pan-fried biscuits from the previous day.

He reflected on the old man, and his senseless murder. Curtis had found enough stones at the riverbank to cover the body. Bowing his head, he offered a silent prayer over the fallen man, then continued his quest.

Now, in his flimsy shelter, he wondered, *What's Veeko doing right about now? He'll have no choice but to stop for the night, same as me.* Recalling the man's many crimes, he could only shake his head in disbelief. *I've met farmers, frontiersmen, scallywags, and Injuns in my life, and all of them hold God-fearing beliefs of one kind or another. This stubby-sized fella is unlike anyone that I've ever met or even heard about. He's just downright bloodthirsty.*

The following morning, the rain had stopped, leaving gray skies overhead, as the Missourian continued his journey. Looking at the river, he saw that recent rains had swollen and quickened its pace.

At midmorning, he spied a mesa rising above the river with an outcropping of rocks. *That's where I'd have sat out the storm last night,* Curtis reckoned. *Wonder if Veeko had the same idea.*

Approaching warily on horseback and with Hawken in hand, he looked for signs. Rounding a large limestone outcropping, he was startled to find an old woman lying face down on the ground. Dressed in brown homespun, her long, braided-hair was gray, and a faded, mud-splattered, sunbonnet lay beside her. Dismounting and turning her over, he found that she was alive, but her breathing was shallow. The woman's face was very pale, except for an angry bruise on her forehead. *This must be Mrs. Hills,* he reasoned, *and more of Veeko's brutal handiwork.*

"Ma'am," he said, "can you hear me? Are you hurt bad?"

There was no response.

He tried to stir her by rubbing her hand, again, with no success. Returning to his horse, he retrieved his bedroll and spread it on the ground next to a big boulder. Picking her up, he gently set her down and

covered her with his blanket and rain slicker. He started a fire and anxiously looked at the old woman. The bruise above her brow appeared to
be the only injury. He cleaned it and wiped her pale face. *She needs food
to help her get some strength back and to warm her. Best I make a broth by boiling
a pot of water and add some of my jerky.*

Walking in a wide circle in search of more firewood, he came to the
other side of the rocks and saw wagon tracks heading east. *Veeko, you wily
son of a rattlesnake, you'll not shake me.*

Returning to the fire, he watched, as the woman slowly regained
consciousness.

Suddenly, her eyes flew open, her face etched with fear. "Who're
you?" she whispered, struggling to sit up. "Where am I?"

"My name is Curtis, ma'am, and I found you here by the river."

"Are you with that evil man, the one who stole our wagon and team?"

"No, ma'am, but I am tracking a short man who has two fingers missing on his left hand and goes by the name of Veeko."

"Veeko," the woman shrieked, trembling and turning away, as tears
flooded her eyes.

"Are you Mrs. Hills?"

Seeing a nod, he continued, "I see the bruise on your face. Do you
hurt anywhere else?"

Thinking for a moment, the woman closed her eyes and replied,
"Yes, my heart is broken."

The answer took him by surprise. For a long time, he watched, as she
turned away, sobbing uncontrollably.

Slowly, she quieted, then whispered in a hoarse voice, "That son of
Satan murdered my husband. We've been married for nearly thirty-four
years, and we always figured that we'd be laid side-by-side in our final
resting place." More tears filled her eyes until she gathered herself again
and continued. "That evil man knows you're chasing after him. A young
fella caught up to us as we were returning over the trail. I heard Veeko
call him Billy Joe, and he told that evil man about you chasing after him."

How in blue-blazes did they find each other, Curtis wondered. *Maybe it was
only by chance. Anyway, that explains the lone set of horse tracks.*

"Right after that, we turned north to the Platte and have been following it ever since. He killed my Rodney, figuring that he'd make tracks while you stopped to bury him. Did you find him? Did you take the time to give him a burial?" she asked, anxiously.

"Yes, I did, ma'am."

"Oh, I'm so glad to hear that. Thank you, young man."

"Here, drink some of this broth," he urged. "It'll help you get your strength back."

"Thanks, it smells good," she said, taking a sip. "That fella stole our rig and team, and he plans to sell them in Independence." Looking at him closely, she asked, "Did you cut Billy Joe's ears?"

Curtis simply looked at the woman.

"I figured as much. That boy had a shirt wrapped around his head and another around his thigh. I tended his wounds, as best I could. Meeting him surprised Veeko. When that murderer learned that you were after him, he was beside himself with anger and kept badgering the young man with questions, one after another, until I could see that Billy Joe was becoming fearful for his own skin.

"And, my Lord, when that evil jackal learned that you knew he was driving our wagon in Captain Fudge's train, he went nearly loco, ranting and raving, just like a mad dog I once saw when I was a wee youngun. No question about it, Mr. Curtis, you've put the fear of an avenging Saint Michael into the head of that ungodly fella from hell."

The woman seemed winded from talking. After sipping more of the warm liquid, she asked, "Why are you chasing after him? He must have harmed you or someone near to you. Is that the reason?"

"Yes, that's right," he replied. "I aim to rid the frontier of that no-good."

"I pray you do. He was following the river east, the last I knew."

"Yes, I saw his tracks. I came across Captain Fudge, and he told me that you folks turned back because of your husband's health, with Veeko driving your wagon."

"Weren't nothing wrong with my Rodney, until that devil-man knocked him on the head and tied him up in the back of the wagon."

Bewildered, she asked, "Why does the Good Lord allow such a mangy, low-down cur to exist among law-abiding, peace-loving folks?"

"I surely don't know the answer, but I've wondered about the same question."

"Veeko left me here, and he figures I'll make you linger."

Curtis remained silent.

For the rest of the morning, they warmed themselves by the crackling fire, as the woman rested under the blanket, sipping broth. Curtis was unsure about his next step. He could not leave the woman alone on the plains. He had already seen the work of wild critters —and then there were other dangers, such as Indians and the weather. *Maybe I can build a travois and drag the litter behind the horse, like the Injuns do. That way, she could rest as we travel, although it'd be a might bumpy trip. But, I need stout tree limbs for the wood rails and bark for webbing.* Looking around, no tree of any size was to be found. *Well, that idea ain't going to happen.* Glancing up at the threatening sky, he reflected, *I wonder how long it'll be before the rains come again.*

"Ma'am, do you think you can ride?" he asked.

"Are you going after Veeko?"

"Yes. I'd like to get moving, if'n you're feeling stronger."

"I'll do anything to help you catch the fella that killed my Rod. Help me up."

Curtis and Mrs. Hills followed the clear, deep tracks in the soft ground. Sometimes he walked, leading the horse with Mrs. Hills riding, and at other times, both rode.

In the afternoon, the woman was dozing in the saddle, and the Missourian was half-awake, rocking with the cadence of the horse. A large shadow passed above them, catching his attention. Looking up, a turkey-sized buzzard flew overhead to join others circling in the sky ahead. *I wonder if someone else has crossed Veeko's path.*

From a distance, they could see a man laid out directly over the wagon wheel tracks. *He certainly didn't want us to miss this fella,* Curtis decided. *That evil spawn from Hell is sure blazing a trail of maim and death.*

Three huge, black birds were already perched near the body, and they lazily walked away as the two approached. *By God, I hate these ugly scavengers,* he thought. Dismounting, he waved his arms and hat at the brutes. They walked away and then, flapping their broad wings, they slowly took flight.

"It's that boy, Billy Joe," the woman said. "Help me down from the horse, and I'll see if'n I can do anything for him."

Curtis handed her down and then swung back into the saddle. Spurring his horse, he examined the tracks ahead.

"MISTER CURTIS, HELP!" the woman shrieked in a high, piercing voice. "OH GOD, PLEASE, HELP ME . . ."

Looking back, he saw her kneeling beside the young man and flailing wildly with her hands and arms. To his astonishment, there was a big prairie rattlesnake striking her and twisting violently near the man on the ground. Galloping back, the Missourian slid his frightened horse to a halt and hit the ground running. Unbelievably, the snake repeatedly coiled and attacked, while violently thrashing about.

He grabbed the screaming woman by the arm and pulled her clear. Only then did he see the rawhide thong tying the snake's tail to a stake in the ground. Lifting his Colt, he took dead aim and fired.

The woman was in shock and unconscious. Quickly, he used his knife to slit the dress sleeve and collar to expose the punctures. There were at least five bites on her arm and neck. A glance at the man confirmed that he had met with a grizzly death. *Look at your reward, Billy Joe—he cut you ear to ear, just like he did old man Hills.*

Carrying the small woman in his arms, Curtis set her down beneath a large bush and covered her with his bedroll. Carefully, he began washing the puncture wounds. Sitting back on his heels, he thought, *she won't last long with those neck bites so close to her heart.*

Coming around, the woman opened her brown eyes. Tears ran down her face. "Oh, I've got pain on my left side and the bites sting." Looking at her arm and shoulder, she continued, "Now, that's a sorry mess. I'm done for, ain't I, young man?"

"Don't you worry, I'm going to clean these wounds, and you'll get better, just you wait and see," he replied, cradling her in his arms.

"Don't whitewash . . . me."

Talking was difficult for her, as he brushed away her tears.

"We both know . . . my time be up."

He held the water bag to her lips, and she sipped. He thought that she might be drifting off to sleep until her eyes suddenly flew open.

"My neck . . . pains me greatly!" she gasped, in a raspy whisper. "Please promise me . . . you'll come back later . . . and lay me to rest beside my Rodney. I can't see . . ."

With tears in his eyes and a heavy heart, he hugged the woman. "I swear it," he said, rocking her gently in his arms.

<hr />

Curtis rode at a fast pace for the next few hours. As he thought about the old settlers, tears filled his eyes. *They most likely were excited and filled with hope, traveling to carve out new lives in an untamed land. It was a tragic turn of events, when the killer crossed their path. I made a promise to Mrs. Hills, and by all that's holy, I'll keep it . . . unless I'm . . .*

The old woman was right. Veeko's a man who's surely kin to the Dark Prince of Hell. Moreover, that's exactly where I'm going to send him. Both the coyote and rattler have more earthly feelings than this fella.

As the afternoon wore on, the Missourian slowed his pace, to spare the horse. The tragic loss of the old couple keenly weighed upon him. Aloud, he shouted, "Keep watching your backside, you demon. I'm coming for you. It's getting mighty tiresome, burying folks that you leave behind, Veeko. I'm going to use everything in my power to send you to the eternal fires of damnation!"

He estimated that Veeko was still a few hours ahead of him, given the speed of an ox-drawn wagon. The old gent at the mercantile came to his mind. *That fella talked about a shortcut across the dogleg between the Platte and Missouri rivers. If I travel over the hills bordering the Platt, I can do the same and shorten the distance.*

A movement in the river caused him to stop and study the swiftly flowing current, carrying debris downriver. *These storms have really churned the water, causing it to flood its banks. The overflow will be even worse when the next cloudburst hits.*

Reining his horse toward the hills, he thought, *If'n they're getting these same storms back home, the rains may damage my crops. I hope my family is helping Judy Beth with the chores on the farm. I have to end this wild chase. My life is in Lost Creek Valley, not out here, traipsing about in the wilds of Nebraska Territory.*

CHAPTER THIRTY-FOUR

Below the windy ridge, Curtis carefully swept the riverbank with his spyglass and suddenly stopped. Nearly a mile away, he saw the distinct white bonnet of a wagon. It stood distinctly against the dark clouds on a cliff above the rain-swollen river. *That has to be him,* he figured, feeling a rush of anticipation. *I have you spotted, you spawn of evil. Prepare yourself to meet your next of kin.*

It was nearly twilight, with dark clouds overhead and the wind swirling about, as the next storm neared. Riding down from the hilltop in the fading light, he reined in and dismounted some distance from the team and wagon. With the hair-trigger on his rifle already positioned, he approached cautiously. *The team is still in harness and the brakes on the wagon look like they're set. Veeko's crafty and devious. He's surely set another trap hereabouts.*

The rig appeared to be the only thing on the high bluff. To his left, there was a distant stand of cottonwood trees. A large limestone rock face framed the right side, with wagon-sized stones littering its base. Guardedly, Curtis made his way to a large boulder, alert for any sound or movement. Cautiously, he stood still and scanned the area, then took a tentative step forward.

Suddenly, the roar of a gunshot stunned him, as the blast whistled past him. Instinctively, his finger squeezed the Hawken's hair-trigger. The instant, back-to-back blasts disintegrated against the limestone face, then returned a hail of jagged stone fragments and shrapnel that peppered the side of his head. Immediately, he felt intense pain. He dropped to his knees, overwhelmed by a loud ringing in his ear and pounding pain in his head. Exploring the side of his head and ear, his fingers came away bloody.

Shaking his head, he closed his eyes and saw exploding stars, as waves of nausea gripped him. He remained motionless, then undid his bandana and pressed it against the bleeding wounds. Leaning against the huge rock for support, he waited for the spell to pass.

He straightened slowly and wondered how long it would take for the loud drumming in his head to stop. Gradually, his mind cleared. Sounds came only through his left ear, as he became aware that a man was shouting at him.

". . . you be the *hombre* that's been chasing me? Who are you, and what's put the burr under your saddle?"

From the tone of Veeko's voice, Curtis figured that the man sounded either angry or scared. *Probably both,* he guessed, remaining silent. *Let him fret in his own stew.* Picking up his Hawken, he found that the flying rock chips had disabled the hammer. *Well, that's just great. He's rendered my rifle useless, and my head feels like a giant is hammering it with a mallet.* Moving it from side to side was no help. In fact, the motion increased his queasiness and added clicking noises in his damaged ear.

He must have blasted me at close range with a scattergun, but the fiend scurried away to hide and reload. He could've jumped me, but I'm guessing that's not his style: bushwhacking—yes; man-to-man—no!

"C'mon, you dimwit, speak up," the outlaw yelled. "You know you can't move from behind that rock face without me getting a clear shot at you. So, mister, answer my question! Why are you chasing after me?"

The wind strengthened to the point that it blew Curtis' hat off, drawing immediate gunfire from Veeko. *I saw the powder smoke right below the high point of that stone outcrop to my right, so that's where the varmint is hiding. It's surprising how fast he's reloaded his gun. Maybe it's double-barreled, or could be he has more than one gun. He's bound to have good firing sight lines from there. He'd have worked all that out when planning his ambush. Somehow, I have to distract him and find another place to take cover—maybe behind the wagon.*

Curtis shouted loudly to be heard over the wind, "I buried your pardn'r, Billy Joe, where you dumped him on the trail. A God-fearing man would have seen to his grave." The sound of his own voice echoed in his head.

"Hooray for you. I didn't want to take the time. I figured you were probably a dumb Christian-believer, and I knew you'd bury him. You Bible-thumpers are all alike."

Mrs. Hills said Veeko was edgy, he recalled. *Think I'll just keep needling this killer and see where it leads.* Fighting back the nausea, he shouted, "I also buried the settlers you murdered. I can't believe you got any satisfaction from killing the old man. And, your snake-trap surprised the woman. They couldn't have given you much trouble. Do you glory in murdering innocent settlers?"

"You got a big mouth for a lamebrain jackass, but I have my reasons. Those old folks were whining and were no more use to me, except to slow you down."

"You're as vicious as anyone I've ever met. How do you live with yourself, when you're such a miserable excuse for being a man?"

Veeko's vexation was evident, as he replied, "You sure jaw a lot for a fella that's trapped behind that rock."

Curtis continued, "Now, you're in a bad fix, ain't you, because I'm going to see that you don't leave here alive. I wouldn't want to be in your boots at this moment."

"You're certainly a chatterbox, but I really don't give a hooting-damn what you think. Why, hell, if'n you've a mind, you can paint yourself gallbladder green for all I care. Your words roll off'n me like a duck sheds water."

The man from Missouri looked around for some way to distract the devil-man. *There's a good-sized rock that I can reach. I'll toss it to the left, while I run the other way for the back of the wagon.*

He tensed and waited for the next clap of lightning. As the jagged bolt arched from the dark clouds overhead filling the land with a rolling and thunderous roar, he threw the rock and raced for the wagon. Each step jarred his head, as the throbbing pain continued. Nearly there, he slipped in the muck and went sprawling.

At that instant, Veeko's gunshot hit the ground nearby, spraying mud.

Rising quickly, the Missourian hurried to the back of the wagon. Thunder continued to rumble and each reverberation hammered his head with sharp pains.

Another lightning bolt lit the wagon's interior, and Curtis saw a rifle lying on the bedding. Picking it up, he checked and found that it was primed and loaded. He also saw an oil lantern and Lucifer sticks. *Well, well,* he thought, *maybe I can use these to flush out this varmint.* Carrying the gun, he stealthily moved forward along the hidden side of the wagon and stopped next to the front wheel.

"What're you aiming to do, stranger," Veeko called out, followed by a mocking laugh. "You can't get out of the fix that you're in. Those slow critters sure ain't going to whisk you off to safety. You picked this fight, and I aim to finish it. You're dying today, and you know it. And I'm going to enjoy seeing you meet your maker, real slow-like."

Curtis shouted back, "That'll be the day! It seems that we both have the same idea, you sow-bellied coward. You could have jumped me at the rock, but you don't have enough pluck and grit to face me."

"You got a big, wagging tongue, you mealy-mouth, misbegotten ass," Veeko yelled.

"You sound like you're rattled. Stalking game is one thing, but hunted as prey—now that takes courage. That's a quality you don't have. By the way, 'Shorty' is exactly the right nickname for a sniveling excuse of a man like you who harms defenseless folks. You're short on decency, short on compassion, and you certainly have no morals, you stumpy ass."

"Are you going to keep chewing the fat till we're both old and sitting in our rocking chairs?"

"Yeah, I can hear it in your voice. You're as nettled as a prickly cactus and plumb rattled, ain't you?"

In a loud voice that carried over the sound of the wind, Veeko demanded, "What riles you so that you've tracked me all these days? And, who the hell are you?"

"A while back, you were in Lost Creek Valley. Do you remember a pretty girl named Ella Mae?"

There was a pause before the man replied. "So what? You must be her kin."

"That's about right."

"Hell, she was a saucy lassie, teasing the daylights out of some calf-mooning farm boy, who was green in the ways of pleasuring a gal want-ing to become a woman. She played him like the dumb oaf that he was—kissing, showing herself, and doing sinful things."

"That's not the way I heard it," Curtis replied, shouting over the ris-ing wind. "You walloped her and left her with the marks of Cain."

"Well, ain't that too bad? Yet, you surely agree, I gave her the one thing she wanted most."

The Missourian saw that the bullwhip was still in the pocket mounted on the side of the rig. *I'll get these animals moving forward, so I can shorten the distance and get on with my plan.* "And what about that fancy woman in Raytown that you beat on?" Curtis shouted. "You're just not much of a man, unless you can pick on someone weaker. Ain't that right?" Disdainfully, he continued, "Preying on them must make a reject like you feel important. You've got a twisted heart, and it's as black as soot."

Curtis untied the reins and released the wagon brake. Reaching up, he grabbed the whip. Then he waited for lightning to strike again. *I sure hope it distracts the killer for an instant.*

"Who're you calling a coward?" Veeko replied, obviously nervous and jumpy. "And what saloon gal are you talking about? It must be Shelley, isn't it, with her brilliant red hair? If'n that's who you mean, she's been handing it out for years to any fella with enough coins jingling in his pocket to buy her favors. How do you know her?"

Suddenly, a jagged bolt tore across the heavens, and again Curtis felt sharp stabs of pain in his head. Ignoring them, he cracked the whip over the animals' backs. "Ha, get up there, you muddy excuses for bulls!" he yelled, loudly. Snapping the whip over the animals' heads once more, he pulled on the lead line, and shouted, "AHA! GET YOUR ASSES MOVING! AHA, MOVE IT!"

Immediately, the wagon began to roll. Curtis moved in-step with the oxen, hunched over at the waist, to avoid being visible and becoming a target. Then, he stood quickly and leveled the long gun over the rump of the nearest bull, fired, and scurried to the rear of the wagon. The team continued its slow pace, heading straight for the short man's hiding place.

"You got to re-arm that muzzle-loader, don't you?" Veeko jeered. "I'm the one chewing the cabbage now. Are you hearing me? How does it feel to know that you're going to die in the next few ticks of the clock?"

The wagon continued to move, while Curtis remained hidden behind the rear gate. He glanced quickly around the wagon's bonnet.

Veeko stood with his gun pointed toward the front of the wagon.

The Missourian gauged the distance and reckoned that he was close enough for the final part of his plan. Scratching a Lucifer stick, he lit the lantern. *Well, here goes,* he thought. Swiftly stepping from behind the wagon, he hurled the lantern in a high arc at the killer.

At the last moment, Veeko changed his aim to the rear of the prairie schooner and blasted away with the scattergun, ignoring the burning lamp in the air.

Lead fragments hit Curtis in the left arm and sent him sprawling in the mud.

The highflying lantern smashed at Veeko's feet, drenching his pants with oil. Fire followed instantly, setting him ablaze.

"Ahh, someone help me!" he screamed, dropping the gun, as he beat his blazing trousers with his hands. Turning, he headed for the river but stopped, obviously remembering that the raging water was far below.

Instead, he dropped to the soft ground and rolled about madly to douse the flames.

Using his teeth and his hand, Curtis knotted a neckerchief tightly around his upper arm to contain the bleeding. He stood and drew the Colt, carefully watching the killer on the ground, shaking with fear, shock, and agony.

Despite their paths crossing repeatedly, it was the first time that he was near enough to study Veeko. *Unsurprisingly, he's short, and I'd say he's ugly looking rather than plain, as Shelly described him. But then, I know him for his murdering and evil ways. His clothes seem in good shape, so his thieving ways have been good to him, until now.* Noticing the killer's weapon, he was surprised. *By Jove, he has an over-and-under, double-barreled scattergun.*

Veeko looked up at him, a murderous expression on his face.

"Stand up, you mangy cur."

"YOU GO STRAIGHT TO HELL!" came his high-pitched shriek.

Curtis fired a shot into the ground, spraying mud into Veeko's face, as the burned man scrambled closer to the steep drop off.

"That was for Mrs. Hills."

"Stop this madness," Veeko rasped, bitterly. "The old folks, they had more than nine hundred dollars in the wagon. You can have it, just let me be."

"This one is for old man Hills," Curtis replied, slowly cocking and firing the long-barreled pistol, nicking the heel of the killer's boot.

The short man stood and hollered, "You must be crazier than a loon. I ain't done you no harm. You and me, we can work out something. I have other money hidden in the wagon. You can have it all."

"I'm not crazy. I'm just a man bent on avenging me and my kin. How about those horses you stole from me some years ago?" Despite the poor light, he saw the baffled look on the man's face.

"Now what in the hell are you raving about? I've never seen or met you before."

"The horses you and your pardn'rs stole that were destined to be sold in Texas," Curtis replied, as the ringing in his ear continued. "And, to boot, you killed my hound and burned down my barn. You remember now, don't you? It's written as plain as day on your face."

"Damn you to hell!"

I'm sure you remember your clash with the leader of the gang. How could anyone ever forget having two of his fingers lopped off with a big old knife? I saw them lying in the muck, all shriveled and gray. That memory surely sticks in your craw, doesn't it, you ring-tailed cur!"

Veeko's face had an odd expression— equal measures of pain, defiance, and wide-eyed fear. "How come—" he stuttered, "—you know all these things?"

"Simple. All your pards have met their fate."

"Even Tucker?"

"Yep—he was scalped the last time I saw him. Then, there's the other time. You remember robbing some hunters in the woods before you hired on to work at the Zacharias place? You likely found your friends sprawled in the glen, exactly where they died. It was me that gunned them down—all three—with this pistol." From the workings on his face, Curtis could almost read the evil man putting the pieces together.

"Have you been following me long? And who in the hell are you?"

"Most times, I'm a farmer," Curtis responded, seeing a look of disbelief on the evil man's face. "You saw fit to change that by wronging me and my family. So now, I've become the reaper, and I'm going to see that you rot in hell. By the way, Shelley asked me to give you a special present when I caught up with you," Curtis added, and again the Colt roared, as the shot nipped the killer's left ear.

"You turnip-growing dirt-grubber! " Veeko hollered, grabbing the side of his head and swaying on his burned legs. "Stop! I'll do anything you say, mister." With tears running down his mud-streaked face, he pleaded, "Stop this madness! Have mercy!"

In the last light, Curtis scoffed, "For someone who regularly shakes hands with Satan, asking for mercy must be a new, stomach-wrenching experience for you."

Sudden gusts of wind swirled around them, and Veeko's hat whipped off his head and over the high cliff.

Curtis' dark hair, blowing straight back, framed his chiseled face.

Then, the skies opened and dense curtains of rain fell, drenching them in the downpour.

"You're nothing but a whelp of a sodbuster's whore," Veeko stammered, visibly trembling.

"Keep it together, Veeko. I ain't finished yet. There's the very important matter of that young gal, Ella Mae," Curtis continued, rain plastering his hair down and running into his eyes. "You've changed her life forever." The gun roared again, the bullet clipping Veeko's other ear.

"Stop!" the short man cried again, as he staggered at the brink of the cliff. "Damn you to hell, you muckraking jackass," he cursed, holding both hands to his head while keeping a wary eye on the Missourian. The killer's voice was raw and shrill with panic, as saliva dribbled from the corner of his mouth.

Another thunderclap lit his pale face, which was a mask of horror. The bluster was gone, as he shrieked, "No! Don't hurt me again. I'm begging you . . . have mercy, mister. I won't harm folks no more. I'll take up the Lord's ways. I promise . . ." Veeko's words trailed off as he saw the barrel of the big Colt lift once more.

"And, I'll never forgive you for what you did to my brother. You know the one. You called him a calf-mooning youngun. His life is changed forever, and I won't let that go unanswered," he said, firing once more.

Instinctively lifting an arm for protection, the bullet struck his hand. "You miserable, Missouri scum!" Veeko screamed. Cradling his shattered limb against his body, he looked around wildly. "Someone make this loco dirt-farmer stop."

"Nobody here except you and me, Veeko, and the river."

In a final moment of clear-headedness, Veeko asked in disbelief, "Damn, how many shots you got in that pistol?"

"Just enough for a polecat that's plumb outlived his time. Here's the last."

"NO!" Veeko screamed.

"YES!" the Missourian shouted back, squeezing the trigger.

Struck in the shoulder, Veeko spun around. Fear etched his face, and his eyes were as big as saucers. Unsteady on the rain-slick cliff, first one foot and then the other slipped. Windmilling his good arm frantically for balance, the little man teetered. "Help me!" he shrieked. "I don't even know your name!"

"CURTIS."

"HELP ME! HELP—"

As the rim broke away, the sound of his piercing scream followed him down the cliff, eerily echoing off the rock walls.

It took a moment for Curtis to gather himself, then he went to the edge and peered down, but the spawn of evil was lost to sight, swept away in the muddy river.

Suddenly, the raging emotions consuming him dissolved. His pains, all but forgotten during the fight, came roaring back.

I avenged the family's honor, he thought, feeling emotionally drained and strangely numb. *The bushwhackers singled me out years ago, and I've dealt with all of them. Still, my Walker and hound are gone. My closest friends—my brothers—no longer share my life. Final punishment has come to the devil-man who did harm to Marion and Ella Mae, yet I can't give them back the lives they wanted. With this gun, God, I've delivered justice, by becoming a grim reaper—an avenger.*

Looking up into the windswept rain, he held the Colt up high. "This isn't my way, Lord. I have family and deep roots in Lost Creek Valley. That's where I belong, not out here on the plains, righting injustices. How do I begin atoning to Thee for my deeds, Lord? Will you show me the way?"

Another thunderbolt split the sky, and the six-shooter's polished barrel reflected the bright streak of light.

Nodding, Curtis had his answer. He flung the pistol in a high arc, far out over the cliff, and watched as it splashed into the raging river below. Again, lightning cracked in the darkened sky above. Undoing the buckle, his leather holster slid into the mud.

END

AUTHOR NOTES

The four novels in the Six Bulls series draw upon family tales of settlers who journeyed across the American frontier in the 1800s. Their stories, passed down through the generations, paint pictures of courageous and adventurous people—a hearty lot—who had perseverance and self-reliance, despite the many dangers they encountered. They overcame their misgivings and fears of the unknown wilderness. Most were not famous nor widely celebrated, yet they carved out homes, farms, and a life on the frontier. In the process, they created a great nation. They are my heroes.

From my research, I have a better understanding of the plight of Native Americans, as westward expansion occurred. Despite being fierce and resourceful, ultimately, the oncoming tide of settlers swept them aside. There came a time for understanding and compassion by the conquering invaders. In too many instances, this did not occur, and that stain is part of our American historical legacy.

Various historical events and individuals are included in my novels. Some found in this story follow ~

Lydia Maria Child (1802-1880)

Author, journalist, editor, abolitionist, and reformer, Mrs. Child's wrote *The American Frugal Housewife* in 1832. Recipes for homemade yeast and carrot pie, as well as remedies for removing warts, splinters, and many other ailments, are included in this small book. It is still available today.

Samuel Colt (1814-1862)

He invented and manufactured revolvers that were revolutionary. Starting in 1834, his company initially sold firearms to the U.S. Army during its Florida campaign with the Seminole Indians. Despite that major sale, the company went bankrupt in 1842.

The Texas Rangers became familiar with the gun during the Florida engagement. At the outbreak of the Mexican-American War (1846-1848), they ordered one thousand revolvers, and Samuel Colt's company was back in business.

Over the years, the firm made many different single-action and double-action revolvers. Perhaps the company's most famous was the .45 caliber Peacemaker, which was the standard U.S. military sidearm for seventy-five years.

Donation Land Claim Act of 1850

Hudson's Bay Company, an English firm formed in the seventeenth century, is the oldest commercial company in North America. During the 1800s, it had jurisdiction over the profitable fur trading business on lands claimed by the English Crown. This included Canada and Oregon Territory (comprising the states of Oregon, Washington, and Idaho).

The company's stranglehold on the Northwest began to end when the first American wagon train reached Oregon, in 1843. Under the threat of military action, as well as diplomacy, the 49th parallel became the border between the United States and Canada, west of the Great Lakes.

The U.S. government adopted the Donation Land Claim Act of 1850, to strengthen and assure its dominion over Oregon. Every man, older than age twenty-one, could file a claim and receive, at no cost, three hundred-twenty acres. A married couple could seek up to double the acreage. The law required that the claimants work the land for four years, after which time the owner received a land patent (deed). In 1855, the program ended.

In 1970, Hudson's Bay Company celebrated its 300th anniversary.

Captain Mabel Gilbert (1797-1870)

Gilbert was born in Tennessee. Early in life, he became a steamboat captain on the Mississippi River, and he retained the title. After inheriting wealth, he was restless and moved to the wilds of Fannin County, Texas, with his wife and seven children. By 1838, he was a successful businessman, rancher, and part-time Texas Ranger. Later, he also served as justice of the peace and county commissioner.

In 1856, he and his second wife became the first settlers in a remote area that later became Wichita County, Texas, and where they built a home on their large cattle ranch located on the banks of the Red River. Conflicts with the Indians were frequent, forcing the family to flee more than once during his lifetime.

The Gilbert family was also one of the earliest to settle in the community that became Dallas, Texas. Some maintain that his wife suggested the city's name in honor of their friend, Commodore Alexander James Dallas of the Texas Navy.

Captain Gilbert sired twenty-one children over the span of his seventy-three years. In Texas, creeks in Fannin and Wichita counties bear his name.

Hawken Rifle

Jacob and Samuel Hawken learned the rifle-smith trade from their father. Together, they opened a blacksmithing business in the fur-trading outpost of St. Louis in about 1814. The brothers were skilled craftsmen, who made or repaired firearms. Initially, they forged gun barrels for other gun manufacturers. When they began making rifles in 1825, each was individually handmade.

The black powder Hawken rifle carried the following specifications:

In-service History	1823-1870
Designer	Samuel Hawken
Number Built	Estimated at 2,000
Barrel Length	33-36 Inches
Caliber	Round Shot-Averaged .54
Action	Flintlock or Percussion Cap
Firing Mechanism	Double Set Trigger
Effective Range	400 Yards
Feed System	Muzzle Loaded
Sight	Open Blade

With a reputation for accuracy and dependability, it was capable of knocking down the big targets of the West. The company made relatively few rifles; yet, it accompanied many renowned explorers and frontiersmen. Over the centuries, it has become legendary, acquiring the moniker "the gun that settled the West." Today, black powder reproductions are available.

Major Frank Parke (1829-1902)

Born in County Leitrim, Ireland, Frank Parke came to America in 1849. Five years later, he journeyed to Fort Smith, Arkansas Territory. Among other pursuits, he volunteered and became a major in the Confederate Army; served as mayor of Skullyville, Choctaw Nation; was a merchant, real estate developer, and owner of a colliery.

He married Sarah Jane Ish in 1856. She was the daughter of early Arkansas pioneers who were killed by Cherokee Indians. As a young woman, she worked at the Asbury Indian Mission located in Eufaula, Indian Territory. It was there that she met Parke. They had nine children.

William Ray (1808-1874)

Today, the city of Raytown has a population of thirty thousand and is a suburb of Kansas City, Missouri. William Ray established a blacksmith shop on the Santa Fe Trail around 1848, by purchasing seven acres for $72.16. He became renowned for his forging skill, and the early settlement bears his name.

In the early history of the American frontier, salt was scarce. It was a necessity in sustaining life, and a vital ingredient in both preserving food and tanning leather. One early source of salt was in New Orleans, and it was hauled upriver by steamboats; another was less expensive and much closer to early frontier lands.

In 1804, explorers Lewis and Clark reported many saltwater springs along the Missouri River, located near the present-day counties of Howard and Saline. Frontiersman Daniel Boone claimed and named one Boone's Lick. His sons later developed the frontier salt business. They, and others, continued to operate the springs for the next fifty years, supplying salt to settlers throughout the formative days of the nation. The process involved boiling off three hundred gallons of brine to produce one bushel of salt.

Raytown (along with the adjacent town of Independence) was the starting point for pioneering trails headed westward, including tandem wagons of salt headed for New Mexico Territory. That, in turn, led to the need for the services of a capable blacksmith named William Ray.

Seneca, Newton County, Missouri
Settlers pioneered the southwest corner of Missouri in the 1830s. For decades, its location *was* the American frontier, adjoining the large geographical region, which the U.S. Government designated *Indian Territory*.

Settlers came to southwest Missouri, drawn by the prospect of cheap, good farmland, which they acquired from the government for $1.25 per acre. Much of the time, the area was a quiet farming community. Notable exceptions occurred during the Civil War and, later, the building of the railroad. Today, it remains a community tucked into the rolling hills of Missouri.

James Henry Sparks (about 1830-1879)
Born in Ireland, James Sparks came to Fort Smith, Arkansas, in 1849. He followed the family tradition and engaged in the mercantile business. The business became bankrupt in 1852. Later, he entered the newspaper publishing business, co-founded the *Fort Smith Herald* newspaper,

and became town mayor. On April 18, 1854, he led the "Fort Smith and California Emigrating Company" to northern California. His leather-bound journal provides a record of the journey, which included forty-eight men and over seven hundred head of cattle. It appears that he survived the journey.

"K"

The next novel by Richard Puz is a love story, based on true events. The story takes place in the farming hamlet of Am Furtt, situated at the toll crossing on the Kupi River, presently the border between Slovenia and Croatia. The story spans centuries, beginning with vicious raids by the Ottoman Empire over several hundred years. In pursuit of their "blood tax," the attacks involved repeated kidnapping of young children.

For half a millennium, families in the Kostel serfdom farmed and labored for absentee landowners in the rich river bottomlands. Families of serfs, tied to specific parcels of farmland, passed the right of use from father to son. Serfdom prevailed until the mid-19th century.

Life was hard. Along with the Turkish raids, crushing taxation, enforced by the fiefdom's garrison and a compliant church, led to a meager existence. During a span of nearly a century, ending in the 1800s, church records provide an insight into the misery of fiefs working the fields for absentee landowners. Data show the average life span at twenty-two years, while the average age for marriage was twenty-four.

This new tale is set against this historical legacy. The publish date for "K" is 2015.

OTHER NOVELS AND SHORT STORIES BY RICHARD PUZ

Six Bulls Series of Novels ~

Six Bulls—The Ohioans (print and e-book versions)

Rafting from Ohio to Missouri down the big rivers of America, pioneers load their families and possessions onto flatboats, seeking a new life on the American frontier. Adventures abound during their exciting and dangerous trip.

The Carolinian (print and e-book versions)Abraham

matures during the Battle of New Orleans and later applies lessons learned on his tobacco plantation in North Carolina. Shunning slavery, he moves his family west. Their adventures produce a riveting account of pioneer life in the wilds of a new country, while battling the ever-present Hooker, the slaver.

Bride by Mail (print and e-book versions)

Independent and spirited, Eva is determined to seek a life that includes adventure and travel. Through fateful twists, she corresponds with Frank, a stranger who lives in the wilds of Washington Territory. As the love story unfolds, he asks her to come west and marry him, but doubts persist. In his letters, Frank captivates her with his adventures—encountering stampedes, cutthroats, and stumbling onto the "silent killer." Adding to the danger is the scheming owner of the Sourdough Wind Mine in the gold mining camp of Yreka.

Short Stories ~

The author's novels are the source of the following e-books:

Abraham

The young, raw-recruit witnesses the terror of war during the Battle of New Orleans. During a key incident, a frontiersman provides the wisdom to help him become a hero.

Arkansas Storm & Captain Jonathan Buzzard

Pioneers encounter a violent storm on the Arkansas River that threatens to take their lives and everything they own. In the second short story, the big, brawny captain takes on the outlaw gang, to save his neighbors.

Beanblossom Creek & Stain

Chief Black Hawk's men are on the warpath, and the captain and his men are waiting. The battle that follows is tragic and larger-than-life. The second tale finds white settlers conflicted over the heartless treatment of Indians.

Canyon of Death

The greatest killer on the Oregon Trail in the 1800s was unexpected, silent, and lethal. This pioneering party comes across a large herd of cattle and drovers who are mysteriously dying. Read the story about *the* greatest killer on the California and Oregon trails.

Danny Boy and Tennie

Whimsical and humorous, a riverbank tavern on the Ohio River is the setting for pioneers quenching their thirst after their long wagon train journey to Indiana. It's a roaring good time, until a fight breaks out to enliven the evening. The second story is about Jonah and the green-eyed gal—Tennie—confronting a violent tornado storm on the trail to Oregon.

Newtonia

Caught between warring armies, a frontier family attempts to survive, hiding in a stone barn, as the Civil War rages. In the midst, they receive the blessing of compassion.

Roaring River

Bushwhackers ambush two men, killing one. The survivor leads a posse to track down the band of killers, resulting in the battle of Roaring River.

Runaway Slave

A tobacco plantation owner makes a split-second decision, which affects the rest of his life.

Smoke

Prairies are one of God's greatest gifts, but they can also be deadly. Rural pioneers take desperate measures, trying to save everything they have created on the wild frontier.

Sourdough Wind Mine

Deep in the bowels of the gold mine, the enforcer confronts bandits.

Three Bells

Settlers on remote farms in Indiana prepare to defend themselves against Chief Blackhawk and his warriors. On a fateful night, an encounter changes everyone, forever.

Please visit my web site.
http://hstrial-rpuz.homestead.com/